NORA ROBERTS

CHRISTMAS *Angels*

SILHOUETTE®

All the characters in this book have no existence outside the imagination of the author, and have no relation whatsoever to anyone bearing the same name or names. They are not even distantly inspired by any individual known or unknown to the author, and all the incidents are pure invention.

Silhouette Books, Eton House, 18-24 Paradise Road, Richmond, Surrey TW9 1SR

ISBN: 978 0 263 86577 6

025-1107

Printed and bound in Spain by Litografia Rosés S.A., Barcelona

Praise for No. 1 *New York Times* bestselling author

NORA ROBERTS

"You can't bottle wish fulfilment, but Nora Roberts certainly knows how to put it on the page."
—*New York Times*

"Roberts' bestselling novels are some of the best in the romance genre. They are thoughtfully plotted, well-written stories featuring fascinating characters."
—*USA TODAY*

"The publishing world might be hard-pressed to find an author with a more diverse style or fertile imagination than Roberts."
—*Publishers Weekly*

"Roberts has a warm feel for her characters and an eye for detail."
—*Chicago Tribune*

"Roberts is indeed a word artist, painting her story and her characters with vitality and verve."
—*Los Angeles Daily News*

"Her stories have fuelled the dreams of twenty-five million readers."
—*Entertainment Weekly*

"Everything Nora Roberts writes turns to gold."
—*Romantic Times*

"Nora Roberts just keeps getting better and better."
—*Milwaukee Journal Sentinel*

Number One *New York Times* bestselling author **Nora Roberts** is "a storyteller of immeasurable diversity and talent" according to *Publishers Weekly*. She has published over one hundred and sixty novels, her work has been optioned and made into films, and her books have been translated into over twenty-five different languages and published all over the world.

CHRISTMAS *Angels*

Also available from Silhouette by

NORA ROBERTS

Rafe & Jared: The MacKade Brothers
Devin & Shane: The MacKade Brothers

The Calhouns: Catherine, Amanda & Lilah
The Calhouns: Suzanna & Megan

Cordina's Royal Family: Gabriella & Alexander
Cordina's Royal Family: Bennett & Camilla

Dream Makers

Gabriel's Angel

To Tom and Ky and Larry
for having the good sense to marry well.

Chapter 1

Damn snow. Gabe downshifted to second gear, slowed the Jeep to fifteen miles an hour, swore and strained his eyes. Through the frantic swing of the wipers on the windshield all that could be seen was a wall of white. No winter wonderland. Snow pelted down in flakes that looked as big and as mean as a man's fist.

There would be no waiting out this storm, he thought as he took the next curve at a crawl. He considered himself lucky that after six months he knew the narrow, winding road from town so well. He could drive almost by feel, but a newcomer wouldn't stand a chance. Even with that advantage, his shoulders and the back of his neck were tight with tension. Colorado snows could be as vicious in spring as they were in the dead of winter, and they could last for an hour or a day. Apparently this one had been a surprise to everyone—residents, tourists and the National Weather Service.

He had only five miles to go. Then he could unload his supplies, stoke his fire and enjoy the April blizzard from the comfort of his cabin, with a hot cup of coffee or an ice cold beer.

The Jeep chugged up the incline like a tank, and he was grateful for its sturdy perseverance. The unexpected snowfall might force him to take three times as long to make the twenty-mile trip from town to home, but at least he'd get there.

The wipers worked furiously to clear the windshield. There were seconds of white vision followed by seconds of white blindness. At this rate there would be better than two feet by nightfall. Gabe comforted himself with the thought that he'd be home long before that, even as the air in the Jeep turned blue from his cursing. If he hadn't lost track of the time the day before, he'd have had his supplies and been able to laugh at the weather.

The road went into a lazy S and Gabe took it cautiously. It was difficult for him to move slowly under any circumstances, but over the winter he had gained a healthy respect for the mountains and the roads that had been blasted through them. The guardrail was sturdy enough, but beneath it the cliffs were unforgiving. He wasn't worried so much about making a mistake himself—the Jeep was solid as a rock—but he thought of others who might be traveling north or south on the pass, pulling over to the side or stopping dead in the middle of the road.

He wanted a cigarette. His hands gripping the wheel

hard, he all but lusted for a cigarette. But it was a luxury that would have to wait. Three miles to go.

The tension in his shoulders began to ease. He hadn't seen another car in more than twenty minutes, and he wasn't likely to now. Anyone with any sense would have taken shelter. From this point on he could almost feel his way home. A good thing. Beside him the radio was squawking about roads closed and activities canceled. It always amazed Gabe that people planned so many meetings, luncheons, recitals and rehearsals on any given day.

But that was human nature, he supposed. Always planning on drawing together, if only to sell a bunch of cakes and cookies. He preferred to be alone. At least for now. Otherwise he wouldn't have bought the cabin and buried himself in it for the last six months.

The solitude gave him freedom, to think, to work, to heal. He'd done some of all three.

He nearly sighed when he saw—or rather felt—the road slant upward again. This was the final rise before his turnoff. Only a mile now. His face, which had been hard and tight with concentration, relaxed. It wasn't a smooth or particularly handsome face. It was too thin and angular to be merely pleasant, and the nose was out of alignment due to a heated disagreement with his younger brother during their teens. Gabe hadn't held it against him.

Because he'd forgotten to wear a hat, his dark blond hair fell untidily around his face. It was long and a bit shaggy over the collar of his parka and had been styled hastily with his fingers hours before. His eyes, a dark, clear green, were starting to burn from staring at the snow.

While his tires swished over the cushioned asphalt he

glanced down at his odometer, saw that there was only a quarter mile left, then looked back to the road. That was when he saw a car coming at him out of control.

He didn't even have time to swear. He jerked the Jeep to the right just as the oncoming car seemed to come out of its spin. The Jeep skimmed over the snow piled on the shoulder, swaying dangerously before the tires chewed down to the road surface for traction. He had a bad moment when he thought the Jeep was going to roll over like a turtle. Then all he could do was sit and watch and hope the other driver was as lucky.

The oncoming car was barreling down the road sideways. Though only seconds had passed, Gabe had time to think of how nasty the impact would be when the car slammed into him. Then the driver managed to straighten out. With only feet between them the car fishtailed and swerved to avoid the collision, then began to slide helplessly toward the guardrail. Gabe set his emergency brake and was out of the Jeep when the car rammed into the metal.

He nearly fell on his face, but his boots held as he raced across the road. It was a compact—a bit more compact now, with its right side shoved in and its hood sprung like an accordion, also on the passenger side. He had another moment to think, and he grimaced at the thought of what would have happened if the car had hit on the driver's side.

Fighting his way through the snow, he managed to make it to the wrecked car. He saw a figure slumped over the wheel, and he yanked at the door. It was locked. With his heart in his throat, he began to pound against the window.

The figure moved. A woman, he saw from the thick

wave of wheat-blond hair that spilled onto the shoulders of a dark coat. He watched her reach up and drag a ski cap from her head. Then she turned her face to the window and stared at him.

She was white, marble white. Even her lips were colorless. Her eyes were huge and dark, the irises almost black with shock. And she was beautiful, stunningly breathtakingly beautiful. The artist in him saw the possibilities in the diamond-shaped face, the prominent cheekbones, the full lower lip. The man in him rejected them and banged on the glass again.

She blinked and shook her head as if to clear it. As the shock passed out of them, he saw that her eyes were blue, a midnight blue. They filled now with a rush of concern. In a quick movement she rolled down the window.

"Are you hurt?" she demanded before he could speak. "Did I hit you?"

"No, you hit the guardrail."

"Thank God." She let her head slump back on the seat for a moment. Her mouth was as dry as dust. And her heart, though she was already fighting to control it, was thudding in her throat. "I started to skid coming down the incline. I thought—I hoped—I might be able to ride it out. Then I saw you and I was sure I was going to hit you."

"You would have if you hadn't swerved away toward the rail." He glanced at the front of her car again. The damage could have been worse, much worse. If she'd been going any faster… There was no use speculating. He turned to her again, studying her face for signs of shock or concussion. "Are you all right?"

"Yes. I think so." She opened her eyes again and

tried to smile at him. "I'm sorry. I must have given you quite a scare."

"At least." But the scare was over now. He was less than a quarter of a mile from hearth and home, and stuck in the snow with a strange woman whose car wasn't going anywhere for several days. "What the hell are you doing out here?"

She took the furiously bitten-off words in stride as she unhooked her seat belt. The long, deep breaths she'd been taking had gone a long way toward steadying her. "I must have gotten turned around in the storm. I was trying to get down to Lonesome Ridge to wait it out, find a place for the night. That's the closest town, according to the map, and I was afraid to pull over on the shoulder." She glanced over at the guardrail and shuddered. "What there is of it. I don't suppose there's any way I'm going to get my car out of here."

"Not tonight."

Frowning, Gabe stuck his hands in his pockets. The snow was still falling, and the road was deserted. If he turned around and walked back to his Jeep, leaving her to fend for herself, she might very well freeze to death before an emergency vehicle or a snowplow came along. However much he'd have liked to shrug off the obligation, he couldn't leave a woman stranded in this storm.

"The best I can do is take you with me." There wasn't an ounce of graciousness in his tone. She hadn't expected any. If he was angry and impatient about nearly being plowed into, and inconvenienced on top of it, he was entitled.

"I'm sorry."

He moved his shoulders, aware that he'd been rude.

"The turnoff for my cabin's at the top of the hill. You'll have to leave your car and ride in the Jeep."

"I'd appreciate it." With the engine off and the window open, the cold was beginning to seep through her clothes. "I'm sorry for the imposition, Mr.—?"

"Bradley. Gabe Bradley."

"I'm Laura." She slipped out of the safety harness that had undoubtedly saved her from injury. "I have a suitcase in the trunk, if you wouldn't mind giving me a hand with it."

Gabe took the keys and stomped back toward the trunk, thinking that if he'd only left an hour earlier that afternoon he'd be home—alone—at this moment.

The case wasn't large, and it was far from new. The lady with only one name traveled light, he thought. He muttered to himself as he hefted it out of the trunk. There was no use being angry with her, or being snotty. If she hadn't managed to skid quite so well, if she hadn't avoided him, they might have been needing a doctor now instead of a cup of coffee and dry feet.

Deciding to be more civil, Gabe turned to tell her to go across to the Jeep. She was standing, watching him, with the snow falling on her uncovered hair. That was when he saw she was not only beautiful, she was very, very pregnant.

"Oh, God" was all he could manage.

"I'm really sorry to be so much trouble," Laura began. "And I want to thank you in advance for the lift. If I could call from your cabin and find a tow truck, maybe we could clear this whole thing up quickly."

He hadn't heard a word she'd said. Not one. All he could do was stare at the ripe slope beneath her dark coat.

"Are you sure you're all right? You didn't tell me you were— Are you going to need a doctor?"

"I'm fine." This time she smiled, fully. The cold had brought the color back into her face. "Really. The baby wasn't hurt. He's annoyed a bit, I'd say from the way he's kicking me, but we hardly felt the impact. We didn't ram the guardrail, we sort of slid into it."

"You might have..." What? he wondered. "Jarred something."

"I'm fine," she said again. "I was strapped in, and the snow, though it started it all, cushioned the hit." Noting that he still seemed unconvinced, she tossed back her snow-covered hair. Her fingers, though they were tucked into subtle, silk-lined leather, were going numb. "I promise, I'm not going to give birth in the middle of the road—unless you plan on standing here for a few more weeks."

She was all right...he hoped. And the way she was smiling at him made him feel like an idiot. Deciding to take her word for it, he offered her a hand. "Let me help you."

The words, such simple words, went straight to her heart. She could have counted on her hands the number of times she had heard them.

He didn't know how to deal with pregnant women. Were they fragile? It had always seemed to him that the opposite must be true, given what they had to go through, but now, faced with one, he was afraid she'd shatter at a touch.

Mindful of the slippery road, Laura took a firm grip on his arm as they started across. "It's beautiful here," she said when they reached the Jeep. "But I have to admit, I'm going to appreciate the snow more from inside." She glanced at the high step below the door of the Jeep. "I think you're going to have to give me a bit of a boost. I'm not as agile as I used to be."

Gabe stowed her case, wondering exactly where to grab her. Mumbling, he put a hand under her elbow and another on her hip. Laura slid into the seat with less fuss than he'd expected.

"Thanks."

He grunted a response as he slammed the door. He skirted the hood, then took his place behind the wheel. It took a little maneuvering, but with a minimum of effort they inched back onto the road.

The dependable Jeep started up the hill. Laura uncurled her hands as they moved along at a steady pace. They'd finally stopped shaking. "I wasn't sure anyone lived along here. If I'd known, I'd have begged a roof long before this. I wasn't expecting a snowstorm in April."

"We get them later than this." He said nothing for a moment. He respected other people's privacy as zealously as his own. But these were unusual circumstances. "You're traveling alone?"

"Yes."

"Isn't that a little risky in your condition?"

"I'd planned on being in Denver in a couple of days." She laid a hand lightly on her belly. "I'm not due for six weeks." Laura took a deep breath. It was a risk to trust him, but she really had no other option. "Do you live alone, Mr. Bradley?"

"Yes."

She shifted her gaze just enough to study him as he turned down a narrow, snow-covered lane. At least she assumed a lane was buried somewhere under all the white. There was something tough and hard about his face. Not rugged, she thought. It was too lean and fine-boned for that. It was coldly sculpted, as she imagined a mythic warrior chief's might be.

But she remembered the stunned male helplessness in his eyes when he'd seen she was pregnant. She believed she'd be safe with him. She had to believe that.

He felt her gaze and read her thoughts easily enough. "I'm not a maniac," he said mildly.

"I appreciate that." She smiled a little, then turned to look out the windshield again.

The cabin could barely be seen through the snow, even when he stopped in front of it. But what Laura could see, she loved. It was a squat rectangle of wood with a covered porch and square-paned windows. Smoke puffed from the chimney.

Though it was buried under snow, there was a path of flat rocks leading from the lane to the front steps. Evergreens mantled with white trooped around the corners. Nothing had ever looked as safe and warm as this snow-decked little cabin in the mountains.

"It's lovely. You must be happy here."

"It does the job." Gabe came around to help her down. She smelled like the snow, he thought, or perhaps more like water, the pure, virginal water that poured down the mountain in the spring. "I'll take you in," he told her, knowing both his reaction and his comparison were ridiculous. "You can warm up by the fire." Gabe opened the front door and waved her in. "Go ahead. I'll bring in the rest."

He left her alone, snow dripping wet from her coat onto the woven mat inside the door.

The paintings. Laura stood just where she was and stared openmouthed at the paintings. They covered the walls, they were stacked in corners, they were piled on tables. Only a few were framed. They didn't need the ornamentation. Some were half finished, as though the artist had lost interest or motivation. There were oils, in colors vivid and harsh, and watercolors in soft, misty hues that might have sprung from dreams. Shrugging out of her coat, Laura moved in for a closer look.

There was a scene from Paris, the Bois de Boulogne. She remembered it from her honeymoon. Looking at it made her eyes swim and her muscles tense. Breathing deeply, she forced herself to look at it until her emotions settled.

An easel was set near the window, where the light would come in and fall on the canvas. She resisted the temptation to go over and steal a look. She already had the sensation that she was trespassing.

What was she going to do? Laura gripped her hands together tightly as she let the despair come. She was stranded, her car wrecked, her money dwindling. And the baby— The baby wasn't going to wait until she made things right.

If they found her now…

They weren't going to find her. Deliberately she unlaced her hands. She'd come this far. No one was going to take her baby, now or ever.

She turned as the door to the cabin opened. Gabe shifted the bags he'd carried inside, leaving them jumbled together in a pile. He, too, shrugged out of his coat and hung it on a hook by the door.

He was as lean as his face had indicated. Though he

might have been a bit under six feet, the spare toughness of his build gave the illusion of more height, more power. More like a boxer than an artist, Laura thought as she watched him kick the clinging snow from his boots. More like a man of the outdoors than one who came from graceful mansions and gentle blood.

Despite what she knew of his aristocratic background, he wore flannel and corduroy and looked perfectly suited to the rustic cabin. Laura, who came from humbler stock, felt fussy and out of place in her bulky Irish knit sweater and tailored wool.

"Gabriel Bradley," she said, and gestured widely toward the walls. "My brain must have been scrambled before. I didn't put it together. I love your work."

"Thanks." Bending, he hefted two of the bags.

"Let me help—"

"No." He strode off into the kitchen, leaving Laura biting her lip.

He wasn't thrilled to have her company, she thought. Then she shrugged. It couldn't be helped. As soon as it was reasonably safe for her to leave, she would leave. Until then… Until then Gabriel Bradley, artist of the decade, would have to make do.

It was tempting just to take a seat and passively stay out of his way. Once she would have done just that, but circumstances had changed her. She followed him into the adjoining kitchen. Counting the baby she carried, there were three of them in the little room, and it was filled to capacity.

"At least let me make you something hot to drink." The ancient two-burner stove looked tricky, but she was determined.

He turned, brushed against her belly and was amazed at the wave of discomfort he felt. And the tug of fascination. "Here's the coffee," he mumbled, handing her a fresh can.

"Got a pot?"

It was in the sink, which was filled with water that had once been sudsy. He had been trying to soak out the stains from the last time he'd used it. He moved to get it, bumped her again and stepped back.

"Why don't you let me take care of it?" she suggested. "I'll put this stuff away and start the coffee, and you can call a tow truck."

"Fine. There's milk. Fresh."

She smiled. "I don't suppose you have any tea."

"No."

"Milk's fine, then. Thank you."

When he left, Laura busied herself in the kitchen. It was too small for it to be complicated. She used her own system in storing the goods since it appeared Gabe had none. She'd only emptied the first bag when he reappeared in the doorway.

"Phone's out."

"Out?"

"Dead. We lose service a lot when there's a storm."

"Oh." Laura stood holding a can of soup. "Is it usually out for long?"

"Depends. Sometimes a couple hours, sometimes a week."

She lifted a brow. Then she realized that he was perfectly serious. "I guess that puts me in your hands, Mr. Bradley."

He hooked his thumbs in his front pockets. "In that case, you'd better call me Gabe."

Laura frowned down at the can in her hand. When things got bad, you made the best of them. "Want some soup?"

"Yeah. I'll, ah…put your things in the bedroom."

Laura simply nodded, then began to search for a can opener.

She was a piece of work, all right, Gabe decided as he carried Laura's suitcase into his room. Not that he was an expert when it came to women, but he wasn't what anyone would have called a novice, either. She hadn't batted an eye when he'd told her that the phone was dead and they were effectively cut off from the outside world. Or, to put it more precisely, that she was cut off from everyone but him.

Gabe glanced into the streaked mirror over his battered dresser. As far as he knew, no one had ever considered him harmless before. A quick, cocky smile flashed over his face. He hadn't always been harmless, when it came right down to it.

This, of course, was an entirely different situation.

Under other circumstances he might have entertained some healthy fantasies about his unexpected guest. That face. There was something haunting, something indefinable, about that kind of beauty. When a man looked at it, he automatically began to wonder and imagine. Even if she hadn't been carrying a child, the fantasies would have remained only that. Fantasies. He'd never been enthusiastic about flings and one-night stands, and he certainly wasn't in any shape for a relationship. Celibacy had been the order of the day for the last few months. The desire to paint had finally seduced him again. Gabe needed no other love affair.

But as for more practical matters, he did have a guest, a lone woman who was very pregnant—and very secretive. He hadn't missed the fact that she'd told him only her first name and hadn't volunteered any information about who she was and where and why she was traveling. Since it was unlikely that she'd robbed a bank or stolen secrets for terrorists, he wouldn't press too hard right now.

But, given the strength of the storm and the seclusion of the cabin, they were likely to be together for a few days. He was going to find out more about the calm and mysterious Laura.

What was she going to do? Laura stared at the empty plate in her hand and saw a hint of her reflection. How could she get to Denver or Los Angeles or Seattle—or any huge, swallowing city that was far enough away from Boston—when she was trapped here? If only she hadn't felt that urgent need to move on this morning. If she'd stayed in that quiet little motel room another day she might still have had some control over what was happening.

Instead, she was here with a stranger. Not just any stranger, Laura reminded herself. Gabriel Bradley, artist—wealthy, respected artist from a wealthy, respected family. But he hadn't recognized her. Laura was certain of that. At least he had yet to recognize her. What would happen when he did, when he found out who she was running from? For all she knew, the Eagletons might be close family friends of the Bradleys. The gesture of her hand over the mound of her stomach was automatic and protective.

They wouldn't take her baby. No matter how much money and how much power they wielded, they wouldn't take her baby. And if she could manage it they would never find her or the child.

Setting down the plate, she turned her attention to the window. How odd it was to look out and see nothing. It gave her a nice, settled feeling to know that no one could see in, either. She was effectively curtained off from everyone. Or nearly everyone, she corrected, thinking again of Gabe.

Perhaps the storm had been a blessing. When there was no choice, she found it best to look on the bright side. No one could follow her trail in this kind of weather. And who would think of looking for her in some tiny, out-of-the-way cabin in the mountains? It felt safe. She would cling to that.

She heard him moving around in the next room, heard the sound of his boots on the hardwood, the thud of a log being added to the fire. After so many months alone she found even the sound of another human being a comfort.

"Mr. Bradley…Gabe?" She stepped through the doorway to see him adjusting the screen in front of the fire. "Could you clear off a table?"

"Clear off a table?"

"So we could eat…sitting down."

"Yeah."

She disappeared again while he tried to figure out what to do with the paints, brushes, canvas stretchers and general disorder on the picnic table that had once served as a dining area. Annoyed at having his space compromised, he spread his equipment throughout the room.

"I made some sandwiches, too." Using a bent cookie sheet as a makeshift tray, she carried in bowls and plates and cups. Embarrassed and edgy, Gabe snatched it from her.

"You shouldn't be carrying heavy things."

Her brows lifted. Surprise came first. No one had ever pampered her. And certainly her life, which had rarely been easy, had been hardest over the last seven months. Then gratitude came, and she smiled. "Thanks, but I'm careful."

"If you were careful, you'd be in your own bed with your feet up and not snowbound with me."

"Exercise is important." But she sat and let him set out the dishes. "And so's food." With her eyes closed, she breathed in the scents. Hot, simple, fortifying. "I hope I didn't put too much of a dent in your supplies, but once I got started I couldn't stop."

Gabe picked up half a sandwich that was thick with cheese, crisp bacon and sliced hothouse tomatoes. "I'm not complaining." The truth was, he'd gotten into the habit of eating right out of the pan over the kitchen sink. Hot food made with more care than hurry tasted one hell of a lot better from a plate.

"I'd like to pay you back, for the bed and the food."

"Don't worry about it." He scooped up clam chowder while he studied her. She had a way of sticking out her chin that made him think of pride and will. It made an interesting contrast with the creamy skin and the slender neck.

"That's kind of you, but I prefer paying my own way."

"This isn't the Hilton." She wore no jewelry, he noted, not even a plain gold band on her finger. "You cooked the meal, so we'll call it even."

She wanted to argue—her pride wanted to argue—but the simple truth was, she had very little cash, except for the baby fund she'd scrupulously set aside in the lining of her suitcase. "I'm very grateful." She sipped at the milk, though she detested it. The scent of his coffee was rich and forbidden. "Have you been here long, in Colorado?"

"Six months, seven, I guess."

That gave her hope. The timing was good, almost too good. From the looks of the cabin, he didn't spend much time poring over the newspapers, and she hadn't noticed a television. "It must be a wonderful place to paint."

"So far."

"I couldn't believe it when I walked in. I recognized your work right away. I've always admired it. In fact, my—someone I knew bought a couple of your pieces. One of them was a painting of a huge, deep forest. It seemed as though you could step right into it and be completely alone."

He knew the work, and, oddly enough, he'd had the same feeling about it. He couldn't be sure, but he thought it had been sold back east. New York, Boston, perhaps Washington, D.C. If his curiosity about her persisted, it would only take a phone call to his agent to refresh his memory.

"You didn't say where you were traveling from."

"No." She continued to eat, though her appetite had fled. How could she have been foolish enough to describe the painting? Tony had bought it, or rather had snapped his fingers and arranged for his lawyers to buy it on his behalf because Laura had admired it. "I've been in Dallas for a while."

She'd been there almost two months before she'd discovered that the Eagletons' detectives were making discreet inquiries about her.

"You don't sound like a Texan."

"No, I suppose I don't. That's probably because I've

lived all over the country." That was true enough, and she was able to smile again. "You're not from Colorado."

"San Francisco."

"Yes, I remember reading that in an article about you and your work." She would talk about him. From her experience men were easily distracted when the conversation centered on themselves. "I've always wanted to see San Francisco. It seems like a lovely place, the hills, the bay, the beautiful old houses." She gave a quick gasp and pressed a hand to her stomach.

"What is it?"

"The baby's just restless." She smiled, but he noted that her eyes were shadowed with fatigue and her complexion was pale again.

"Look, I don't know anything about what you're going through, but common sense tells me you should be lying down."

"Actually, I am tired. If you wouldn't mind, I'd like to rest for a few minutes."

"The bed's through here." He rose and, not certain she could get up and down on her own, offered her a hand.

"I'll take care of the dishes later if…" Her words trailed off as her knees buckled.

"Hold on." Gabe put his arms around her and had the odd, rather humbling sensation of having the baby move against him.

"I'm sorry. It's been a long day, and I guess I pushed it further than I should have." She knew she should move away, pull back on her own, but there was something exquisite about leaning against the hard, sturdy body of a man. "I'll be fine after a nap."

She didn't shatter as he'd once thought she might, but now she seemed so soft, so delicate, that he imagined her dissolving in his hands. He would have liked to comfort her, would have liked to go on holding her like that while she leaned into him, trusting, depending. Needing him. Calling himself a fool, he picked her up.

Laura started to protest, but it felt so good to be off her feet. "I must weigh a ton."

"That's what I was expecting, but you don't."

She found she could laugh, even though the fatigue was smothering her. "You're a real charmer, Gabe."

His own awkwardness began to fade as he moved through the door to the bedroom. "I haven't had many opportunities to flirt with pregnant ladies."

"That's all right. You redeemed yourself by rescuing this one from a snowstorm." With her eyes half closed, she felt herself being lowered onto a bed. It might be nothing more than a mattress and a rumpled sheet, but it felt like heaven. "I want to thank you."

"You've been doing that on an average of every five minutes." He pulled a slightly ragged comforter over her. "If you really want to thank me, get some sleep and don't go into labor."

"Fair enough. Gabe?"

"Yeah."

"Will you keep trying the phone?"

"All right." She was nearly asleep. He had a moment's attack of guilt for wanting to press her while she was vulnerable. Right now, she didn't look as though she had the strength to brush away a fly. "Do you want me to call anyone for you? Your husband?"

She opened her eyes at that. Though they were clouded with fatigue, they met his levelly, and he saw that she wasn't down for the count yet.

"I'm not married," she said, very clearly. "There's no one to call."

Chapter 2

In the dream she was alone. That didn't frighten her. Laura had spent a large portion of her life alone, so she was more comfortable in solitude than in a crowd. There was a soft, misty quality to the dream—like the seascape she had seen on the wall of Gabe's cabin.

Oddly, she could even hear the ocean, purring and lapping off in the distance, though a part of her knew she was in the mountains. She walked through a pearl-colored fog, listening to the waves. Under her feet sand shifted, warm and soft. She felt safe and strong and strangely unencumbered. It had been a long, long time since she had felt so free, so at ease.

She knew she was dreaming. That was the best part. If she could have managed it, she would have stayed there, in the soft-focused fantasy of it, forever. It would be so easy to keep her eyes closed and cling to the utter peace of the dream.

Then the baby was crying. Screaming. A pulse began to beat in her temple as she listened to the high, keening wails. She started to sweat, and the clean white fog changed to a dark, threatening gray. No longer warm, the air took on a chill that whipped straight to the bone.

The cries seemed to come from everywhere and nowhere, echoing and rebounding as she searched. Sobbing for breath, she fought her way through the mist as it circled and thickened. The cries became louder, more urgent. Her heart was beating in her throat, and her breath rasped and her hands shook.

Then she saw the bassinet, with its pretty white skirt and its lacy pink and blue ruffles. The relief was so great that her knees sagged.

"It's all right," she murmured as she gathered the child in her arms. "It's all right. I'm here now." She could feel the baby's warm breath against her cheek, could feel the weight in her arms as she rocked and soothed. The fine scent of powder surrounded her. Gently she cradled the child, murmuring and comforting as she began to lift the concealing blanket from its face.

And there was nothing, nothing in her arms but an empty blanket.

Gabe was sitting at the picnic table, sketching her face, thinking of her, when he heard her cry out. The moan was so long, so desperate, that he snapped the pencil in two before he jumped up and raced to the bedroom.

"Hey, come on." Feeling awkward, he took her by the shoulders. She jerked so hard that he had to fight back his own panic, as well as hers, to hold on to her. "Laura, take it easy. Are you in pain? Is it the baby? Laura, tell me what's going on."

"They took my baby!" There was hysteria in her voice, but it was a hysteria that was laced with fury. "Help me! They took my baby!"

"No one took your baby." She was still fighting him, with a strength that awed him. Moving on instinct, he wrapped his arms around her. "You're having a dream. No one took your baby. Here." He clamped a hand around her wrist, where her pulse was beating like a jackhammer, and dragged her hand to her belly. "You're safe, both of you. Relax before you hurt yourself."

When she felt the life beneath her palms, she slumped against him. Her baby was safe, still inside her, where no one could touch him. "I'm sorry. It was a dream."

"It's okay." Without being aware of it, he was stroking her hair, cradling her as she had cradled the baby of her imagination, rocking her gently in an age-old comforting motion. "Do us both a favor and relax."

She nodded, feeling protected and sheltered. Those were two sensations she had experienced very rarely in her twenty-five years. "I'm all right, really. It must have been the shock from the accident catching up with me."

He drew her away, angry with himself because he wanted to go on holding her, shielding her. When she had asked him for help, he had known, without understanding why, that he would do anything to protect her. It was almost as though he had been dreaming himself, or had been caught up in her dream.

The snow was still falling in sheets outside the window and the only light was what came slanting through the bedroom door from the main cabin. It was dim and slightly yellow, but he could see her clearly, and he wanted to be certain that she saw him, as well. He wanted answers, and he wanted them now.

"Don't lie to me. Under normal circumstances you'd be entitled to your privacy, but right now you're under my roof for God knows how long."

"I'm not lying to you." Her voice was so calm, so even, that he nearly believed her. "I'm sorry if I upset you."

"Who are you running from, Laura?"

She said nothing, just stared at him with those dark blue eyes. He swore at her, but she didn't flinch. He sprang up to pace the room, but she didn't shudder. Abruptly he dropped down on the bed again and caught her chin in his hand. She went absolutely still. Gabe would have sworn that for an instant she stopped breathing. Though it was ridiculous, he had the odd sensation that she was bracing for a blow.

"I know you're in trouble. What I want to know is how big. Who's after you, and why?"

Again she said nothing, but her hand moved instinctively to protect the child she carried.

Since the baby was obviously the core of the problem, they would begin there. "The baby's got a father," he said slowly. "You running from him?"

She shook her head.

"Then who?"

"It's complicated."

He lifted a brow as he jerked his head toward the window. "We've got nothing but time here. This keeps up, it could be a week before the main roads are open."

"When they do, I'll go. The less you know, the better off we'll both be."

"That won't wash." He was silent a moment, trying to organize his thoughts. "It seems to me that the baby is very important to you."

"Nothing is or can be more important."

"Do you figure the strain you're carrying around is good for it?"

He saw the regret in her eyes instantly, saw the concern, the almost imperceptible folding into herself. "There are some things that can't be changed." She took a long breath. "You have a right to ask questions."

"But you don't intend to answer them."

"I don't know you. I have to trust you, to a point, because I have no choice. I can only ask you to do the same."

He moved his hand away from her face. "Why should I?"

She pressed her lips together. She knew he was right. But sometimes right wasn't enough. "I haven't committed a crime, I'm not wanted by the law. I have no family, no husband looking for me. Is that enough?"

"No. I'll take that much tonight because you need to sleep, but we'll talk in the morning."

It was a reprieve—a short one, but she'd learned to be grateful for small things. With a nod, she waited for him to walk to the door. When it shut and the darkness was full again, she lay down. But it was a long, long time before she slept.

It was silent, absolutely silent, when Laura woke. She opened her eyes and waited for memory to return. There had been so many rooms, so many places where she'd slept, that she was used to this confusion upon waking.

She remembered it all…Gabriel Bradley, the storm, the cabin, the nightmare. And the sensation of waking in fear to find herself safe, in his arms. Of course, the safety was only temporary, and his arms weren't for her. Sighing, she turned her head to look out the window.

The snow was still falling. It was almost impossible to believe, but she lay and watched it, thinner now, slower, but still steady. There would be no leaving today.

Tucking her hand under her cheek, she continued to watch. It was easy to wish that the snow would never stop and that time would. She could stay here, cocooned, isolated, safe. But time, as the child she carried attested, never stopped. Rising, she opened her suitcase. She would put herself in order before she faced Gabe.

The cabin was empty. She should have felt relieved at that. Instead, the cozy fire and polished wood made her feel lonely. She wanted him there, even if it was just the sound of his movements in another room. Wherever he had gone, she reminded herself, he would be back. She started to walk into the kitchen to see what could be done about breakfast.

She saw the sketches, a half dozen of them, spread out on the picnic table. His talent, though raw in pencil or charcoal drawing, was undeniable. Still, it made her both uneasy and curious to see how someone else—no, how Gabriel Bradley—perceived her.

Her eyes seemed too big, too haunted. Her mouth was too soft, too vulnerable. She rubbed a finger over it as she frowned at the drawing. She'd seen her face countless times, in glossy photographs, posed for the best angle.

She'd been draped in silks and furs, drenched in jewels. Her face and form had sold gallons of perfume, hawked fortunes in clothes and gems.

Laura Malone. She'd nearly forgotten that woman, the woman they'd said would be the face of the nineties. The woman who had, briefly, held her own destiny in her hands. She was gone, erased.

The woman in the sketches was softer, rounder and infinitely more fragile. And yet she seemed stronger. Laura lifted a sketch and studied it. Or did she just want to see the strength, need to see it?

When the front door opened, she turned, still holding the pencil sketch. Gabe, covered with snow, kicked the door shut again. His arms were loaded with wood.

"Good morning. Been busy?"

He grunted and stomped the worst of the snow from his boots, then walked, leaving a wet trail, to the firebox to dump his wood. "I thought you might sleep longer."

"I would have." She patted her belly. "He wouldn't. Can I fix you some breakfast?"

Drawing off his gloves, he tossed them down on the hearth. "Already had some. You go ahead."

Laura waited until he'd stripped off his coat. Apparently they were back on friendly terms again. Cautiously friendly. "It seems to be letting up a little."

He sat on the hearth to drag his boots off. Snow was caked in the laces. "We've got three feet now, and I wouldn't look for it to stop before afternoon." He drew out a cigarette. "Might as well make yourself at home."

"I seem to be." She held up the sketch. "I'm flattered."

"You're beautiful," he said offhandedly as he set his

boots on the hearth to dry. "I can rarely resist drawing beautiful things."

"You're fortunate." She dropped the sketch back on the table. "It's so much more rewarding to be able to depict beauty than it is to be beautiful." Gabe lifted a brow. There was a trace, only a trace, of bitterness in her tone. "Things," she explained. "It's strange, but once people see you as beautiful, they almost always see you as a thing."

Turning, she slipped into the kitchen, leaving him frowning after her.

She brewed him fresh coffee, then idled away the morning tidying the kitchen. Gabe gave her room. Before night fell again, he would have some answers, but for now he was content to have her puttering around while he worked.

She seemed to need to be busy. He had thought a woman in her condition would be content to sleep or rest or simply sit and knit for most of the day. He decided it was either nervous energy or her way of avoiding the confrontation he'd promised her the night before.

She didn't ask questions or stand over his shoulder, so they rubbed along through the morning without incident. Once he glanced over to see her tucked into a corner of the sagging sofa reading a book on childbirth. Later she threw some things together in the kitchen and produced a thick, aromatic stew.

She said little. He knew she was waiting, biding her time until he pushed open the door he'd unlocked the night before. He, too, was waiting, biding his time. By midafternoon he decided she looked rested. Taking up his sketch pad and a piece of charcoal, he began to work while she sat across from him peeling apples.

"Why Denver?"

The only sign of her surprise was a quick jerk of the paring knife. She didn't look up or stop peeling. "Because I've never been there."

"Under the circumstances, wouldn't you be better off in some place that's familiar?"

"No."

"Why did you leave Dallas?"

She set the apple down and picked up another. "Because it was time."

"Where's the baby's father, Laura?"

"Dead." There wasn't even a shadow of emotion in her voice.

"Look at me."

Her hands stilled as she lifted her gaze, and he saw that that much, at least, was true.

"You don't have any family who could help you?"

"No."

"Didn't he?"

Her hand jerked again. This time the blade nicked her finger. The blood welled up as Gabe dropped his pad to take her hand. Once again she saw her face in the sweeping charcoal lines.

"I'll get you a bandage."

"It's only a scratch," she began, but he was already up and gone. When he returned he dabbed at the wound with antiseptic. Again Laura was baffled by the care he displayed. The sting came and went; his touch remained gentle.

He was kneeling in front of her, his brows drawn

together as he studied the thin slice in her finger. "Keep this up and I'll think you're accident-prone."

"And I'll think you're the original Good Samaritan." She smiled when he looked up. "We'd both be wrong."

Gabe merely slipped a bandage over the cut and took his seat again. "Turn your head a little, to the left." When she complied, he picked up his pad and turned over a fresh sheet. "Why do they want the baby?"

Her head jerked around, but he continued to sketch.

"I'd like the profile, Laura." His voice was mild, but the demand in it was very clear. "Turn your head again, and try to keep your chin up. Yes, like that." He was silent as he formed her mouth with the charcoal. "The father's family wants the baby. I want to know why."

"I never said that."

"Yes, you did." He had to hurry if he was going to capture that flare of anger in her eyes. "Let's not beat that point into the ground. Just tell me why."

Her hands were gripped tightly together, but there was as much fear as fury in her voice. "I don't have to tell you anything."

"No." He felt a thrill of excitement—and, incredibly, one of desire—as he stroked the charcoal over the pad. The desire puzzled him. More, it worried him. Pushing it aside, he concentrated on prying answers from her. "But since I'm not going to let it drop, you may as well."

Because he knew how to look, and to see, he caught the subtle play of emotions over her face. Fear, fury, frustration. It was the fear that continued to pull him over the line.

"Do you think I'd bundle you and your baby off to

them, whoever the hell they are? Use your head. I haven't got any reason to."

He'd thought he would shout at her. He'd have sworn he was on the verge of doing so. Then, in a move that surprised them both, he reached out to take her hand. He was more surprised than she to feel her fingers curl instinctively into his. When she looked at him, emotions he'd thought unavailable to him turned over in his chest.

"You asked me to help you last night."

Her eyes softened with gratitude, but her voice was firm. "You can't."

"Maybe I can't, and maybe I won't." But as much as it went against the grain of what he considered his character, he wanted to. "I'm not a Samaritan, Laura, good or otherwise, and I don't like to add someone else's problems to my own. But the fact is, you're here, and I don't like playing in the dark."

She was tired, tired of running, tired of hiding, tired of trying to cope entirely on her own. She needed someone. When his hand was covering hers and his eyes were calm and steady on hers, she could almost believe it was him she needed.

"The baby's father is dead," she began, picking her way carefully. She would tell him enough to satisfy him, she hoped, but not all. "His parents want the baby. They want…I don't know, to replace, to take back, something that they've lost. To…to ensure the lineage. I'm sorry for them, but the baby isn't their child." There was that look again, fierce, protective. A mother tiger shielding her cub. "The baby's mine."

"No one would argue with that. Why should you have to run?"

"They have a lot of money, a lot of power."

"So?"

"So?" Angry again, she pushed away. The contact that had been so soothing for both of them was broken. "It's easy to say that when you come from the same world. You've always had. You've never had to want and to wonder. No one takes from people like you, Gabe. They wouldn't dare. You don't know what it's like to have your life depend on the whims of others."

That she had was becoming painfully obvious. "Having money doesn't mean you can take whatever you want."

"Doesn't it?" She turned to him, her face set and cold. "You wanted a place to paint, somewhere you could be alone and be left alone. Did you have to think twice about how to arrange it? Did you have to plan or save or make compromises, or did you just write a check and move in?"

His eyes were narrowed as he rose to face her. "Buying a cabin is a far cry from taking a baby from its mother."

"Not to some. Property is property, after all."

"You're being ridiculous."

"And you're being naive."

His temper wavered, vying with amusement. "That's a first. Sit down, Laura, you make me nervous when you swing around."

"I'm not going to break," she muttered, but she eased into a chair. "I'm strong, I take care of myself. I had an examination just before I left Dallas, and the baby and I are fine. Better than fine. In a few weeks I'm going to check into a hospital in Denver and have my baby. Then we're going to disappear."

He thought about it. He almost believed the woman sitting across from him could accomplish it. Then he remembered how lost and frightened she'd been the night before. There was no use pointing out the strain she'd been under and its consequences for her. But he knew now what button to push.

"Do you think it's fair to the baby to keep running?"

"No, it's horribly, horribly unfair. But it would be worse to stop and let them take him."

"Why are you so damn sure they would, or could?"

"Because they told me. They explained what they thought was best for me and the child, and they offered to pay me." The venom came into her voice at that, black and bitter. "They offered to give me money for my baby, and when I refused they threatened to simply take him." She didn't want to relive that dreadful, terrifying scene. With an effort she cleared it from her mind.

He felt a swift and dark disgust for these people he didn't even know. He buried it with a shake of his head and tried to reason with her. "Laura, whatever they want, or intend, they couldn't just take what isn't theirs. No court would just take an infant from its mother without good cause."

"I can't win on my own." She closed her eyes for a moment because she wanted badly to lay her head down and weep out all the fear and anguish. "I can't fight them on their own ground, Gabe, and I won't put my child through the misery of custody suits and court battles, the publicity, the gossip and speculation. A child needs a home, and love and security. I'm going to see to it that mine has all of those things. Whatever I have to do, wherever I have to go."

"I won't argue with you about what's right for you and the baby, but sooner or later you're going to have to face this."

"When the time comes, I will."

He rose and paced over to the fire to light another cigarette. He should drop it, just leave it—her—alone and let her follow her own path. It was none of his business. Not his problem. He swore, because somehow, the moment she'd taken his arm to cross the road, she'd become his business.

"Got any money?"

"Some. Enough to pay a doctor, and a bit more."

He was asking for trouble. He knew it. But for the first time in almost a year he felt as though something really mattered. Sitting on the edge of the hearth, he blew out smoke and studied her.

"I want to paint you," he said abruptly. "I'll pay you the standard model's fee, plus room and board."

"I can't take your money."

"Why not? You seem to think I have too much for my own good, anyway."

Shame brought color flooding into her cheeks. "I didn't mean it—not like that."

He brushed her words aside. "Whatever you meant, the fact remains that I want to paint you. I work at my own pace, so you'll have to be patient. I'm not good at compromise, but owing to your condition I'm willing to make some concessions and stop when you're tired or uncomfortable."

It was tempting, very tempting. She tried to forget that she'd traded on her looks before and concentrate on what the extra money would mean to the baby. "I'd like to agree, but the fact is, your work is well-known. If the portrait was shown, they'd recognize me."

"True enough, but that doesn't mean I'd be obliged to tell anyone where we'd met or when. You have my word that no one will ever trace you through me."

She was silent for a moment, warring with herself. "Would you come here?"

Hesitating only a moment, he tossed his cigarette into the fire. He rose, walked over, then crouched in front of her chair. She, too, had learned how to read a face. "Your word?"

"Yes."

Some risks were worth taking. She held both hands out to his, putting her trust into them.

With the continuing fall of snow, it was a day without a sunrise, a sunset, a twilight. The day stayed dim from morning on, and then night closed in without fanfare. And the snow stopped.

Laura might not have noticed if she hadn't been standing by the window. The flakes didn't appear to have tapered off, but to have stopped as if someone had thrown a switch. There was a vague sense of disappointment, the same she remembered feeling as a young girl when a storm had ended. On impulse, she bundled herself in her boots and coat and stepped out onto the porch.

Though Gabe had shoveled it off twice during the day, the snow came almost to her knees. Her boots sank in and disappeared. She had the sensation of being swallowed up by a soft, benign cloud. She wrapped her arms around her chest and breathed in the thin, cold air.

There were no stars. There was no moon. The porch light tossed its glow only a few feet. All she could see was white. All she could hear was silence. To some the high blanket of snow might have been a prison, something to chafe against. To Laura it was a fortress.

She'd decided to trust someone other than herself again. Standing there, soaking up the pure dark, the pure quiet, she knew that the decision had been the right one.

He wasn't a gentle man, or even a contented man, but he was a kind one, and, she was certain, a man of his word. If they were using each other, her for sanctuary, him for art, it was a fair exchange. She needed to rest. God knew she needed whatever time she could steal to rest and recover.

She hadn't told him how tired she was, how much effort it took for her just to keep on her feet for most of the day. Physically the pregnancy had been an easy one. She was strong, she was healthy. Otherwise she would have crumpled long before this. But the last few months had drained every ounce of her emotional and mental reserves. The cabin, the mountains, the man, were going to give her time to build those reserves back up again.

She was going to need them.

He didn't understand what the Eagletons could do, what they could accomplish with their money and their power. She'd already seen what they were capable of. Hadn't they paid and maneuvered to have their son's mistakes glossed over? Hadn't they managed, with a few phone calls and a few favors called in, to have his death, and the death of the woman with him, turned from the grisly waste it had been into a tragic accident?

There had never been any mention in the press about alcohol and adultery. As far as the public was concerned, Anthony Eagleton, heir to the Eagleton fortune, had died as a result of a slippery road and faulty steering, and not his criminally careless drunk driving. The woman who had died with him had been turned from his mistress into his secretary.

The divorce proceedings that Laura had started had been erased, shredded, negated. No shadow of scandal would fall over the memory of Anthony Eagleton or over the family name. She'd been pressured into playing the shocked and grieving widow.

She had been shocked. She had grieved. Not for what had been lost—not on a lonely stretch of road outside of Boston—but for what had been lost so soon after her wedding night.

There was no use looking back, Laura reminded herself. Now, especially now, she had to look forward. Whatever had happened between her and Tony, they had created a life. And that life was hers to protect and to cherish.

With the spring snow glistening and untouched as far as she could see, she could believe that everything would work out for the best.

"What are you thinking?"

Startled, she turned toward Gabe with a little laugh. "I didn't hear you."

"You weren't listening." He pulled the door closed behind him. "It's cold out here."

"It feels wonderful. How much is there, do you think?"

"Three and a half, maybe four feet."

"I've never seen so much snow before. I can't imagine it ever melting and letting the grass grow."

His hands were bare. He tucked them in the pockets of his jacket. "I came here in November and there was already snow. I've never seen it any other way."

She tried to imagine that, living in a place where the snow never melted. No, she thought, she would need the spring, the buds, the green, the promise. "How long will you stay?"

"I don't know. I haven't thought about it."

She turned to smile at him, though she felt a touch of envy at his being so unfettered. "All those paintings. You'll need to have a show."

"Sooner or later." He moved his shoulders, suddenly restless. San Francisco, his family, his memories, seemed very far away. "No hurry."

"Art needs to be seen and appreciated," she murmured, thinking out loud. "It shouldn't be hidden up here."

"And people should?"

"Do you mean me, or is that what you're doing, too? Hiding?"

"I'm working," he said evenly.

"A man like you could work anywhere, I think. You'd just elbow people aside and go to it."

He had to grin. "Maybe, but now and again I like to have some space. Once you make a name, people tend to look over your shoulder."

"Well, I, for one, am glad you came here, for whatever reason." She brushed the hair away from her face. "I should go back in, but I don't want to." She was smiling as she leaned back against the post.

His eyes narrowed. When he cupped her face in his hands, his fingers were cold and firm. "There's something about your eyes," he murmured, turning her face fully into the light. "They say everything a man wants a woman to say, and a great deal he doesn't. You have old eyes, Laura. Old, sad eyes."

She said nothing, not because her mind was empty, but because it was suddenly filled with so many things, so many thoughts, so many wishes. She hadn't thought she could feel anything like this again, and certainly not this longing for a man. Her skin warmed with it, even though his touch was cool, almost disinterested.

The sexual tug surprised her, even embarrassed her a little. But it was the emotional pull, the slow, hard drag of it, that kept her silent.

"I wonder what you've seen in your life."

As if of their own volition, his fingers stroked her cheek. They were long, slender, artistic, but hard and strong. Even so, he might merely have been familiarizing himself with the shape of her face, with the texture of her skin. An artist with his subject.

The longing leaped inside her, the foolish, impossible longing to be loved, held, desired, not for her face, not for the image a man could see, but for the woman inside.

"I'm getting tired," she said, managing to keep her voice steady. "I think I'll go to bed now."

He didn't move out of her way immediately. And his hand lingered. He couldn't have said what kept him there, staring at her, searching the eyes he found so fascinating. Then he stepped back quickly and shoved the door open for her.

"Good night, Gabe."

"Good night."

He stayed out in the cold, wondering what was wrong with him. For a moment, damn it, for a great deal longer than a moment, he'd found himself wanting her. Filled with self-disgust, he pulled out a cigarette. A man had to be sinking low to think about making love to a woman who was more than seven months along with another man's child.

But it was a long time before he could convince himself he'd imagined it.

Chapter 3

He wondered what she was thinking. She looked so serene, so quietly content. The pale pink sweater she wore fell into a soft cowl at her throat. Her hair shimmered to her shoulders. Again she wore no jewelry, nothing to draw attention away from her, nothing to draw attention to her.

Gabe rarely used models in his work, because even if they managed to hold the pose for as long as he demanded they began to look bored and restless. Laura, on the other hand, looked as though she could sit endlessly with that same soft smile on her face.

That was part of what he wanted to capture in the portrait. That inner patience, that…well, he supposed he could call it a gracious acceptance of time—what had come before, and what was up ahead. He'd never had much patience, not with people, not with his work, not with himself. It was a trait he could admire in her without having the urge to develop it himself.

Yet there was something more, something beyond the utterly feminine beauty and the Madonna-like calm. From time to time he saw a fierceness in her, a warrior-like determination. He could see that she was a woman who would do whatever was necessary to protect what was hers. Judging from her story, all that was hers was the child she carried.

She had more to tell, he mused as he ran the pencil over the pad. The bits and pieces she'd offered had only been given to keep him from asking more. He hadn't asked for more. It wasn't his usual style, once he'd decided an explanation was called for, to accept a partial one. He couldn't quite make himself push for the whole when even the portion she'd given him had plainly cost her so much.

There was still time. The radio continued to squawk about the roads that were closed and the snow that was yet to come. The Rockies could be treacherous in the spring. Gabe estimated it would be two weeks, perhaps three, before a trip could be managed with real safety.

It was odd, but he would have thought the enforced company would annoy him. Instead, he found himself pleased to have had his self-imposed solitude broken. It had been a long time since he'd done a portrait. Maybe too long. But he hadn't been able to face flesh and blood, not since Michael.

In the cabin, cut off from memories and reminders, he'd begun the healing process. In San Francisco he hadn't been able to pick up a brush. Grief had done more than make him weak. For a time it had made him…blank.

But here, secluded, solitary, he'd painted landscapes, still lifes, half-remembered dreams and seascapes from old sketches. It had been enough. Not until Laura had he felt the need to paint the human face again.

Once he'd believed in destiny, in a pattern of life that was meant to be even before birth. Michael's death had changed that. From that point, Gabe had had to blame something, someone. It had been easiest, and most painful, to blame himself. Now, sketching Laura, thinking over the odd set of circumstances that had brought her into his life, he began to wonder again.

And what, he asked himself yet again, was she thinking?

"Are you tired?"

"No." She answered, but she didn't move. He'd stationed a chair by the window, angling it so that she was facing him but still able to look out. The light fell over her, bringing no shadows. "I like to look at the snow. There are tracks in it now, and I wonder what animals might have passed by without us seeing. And I can see the mountains. They look so old and angry. Back east they're more tame, more good-natured."

He absently murmured his agreement as he studied his sketch. It was good, but it wasn't right, and he wanted to begin working on canvas soon. He set the pad aside and frowned at her. She stared back, patient and—if he wasn't reading her incorrectly—amused. "Do you have anything else to wear? Something off-the-shoulder, maybe?"

The amusement was even more evident now. "Sorry, my wardrobe's a bit limited at the moment."

He rose and began to pace, to the fire, to the window, back to the table. When he strode over to take her face in his hand and turn it this way and that, she sat obligingly. After three days of posing, she was used to it. She might have been an arrangement of flowers, Laura thought, or a bowl of fruit. It was as if that one moment of awareness on the snow-covered porch had never happened. She'd already convinced herself that she'd imagined that look in his eyes—and, more, her response to it.

He was the artist. She was the clay. And she'd been there before.

"You have a completely feminine face," he began, talking more to himself than to her. "Alluring and yet composed, and soft, even with the angular shape and those cheekbones. It's not threatening, and yet, it's utterly distracting. This—" his thumb brushed casually over her full lower lip "—says sex, even while your eyes promise love and devotion. And the fact that you're ripe—"

"Ripe?" She laughed, and the hands that had clenched in her lap relaxed again.

"Isn't that what pregnancy is? It only adds to the fascination. There's a promise and a fulfillment and—despite education and progress—a compelling mystery to a woman with child. Like an angel."

"How?"

As he spoke, he began to fuss with her hair, drawing it back, piling it up, letting it fall again. "We see angels as ethereal creatures, mystic, above human desires and flaws, but the fact is, they were human once."

His words appealed to her, made her smile. "Do you believe in angels?"

His hand was still in her hair, but he'd forgotten, totally forgotten, the practical reason for it. "Life wouldn't be worth much if you didn't." She had the hair of an angel, shimmery-blond, cloud-soft. Feeling suddenly awkward, he drew his hand away and tucked it in the pocket of his baggy corduroys.

"Would you like to take a break?" she asked him. Her hands were balled in her lap again.

"Yeah. Rest for an hour. I need to think this through." He stepped back automatically when she rose. When he wasn't working, he took great care not to come into physical contact with her. It was disturbing how much he wanted to touch her. "Put your feet up." When she lifted a brow at that, he shifted uncomfortably. "It recommended it in that book you leave lying around. I figured it wouldn't hurt for me to glance through it, under the circumstances."

"You're very kind."

"Self-preservation." Things happened to him when she smiled like that. Things he recognized but didn't want to acknowledge. "The more I make sure you take care of yourself, the less chance there is of you going into labor before the roads are clear."

"I've got more than a month," she reminded him. "But I appreciate you worrying about me—about us."

"Put your feet up," he repeated. "I'll get you some milk."

"But I—"

"You've only had one glass today." With an impatient gesture, he motioned her to the sofa before he walked into the kitchen.

With a little sigh of relief, Laura settled back against the cushions. Putting her feet up wasn't as easy as it once had been, but she managed to prop them on the edge of the coffee table. The heat from the fire radiated toward her, making her wish she could curl up in front of it. If she did, she thought wryly, it would take a crane to haul her back up again.

He was being so kind, Laura thought as she turned her head toward the sound of Gabe rummaging in the kitchen. He didn't like her to remind him of it, but he was. No one had ever treated her quite like this—as an equal, yet as someone to be protected. As a friend, she thought, without tallying a list of obligations, a list of debts that had to be paid. Whether he listed them or not, someday, when she was able, she'd find a way to pay him back. Someday.

She could see the future if she closed her eyes and thought calm thoughts. She'd have a little apartment somewhere in the city. Any city. There would be a room for the baby, something in sunny yellows and glossy whites, with fairy-tale prints on the walls. She'd have a rocking chair she could sit in with the baby during the long, quiet nights, when the rest of the world was asleep.

And she wouldn't be alone anymore.

Opening her eyes, she saw Gabe standing over her. She wanted, badly, to reach up, to take his hands and draw in some of the strength and confidence she felt radiating from him. She wanted, more, for him to run his thumb along her lip again, slowly, gently, as though she were a woman, rather than a thing to be painted.

Instead, she reached up to take the glass of milk he held. "After the baby's born and I finish nursing, I'm never going to drink a drop of milk again."

"This is the last of the fresh," he told her. "Tomorrow you go on powdered and canned."

"Oh, joy." Grimacing, she downed half the contents of

the glass. "I pretend it's coffee, you know. Strong, black coffee." She sipped again. "Or, if I'm feeling reckless, champagne. French, in fluted crystal."

"It's too bad I don't have any wineglasses handy. It would help the illusion. Are you hungry?"

"It's a myth about eating for two, and if I gain much more weight I'll begin to moo." Content, she settled back again. "That painting of Paris…did you do it here?"

He glanced over at the work. So she'd been there, he thought. It was a moody, almost surreal study of the Bois de Boulogne. "Yes, from old sketches and memory. When were you there?"

"I didn't say I'd been to Paris."

"You wouldn't have recognized it otherwise." He took the empty glass out of her hand and set it aside. "The more secretive you are, Laura, the more it makes me want to dig."

"A year ago," she said stiffly. "I spent two weeks there."

"How did you like it?"

"Paris?" She ordered herself to relax. It had been a lifetime ago, almost long enough that she could imagine it had all happened to someone else. "It's a beautiful city, like an old, old woman who still knows how to flirt. The flowers were blooming, and the smells were incredible. It rained and rained, for three days, and you could sit and watch the black umbrellas hurrying by and the blossoms opening up."

Instinctively he put a hand over hers to calm the agitated movement of her fingers. "You weren't happy there."

"Paris in the spring?" She concentrated on making her hands go limp. "Only a fool wouldn't be happy there."

"The baby's father…was he with you there?"

"Why does it matter?"

It shouldn't have mattered. But now, whenever he looked at the painting, he would think of her. And he had to know. "Did you love him?"

Had she? Laura looked back at the fire, but the only answers were within herself. Had she loved Tony? Her lips curved a little. Yes, she had, she had loved the Tony she'd imagined him to be. "Very much. I loved him very much."

"How long have you been alone?"

"I'm not." She laid a hand on her stomach. When she felt the answering movement, her smile widened. Taking Gabe's hand, she pressed it against her. "Feel that? Incredible, isn't it? Someone's in there."

He felt the stirring beneath his hand, gentle at first, then with a punch that surprised him. Without thinking, he moved closer. "That felt like a left jab. Makes you feel as though it's fighting to get out." He knew the feeling, the impatience, the frustration at being trapped in one world while you longed for another. "How does it feel from the other side?"

"Alive." Laughing, she left her hand over his. "In Dallas they put a monitor on, and I could hear the baby's heartbeat. It was so fast, so impatient. Nothing in the world ever sounded so wonderful. And I think…"

But he was looking at her now, deeply, intently. Their hands were still joined, their bodies just brushing. Even as the life inside her quickened, so did her pulse. The warmth, the intimacy, of the moment washed over her, leaving her breathless and full of needs.

He wanted to hold her, badly. The urge to gather her close and just hold on was so sharp, so intense that he hurt. He dreamed of her every night when he struggled for sleep on the floor of the spare room. In his dreams they were curled in bed together, with her breath warm on his cheek and her hair tangled in his hands. And when he woke from the dreams he told himself he was mad. He told himself that again now and moved aside.

Though they were no longer touching, he could feel, as well as hear, her long, quiet sigh.

"I'd like to work some more, if you're up to it."

"Of course." She wanted to weep. That was natural, she told herself. Pregnant women wept easily. Their emotions ran on the surface, to be bruised and battered without effort, and often without cause.

"I've got something in mind. Hold on a minute."

She waited, still sitting, while he went into the spare room. Moments later he came back holding a navy blue shirt.

"Put this on. I think the contrast between the man's shirt and your face might be the answer."

"All right." Laura went into the bedroom and stripped off the big pink sweater. She started to draw an arm through the sleeve and then she caught his scent. It was there, clinging to the heavy cotton. Tough, and unapologetically sexual. Man. Unable to resist, she rubbed her cheek over it. The material was soft. The scent was not, but somehow even the scent of him made her feel safe. And yet, foolish as it seemed, it made her feel a dull, deep tremor of desire.

Wasn't it wrong to want as a woman, to want Gabe as a man, when she carried such a responsibility? But it didn't seem wrong when she felt so close to him. He had sorrows, too. She could see them, sense them. Perhaps it was that common ground, and their isolation, that made her feel as though she'd known him, cared about him, for so long.

With a sigh, she slipped into the shirt. What did she know about her own feelings? The first, the only, time she'd trusted them completely had brought misery. Whatever emotions Gabe stirred in her, she would be wise to keep gratitude in the forefront.

When she stepped back into the main cabin, he was going through his sketches, rejecting, considering, accepting. He glanced up and realized that his conception of Laura fell far, far short of the mark.

She looked like the angel he'd spoken of, illusory, golden, yet tied now to the earth. He preferred to think of her as an illusion rather than as a woman, one who stirred him.

"That's more of the look I want," he said, managing to keep his voice steady. "The color's good on you, and the straight-line masculine style is a nice contrast."

"You may not get it back anytime soon. It's wonderfully comfortable."

"Consider it a loan."

He walked over to the chair as she sat and shifted into the precise pose she'd been in before the break. Not for the first time, Gabe wondered if she'd modeled before. That was another question, for another time.

"Let's try something else." He shifted her, mere inches, muttering to himself. Laura nearly smiled. She was back to being a bowl of fruit.

"Damn, I wish we had some flowers. A rose. Just one rose."

"You could imagine one."

"I may." He tilted her head a fraction to the left before he stood back. "This feels right, so I'm going to draw it on canvas. I've wasted enough time on rough sketches."

"Three whole days."

"I've completed paintings in half that time when things clicked."

She could see it, him sitting on a tall stool at an easel, working feverishly, brows lowered, eyes narrowed, those long, narrow hands creating. "There are some in here you haven't finished at all."

"Mood changed." He was already making broad strokes on canvas with his pencil. "Do you finish everything you start?"

She thought about that. "I suppose not, but people are always saying you should."

"When something's not right, why drag it out to the bitter end?"

"Sometimes you promise," she murmured, thinking of her marriage vows.

Because he was watching her closely, he saw the swift look of regret. As always, though he tried to block it, her emotions touched a chord in him. "Sometimes promises can't be kept."

"No. But they should be," she said quietly. Then she fell silent.

He worked for nearly an hour, defining, refining, perfecting. She was giving him the mood he wanted. Pensive, patient, sensuous. He already knew, even before the first brush stroke, that this would be one of his best. Perhaps his very best. And he knew he would have to paint her again, in other moods, in other poses.

But that was for tomorrow. Today, now, he needed to capture the tone of her, the feel, the simplicity. That was pencil lines and curves. Black against white, and a few shades of gray. Tomorrow he would begin filling in, adding the color, the complexities. When he had finished he would have the whole of her on canvas, and he would know her fully, as no one had ever before or would ever again.

"Will you let me see it as you go along?"

"What?"

"The painting." Laura kept her head still but shifted her eyes from the window to him. "I know artists are supposed to be temperamental about showing their work before it's finished."

"I'm not temperamental." He lifted his gaze to hers, as if inviting her to disagree.

"Anyone could see that." Though she kept her expression sober, he could hear the amusement in her voice. "So will you let me see it?"

"Doesn't matter to me. As long as you realize that if you see something you don't like I won't change it."

This time she did laugh, more freely, more richly than before. His fingers tightened on the pencil. "You mean if I see something that wounds my vanity? You don't have to worry about that. I'm not vain."

"All beautiful women are vain. They're entitled."

"People are only vain if their looks matter to them."

This time he laughed, but cynically. He set down his pencil. "And yours don't matter to you?"

"I didn't do anything to earn them, did I? An accident of fate, or a stroke of luck. If I were terribly smart or talented somehow I'd probably be annoyed with my looks, because people look at them and nothing else." She shrugged, then settled with perfect ease into the pose again. "But since I'm neither of those, I've learned to accept that looking a certain way is…I don't know, a gift that makes up for a lack of other things."

"What would you trade your beauty for?"

"Any number of things. But then, a trade isn't earning, either, so it wouldn't count. Will you tell me something?"

"Probably." He took a rag out of his back pocket and dusted off his hands.

"Which are you more vain about, your looks or your work?"

He tossed the rag aside. It was odd that she could look so sad, so serious, and still make him laugh. "No one's ever accused me of being beautiful, so there's no contest." He started to turn the easel. When she began to rise, he motioned her back. "No, relax. Look from there and tell me what you think."

Laura settled back and studied. It was only a sketch, less detailed than many of the others he'd done. It was her face and torso, her right hand resting lightly just below her left shoulder. For some reason it seemed a protective pose, not defensive, but cautious.

He'd been right about the shirt, she realized. It made her seem more of a woman than any amount of lace or silks could have. Her hair was long and loose, falling in heavy, disordered curls that contradicted the pose. She hadn't expected to find any surprises in her face, but as she studied his conception of it, she shifted uncomfortably in her chair.

"I'm not as sad as you make me look."

"I've already warned you I wouldn't change anything."

"You're free to paint as you please. I'm simply telling you that you have a misconception."

There was a huffiness in her voice that amused him. He turned the easel around again but didn't bother to look at his work. "I don't think so."

"I'm hardly tragic."

"Tragic?" He rocked back on his heels as he studied her. "There's nothing tragic about the woman in the painting. *Valiant* is the word."

She smiled at that and pushed herself out of the chair. "I'm not valiant, either, but it's your painting."

"We agree on that."

"Gabe!"

She flung out a hand. The urgency in her voice had him crossing to her quickly and gripping her hand. "What is it?"

"Look, look out there." She turned to him, using her free hand to point.

Not urgency, Gabe realized. He was tempted to strangle her. Excitement. The excitement of seeing a solitary buck less than two yards from the window. It stood deep in snow, its head lifted, scenting the air. Arrogantly, and without a trace of fear, it stared at them through the glass.

"Oh, he's wonderful. I've never seen one so big before, or so close."

It was easy to share the pleasure. A deer, a fox, a hawk circling overhead…those were some of the things that had helped him over his own grief.

"A few weeks ago I hiked down to a stream about a mile south of here. I came across a whole family. I was downwind, and I managed three sketches before the doe spotted me."

"This whole place belongs to him. Can you imagine it? Acres and acres. He must know it, even enjoy it, or else he wouldn't look so sure of himself." She laughed again, and pressed her free hand to the frosted glass. "You know, it's as if we were exhibits and he'd come to take a quick look around the zoo."

The deer nosed down in the snow, perhaps looking for the grass that was buried far beneath, perhaps scenting another animal. He moved slowly, confident in his solitude. Around him the trees dripped with ice and snow.

Abruptly he raised his head, his crown of antlers plunging high in the air. In bounds and leaps he raced across the snow and disappeared into the woods beyond.

Laughing, Laura turned, then instantly forgot everything.

She hadn't realized they had moved so close together. Nor had he. Their hands were still linked. Beside them the sun streamed in, losing power as the afternoon moved toward evening. And the cabin, like the woods beyond, was absolutely silent.

He touched her. He hadn't known he would, but the moment his fingers grazed her cheek he knew he needed to. She didn't move away. Perhaps he would have accepted it if she had. He wanted to believe he would have accepted it. But she didn't move.

There were nerves. He felt them in the hand that trembled in his. He had them, too. Another new experience. How did he approach her, when he knew he had no business approaching her? How did he resist what common sense told him he had to resist?

Yet her skin was warm under his touch. Real. Not a portrait, but a woman. Whatever had happened in her life, whatever had made her into the woman she was, that was yesterday. This was now. Her eyes, wide and more than a little frightened, were on his. She didn't move. She waited.

He swore at himself even as he slowly, ever so slowly, lowered his lips to hers.

It was madness to allow it. It was more than madness to want it. But even before his lips touched hers she felt herself give in to him. As she gave, she braced herself, not knowing what to expect for herself, or for him.

It might have been the first. That was her one and only thought as his mouth closed over hers. Not just the first with him but the first with anyone. No one had ever kissed her like this. She had known passion, the quick, almost painful desire that came from heat and frenzy. She had known demands, some that she could answer, some that she could not. She had known the anger and the hunger a man could have for a woman, but she had never known, had never imagined, this kind of reverence.

And yet, even with that, there were hints of darker needs, needs held down by chains, that made the embrace more exciting, more involving, than any other. His hands were in her hair, searching, exploring, while his lips moved endlessly over hers. She felt the world tip and knew instinctively that he would be there to right it again.

He had to stop. He couldn't stop. One taste, just one taste, and he craved more. It seemed he'd been empty, without knowing it, and now—incredibly, swiftly, terrifyingly—he was filled.

Her hands, hesitant, somehow innocent, slipped over

his arms to his shoulders. When she parted her lips, there was that same curious shyness in the invitation. He could smell the spring, though it was still buried beneath the snow, could smell it in her hair, on her skin. Even the woodsmoke that always tinted the air in the cabin couldn't overwhelm it. Logs shifted in the grate, and the wind that came up with evening began to moan against the window. And Laura, her mouth warm and giving under his, sighed.

He wanted to play out the fantasy, to draw her up into his arms and take her to bed. To lie with her, to slip his shirt from her and feel her skin against his own. To have her touch him, hold on to him. Trust him.

The war inside him raged on. She wasn't merely a woman, she was a woman who was carrying a child. And growing inside her was not merely a child, but the child of another man, one she had loved.

She wasn't his to love. He wasn't hers to trust. Still, she pulled at him, her secrets, her eyes, eyes that said much, much more than her words, and her beauty, which she didn't seem to understand went far beyond the shape and texture of her face.

So he had to stop, until he resolved within himself exactly what he wanted—and until she trusted him enough to tell him the whole truth.

He would have drawn her away from him, but she pressed her face into his shoulder. "Please don't say anything, just for a minute."

There were tears in her voice, and they left him more shaken than the kiss had. The tug-of-war increased, and finally he lifted a hand to stroke her hair. The baby turned, moving inside her, against him, and he wondered what in God's name he was going to do.

"I'm sorry." Her voice was under control again, but she didn't let go. How could she have known how badly she needed to be held, when there had been so few times in her life when anyone had bothered? "I don't mean to cling."

"You're not."

"Well." Drawing herself up straight, she stepped back. There were no tears, but her eyes glimmered with the effort it took to hold them in. "You were going to say that you didn't mean for that to happen, but it's all right."

"I didn't mean for that to happen," he said evenly. "But that's not an apology."

"Oh." A little nonplussed, she braced a hand on the back of the chair. "I suppose what I meant is that I don't want you to feel—I don't want you to think that I— Hell." With that, she gave in and sat. "I'm trying to say that I'm not upset that you kissed me and that I understand."

"Good." He felt better, much better than he'd thought he would. Casually he dragged over another chair and straddled it. "What do you understand, Laura?"

She'd thought he would let it go at that, take the easy way out. She struggled to say what she felt without saying too much. "That you felt a little sorry for me, and involved a bit, because of the situation, and the painting, too." Why couldn't she relax again? And why was he looking at her that way? "I don't want you to think that I misunderstood. I would hardly expect you to be..." The ground was getting shakier by the minute. She was ready to shut up entirely, but he quirked a brow and gestured with his hands, inviting her, almost challenging her, to finish.

"I realize you wouldn't be attracted to me—physically, that is—under the circumstances. And I don't want to think that I interpreted what just happened as anything other than a—a sort of kindness."

"That's funny." As if he were considering the idea, Gabe reached up and scratched his chin. "You don't look stupid. I'm attracted to you, Laura, and there's a part of that attraction that's very, very physical. Making love with you may not be possible under the circumstances, but that doesn't mean that the desire to do so isn't there."

She opened her mouth as if to speak, but ended up just lifting her hands and then letting them fall again.

"The fact that you're carrying a child is only part of the reason I can't make love with you. The other, though not as obvious, is just as important. I need the story, Laura, your story. All of it."

"I can't."

"Afraid?"

She shook her head. Her eyes glimmered, but her chin lifted. "Ashamed."

He would have expected almost any other reason than that. "Why? Because you weren't married to the baby's father?"

"No. Please don't ask me."

He wanted to argue, but he bit the words back. She was looking pale and tired and just too fragile. "All right, for now. But think about this. I have feelings for you, and they're growing much faster than either of us might like. Right now I'm damned if I know what to do about it."

When he rose, she reached up and touched his arm.

"Gabe, there's nothing to do. I can't tell you how much I wish it were otherwise."

"Life's what you make it, angel." He touched her hair then stepped away. "We need more wood."

Laura sat in the empty cabin and wished more than she had ever wished for anything that she had made a better job of hers.

Chapter 4

More snow had fallen during the night. It was, compared to what had come before, hardly more than a dusting. The fresh inches lay in mounds and drifts over the rest, where the wind had blown them. In places the snow was as high as a man. Miniature mountains of it lay cozily against the windowpanes, shifting constantly in the wind.

Already the sun was melting the fresh fall, and if Laura listened she could hear the water sliding down the gutters from the roof like rain. It was a friendly sound, and it made her think of hot tea by a sizzling fire, a good book read on a lazy afternoon, a nap on the sofa in early evening.

But this was morning, only an hour or two past dawn. As usual, she had the cabin to herself.

Gabe was chopping wood. From the kitchen, where she was optimistically heating milk and a chocolate bar in a pan, she could hear the steady thud of the ax. She knew the woodbox was full, and the stack of logs outside the rear door was still high. Even if the snow lasted into June, they would still have an ample supply. Artist or not, he was a physical man, and she understood his need to do something manual and tiring.

It seemed so…normal, she thought. Her cooking in the kitchen, Gabe splitting logs, icicles growing long and shiny on the eaves outside the window. Their little world was so well tuned, so self-contained. It was like this every morning. She would rise to find him already outdoors, shoveling, chopping, hauling. She would make fresh coffee or warm what he'd left in the pot. The portable radio would bring her news from the outside, but it never seemed terribly important. After a little while he would come in, shake and stomp the snow off, then accept the cup of coffee she offered him. The routine would continue with him taking his place in behind the easel and Laura taking hers by the window.

Sometimes they would talk. Sometimes they would not.

Beneath the routine, she sensed some kind of hurry in him that she couldn't understand. Though he might paint for hours, his movements controlled and measured, he still seemed impatient to finish. The fact was, the portrait was coming along faster than she could ever have imagined. She was taking shape on canvas—or rather the woman he saw when he looked at her was taking shape. Laura couldn't understand why he had chosen to make her look so otherworldly, so dreamy. She was very much a part of the world. The child she carried grounded her to it.

But she'd learned not to complain, because he didn't listen.

He'd done other sketches, as well, some full-length, some just of her face. She told herself he was entitled, particularly if that was all the payment she could give him for the roof over her head. A few of the sketches made her uneasy, like the one he'd drawn when she'd fallen asleep on the sofa late one afternoon. She'd looked so…defenseless. And she'd felt defenseless when she'd realized that he'd watched her and drawn her while she was unaware of it.

Not that she was afraid of him. Laura poked halfheartedly at the mixture of powdered milk, water and chocolate. He'd been kinder to her than she'd had any right to expect. And, though he could be terse and brusque, he was the gentlest man she'd ever known.

Perhaps he was attracted to her. Men had often been attracted to her face. But whether he was or not he treated her with respect and care. She'd learned not to expect those things when there was attraction.

With a shrug, she poured the liquid into a mug. Now wasn't the time to focus on the feeling Gabe might or might not have. She was on her own. Fixing a mental image of creamy hot chocolate in her mind, Laura downed half the contents of the mug. She made a face, sighed, then lifted the mug again. In a matter of days she would be on her way to Denver again.

A sudden pain had her gripping the side of the counter for support. She held on, fighting back the instinctive need to call for Gabe. It was nothing, she told herself as it began to ease. Moving carefully, she started into the living room. Gabe's chopping stopped. It was in that silence that she heard the other sound. An engine?

The panic came instantly, and almost as quickly was pushed down. They hadn't found her. It was ridiculous to even think it. But she walked quickly, quietly, to the front window to look out.

A snowmobile. The sight of it, shiny and toylike, might have amused and pleased her if she hadn't seen the uniformed state trooper on it. Preparing to stand her ground if it came to that, Laura moved to the door and opened it a crack.

Gabe had worked up a warm, healthy sweat. He appreciated being outdoors, appreciated the crisp air, the rhythm of his work. He couldn't say that it kept his mind off Laura. Nothing did. But it helped him put the situation into perspective.

She needed help. He was going to help her.

There were some who knew him who would have been more than a little surprised by his decision. It wasn't that anyone would have accused him of being unfeeling. The sensitivity in his paintings was proof of his capacity for emotion, passion, compassion. But few would have thought him capable of unconditional generosity.

It was Michael who had been generous.

Gabe had always been self-absorbed—or, more accurately, absorbed in his art, driven to depict life, with all its joys and pains. Michael had simply embraced life.

Now he was gone. Gabe brought the ax down, his breath whistling through his teeth and puffing white in the thin air. And Michael's leaving had left a hole so big, so great, that Gabe wasn't certain it could ever be filled.

He heard the engine when his ax was at the apex of his swing. Distracted, he let it fall so that the blade was buried in wood. Splinters popped out to join others on the trampled snow. With a quick glance toward the kitchen window, Gabe started around the cabin to meet the visitor.

He didn't make a conscious decision to protect the woman inside. He didn't have to. It was the most natural thing in the world.

"How ya doing?" The cop, his full cheeks reddened by wind and cold, shut off the engine and he nodded to Gabe.

"Well enough." He judged the trooper to be about twenty-five and half frozen. "How's the road?"

Giving a short laugh, the trooper stepped off the snowmobile. "Let's just say I hope you've got no appointments to keep."

"Nothing pressing."

"Good thing." He offered a gloved hand. "Scott Beecham."

"Gabe Bradley."

"I heard somebody bought the old McCampbell place." With his hands on his hips, Beecham studied the cabin. "A hell of a winter to pick for moving in. We're swinging by to check on everybody on the ridge, seeing if they need supplies or if anyone's sick."

"I stocked up the day of the storm."

"Good for you." He gestured toward the Jeep. "At least you've got a fighting chance in a four-wheel drive. Could've filled a used car lot with some of the vehicles towed in. We're checking around on a compact, an '84

Chevy that took a spin into the guardrail about a quarter mile from here. Abandoned. Driver might have wandered out and got lost in the blizzard."

"My wife," Gabe said. In the doorway, Laura opened her eyes wide. "She was worried that something had happened to me and got the idea of driving into town." Gabe grinned and drew out a cigarette. "Damn near ran into me. At the rate things were going, I figured it was best to leave the car where it was and get us back here. Haven't been able to get back out to check on the damage."

"Not as bad as some I've seen the last few days. Was she hurt?"

"No. Scared ten years off both of us, though."

"I'll bet. Afraid we're going to have to tow the vehicle in, Mr. Bradley." He glanced toward the house. His voice was casual, but Gabe sensed that he was alert. "Your wife, you say?"

"That's right."

"Name on the registration was Malone, Laura Malone."

"My wife's maiden name," Gabe said easily.

On impulse, Laura pushed open the door. "Gabe?"

Both men turned to look at her. The trooper pulled off his hat. Gabe merely scowled.

"I'm sorry to interrupt—" she smiled "—but I thought the officer might like some hot coffee."

The trooper replaced his hat. "That's mighty tempting, ma'am, and I appreciate it, but I have to get along. Sorry about your car."

"My own fault. Can you tell us when the road will be open?"

"Your husband ought to be able to manage a trip into

town in a day or two," Beecham said. "I wouldn't recommend the drive for you, ma'am, for the time being."

"No." She smiled at him and hugged her elbows. "I don't think I'll be going anywhere for a little while yet."

"I'll just be on my way." Beecham straddled the snowmobile again. "You got a shortwave, Mr. Bradley?"

"No."

"Might not be a bad idea to pick one up next time you're in town. More dependable than the phones. When's your baby due?"

Gabe just stared for a moment. The pronoun had stunned him. "Four or five weeks."

"You got yourself plenty of time, then." With a grin, Beecham started the engine. "This your first?"

"Yes," Gabe murmured. "It is."

"Nothing quite like it. Got myself two girls. Last one decided to be born on Thanksgiving. Hardly had two bites of pumpkin pie when I had to drive to the hospital. My wife still says it was my mother's sausage stuffing that started her off." He raised a hand and his voice. "Take care, Mrs. Bradley."

They watched, Gabe from the yard, Laura from the doorway, as the snowmobile scooted up the lane. And then they were alone.

Clearing his throat, Gabe started up the stairs. Laura said nothing, but she stepped out of the way and closed the door behind him. She waited until he was sitting on the low stone hearth, unlacing his boots.

"Thank you."

"For what?"

"You told the trooper that I was your wife."

Still frowning, he pried off a boot. "It seemed less complicated that way."

"For me," Laura agreed. "Not for you."

He shrugged his shoulders and then rose to go into the kitchen. "Any coffee?"

"Yes." She heard the glass pot chink against the mug, heard the liquid pour into the stoneware. He'd lied for her, protected her, and all she had done was take from him. "Gabe." Praying that her instincts and her conscience were right, she walked to the doorway.

"What the hell is this?" He had the pan she'd used to heat the milk in his hand.

For a moment the tension fled. "If you're desperate enough, it's hot chocolate."

"It looks like… Well, never mind what it looks like." He set it back on the stove. "That powdered stuff tastes filthy, doesn't it?"

"It's hard to argue with the truth."

"I'll try to make it into town tomorrow."

"If you do, could you…" Embarrassed, she let her words trail off.

"What do you want?"

"Nothing. It's stupid. Listen, could we sit down a minute?"

He took her hand before she could back away. "What do you want from town, Laura?"

"Marshmallows, to toast in the fireplace. I told you it was stupid," she murmured, and tried to tug her hand away.

He wanted, God, he wanted just to fold her into his arms. "Is that a craving or just a whim?"

"I don't know. It's just that I look at the fireplace and

think about marshmallows." Because he wasn't laughing at her, it was easy to smile. "Sometimes I can almost smell them."

"Marshmallows. You don't want anything to go with them? Like horseradish?"

She made a face at him. "Another myth."

"You're spoiling all my preconceptions." He wasn't sure when he'd lifted her hand to his lips, but after the faintest taste of her skin he dropped it again. "And you're not wearing the shirt."

Though he was no longer touching it, her hand felt warm, warm and impossibly soft. "Oh." She took a long breath. He was thinking of the painting, not of her. He was the artist with his subject again. "I'll change."

"Fine." More than a little shaken by the extent of his desire for her, he turned back to the counter and his coffee.

The decision came quickly, or perhaps it had been made the moment she'd heard him lie for her, protect her. "Gabe, I know you want to work right away, but I'd like…I feel like I should…I want to tell you everything, if you still want to hear it."

He turned back, his eyes were utterly clear and intent. "Why?"

"Because it's wrong not to trust you." Again the breath seemed to sigh out of her. "And because I need someone. We need someone."

"Sit down," he said simply, leading her to the couch.

"I don't know where to start."

It would probably be easier for her to start further back, he thought as he tossed another log in the fire. "Where do you come from?" he asked when he joined her on the couch.

"I've lived a lot of places. New York, Pennsylvania, Maryland. My aunt had a little farm on the Eastern Shore. I lived with her the longest."

"Your parents?"

"My mother was very young when I was born. Unmarried. She…I went to live with my aunt until…until things became difficult for her, financially. There were foster homes after that. That isn't really the point."

"Isn't it?"

She took a steadying breath. "I don't want you to feel sorry for me. I'm not telling you this so that you'll feel sorry for me."

The pride was evident in the tilt of her head, in the tone of her voice—the same quiet pride he was trying to capture on canvas. His fingers itched for his sketchpad, even as they itched to touch her face. "All right, I won't."

With a nod, she continued. "From what I can gather, things were very hard on my mother. Even without the little I was told, it's easy enough to imagine. She was only a child. It's possible that she wanted to keep me, but it didn't work out. My aunt was older, but she had children of her own. I was essentially another mouth to feed, and when it became difficult to do so, I went into foster care."

"How old were you?"

"Six the first time. For some reason it just never seemed to work out. I would stay in one place for a year, in another for two. I hated not belonging, never being a real part of what everyone else had. When I was about twelve I went back with my aunt for a short time, but her husband had problems of his own, and it didn't last."

He caught something in her voice, something that made him tense. "What sort of problems?"

"They don't matter." She shook her head and started to rise, but Gabe put his hand firmly on hers.

"You started this, Laura, now finish it."

"He drank," she said quickly. "When he drank he got mean."

"Mean? Do you mean violent?"

"Yes. When he was sober, he was discontented and critical. Drunk, he was—could be—vicious." She rubbed a hand over her shoulder, as if she were soothing an old wound. "My aunt was his usual target, but he often went after the children."

"Did he hit you?"

"Unless I was quick enough to get out of his way." She managed a ghost of a smile. "And I learned to be quick. It sounds worse than it was."

He doubted it. "Go on."

"The social services took me away again and placed me in another home. It was like being put on hold. I remember when I was sixteen, counting the days until I'd be of age and able to at least fend for myself. Make…I don't know, make some of my own decisions. Then I was. I moved to Pennsylvania and got a job. I was working as a clerk in a department store in Philadelphia. I had a customer, a woman, who used to come in regularly. We got friendly, and one day she came in with a man. He was short and balding—looked like a bulldog. He nodded to the woman and told her she'd been absolutely right. Then he handed me a business card and told me to come to his studio the next day.

Of course, I had no intention of going. I thought…that is, I'd gotten used to men…"

"I imagine you did," Gabe said dryly.

It still embarrassed her, but since he seemed to take it in stride she didn't dwell on it. "In any case, I set the card aside and would have forgotten about it, but one of the girls who worked with me picked it up later and went wild. She told me who he was. You might know the name. Geoffrey Wright."

Gabe lifted a brow. Wright was one of the most respected fashion photographers in the business—no, *the* most. Gabe might not know much about the fashion business, but a name like Geoffrey Wright's crossed boundaries. "It rings a bell."

"When I found out he was a professional, a well-known photographer, I decided to take a chance and go to see him. Everything happened at once. He was very gruff and had me in makeup and under the lights before I could babble an excuse. I was terribly embarrassed, but he didn't seem to notice. He barked out orders, telling me to stand, sit, lean, turn. He had a fur in his vault—a full-length sable. He took it out and tossed it around my shoulders. I thought I was dreaming. I must have said so aloud, because while he was shooting he laughed and told me that in a year I could wear sable to breakfast."

Saying nothing, Gabe settled back. With his eyes narrowed, he could see her, enveloped in furs. There was a twist in his stomach as he thought about her becoming one of Wright's young and casually disposable mistresses.

"Within a month I had done a layout for *Mode* magazine. Then I did another for *Her*, and one for *Charm.* It was incredible. One day I was selling linens and the next I was having dinner with designers."

"And Wright?"

"No one in my life had ever been as good to me as Geoffrey. Oh, I knew he saw me as a commodity half the time, but he set himself up as, I don't know, a watchdog. He had plans, he'd tell me. Not too much exposure too quickly. Then, in another two years, there wouldn't be a person in the Western world who wouldn't recognize my face. It sounded exciting. Most of my life I'd been essentially anonymous. He liked that, the fact that I'd come from nothing, from nowhere. I know some of his other models saw him as cold. He often was. But he was the closest thing I'd ever had to a father."

"Is that how you saw him?"

"I suppose. And then, after all he'd done for me, after all the time he'd invested, I let him down." She started to rise again, and again Gabe stopped her.

"Where are you going?"

"I need some water."

"Sit. I'll get it."

She used the time to compose herself. Her story was only half done, and the worst part, the most painful part, was yet to come. He brought her a clear glass with ice swimming in it. Laura took two long sips, then continued.

"We went to Paris. It was like being Cinderella and being told midnight never had to come. We were scheduled to be there for a month, and because Geoffrey wanted a very French flavor to the pictures we went all over Paris for the shoot. We went to a party one night. It was one of those gorgeous spring nights when all the women are beautiful and the men handsome. And I met Tony."

He caught the slight break in her voice, the shadow of pain in her eyes, and knew without being told that she was speaking now of her baby's father.

"He was so gallant, so charming. The prince to my Cinderella. For the next two weeks, whenever I wasn't working, I was with Tony. We went dancing, we ate in little cafés and walked in the parks. He was everything I'd thought I'd wanted and knew I could never have. He treated me as though I were something rare and valuable, like a diamond necklace. There was a time when I thought that was love."

She fell silent for a moment, brooding. That had been her mistake, her sin, her vanity. Even now, a year later, it cut at her.

"Geoffrey grumbled and talked about rich young pups sowing wild oats, but I wouldn't listen. I wanted to be loved, I wanted so terribly for someone to care, to want me. When Tony asked me to marry him, I didn't think twice."

"You married him?"

"Yes." She looked at him again. "I know I led you to believe that I hadn't married the baby's father. It seemed easiest."

"You don't wear a ring."

Color washed into her face. The shame of it. "I sold them."

"I see." There was no condemnation in the two words, but she felt it nonetheless.

"We stayed in Paris for our honeymoon. I wanted to go back to the States and meet his family, but he said we should stay where we were happy. It seemed right. Geoffrey was furious with me, lectured and shouted about me wasting myself. At the time I thought he meant my career, and I ignored him. It was only later that I realized he meant my life."

She jumped when a log fell apart in the fire. It was easier to continue if she looked at the flames, she discovered. "I thought I'd found everything I'd ever wanted. When I look back I realize that those weeks we spent in Paris were like a kind of magic, something that's not quite real but that you believe because you aren't clever enough to see the illusion. Then it was time to come home."

She linked her hands together and began to fidget. He had come to recognize it as a sign of inner turmoil. Though the urge was there, he didn't take them in his to calm her. "The night before we were to leave, Tony went out. He said he had some business to tie up. I waited for him, feeling a little sorry for myself that my new husband would leave me alone on our last night in Paris. Then, as it got later and later, I stopped feeling sorry for myself and started feeling frightened. By the time he got back, it was after three and I was angry and upset."

She fell silent again. Gabe pulled the afghan from the back of the couch and spread it over her lap. "You had a fight."

"Yes. He was very drunk and belligerent. I'd never seen him like that before, but I was to see him like that again. I asked him where he'd been and he said—essentially he told me it was none of my business. We started shouting at each other, and he told me he'd been with another woman. At first I thought he said that just to hurt me, but then I saw that it was true. I started to cry."

That was the worst of it, Laura thought, looking back on the way she'd crumbled and wept. "That only made him angrier. He tossed things around the suite, like a little boy having a tantrum. He said things, but the gist of it was that I'd have to get used to the way he lived, and that I hardly had a right to be upset when I'd been Geoffrey's whore."

Her voice broke on the last word, so she lifted the glass and cooled her throat with the water. "That hurt the most," she managed. "Geoffrey was almost like a father to me, never, never anything else. And Tony knew, he knew that I'd never been with anyone before our wedding night. I was so angry then, I stood up and began to shout at him. I don't even know what I said, but he went into a rage. And he—"

Gabe saw her fingers tighten like wires on the soft folds of the afghan. Then he saw how she deliberately, and with great care, relaxed them again. With an effort, he kept his voice calm. "Did he hit you, Laura?"

She didn't answer, couldn't seem to push the next words out. Then he touched a hand to her cheek and turned her face to his. Her eyes were brimming over.

"It was so much worse than with my uncle, because I couldn't get away. He was so much stronger and faster. With my uncle, he'd simply struck out at anyone who didn't get out of the way in time. With Tony, there was something viciously deliberate in the way he tried to hurt me. Then he—" But she couldn't bring herself to speak of what had happened next.

It was a moment before she went on, and Gabe sat in

silence as the rage built and built inside him until he thought he'd explode. He understood temper, he had a hair-trigger one of his own, but he could never understand, never forgive, anyone who inflicted pain on someone smaller, weaker.

"When it was over," she continued, calmer now, "he just went to sleep. I lay there, not knowing what to do. It's funny, but later, when I talked with other women who had had some of the same experiences, I found out that it's fairly common to believe you had it coming somehow.

"The next morning, he wept and he apologized, promised that it would never happen again. That became the pattern for the time we were together."

"You stayed with him?"

The color came and went in her face, and part of that, too, was shame. "We were married, and I thought I could make it work. Then we went back to his parents' home. They hated me right from the start. Their son, the heir to the throne, had gone behind their back and married a commoner. We lived with them, and though there was talk about getting our own house, nothing was ever done about it. You could sit at the same table, hold a conversation with them, and be totally ignored. They were amazing. Tony got worse. He began to see other women, almost flaunting them. They knew what he was doing, and they knew what was happening to me. The cycle got uglier and uglier, until I knew I had to get out. I told him I wanted a divorce.

"That seemed to snap him out of it for a while. He made promises, swore he'd go into therapy, see a marriage counselor, anything I wanted. We even began to look at houses.

I have to admit that I'd stopped loving him by this time, and that it was wrong, very wrong, for me to stay with him, to make promises myself. What I didn't realize was that his parents were pulling on the other end. They held the financial strings and were making it difficult for him to move out. Then I discovered I was pregnant."

She laid a hand over her belly, her fingers spread. "Tony was, well, at best ambivalent about the idea of having a child. His parents were thrilled. His mother immediately started redecorating a nursery. She bought antique cribs and cradles, silver spoons, Irish linen. Though it made me nervous, the way she was taking over, I thought that the baby might be the way to help us come together. But they weren't looking at me as the baby's mother, any more than they'd looked at me as Tony's wife. It was *their* grandchild, *their* legacy, *their* immortality. We stopped looking for houses, and Tony began to drink again. I left the night he came home drunk and hit me."

She drew a careful breath and continued to stare at the fire. "It wasn't just me he was hitting now, but the child. That made all the difference. In fact, it made it incredibly easy to walk out. I called Geoffrey, buried my pride and asked for a loan. He wired me two thousand dollars. I got an apartment of my own, found a job and started divorce proceedings. Ten days later, Tony was dead."

The pain came, dull and low. Laura shut her eyes and rode it out. "His mother came to see me, begged me to bury the divorce papers, to come to the funeral as Tony's widow. His reputation, his memory, were all that was important now. I did what she asked, because—because I could still remember those first days in Paris. After the funeral I went back to their house. They'd told me there were things we needed to talk about. That was when they told me what they wanted, what they intended to have. They said they would pay all my medical expenses, that I would have the best possible care. And that after the baby was born they would give me a hundred thousand dollars to step aside. When I refused, when I had the nerve to be angry at what they were suggesting, they explained that if I didn't cooperate they would simply take the baby. Tony's baby. They made it very clear that they had enough money and influence to win a custody suit. They would bring out the 'fact' that I had been Geoffrey's mistress, that I had taken money from him. They'd checked my background and would show that due to my upbringing I would be an unstable influence on a child. That they, as the child's grandparents, could provide a better environment. They gave me twenty-four hours to think it over. And I ran."

He didn't speak for several minutes. What she had told him had left a bitter taste in his mouth. He had asked for her story, had all but demanded it. Now that he had it, he wasn't at all sure he could handle it.

"Laura, no matter what you were told, how you were threatened, I don't believe they could take the child."

"That isn't enough? Don't you see? As long as there's a chance, I can't risk it. I'd never be able to fight them on their terms. I don't have the money, the connections."

"Who are they?" When she hesitated, he took her hand again. "You've trusted me with this much."

"Their name is Eagleton," she said. "Thomas and Lorraine Eagleton of Boston."

His brows drew together. He knew the name. Who didn't? But because of his family's position, it was more than a name, more than an image. "You were married to Anthony Eagleton?"

"Yes." She turned to him then. "You knew him, didn't you?"

"Not well. Barely. He was more—" More Michael's age, he'd started to say. "He was younger. I met him once or twice when he came to the Coast." And what he had seen hadn't impressed him enough to have him form any opinion. "I read that he had been killed in a car accident, and I suppose a wife was mentioned, but this past year has been a little difficult, and I didn't pay attention. My family has socialized with the Eagletons occasionally, but they aren't well acquainted."

"Then you know they're an old, well-established family with old, well-established money. They consider this child a part of their…holdings. They've had me followed all across the country. Every time I would settle in a place and begin to relax I'd discover that detectives were making inquiries about me. I can't—I won't—let them find me."

He rose, to pace, to light a cigarette, to try to organize his thoughts and, more, his feelings. "I'd like to ask you something."

She sighed tiredly. "All right."

"Once before, when I asked you if you were afraid, you said no, that you were ashamed. I want to know why."

"I didn't fight back, and I didn't try hard enough to fix what was wrong. I just let it happen to me. You have no idea how difficult it is to sit here and admit that I let myself be used, that I let myself be beaten, that I let myself be driven down so low that I accepted it all."

"Do you still feel that way?"

"No." Her chin lifted. "No one's ever going to take control of my life again."

"Good." He sat on the hearth. The smoke from his cigarette disappeared up the draft. "I think you've had a hell of a time, angel, worse than anyone deserves. Whether you brought some of it on yourself, as you choose to think, or if it was just a matter of circumstances, doesn't really matter at this point. It's over."

"It's not as easy as that, Gabe. I don't just have myself to worry about now."

"How far are you willing to go to fight them?"

"I've told you I can't—"

He interrupted her with a wave of his hand. "If you had the means. How far?"

"All the way. As far and as long as it takes. But that isn't the point, because I don't have the means."

He drew on his cigarette, studied it with apparent interest, then tossed it into the fire. "You would, if you were married to me."

Chapter 5

She said nothing, could say nothing. He sat on the hearth, his legs folded up, his eyes very cool, very calm, on her face. Part of the enormity of his talent was his ability to focus on an expression and draw the underlying emotions out of it. Perhaps because he did it so well, he also knew how to mask emotions when they were his own.

She could hear the logs sizzling behind him. The mid-morning sunlight sparkled through the frost on the windowpanes and landed at his feet. He seemed totally at ease, as though he'd just suggested that they have soup for lunch. If her life had depended upon it, Laura couldn't have said whether it meant any more to him than that.

Using the table for leverage, she rose.

"I'm tired. I'm going in to lie down."

"All right. We can talk about this later."

She whirled around, and it wasn't anguish or fear he saw on her face now, it was fury, livid and clear. "How could you sit there and say something like that to me after everything I've told you?"

"You might consider that I said it because of everything you've told me."

"Oh, the Good Samaritan again." She detested the bitterness in her voice, but she could do nothing to stop it. "The white knight, riding in full of chivalry and good intentions to save the bumbling, inept female. Do you think I should fall on my knees and be grateful? That I would blindly let myself be taken over again, fall back into the same pitiful, destructive pattern a second time, because a man offers me a way out?"

He thought about controlling his temper, then rose, deciding to let her see it. "I have no desire to control you, and I'll be damned if you're going to stand there and compare me with some weak-minded alcoholic wife-beater."

"What then—the knight on a white charger, selflessly rescuing damsels in distress?"

He laughed at that, but his anger was still on the edge. "No one's ever accused me of that. I'm very selfish, which is another reason for my suggestion. I'm moody—you've been around me long enough to know that. I have a temper and I can get angry. But I don't hit women, and I don't use them."

With an effort, she pulled her emotions back in and forced them to settle. "I didn't mean to imply that you did, or to compare you with someone else. It's the situation that's comparable."

"One has nothing to do with the other. The fact that I have money only works to your advantage."

"I didn't marry Tony for his money."

"No." His tone softened. "No, I'm sure you didn't. But in this case I'm willing to accept that you marry me for mine."

"Why?"

Something flickered in his eyes and was gone before she could read it. "That might have been the wisest question to ask first."

"Maybe you're right." She already regretted the outburst of temper and harsh words, as she invariably did. "I'm asking it now."

With a nod, he roamed the room, stopping before the nearly completed portrait. He stared at it, as he had stared at it countless times before, trying to understand, to define, not only Laura, but himself.

"I feel something for you. I'm not sure what it is, but it's very strong. Stronger than anything I've felt before." He lifted a finger to the face on canvas. He wished he could explain himself completely, to himself, to her, but he'd always expressed himself best through painting. "I'm attracted to you, Laura, and I've discovered recently that I've been alone long enough."

"That might be enough, almost enough, for marriage, but not for me, not to me. Not with what you'd be taking on."

"I have some debts to pay," he murmured, then turned to her again. "Helping you, and the child, might just clear the slate."

Whatever anger she'd felt evaporated. It only took the kindness and the grief in his eyes. "You've already helped us, more than I can ever repay."

"I don't want payment." The impatience, the edge, was back in his voice. "What I want is you. How many ways do you want me to say it?"

"I don't think I want you to say it." The nerves began to eat at her again, and she twisted her fingers together. He meant it. She had no doubt that he meant what he said. The prospect of being wanted by him both thrilled and terrified her. "Don't you see, I've already made one terrible mistake."

He crossed to her, gently drawing her hands apart and into his. "You're not indifferent to me?"

"No, but—"

"You're not afraid of me?"

Some of the tension seeped out of her. "No."

"Then let me help you."

"I'm going to have another man's child."

"No." He took her face in his hands because he wanted her eyes on his. "Marry me, and the child is ours. Privately, publicly, totally."

The tears came back. "They'll come."

"Let them. They won't touch you again, and they won't take the baby."

Safety. Could what had always eluded her really be only a promise away? She opened her mouth, knowing that agreement was on her tongue. Then her heart turned over in her chest and she lifted a hand to his cheek. "How could I do this to you?"

For an answer, he put his lips to hers. The need was there, she couldn't deny it, couldn't pretend it away. She tasted it as his mouth drew from hers. She felt it when his hand skimmed through her hair to brace, both possessive and supportive, at the back of her neck. Instinctively, wanting to give, she lifted her other hand to his face. They rested there, comforting.

She wasn't the only one who had demons, Laura thought. She wasn't the only one who needed love and understanding. Because he was strong, it was easy to forget that he, too, might have pain. Seeking to soothe, she drew him closer into her arms.

He could have sunk into her, into the softness, the generosity. This was what he wanted to capture on canvas, her warmth, her spirit. And this was what he was forced to admit he would never have the skill to translate. This part of her beauty, this most essential part, could never be painted. But it could be cherished.

"You need me," he murmured as he drew her away. "And I need you."

She nodded, then rested her head on his shoulder, because that seemed to say it all.

Due to fresh flurries, it was three days before Gabe risked a trip into town. Laura watched him as he downed a final cup of coffee before pulling on his coat.

"I'll be as quick as I can."

"I'd rather you took your time and paid attention to the roads."

"The Jeep drives like a tank." He accepted the gloves she held out to him but didn't put them on. "I don't like leaving you alone."

"Gabe, I've been taking care of myself for a long time."

"Things have changed. My lawyers have probably sent the marriage license."

Immediately she began to fuss with the breakfast dishes. "That would be quick work."

"They get paid to work fast, and it's been three days since I contacted them. If I can arrange it, I'd like to bring a justice of the peace back here with me."

A cup slipped out of her hand and plopped into the soapy water. "Today?"

"You haven't changed your mind?"

"No, but—"

"I want my name on the birth certificate." He had a moment of panic, vague and disturbing, at her hesitation. "It would be less complicated if we were married before the baby's born."

"Yes, that makes sense." It seemed so rushed. She plunged her hands into the water and began to wash. Her first wedding had been rushed, too, a whirlwind of flowers and champagne and white silk.

"I realize you might prefer something a little more festive, but under the circumstances—"

"No." She turned and managed a smile. "No, I don't care about that. If you can arrange it for today, here, that's fine."

"All right, then. Laura, I'd feel better if you rested until I got back. You didn't sleep well."

She turned back again. No, she hadn't slept well. The nightmare had come back, and she hadn't rested until Gabe had come in and finally slipped into bed with her. "I won't overdo."

"I don't think it would tax your strength for you to kiss me goodbye."

That made her smile. She turned, her hands still dripping, to lift her lips to his.

"Not even married yet and you're already kissing me as though we've been together twenty years." He changed the mood simply by nipping her lip. In seconds she was clinging to him, and there was nothing casual about the embrace.

"Better," he murmured. "Now go lie down. I'll be back in less than two hours."

"Be careful."

He closed the door. In moments she heard the sound of the Jeep's engine chugging to life. Moving into the living room, she watched Gabe drive away.

Strangely enough, even as the quiet settled over the cabin, she didn't feel alone. She felt nervous, she admitted with a little laugh. Brides were entitled to nerves. If Gabe had his way—and she'd come to believe that he nearly always did—they would be married that afternoon.

And her life, Laura realized, would change yet again.

This time it would be better. She would make it better.

As the ache in her lower back grew worse, she pressed her hand against it. Blaming the discomfort she'd been feeling all morning on the mattress and a restless night, she walked over to the portrait.

He'd finished it the day before. She knew, because he'd explained it to her, that the paint would take a few days to set and dry completely, so she didn't touch it. She sat on the stool Gabe sometimes used and studied her own face.

So this was how he saw her, she thought. Her skin was pale, with only a faint shadow of color along her cheekbones. It was partly that whiteness, that translucence, that made her appear like the angel he sometimes called her. She looked as though she were caught in a daydream, one of the many she'd indulged in during the hours Gabe had painted. As she had told him—as she had complained—there was too much vulnerability. It was in her eyes, around her mouth. There was something strong and independent about the pose, about the way her head was tilted, but that lost, sad look in her eyes seemed to negate the strength.

She was reading too much into it, Laura decided as the pain dug, deep and dull, into her back. Rubbing at it, she rose to look around the cabin.

She would be married here, in a matter of hours. There would be no crowd of well-wishers, no pianist playing romantic songs, no trail of rose petals. Yet, with or without the trimmings, she would be a bride. She might not be able to make it look festive, but at least she could tidy up.

The pain in her back drove her to lie down. Two hours later she heard the Jeep coming down the lane. For a moment longer she lay there, working to block out the discomfort. Later, she told herself, she would soak the ache away in a hot tub. She walked into the living room just as Gabe ushered an elderly couple into the cabin.

"Laura, this is Mr. and Mrs. Witherby. Mr. Witherby is a justice of the peace."

"Hello. It's so nice of you to come all this way."

"Part of the job," Mr. Witherby said, adjusting his fogging glasses. "'Sides that, your young man here wasn't going to take no for an answer."

"Don't you worry about this old man here." Mrs. Witherby patted her husband's arm and studied Laura. "He loves to complain."

"Can I get you something, some coffee?"

"Don't you fuss. Mr. Bradley's got a carload of supplies. You just sit down and let him take care of it." She had already walked over to lead Laura to the couch with her frail hands. "Man's nervous as a goose at Christmas," she confided. "Let him keep busy for a spell."

Though she couldn't imagine Gabe being nervous about anything, she thought the Witherbys would expect such emotion from a man about to marry. Laura listened to Gabe rattling bags and cans in the kitchen. "Maybe I should help him."

"Now, you sit right here." Mrs. Witherby motioned to her husband to sit, as well. "A woman's entitled to be waited on when she's carrying. The good Lord knows you won't have much time to sit once that baby's born."

Grateful, Laura shifted to ease the throbbing in her back. "You have children?"

"Had six of them. Now we've got twenty-two grandchildren and five great-grandchildren."

"And another on the way," Mr. Witherby stated, pulling out a pipe.

"You can just put that smelly thing away," his wife told him. "You aren't smoking up this room with this lady expecting."

"I wasn't going to light it," he said, and began to chew on the stem.

Satisfied that her husband had been put in his place, Mrs. Witherby turned back to Laura. "That's a pretty picture there." She indicated a sprawling landscape that might very well sell for an amount in six figures. "Your man's an artist fellow?"

Her man. Laura experienced a twinge of panic and a glow of pleasure at the phrase. "Yes, Gabe's an artist."

"I like pictures," she said comfortably. "Got me one of the seashore over my sofa."

Gabe walked back in carrying an armful of flowers. Feeling awkward, he cleared his throat. "They sold them at the market."

"And he bought them out, too," Mrs. Witherby cackled. Then, with a few wheezes, she heaved herself off the couch. "You got a vase? She can't be carrying all of them."

"No, at least…I don't know."

"Men." She sighed and then winked at Laura. "Give them to me and let me take care of it. You can do something useful, like putting more wood on that fire. Wouldn't want your lady to catch a chill."

"Yes, ma'am."

If he'd ever felt more of a fool, he couldn't remember when. Wanting to keep his hands busy, he moved to the fire.

"Don't let her browbeat you, boy," Mr. Witherby advised him from the comfort of his chair. "She's already spent fifty-two years nagging me."

"Somebody had to," Mrs. Witherby called out from the kitchen, and he chuckled.

"Sure you two know what you're getting into?"

Gabe dusted his hands on the thighs of his jeans and grinned. "No."

"That's the spirit." Witherby laughed and rested his head against the back of the chair. "Essie, get that bag of bones you call a body moving, will you? These two people want to get married while they're still young."

"Keep your tongue in your mouth," she muttered. "Already lost his teeth." She came in carrying a watering can filled with flowers. She set it in the middle of the coffee table, nodded her approval, then handed Laura a single white carnation.

"Thank you. They're lovely." She started to rise and nearly winced at the stab of pain in her back. Then Gabe was there to take her hand and draw her to his side.

They stood in front of the fire with wood crackling and the scent of the flowers merging with that of the smoke. The words were simple and very old. Despite the countless weddings she'd been to, Mrs. Witherby dabbed at her eyes.

To love. To honor. To cherish.

For richer. For poorer.

Forsaking all others.

The ring he slipped onto her finger was very plain, just a gold band that was a size too large. Looking at it, Laura felt something grow inside her. It was warm and sweet and tremulous. Curling her hand into his, she repeated the words, and meant them, from her heart.

Let no man put asunder.

"You may kiss the bride," Witherby told him, but Gabe didn't hear.

It was done. It was irrevocable. And until that moment he hadn't been completely aware of how much it would mean to him.

With her hand still caught in his, he kissed her and sealed the promise.

"Congratulations." Mrs. Witherby brushed her dry lips over Gabe's cheek, then Laura's. "Now you sit down, Mrs. Bradley, and I'm going to fix you a nice cup of tea before we drag your husband off again."

"Thank you, but we don't have any tea."

"I bought some," Gabe put in.

"That and everything else he could lay his hands on. Come on, Ethan, give me a hand."

"You ought to be able to fix a cup of tea by yourself."

Mrs. Witherby rolled her eyes. "You'd think the old goat would have a little more romance, seeing as he's married more'n five hundred couples in his time. In the kitchen, Ethan, and give these young people five minutes alone."

He grumbled about wanting his supper, but he followed her.

"They're wonderful," Laura murmured.

"I don't think I'd have gotten him away from his TV if she hadn't shoved him out the door."

Silence followed, awkward. "It was nice of you to think of flowers...and the ring."

He lifted her hand and studied it. "They don't have a jewelry store in Lonesome Ridge. They sell these at the hardware in a little case next to sixpenny nails. It may just turn your finger green."

She laughed and knew she'd treasure it even more now. "You may not believe it, but you may have saved my life by buying that tea."

"I got some marshmallows, too."

She hated it, despised herself for not being able to control it, but she started to cry. "I'm sorry. I can't seem to do anything about this."

Discomfort surged through him. He was feeling edgy himself, and tears did nothing to help matters. "Look, I know it wasn't exactly the wedding of the century. We can have some sort of party or reception back in San Francisco."

"No, no, that's not it." Though she urged her hands

over her face, the tears kept coming. "It was lovely and sweet and I don't know how to thank you."

"Not crying would be a good start." He had a bandanna in his pocket, one that he used more often than not as a paint rag. He drew it out and offered it to her. "Laura, we're legally married. That means you don't have to be grateful for every bunch of daisies I hand you."

She sniffled into the cloth and tried to smile. "I think it was the marshmallows that did it."

"Keep this up and you won't get any more."

"I want you to know…" She dried her face and managed to compose herself. "I want you to know that I'm going to do everything I can to make you happy, to make you comfortable, so that you never regret what you did today."

"I'm going to regret it," he said suddenly impatient, "if you keep making it sound as though I gave someone else the last life jacket as the ship was sinking. I married you because I wanted to, not to be noble."

"Yes, but I—"

"Shut up, Laura." To make certain she did, he closed his mouth over hers. And for the first time she felt the true strength of his passion and need and desire. With a little murmur of surprise, she drew him closer.

This was what he had needed, all he had needed, to settle him. Yet even as the first layer of tension dissolved, a new layer, one built on desire, formed.

"Before too much longer," he said against her mouth, "we're going to finish this. I want to make love with you, Laura. And after I do you won't have the strength to thank me."

Before she could think of a response, Mrs. Witherby came in with her tea. "Now let the poor thing rest and drink this while it's hot." She set the cup on the table in front of Laura. "I hate to drag you out on your wedding day, Mr. Bradley, but the sooner you drive us back to town, the sooner you can get back and fix your wife that nice steak you bought for supper."

She moved over to gather up her coat. On impulse, Laura drew one of the flowers from the watering can and took it to her. "I'm never going to forget you, Mrs. Witherby."

"There now." Touched, she sniffed at the flower. "You just take care of yourself and that baby of yours. Shake a leg, Ethan."

"I should only be an hour," Gabe told her. "The roads aren't too bad. I really think you should rest, Laura. You look exhausted."

"I'm supposed to look glowing, but I promise I won't lift anything heavier than a teacup until you get back."

This time she watched the Jeep drive away, running her finger over and over her wedding ring. It took so little, she thought, to change so much. She bent, trying to ease the ache in her back, then she crossed the room to finish her tea.

Her back had never ached like this, not even after she'd worked a full day on her aunt's farm. The pain was constant and deep. She tried stretching out, then curling up, then stretching out again. Impatient with herself, she tried to ignore it, concentrating instead on roasting marshmallows and warming tea.

She'd been alone less than ten minutes when the first contraction hit.

It wasn't the vague warning pain she'd read about. It was sharp and long. Caught off guard, she had no time to breathe her way over it. Instead, she tensed, fought against it, then collapsed against the cushions when it faded.

It couldn't be labor. Her forehead broke out in sweat as she tried to dismiss the idea. It was too early, a month too early, and it had come on so suddenly. False labor, she assured herself. Brought on by nerves and by the excitement of the day.

But the back pain. Struggling to keep calm, she pushed herself into a sitting position. Was it possible she'd been having back labor all morning?

No, it had to be false labor. It had to be.

But when the second contraction hit she began to time them.

She was in bed when Gabe returned, but she couldn't call out to him, because she was riding out the latest contraction. The fear that had gripped her in a stranglehold for the past hour faded a bit. He was here, and somehow that meant that everything would be all right. She heard him toss a log on the fire, took a last cleansing breath as the pain passed and called out.

The urgency in her voice had him across the room in three strides. At the bedroom door he paused, and his heart jumped into his throat.

She was propped against the pillows, half lying, half sitting. Her face was bathed in sweat. Her eyes, always dark, were sheened with moisture and nearly black.

"I have to go back on our deal," she managed, struggling with a smile because she saw the same blank fear she felt reflected on his face. "The baby's decided to come a little early."

He didn't ask if she was sure or fumble with reasons why it wasn't a good idea. He wanted to, but he found himself beside the bed, with her hand gripped in his. "Take it easy. Just hold on and I'll phone for a doctor."

"Gabe, the phone's out." Nerves skipped in and out of her voice. "I tried it when I realized this was happening so fast."

"Okay." Fighting for calm, he brushed the damp hair away from her face. "There was an accident on the way into town. Lines must have gone down. I'll get some extra blankets and I'll take you in."

She pressed her lips together. "Gabe, it's too late. I couldn't make the trip." She tried to swallow, but fear had dried up the moisture in her mouth and throat. "I've been in labor for hours, all morning, and I didn't know it. It was back labor, and I didn't pay attention. With everything that was going on, I thought it was nerves and the restless night I'd had."

"Hours," he murmured, and eased himself down on the edge of the bed. His mind went blank, but then her fingers tightened on his. "How far apart are the pains?"

"Five minutes. I've been—" She let her head fall back and began to breathe in short, deep gasps. Gabe slipped his hand over her and felt the hardening of her abdomen.

He'd glanced through the birth and baby books she'd brought with her. To pass the time, he'd told himself, but there had been something deep inside him that had been compelled to understand what she was going through. Perhaps it was instinct that had had him absorbing the advice, the details, the instructions. Now, seeing her in pain, everything he'd read seemed to slip away from him.

When the contraction passed, her face was shiny with fresh sweat. "Getting closer," she whispered. "There's not much time." Though she bit down on her lips, a sob escaped her. "I can't lose the baby."

"The baby's going to be fine, and so are you." He squeezed her hand once reassuringly. They would need towels, lots of them. String and scissors had to be sterilized. It was really very simple when you thought about it. He only hoped it was as simple when you put it into practice.

"Just hang on. I have to get some things." He saw the doubt flash in her eyes, and he leaned over her. "I'm not going to leave you. I'm going to take care of you, Laura. Trust me."

She nodded, and with her head slumped back on the pillow, she closed her eyes.

When he came back, her eyes were focused on the ceiling and she was panting. After setting fresh towels on the foot of the bed, he spread another blanket over her. "Are you cold?"

She shook her head. "The baby will need to be kept warm. He's not full-term."

"I've built up the fire, and there are plenty of blankets." Gently he wiped her face with a cool, damp cloth. "You've talked to doctors, you've read the books. You know what to expect."

She looked up at him, trying to swallow past a dry throat. Yes, she knew what to expect, but reading about it, imagining it, was a far cry from the experience.

"They lied." Her mouth moved into a weak smile when

his brows drew together. "They try to tell you it doesn't hurt so much if you ride out the pain."

He brought her hand to his lips and held it there. "Yell all you want. Scream the roof down. Nobody's going to hear."

"I'm not screaming this baby into the world." Then she gasped, and her fingers dug into his. "I can't—"

"Yes, you can. Pant. Pant, Laura. Squeeze my hand. Harder. Concentrate on that." He kept his eyes locked on hers while she pushed air out. "You're doing fine, better than fine." When her body went lax, he moved to the foot of the bed. "The pains are closer?" As he spoke, he knelt on the mattress and shifted the blanket.

"Almost on top of each other."

"That means it's almost over. Hold on to that."

She tried to moisten her dry lips, but her tongue was thick. "If anything happens to me, promise you'll—"

"Nothing's going to happen." He bit off the words. Their eyes met again, hers glazed with pain, his dark with purpose. "Damn it, I'm not going to lose either of you now, understand? The three of us are going to pull this off. Now, you've got work to do, angel."

Each time the pains hit her, he shuddered with it. Time seemed to drag as she struggled through them, then race again as she rested. Gabe moved back and forth, to arrange her pillows, to wipe her face, then knelt again to check the progress of birth.

He could hear the fire roaring in the next room, but he still worried that the cabin would be too cold. Then he worried about the heat, because Laura's laboring body was like a furnace.

He hadn't known birth could be so hard on a woman.

He knew she was close to total exhaustion, but she managed to pull herself through time after time, recharging somehow during the all-too-brief moments between contractions. Pain seemed to tear through her, impossibly hard, impossibly ruthless. His own shirt was soaked with sweat, and he swore constantly, silently, as he urged her to breathe, to pant, to concentrate. All his ambitions, his joys, his griefs, whittled down to focus on that one room, that one moment, that one woman.

It seemed to him that she should weaken, with her body being battered by the new life fighting to be born. But as the moments passed she seemed to draw on new reserves of strength. There was something fierce and valiant about her face as she pushed herself forward and braced for whatever happened next.

"Do you have a name picked out?" he asked, hoping to distract her.

"I made lists. Sometimes at night I'd try to imagine what the baby would look like and try to— Oh, God."

"Hold on. Breathe, angel. Breathe through it."

"I can't. I have to push."

"Not yet, not yet. Soon." From his position at the foot of the bed, he ran his hands over her. "Pant, Laura."

Her concentration kept slipping in and out. If she stared into his eyes, if she pulled the strength from them, she would make it. "I can't hold off much longer."

"You don't have to. I can see the head." There was wonder in his voice when he looked back at her. "I can see it. Push with the next one."

Giddy, straining with the effort, she bore down. She heard the long, deep-throated moan, but she didn't know it was her own voice. Gabe shouted at her, and in response she automatically began to pant again.

"That's good, that's wonderful." He barely recognized his own voice, or his own hands. Both were shaking. "I have the head. Your baby's beautiful. The shoulders come next."

She braced herself, desperate to see. "Oh, God." Tears mixed with sweat as she steepled her hands over her mouth. "It's so little."

"And strong as an ox. You have to push the shoulders out." Sweat dripped off his forehead as he cupped the baby's head in his hand and leaned over it. "Come on, Laura, let's have a look at the rest of it."

Her fingers dug into the blankets, and her head fell back. And she gave birth. Over her own gasping breaths she heard the first cry.

"A boy." Gabe's eyes were wet as he held the squirming new life in his hands. "You have a son."

As the tears rolled, she began to laugh. The pain and the terror were forgotten. "A boy. A little boy."

"With a loud mouth, ten fingers and ten toes." He reached for her hand and gripped it hard. "He's perfect, angel."

Their fingers linked over the baby, and the cabin echoed with the high, indignant wails of the newborn.

She couldn't rest. Laura knew Gabe wanted her to sleep, but she couldn't shut her eyes. The baby, nearly an hour old now, was wrapped in blankets and tucked in the curve of her arm. He was sleeping, she thought, but she couldn't stop herself from tracing a fingertip over his face.

So tiny. Five pounds, seven ounces, on the vegetable

scale that Gabe had unearthed and scrubbed down. Seventeen and a half inches tall, and with only a bit of pale blond peach fuzz covering his head. She couldn't stop looking at him.

"He's not going to disappear, you know."

Laura glanced up at the doorway and smiled. Fatigue had left her skin almost pale enough to see through. Triumph had given her eyes a rich glow. "I know." She held out a hand in invitation. "I'm glad you came in," she said as he sat on the bed. "I know you must be exhausted, but I'd like you to stay a minute."

"You did all the work," he murmured, running a finger down the baby's cheek.

"That's not true, and that's the first thing I want to say. We wouldn't have made it without you."

"Of course you would have. I was basically a cheerleader."

"No." Her hand tightened on his, demanding that he look at her. "You were as responsible for his life as I was. I know what you said about having your name on the birth certificate, about helping us, but I want you to know it's more than that. You brought him into the world. There's nothing I can ever do or say that could be enough. Don't look like that." She gave a quiet laugh and settled back among the pillows. "I know you hate to be thanked, and that's not what I'm doing."

"Isn't it?"

"No." She shifted the baby from her arm to his. It was a gesture that said more, much more, than the words that followed it. "I'm telling you that you got more than a wife today."

The baby went on sleeping peacefully, cupped between them.

He didn't know what to say. He touched the tiny hand and watched it curl reflexively. As an artist he'd thought he understood the full range of beauty. Until today.

"I've been reading about preemies," he began. "His weight is good, and from what the book says a baby born after the thirty-fourth week is in pretty good shape, but I want to get you both into a hospital. Will you be strong enough to travel into Colorado Springs tomorrow?"

"Yes. We'll both be strong enough."

"We'll leave in the morning, then. Do you think you could eat now?"

"Only a horse."

He grinned, but he couldn't quite bring himself to give her back the baby. "You may have to settle for beefsteak. Isn't he hungry?"

"I imagine he'll let us know."

Just as Laura had been, he was compelled to trace the shape of the child's face. "What about that name? We can't keep calling him *he*."

"No, we can't." Laura stroked the soft down on his head. "I was wondering if you'd like to pick his name."

"Me?"

"Yes, you must have a favorite, or a name of someone who's important to you. I'd like you to choose."

"Michael," he murmured, looking down at the sleeping infant.

Chapter 6

San Francisco. It was true that Laura had always wanted to see it, but she had never expected to arrive there with a two-week-old son and a husband. And she had never expected to be shown into a tall, gracious house near the Bay.

Gabe's house. Hers, too, she thought as she rubbed her thumb nervously over her wedding ring. It was foolish to be jumpy because the house was beautiful and big. It was ridiculous to feel small and insecure because you could taste the wealth and the prominence just by breathing the air.

But she did.

She stepped into the tiled foyer and wished desperately for the comfort of the tiny cabin. It had begun to snow again the day they'd left Colorado, and though the mild spring breeze and the tiny buds here were wonderful, she found herself wishing for the cold and ferocity of the mountains.

"It's lovely," she managed, glancing up at the gentle curve of the stairs.

"It was my grandmother's." Gabe set down the luggage and took in the familiar surroundings. It was a house he'd always appreciated for its beauty and its balance. "She held on to it after her marriage. Shall I show you around, or would you rather rest?"

She nearly winced. It was as though he were talking to a guest. "If I rested as much as you'd like, I'd sleep my way through the rest of the year."

"Then why don't I show you the upstairs." He knew he sounded polite, overly polite, but he'd been edgy ever since they'd stepped off the plane. The farther away from Colorado they'd gotten, the farther Laura had withdrawn from him. It was nothing he could put his finger on, but it was there.

Hefting two cases, he started up the stairs. He was bringing his wife, and his son, home. And he didn't know quite what to say to either of them. "I've used this bedroom." He strode in and set the cases at the foot of a big oak bed. "If there's another you'd prefer, we can arrange it."

She nodded, thinking that though they'd shared a motel room while the baby had been in the hospital they had only shared a bed in the cabin, the night before Michael had been born. It would be different here. Everything would be different here.

"It's a beautiful room."

Her voice was a little stiff, but she smiled, trying to soften it. The room was lovely, with its high ceilings and the glossy antiques. There was a terrace, and through the glass doors she could see a garden below, with green leaves already formed. The floors were dark with age and gleaming, just as the Oriental rug was faded with age and rich with heritage.

"The bath's through there," Gabe told her as she ran a finger down the carving in an old chifforobe. "My studio's at the end of the hall. The light's best there, but there's a room next to this that might do as a nursery."

When they spoke of the baby, things always relaxed between them. "I'd love to see it. After all those days in the incubator, Michael deserves a room of his own."

She followed Gabe out and into the next room. It was decorated in blues and grays with a stately four-poster and a many-cushioned window seat. As with the other rooms she'd seen, paintings hung on the wall, some of them Gabe's, others by artists he respected.

"It's beautiful, but what would you do with all these things?"

"They can be stored." He dismissed the furnishings with a shrug. "Michael can stay in our room until his is finished."

"You don't mind? He's bound to wake during the night for weeks yet."

"I could stick the pair of you in a hotel until it's convenient."

She started to speak, but then she recognized the look in his eyes. "Sorry. I can't get used to it."

"Get used to it." He moved over to cup her face in his hand. Whenever he did that, she was almost ready to believe that dreams came true. "I may not have the equipment to feed him, but I figure I can learn to change a diaper." He stroked a thumb under her jawline. "I've been told I'm clever with my hands."

The heat rushed into her face. She was torn between stepping into his arms and backing away. The baby woke and decided her. "Speaking of feeding…"

"Why don't you use the bedroom, where you can be comfortable? I have some calls to make."

She knew what was coming. "Your family?"

"They're going to want to meet you. Are you up to it this evening?"

She wanted to snap that she wasn't an invalid, but she knew he wasn't speaking of her physical health. "Yes, of course."

"Fine. I'll make arrangements about the nursery. Did you have any colors in mind?"

"Well, I…" She expected to paint the room herself. She'd wanted to. Things were different now, she reminded herself. The cabin had easily become theirs, but the house was his. "I'd like yellow," she told him. "With white trim."

She sat in a chair by the window while Michael suckled hungrily. It was so good to have him with her all the time instead of having to go to the hospital to feed him, touch him, watch him. It had been so hard to leave him there and go back to a hotel room and wait until she could go back and see him again.

Smiling, she looked down at him. His eyes were closed, and his hand was pressed against her breast.

He was already gaining weight. Healthy, the doctor in Colorado Springs had said. Sound as a dollar. And the tag on his little wristband had read Michael Monroe Bradley.

Who was Michael? she wondered. Gabe's Michael. She hadn't asked, but knew that the name, the person, was important.

"You're Michael now," she murmured as the baby began to doze at her breast.

Later she laid him on the bed, surrounding him with pillows though she knew he couldn't roll yet. Going to her suitcase, she took out her hairbrush. It was silly, of course, to feel compelled to leave some mark of herself on the room. But she set the brush on Gabe's bureau before she left.

She found him downstairs, in a dark-paneled library with soft gray carpet. Because he was on the phone, she started to back out, but he waved her in and continued to talk.

"The paintings should be here by the end of the week. Yes, I'm back in harness again. I haven't decided. You take a look first. No, I'm going to be tied up here for a few days, thanks anyway. I'll let you know." He hung up, then glanced at Laura. "Michael?"

"He's asleep. I know there hasn't been time, but he's going to need his own bed. I thought I could run out and buy something if you could watch him for a little while."

"Don't worry about it. My parents are coming over soon."

"Oh."

He sat on the edge of the desk and frowned at her. "They're not monsters, Laura."

"Of course not, it's just that… It seems we're so out in the open," she blurted out. "The more people who know about Michael, the more dangerous it is."

"You can't keep him in a glass bubble. I thought you trusted me."

"I did. I do," she amended quickly, but not quickly enough.

"Did," Gabe repeated. It wasn't anger he felt so much as pressing regret. "You made a decision, Laura. On the day he was born, you gave him to me. Are you taking him back?"

"No. But things are different here. The cabin was—"

"An excellent place to hide. For both of us. Now it's time to deal with what happens next."

"What does happen?"

He picked up a paperweight, an amber ball with darker gold streaks in the center. He set it down again, then crossed to her. She'd shed weight quickly. Her stomach was close to flat, her breasts were high and full, her hips were impossibly narrow. He wondered how it would feel to hold her now, now that the waiting was over.

"We might start with this."

He kissed her, gently at first, until he felt her first nerves fade into warmth. That was what he'd been desperate for, that promise, that comfort. When he gathered her close, she fitted against him as he'd once imagined she would. Her hair, bound up, was easily set free with a sweep of his hand. She made a small sound—a murmur of surprise or acceptance—and then her arms went around him.

And the kiss was no longer gentle.

Passion, barely restrained, and hunger, far from sated, rippled from him into her. An ache, long buried, grew in her until she was straining against him, whispering his name.

Then his lips were roaming over her face, raking over her throat, searing her skin, then cooling it, then searing it again, while his hands stroked and explored with a new freedom.

Too soon. Some sane part of him knew it was too soon for anything more than a touch, a taste. But the more he indulged in her, the more his impatience grew. Taking her by the shoulders, he drew her away and fought to catch his breath.

"You may not trust me as you once did, angel, but trust this. I want you."

Giving in to the need, she held on to him, pressing her face into his shoulder. "Gabe, is it so wrong of me to wish it was just the three of us?"

"Not wrong." He stared over the top of her head as he stroked her hair. "Just not possible, and less than fair to Michael."

"You're right." Drawing a breath, she stepped back. "I want to go check on him."

Shaken by the emotions he pulled out of her, she started back up the stairs. Halfway up, she stopped, stunned.

She was in love with him. It wasn't the love she'd come to accept, the kind that came from gratitude and dependence. It wasn't even the strong, beautiful bond that had been forged when they'd brought Michael into the world. It was more basic than that, the most elemental love of woman for man. And it was terrifying.

She had loved once before, briefly, painfully. That love had kept her chained down. All her life she'd been a victim, and her marriage had both accented that and ultimately freed her. She'd learned through necessity how to be strong, how to take the right steps.

She couldn't be that woman again, she thought as her fingers gripped the banister. She wouldn't. That was what had bothered her most about the house, about the things in it. She had stepped into a house like this before, a house in which she had been out of place and continually helpless.

Not again, she told herself, and shut her eyes. Never again.

Whatever she felt for Gabe, she wouldn't allow it to change her back into that kind of woman. She had a child to protect.

The doorbell rang. Laura sent one swift look over her shoulder, then fled up the stairs.

When Gabe opened the door, he was immediately enveloped in soft fur and strong perfume. It was his mother, a woman of unwavering beauty and unwavering opinions. She didn't believe in brushing cheeks, she believed in squeezing, hard and long.

"I've missed you. I didn't know what it would take to drag you off that mountain, but I didn't think it would be a wife and a baby."

"Hello, Mother." He smiled at her, giving her a quick sweeping look that took in her stubbornly blond hair and her smooth cheeks. She had Michael's eyes. They were a darker green than his own, with touches of gray. Seeing them brought a pang and a pleasure. "You look wonderful."

"So do you, except for the fact that you've lost about ten pounds and can't afford to. Well, where are they?" With that, Amanda Bradley marched inside.

"Give the boy a chance, Mandy." Gabe exchanged bear hugs with his father, a tall, spare man with a hangdog expression and a razor-sharp mind. "Glad you're back. Now she'll take to rattling your cage instead of mine."

"I can handle you both." She was already slipping off her gloves with short, quick little motions. "We brought a bottle of champagne over. I thought since we missed the wedding, the birth and everything else, we should at least toast the homecoming. For heaven's sake, Gabe, don't just stand there, I'm dying to see them."

"Laura went up to check the baby. Why don't we go in and sit down?"

"This way, Mandy," Cliff Bradley said, taking his wife's arm when she started to object.

"Very well, then. You can hold me off for five minutes by telling me how your work's been going."

"Well." He watched his parents sit but couldn't relax enough to follow suit. "I've already called Marion. The paintings I finished in Colorado should be delivered to her gallery by the end of the week."

"That's wonderful. I can't wait to see them."

His hands were in his pockets as he moved around the room with a restlessness both of his parents recognized. "There's one piece in particular I'm fond of. I plan to hang it in here, over the fire."

Amanda lifted a brow and glanced at the empty space above the mantel. Gabe had always claimed that nothing suited that spot. "It must be very special."

"You'll have to judge for yourself." He drew out a cigarette, then set it down when Laura moved into the doorway.

She said nothing for a moment, just studied the couple on the couch. His parents. His mother was lovely, her smooth skin almost unlined, her hair swept back to accent her aristocratic features and fine bones. There were emeralds at her ears and at her throat. She wore a rose silk suit with a fox stole carelessly thrown over her shoulders.

His father was tall and lean, like Gabe. Laura saw a diamond wink at his pinky. He looked sad and quiet, but she saw his eyes sharpen as he studied her.

"This is my wife, Laura, and our son."

Braced for whatever was to come, holding the baby protectively against her breasts, she stepped into the room. Amanda rose first, only because she always seemed to move quicker than anyone else.

"It's so nice to meet you at last." Amanda had reservations, a chestful of them, but she offered a polite smile. "Gabe didn't mention how lovely you were."

"Thank you." She felt a little trip-hammer of fear in her throat. Laura knew formidable when she saw it. Instinctively she lifted her chin. "I'm glad you could come. Both of you."

Amanda noted the little gesture of pride and defiance and approved. "We wanted to meet you at the airport, but Gabe put us off."

"Rightly so," Cliff added in his soothing take-your-time voice. "If I'd been able to, I'd have held Mandy off another day."

"Nonsense. I want to see my grandchild. May I?"

Laura's arms had tightened automatically. Then she looked at Gabe and relaxed her hold. "Of course." With care and caution, she shifted the slight weight into Amanda's arms.

"Oh, how beautiful." The cool, sophisticated voice wavered. "How precious." The scents, the baby scents of talc and mild soap and fragile skin, made her sigh. "Gabe said he was premature. No problems?"

"No, he's fine."

As if to prove it, Michael opened his eyes and stared out owlishly.

"There, he looked right at me." With emeralds glowing

on her skin, Amanda grinned foolishly and cooed. "Looked right at your gran, didn't you?"

"He looked at me." Cliff leaned closer to chuck the baby under the chin.

"Nonsense. Why should he want to look at you? Do something useful, Cliff, like opening the champagne." She clucked and cooed at the baby while Laura stood twisting her hands. "I hope you don't object to the wine. I didn't ask if you were nursing."

"Yes, I am, but I don't think a sip would hurt either of us."

Approving a second time, Amanda started for the couch. Laura took an instinctive step forward, then made herself stop. This wasn't Lorraine Eagleton, and she wasn't the same woman who had once cowered. But as hard as she tried to dispel the image, she saw herself standing just outside the family circle.

"I'd get glasses," she said lamely, "but I don't know where they are."

Saying nothing, Gabe went to a cabinet and drew out four champagne flutes.

Cliff took Laura's arm. "Why don't you sit down, dear? You must be tired after traveling."

"You sound like Gabe." Laura found herself smiling as she eased into a chair.

Glasses were passed. Amanda lifted hers. "We'll drink to— For goodness' sake, I don't know the child's name."

"It's Michael," Laura offered. She saw the grief flash into Amanda's eyes before she closed them. When she opened them again, they were wet and brilliant.

"To Michael," she murmured, and after a sip she leaned down to kiss the baby's cheek. Looking up, she smiled at Gabe. "Your father and I have something in the car for the baby. Would you get it?"

Though they didn't touch, and the glance lasted only a moment, Laura saw something pass between them. "I'll just be a minute."

"We won't eat her, for heaven's sake," Amanda muttered as her son left the room.

With a laugh, Cliff rubbed her shoulder. There was something familiar about the gesture. It was Gabe's, Laura realized. The same casual intimacy.

"Have you been to San Francisco before?" he asked Laura, snapping her back to the present.

"No, I— No. I'd like to offer you something, but I don't know what we have." Or even where the kitchen is, she thought miserably.

"Don't worry about it." Cliff draped his arm comfortably over the back of the chair. "We don't deserve anything after barging in on your first day home."

"Families don't barge," Amanda put in.

"Ours does." Grinning, he leaned over and chucked the baby under the chin again. "Smiled at me."

"Grimaced, you mean." With a laugh of her own, Amanda kissed her husband's cheek. "Granddad."

"I take it the cradle's for Michael and the roses are for me." Gabe strode in, carrying a dark pine cradle heaped with frilly sheets and topped with a spray of pink roses.

"Oh, the flowers. I completely forgot. And no, they're certainly not for you, but for Laura." Amanda handed the baby to her husband and rose. Though she moved to rise, Laura saw Cliff tuck the baby easily in the crook of his arm. "We'll need some water for these," Amanda decided. "No, no, I'll get it myself."

No one argued with her as she marched out of the room, carrying the flowers.

"It's very lovely," Laura began, bending from the chair to run a finger along the smooth wood of the cradle. "We were just talking about the baby needing a bed of his own."

"The Bradley bed," Cliff stated. "Fix those sheets, Gabe, and let's see how he takes to it."

"This cradle's a family tradition." Obediently Gabe lifted out the extra sheets and smoothed on white linen. "My great-grandfather built it, and all the Bradley children have had their turn rocking in it." He took the baby from his father. "Let's see how you fit, old man."

Laura watched Gabe set the baby down and give the cradle a gentle push. Something seemed to break inside her. "Gabe, I can't."

Crouched at her feet beside the cradle, he looked up. There was a dare in his eyes, a challenge, and, she was certain, a buried anger. "Can't what?"

"It isn't right, it isn't fair." She drew the baby from the cradle into her arms. "They have to know." She might have fled right then and there, but Amanda came back into the room holding a crystal vase filled with roses. Sensing tension, and intrigued by it, she continued in.

"Where would you like these, Laura?"

"I don't know, I can't— Gabe, please."

"I think they'll look nice by the window," she said mildly, then moved over to arrange them to her satisfaction. "Now, then, don't you three gentlemen think you could find something to occupy yourselves while Laura and I have a little talk?"

Panic leaping within, Laura looked from one to the other, then back at her husband. "Gabe, you have to tell them."

He took the baby and settled him on his shoulder. His eyes, very clear and still sparking with anger, met hers. "I already have." Then he left her alone with his mother.

Amanda settled herself on the sofa again. She crossed her legs and smoothed her skirts. "A pity there isn't a fire. It's still cool for this time of year."

"We haven't had a chance—"

"Oh, dear, don't mind me." She waved a hand vaguely at a chair. "Wouldn't you rather sit?" When Laura did so without a word, she lifted a brow. "Are you always so amenable? I should certainly hope not, as I liked you better when you stuck your chin out at me."

Laura folded her hands in her lap. "I don't know what to say. I hadn't realized Gabe had explained things to you. The way you were acting…" She let her words trail off. Then, when Amanda continued to wait patiently, she tried again. "I thought you believed that Michael was, well, biologically Gabe's."

"Should that make such a big difference?"

She was calm again, at least outwardly, and able to meet Amanda's eyes levelly. "I would have expected it to, especially with a family like yours."

Amanda drew her brows together as she thought that through. "Shall I tell you that I'm acquainted with Lorraine Eagleton?" She saw the instant, overwhelming fear and backed up. She wasn't often a tactful woman, but she wasn't cruel. "We'll save talk of her for another time. Right now, I think I should explain myself instead. I'm a pushy woman, Laura, but I don't mind being pushed back."

"I'm not very good at that."

"Then you'll have to learn, won't you? We may be friends, or we may not, I can't tell so soon, but I love my son. When he left all those months ago, I wasn't sure I'd ever have him back. You, for whatever reason, brought him back, and for that I'm grateful."

"He would have come when he was ready."

"But he might not have come back whole. Let's leave that." Again, the vague gesture. "And get to the point. Your son. Gabe considers the child his. Do you?"

"Yes."

"No hesitation there, I see." Amanda smiled at her, and Laura was reminded of Gabe. "If Gabe considers Michael his son, and you consider Michael his son, why should Cliff and I feel differently?"

"Bloodlines."

"Let's leave the Eagletons out of this for the time being," Amanda said. Laura merely stared, surprised that the mark had been hit so directly. "If Gabe had been unable to have children and had adopted one, I would love it and think of it as my grandchild. So, don't you think you should get past this nonsense and accept it?"

"You make it sound very simple."

"It sounds to me as though your life's been complicated enough." Amanda picked up the glass of champagne she'd discarded before. "Do you have any objections to our being Michael's grandparents?"

"I don't know."

"An honest woman." Amanda sipped.

"Do you have any objections to me being Gabe's wife?"

With the slightest of smiles, Amanda raised her glass to Laura. "I don't know. So I suppose we'll both have to wait and see. In the meantime, I'd hate to think that I'd be discouraged from seeing Gabe or Michael because we haven't made up our minds about each other."

"No, of course not. I wouldn't do that. Mrs. Bradley, no one's ever been as kind or as generous with me as Gabe. I swear to you I won't do anything to hurt him."

"Do you love him?"

Uneasy, Laura cast a look toward the doorway. "We haven't…Gabe and I haven't talked about that. I needed help, and I think he needed to give it."

Pursing her lips, Amanda studied her glass. "I don't believe that's what I asked you."

The chin came up again. "That's something I should discuss with Gabe before anyone else."

"You're tougher than you look. Thank God for that." Finishing off the sparkling beverage, she set down the empty glass. "I might just like you at that, Laura. Or, of course, we might end up detesting each other. But whatever is between the two of us doesn't change the fact that Gabe has committed himself to you and the child. You're family." She sat back, lifting both brows, but inside she felt a faint twist of sympathy. "From the look on your face, that doesn't thrill the life out of you."

"I'm sorry. I'm not used to being in a family."

"You've had a very rough time, haven't you?" There was compassion there, but not so much that it made Laura uncomfortable. Mentally Amanda made a note to do a little digging on the Eagletons.

"I'm trying to put that behind me."

"I hope you succeed. Some things in the past need to be remembered. Others are best forgotten."

"Mrs. Bradley, may I ask you something?"

"Yes. On the condition that after this question call me Amanda or Mandy or anything—except, please God, Mother Bradley."

"All right. Who was Michael named for?"

Amanda's gaze drifted to the empty cradle and lingered there. There was a softening, a saddening, in her face that compelled Laura to touch her hand. "My son, Gabe's younger brother. He died just over a year ago." With a long sigh, she rose. "It's time we left you to settle in."

"Thank you for coming." She hesitated because she was never quite sure what people expected. Then listening to her heart, she kissed Amanda's cheek. "Thank you for the cradle. It means a great deal to me."

"And to me." She brushed her hand over it before she left the room. "Clifton, aren't you the one who said we shouldn't stay more than a half hour?"

His voice carried, muffled, from upstairs. Clucking her tongue, Amanda pulled on her gloves. "Always poking around in Gabe's studio. The poor dear doesn't know a Monet from a Picasso, but he loves to look over Gabe's work."

"He did some beautiful things in Colorado. You must be so proud of him."

"More every day." She heard her husband coming and glanced upstairs. "Do let me know if you want any help setting up the nursery or finding a good pediatrician. I also expect you'll understand if I buy out the baby boutiques."

"I don't—"

"Not understand, then, but you'll have to tolerate. Kiss your new daughter-in-law goodbye, Cliff."

"You don't have to tell me that." Rather than the formal, meaningless kiss she was expecting, Laura received a hearty hug that left her dazed and smiling. "Welcome to the Bradleys, Laura."

"Thank you." She had an urge to hug him back, to just throw her arms around his neck and breath in that nice, spicy after-shave she'd caught on his throat. Feeling foolish, she folded her hands instead. "I hope you'll come back, maybe next week for dinner, when I've had a chance to find things."

"Cooks, too?" He pinched Laura's cheek. "Nice work, Gabe."

When they were gone, she stood in the foyer, rubbing a finger over her cheek. "They're very nice."

"Yes, I've always thought so."

The sting was still in his voice, so she steadied herself and looked at him. "I owe you an apology."

"Forget it." He started to stride back into the library, then stopped and turned around. He'd be damned if he'd forget it. "Did you think I would lie to them about Michael? That I would have to?"

She accepted his anger without flinching. "Yes."

He opened his mouth, rage boiling on his tongue. Her answer had him shutting it again. "Well, you shoot straight from the hip."

"I did think so, and I'm glad I was wrong. Your mother was very kind to me, and your father…"

"What about my father?"

He hugged me, she wanted to say, but she didn't believe he could possibly understand how much that had affected her. "He's so much like you. I'll try not to disappoint them, or you."

"You'd do better not to disappoint yourself." Gabe dragged a hand through his hair. It fell in a tumble of dark blond disorder, the way she liked it best. "Damn it, Laura, you're not on trial here. You're my wife, this is your home, and for better or worse the Bradleys are your family."

She set her teeth. "You'll have to give me time to get used to it," she said evenly. "The only families I've ever known barely tolerated me. I'm through with that." She swung away to start up the stairs, then called over her shoulder, "And I'm painting Michael's nursery myself."

Not certain whether to laugh or swear, Gabe stood at the foot of the stairs and stared after her.

Chapter 7

Laura brushed the glossy white enamel paint over the baseboard. In her other hand she held a stiff piece of cardboard as a guard against smearing any of the white over the yellow walls she'd already finished.

On the floor in the far corner was a portable radio that was tuned to a station that played bouncy rock. She'd kept the volume low so that she could hear Michael when he woke. It was the same radio Gabe had kept on the kitchen counter in the cabin.

She wasn't sure which pleased her more, the way the nursery was progressing or the ease with which she could bend and crouch. She'd even been able to use part of her hospital fund to buy a couple of pairs of slacks in her old size. They might still be a tad snug in the waist, but she was optimistic.

She wished the rest of her life would fall into order as easily.

He was still angry with her. With a shrug, Laura dipped her brush into the paint can again. Gabe had a temper, he had moods. He had certainly never attempted to deny or hide that. And the truth was, she'd been wrong not to trust him to do the right thing. So she'd apologized. She couldn't let his continuing coolness bother her. But, of course, it did.

They were strangers here, in a way that they had never been strangers in the little cabin in Colorado. It wasn't the house, though a part of her still blamed the size and the glamour of it. Before, the simple mechanics of space had required them to share, to grow close, to depend on each other. Being depended on had become important to Laura, even if it had only been to provide a cup of coffee at the right time. Now, beyond her responsibilities to Michael, there was little for her to do. She and Gabe could spend hours under the same roof and hardly know each other existed.

But it wasn't walls and floors and windows that made the difference. It was quite simply the difference—the difference between them. She was still Laura Malone, from the wrong side of the tracks, the same person who had been moved and shuffled from house to house, without ever being given the chance to really live there. The same person who had been handed from family to family without ever being given the chance to really belong.

And he was… Her laugh was a bit wistful. He was Gabriel Bradley, a man who had known his place from the moment he'd been born. A man who would never wonder if he'd have the same place tomorrow.

That was what she wanted for Michael, only that. The money, the name, the big, sprawling house with the stained-glass windows and the graceful terraces, didn't matter. Belonging did. Because she wanted it, was determined to have it for her son, she was willing to wait to belong herself. To Gabe.

The only time they were able to pull together was when Michael was involved. Her lips curved then. He loved the baby. There could be no doubt about that. It wasn't pity or obligation that had him crouching beside the cradle or walking the floor at three in the morning. He was a man capable of great love, and he had given it unhesitatingly to Michael. Gabe was attentive, interested, gentle and involved. When it came to Michael.

It was only with her, when they had to deal with each other one on one, that things became strained.

They didn't touch. Though they lived in the same house, slept in the same bed, they didn't touch, except in the most casual and impersonal of ways. As a family they had gone out to choose all the things Michael would need—the crib and other nursery furniture, blankets, a windup swing that played a lullaby, soft stuffed animals that Michael would undoubtedly ignore for months. It had been easy, even delightful, to discuss high chairs and playpens and decide together what would suit. Laura had never expected to be able to give her son so much or to be able to share in that giving.

But when they'd come home the strain had returned.

She was being a fool, Laura told herself. She'd been

given a home, protection and care, and, most of all, a kind and loving father for her son. Wishing for more was what had always led her to disappointment before.

But she wished he would smile at her again—at her, not at Michael's mother, not at the subject of his painting.

Perhaps it was best that they remained as they were, polite friends with a common interest. She wasn't entirely sure how she would manage when the time came for him to turn to her as a woman. The time would come, his desire was there, and he was too physical a man to share the bed with her without fully sharing it much longer.

Her experience with lovemaking had taught her that man demanded and woman submitted. He wouldn't have to love her, or even hold her in affection, to need her. God, no one knew better how little affection, how little caring, there could be in a marriage bed. A man like Gabe would have many demands, and loving him as she did she would give. And the cycle she'd finally managed to break would begin again.

Gabe watched her from the doorway. Something was wrong, very wrong. He could see the turmoil on her face, could see it in the set of her shoulders. It seemed that the longer they were here the less she relaxed. She pretended well, but it was only pretense.

It infuriated him, and the harder he held on to his temper the more infuriated he became. He hadn't so much as raised his voice to her since their first day in the house, and yet she seemed continually braced for an outburst.

He'd given her as much room as was humanly possible, and it was killing him. Sleeping with her, having her turn to him during the night, her skin separated from his only by the fragile cotton of a nightgown, had given new meaning to insomnia.

He'd taken to working during the middle of the night and spending his free time in the studio or at the gallery, anywhere he wouldn't be tempted to take what was his only legally.

How could he take when she was still so delicate, physically, emotionally? However selfish he'd always been, or considered himself, he couldn't justify gratifying himself at her expense—or frightening her by letting her see just how desperately, how violently, he wanted her.

Yet there was passion in her, the dark, explosive kind. He'd seen that, and other things, in her eyes. She needed him, as much as he needed her. He wasn't sure either of them understood where their need might take them.

He could be patient. He was aware that her body needed time to heal, and he could give her that. But he wasn't sure he could give her the time it might take for her mind to heal.

He wanted to cross to her, to sit down beside her and stroke his hand over her hair. He wanted to reassure her. But he had no idea what words to use. Instead, he tucked his hands into his pockets.

"Still at it?"

Laura started, splattering paint on her hand. She sat back on her heels. "I didn't hear you come in."

"Don't get up," he told her. "You make quite a picture." He stepped into the room, glancing at the sunny walls before looking down at her. She wore an old pair of jeans, obviously his. He could see the clothesline she'd used to secure the waist. One of his shirts was tented over her, its hem torn at her hip.

"Mine?"

"I thought it would be all right." She picked up a rag to wipe the paint from her hand. "I could tell from the splatters on them they'd already been worked in."

"Perhaps you don't know the difference between painting and—" he gestured toward the wall "—painting."

She'd nearly fumbled out an apology before she realized he was joking. So the mood had passed. Perhaps they were friends again. "Not at all. I thought your pants would give me artistic inspiration."

"You could have come to the source."

She set the brush on top of the open paint can. Relief poured through her. Though he didn't know, Gabe had found exactly the right words to reassure her. "I would never have suggested that the celebrated Gabriel Bradley turn his genius to a lowly baseboard."

It seemed so easy when she was like this, relaxed, with a hint of amusement in her eyes. "Obviously afraid I'd show you up."

She smiled, a bit hesitantly. He hadn't looked at her in quite that way for days. Then she was scrambling back up on her knees as he joined her on the floor. "Oh, Gabe, don't. You'll get paint all over you, and you look so nice."

He had the brush in his hand. "Do I?"

"Yes." She tried to take it away from him, but he didn't give way. "You always look so dashing when you go to the gallery."

"Oh, God." The instant disgust on his face made her laugh.

"Well, you do." She checked the urge to brush at the hair on his forehead. "It's quite different from the rugged-outdoorsman look you had in Colorado, though that was nice, too."

He wasn't certain whether to smile or sneer. "Rugged outdoorsman?"

"That's right. The cords and the flannel, the untidy hair and the carelessly unshaven face. I think Geoffrey would have loved to photograph you with an ax…." She was staring at him, seeing him as he'd been and as he was. Abruptly she became aware that her hand was still covering his on the handle of the brush. Drawing it away, she struggled to remember her point. "You're not dressed for work now, and I was in the fashion business long enough to recognize quality. Those pants are linen, and you'll ruin them."

He was well aware of the sudden tension in her fingers and the look that had come into her eyes, but he only lifted a brow. "Are you saying I'm sloppy?"

"Only when you paint."

"Pot calling the kettle," he murmured, ignoring the way she jumped when he ran a finger down her cheek. He held it up to prove his point.

Laura wrinkled her nose at the smear of white paint on his fingertip—and tried to ignore the heat on her skin where his finger had brushed. "I'm not an artist." With a rag in one hand, she took his wrist in the other to clean the paint from his fingertip.

Such beautiful hands, she thought. She could imagine how it would feel to have them move over her, slowly, gently. To have them stroke and caress the way a man's might if he cared deeply about the woman beneath the skin he was touching. Her imagination had her moistening her lips as she lifted her gaze to his.

They knelt knee to knee on the drop cloth, with his hand caught in hers. It amazed her when she felt his pulse begin to thud. In his eyes she saw what he hadn't allowed her to see for days. Desire, pure and simple. Unnerved by it, drawn to it, she leaned toward him. The rag slipped out of her hand.

And the baby cried out.

They both jerked, like children caught raiding the cookie jar.

"He'll be hungry, and wet, too, I imagine," she said as she started to rise. Gabe shifted his hand until it captured hers.

"I'd like you to come back here after you've tended to him."

Longing and anxiety tangled, confusing her. "All right. Don't worry about the mess. I'll finish up later."

She was more than an hour with Michael, and she was a bit disappointed that Gabe didn't come in, as he often did, to hold the baby or play with him before he slept again. Those were the best times, those simple family times. Tucking the blankets around her son, she reminded herself that she couldn't expect Gabe to devote every free minute to her and the child.

Satisfied that the baby was dry and content, she left him to go into the adjoining bath and freshen up. After she'd washed the paint from her face, she studied herself in the mirrored wall across from the step-down tub. She didn't look seductive in baggy, masculine clothes, with her hair tugged back in a ponytail. Regardless of that, for an instant in the nursery, Gabe had been seduced.

Was that what she wanted?

How could she know what she wanted? She pressed her fingers to her eyes and tried to sort out her feelings. Confusion, and little else. One moment she imagined what it would be like, being with Gabe, making love with him. The next moment she was remembering the way it had been before, when love had had little to do with it.

It was wrong to continually let memories intrude. She told herself she was too sensible for that. Or wanted to be. She'd been in therapy, she'd talked to counselors and other women who had been in situations all too similar to her own. Because she'd had to stay on the move, she hadn't been able to remain with any one group for long, but they had helped her. Just learning that she wasn't alone in what had happened to her, seeing and talking with others who had turned their lives around again, had given her the strength to go on.

She knew—intellectually she knew—that what had happened to her was the result of a man's illness and her own insecurity. But it was one thing to know it and another to accept it and go on, to risk another relationship.

She wanted to be normal, was determined to be. That had been the communal cry from all the sessions in all the towns. Along with the fear and the anger and the self-disgust, there had been a desperate mutual need to be normal women again.

But that step, that enormous, frightening step from past to future, was so difficult to take. Only she could do it, Laura told herself as she continued to stare into her own eyes. With Gabe, and her feelings for him, she had a chance. If she was willing to take it.

How could she know how close they could be, how

much they could mean to each other, if she didn't allow herself to want the intimacy?

Catching her lower lip between her teeth, she turned to study the lush bath. It was nearly as large as many of the rooms she'd lived in during her life. White on white on white, it gleamed and glistened and invited indulgence. She could sink into hot, deep water in the tub and soak until her skin was soft and pink. She still had most of a bottle of perfume, French and suggestive, that Geoffrey had bought her in Paris. She could dab it on her damp skin so that the scent seeped into her pores. Then she could…what?

She had nothing lovely or feminine to wear. The only clothes she hadn't taken to thrift shops or secondhand stores during her cross-country flight were maternity clothes. The two pairs of slacks and the cotton blouses didn't count.

In any case, what would it matter if she had a closetful of lace negligees? She wouldn't know what to do or say. It had been so long since she'd thought of herself strictly as a woman. Perhaps she never had. And surely it was better to try to reestablish that early friendship with Gabe before they attempted intimacy.

If that was what he wanted. What she wanted.

Turning away from the mirror, she went to find him.

She couldn't have been more surprised when she walked into the nursery and found the painting finished, the cans sealed and the brushes cleaned. As she stared, Gabe folded the drop cloth.

"You finished it," she managed.

"I seem to have struggled through without doing any damage."

"It's beautiful. The way I'd always imagined." She stepped into the empty room and began arranging furniture in her head. "There should be curtains, white ones, though I suppose dotted swiss is too feminine for a boy."

"I couldn't say, but it sounds like it. It's warm enough, so I've left the windows open." He tossed the drop cloth over a stepladder. "I don't want to put Michael in here until the smell of the paint's gone."

"No," she agreed absently, wondering if the crib should go between the two windows.

"Now that this is out of the way, I have something for you. A belated Mother's Day present."

"Oh, but you gave me the flowers already."

He took a small box out of his pocket. "There wasn't the time or the opportunity for much else then. We were living out of a suitcase and spending all of our time at the hospital. Besides, the flowers were from Michael. This is from me."

That made it different. Intimate. Again she found herself drawn to him, and again she found herself pulled away. "You don't have to give me anything."

The familiar impatience shimmered. He barely suppressed it. "You're going to have to learn how to take a gift more graciously."

He was right. And it was wrong of her to continue to compare, but Tony had been so casual, so lavish, in his gifts. And they had meant so little. "Thank you." She took the box, opened it and stared.

The ring looked like a circle of fire, with its channel-linked diamonds flashing against its gold band and nestled in velvet. Instinctively she ran a fingertip over it and was foolishly amazed that it was cool to the touch.

"It's beautiful. Absolutely beautiful. But—"

"There had to be one."

"It's just that it's a wedding ring, and I already have one."

He took her left hand to examine it. "I'm surprised your finger hasn't fallen off from wearing this thing."

"There's nothing wrong with it," she said, and nearly snatched her hand away.

"So sentimental, angel?" Though his voice had gentled, his hand was firm on hers. Now, perhaps, he would be able to dig a bit deeper into what she was feeling for him, about him. "Are you so attached to a little circle of metal?"

"It was good enough for us before. I don't need anything else."

"It was a temporary measure. I'm not asking you to toss it out the window, but be a little practical. If you weren't always curling your finger up, it would fall right off."

"I could have it sized."

"Suit yourself." He slipped it from her finger, then replaced it with the diamond circle. "Just consider that you have two wedding rings." When he offered her the plain band, Laura curled it into her fist. "The new one holds the same intentions."

"It is beautiful." Still, she pushed the old ring onto the index finger of her right hand, where it fit more snugly. "Thank you, Gabe."

"We did better than that before."

She didn't have to be reminded. Yet the memories flooded back when he slipped his arms around her. Emotions poured through with those memories the moment his mouth was on hers. His lips were firm and warm and hinted, just hinted, at his impatience as they slanted across hers. Though his arms remained gentle around her, his touch light and testing, she sensed a volcano in him, simmering and smoking.

As if to soothe, she leaned into him and lifted a hand to his cheek. Understanding. Acceptance.

Her touch triggered the need crawling inside him, and his arms tightened and his mouth crushed down on hers. She responded with a moan that he barely heard, with a shudder that he barely felt. Tense, hungry, he fell victim to her as much as to his own demands.

He had wanted before, casually and desperately and all the degrees in between. Why, then, did this seem like a completely new experience? He had held women before, known their softness, tasted their sweetness. But he had never known a softness, never experienced a sweetness, like Laura's.

He took his mouth on a slow, seeking journey over her face, along her jawline, down her throat, drinking in, then devouring. His hands, long and limber, slipped under her full shirt, then roamed upward. At first the slender line of her back was enough, the smooth skin and the quick tremors all he required. Then the need to touch, to possess, grew sharper. As his mouth came back to hers, he slid his hand around to cup, then claim, her breast.

The first touch made her catch her breath, pulling air in quickly, then letting it out again in a long, unsteady sigh. How could she have known, even blinded by love and longings, how desperately she'd need to have his hands on her? This was what she wanted, to be his in every way, in all ways. The confusion, the doubts, the fears, drained away. No memories intruded when he held her like this.

No whispers of the past taunted her. There was only him, and the promise of a new life and an enduring love.

Her knees were trembling so she braced her body against his, arching in an invitation so instinctive that only he recognized it.

The room smelled of paint and was bright with the sun that streamed through the uncurtained windows. It was empty and quiet. He could fantasize about pulling her to the floor, tugging at her clothes until they were skin-to-skin on the polished hardwood. He could imagine taking her in the sun-washed room until they were both exhausted and replete.

With another woman he might have done so without giving a thought to where or when, and little more to how. But not with Laura.

Churning, he drew her away from him. Her eyes were clouded. Her mouth was soft and full. With a restraint he hadn't known he possessed, Gabe swore only in his mind.

"I have work to do."

She was floating, drifting on a mist so fine it could only be felt, not seen. At his words, she began the quick, confused journey back to earth. "What?"

"I have work to do," he repeated, stepping carefully away from her. He detested himself for taking things so far when he knew she was physically unable to cope with his demands. "I'll be in the studio if you need me."

If she needed him? Laura thought dimly as his footsteps echoed down the hall. Hadn't she just shown him how much she needed him? It wasn't possible that he hadn't felt it, that he hadn't understood it. With an oath, she turned and walked to the window. There she huddled on the small, hard seat and stared down at the garden, which was just beginning to bloom.

What was there about her, she wondered, that made men look at her as a thing to be taken or rejected at will? Did she appear so weak, so malleable? She curled her hands into fists as frustration spread through her. She wasn't weak, not any longer, and a long time, in some ways a lifetime, had passed since she had been malleable. She wasn't a young girl caught up in fairy-tale lies now. She was a woman, a mother, with responsibilities and ambitions.

Perhaps she loved, and perhaps this time would be as unwise a love as before. But she wouldn't be used, she wouldn't be ignored, and she wouldn't be molded.

Talk was cheap, Laura thought as she propped her chin on her knees. Doing something about it was a little costlier. She should go in to Gabe now and make herself clear. She cast a look at the door, then turned back to the window. She didn't have the courage.

That had always been her problem. She could say what she would or would not do, but when it came down to acting on it she found passivity easier than action. There had been a time in her life when she'd believed that the passive way was best for her. That had been until her marriage to Tony had fallen viciously apart. She'd done something then, Laura reminded herself, or had begun to do something, then had allowed herself to be pressured and persuaded to erase it.

It had been like that all her life. As a child she hadn't had a choice. She'd been told to live here or live there, and she had. Each house had had its own sets of rules and values, and she'd had to conform. Like one of those rubber dolls, she thought now, that you could bend and twist into any position you liked.

Too much of the child had remained with the woman, until the woman had been with child.

The only positive action she felt she'd ever taken in her life had been to protect the baby. And she had done it, Laura reminded herself. It had been terrifying and hard, but she hadn't backed down. Didn't that mean that buried beneath years of quiet compliance was the strength she'd always wanted to have? She had to believe that and, if she did, to act on it.

Loving Gabe didn't mean, couldn't mean, that she would sit quietly by while he made decisions for her. It was time to take a stand.

Rising, she walked out of the empty nursery and started down the hall. With each step her resolve wavered and had to be shored up again. At the door to his studio, she hesitated again, rubbing the heel of her hand on her chest, where the ache of uncertainty lodged. Taking one last breath, she opened the door and walked in.

He was by the long bank of windows, a brush in his hand, working on one of the paintings that had been stacked half-finished against the wall of the cabin. She remembered it. It was a snow scene, very stark and lonely and somehow appealing. The whites and cold blues and silvers gave a sense of challenge.

Laura was glad of it. A sense of challenge was precisely what she needed.

He hadn't heard her come in, so intent was he on his work. There were no sweeping strokes or bold slashes now, only a delicacy. He was adding details so minute, so exact, that she could almost hear the winter wind.

"Gabe?" It was amazing how much courage it could take to say a name.

He stopped immediately, and when he turned the annoyance on his face was very apparent. Interruptions were never tolerated here. Living alone, he hadn't had to tolerate them.

"What is it?" He clipped the words off, and he didn't set down his brush or move from the painting. It was obvious that he intended to continue exactly where he'd left off the moment he'd nudged her out of his way.

"I need to talk to you."

"Can't it wait?"

She nearly said yes, but then she brought herself up short. "No." She left the door open in case the baby should cry out and walked to the center of the room. Her stomach twisted, knotted. Her chin came up. "Or, if it can, I don't want it to."

He lifted a brow. He'd heard that tone in her voice only a handful of times in the weeks they'd been together. "All right, but make it fast, will you? I want to finish this."

Her temper flared too quickly to surprise her. "Fine, then, I'll sum it up in one sentence. If I'm going to be your wife, I want you to treat me like one."

"I beg your pardon?"

She was too angry to see that he was stunned, and too angry to recognize her own shock at her words. "No, you don't. You've never begged anyone's pardon in your life. You don't have to. You do exactly what suits you. If that means being kind, you can be the kindest man I've ever known. If it means being arrogant, you take that just as far."

With deliberate care, he set his brush down. "If there's a point to this, Laura, I'm missing it."

"Do you want me or don't you?"

He only stared at her. If she continued to stand in the pool of light, her eyes dark and defiant, her cheeks flushed with color, he might beg. "That's the point?" he said steadily.

"You tell me you want me, then you ignore me. You kiss me, then you walk away." She dragged a hand through her hair. When her fingers tangled with the ribbon that held it back, she tugged it out in annoyance. Pale and fragile, her hair fell around her shoulders. "I realize the main reason we're married is because of Michael, but I want to know where I stand. Am I to be a guest here who's alternately indulged and ignored, or am I to be your wife?"

"You are my wife." With his own temper rising, he pushed himself off his stool. "And it's not a matter of me ignoring you. I've simply got a lot of work to catch up on."

"You don't work twenty-four hours a day. At night—" Her courage began to fail. She thrust out the rest of the words. "Why won't you make love with me?"

It was fortunate that he'd set his brush down, or else he might have snapped it in half. "Do you expect performance on demand, Laura?"

Embarrassed color flooded her cheeks. That had once been expected of her, and it shamed her more than she could say to think she'd demanded it. "No. I didn't mean it to sound that way. I only thought it was best that you know how I felt." She took a step back, then turned to go. "I'll let you get back to work."

"Laura." He preferred, much preferred, her anger to the humiliation he'd seen. And caused. "Wait." He started after her when she whirled around.

"Don't apologize."

"All right." There was still fire in her, he saw, and he wasn't entirely sure he should be relieved. "I'll just give you a more honest explanation."

"It isn't necessary." She started toward the door again, but he grabbed her arm and yanked her around. He saw it and cursed at it—the instant fear that leaped into her eyes.

"Damn it, don't look at me like that. Don't ever look at me like that." Without his realizing it, his fingers had tightened on her arm. When she winced, he released her, dropping his hands to his side. "I can't make myself over for you, Laura. I'll yell when I need to yell and fight when I need to fight, but I told you once before, and I'll say it again. I don't hit women."

The fear had risen, a bitter bile in her throat. It was detestable. She waited for it to pass before she spoke. "I don't expect you to, but I can't make myself over for you, either. Even if I could, I don't know what you want. I know I should be grateful to you."

"The hell with that."

"I should be grateful," she continued, calm again. "And I am, but I've found out something about myself this past year. I'll never be anyone's doormat ever again. Not even yours."

"Do you think that's what I want?"

"I can't know what you want, Gabe, until you know yourself." She'd gone this far, Laura told herself, and she would finish. "Right from the beginning you expected me to trust you. But after everything we've been through you still haven't been able to make yourself trust me. If we're ever going to be able to make this marriage work you're going to have to stop looking at me as a good deed and start seeing me as a person."

"You have no idea how I see you."

"No, I probably don't." She managed a smile. "Maybe when I do it'll be easier for both of us." She heard the baby crying and glanced down the hall. "He doesn't seem to be able to settle today."

"I'll get him in a minute. He can't be hungry again. Wait." If she could be honest, he told himself, then so could he. He put a hand on her arm to hold her there. "It's easy enough to clear up one misunderstanding. I haven't made love with you, not because I haven't wanted to, but because it's too soon."

"Too soon?"

"For you."

She started to shake her head. Then his meaning became clear. "Gabe, Michael's over four weeks old."

"I know how old he is. I was there." He held up a hand before she could speak. "Damn it, Laura, I saw what you went through. How hard it was on you. However I feel, it simply isn't possible for me to act on it until I know you're fully recovered."

"I had a baby, not a terminal illness." She let out a huff of breath, but she found it wasn't annoyance or even amusement she felt. It was pleasure, the rare and wonderful pleasure of being cared for. "I feel fine. I am fine. In fact, I've probably never been better in my life."

"Regardless of how you feel, you've just had a baby. From what I've read—"

"You've read about this, too?"

That infuriated him—that wide-eyed wonder and the trace of humor in her eyes. "I don't intend to touch you," he said stiffly, "until I'm sure you're fully recovered."

"What do you want, a doctor's certificate?"

"More or less." He started to touch her cheek, then thought better of it. "I'll see to Michael."

He left her standing in the hall, unsure whether she was angry or amused or delighted. All that she was sure of was that she was feeling, and her feelings were all for Gabe.

Chapter 8

"I can't believe how fast he's growing." Feeling very grandmotherly but sporting a sleek new hairstyle, Amanda sat in the bentwood rocker in Michael's new nursery and cuddled the baby.

"He's making up for being premature." Still not quite certain how she felt about her mother-in-law, Laura continued to fold tiny clothes that were fresh from the laundry. "We had our checkup today, and the doctor said Michael was healthy as a horse." She pressed a sleeper to her cheek. It was soft, almost as soft as her son's skin. "I wanted to thank you for recommending Dr. Sloane. She's wonderful."

"Good. But I don't need a pediatrician to tell me this child's healthy. Look at this grip." Amanda chuckled as Michael curled his fingers around hers, but she stopped short of allowing him to suck on her sapphire ring. "He has your eyes, you know."

"Does he?" Delighted, Laura moved to stand over them. The baby smelled of talc—Amanda of Paris. "It's too early to tell, I know, but I'd hoped he did."

"No doubt about it." Amanda continued to rock as she studied her daughter-in-law. "And what about *your* checkup? How are you?"

"I'm fine." Laura thought about the slip of paper she'd tucked into the top drawer of her dresser.

"Looking a bit tired to me." There wasn't any sympathy in the voice; it was brusque and matter-of-fact. "Haven't you done anything about getting some help?"

Laura's spine straightened automatically. "I don't need any help."

"That's absurd, of course. With a house this size, a demanding husband and a new baby, you can use all the help you can get, but suit yourself." Michael began to coo, pleasing Amanda. "Talk to Gran, sweetheart. Tell Gran just how it is." The baby responded with more gurgles. "Listen to that. Before long you'll have plenty to say for yourself. Just make sure 'My gran's beautiful' is one of the first. There's a sweet boy." She dropped a kiss on his brow before looking up at Laura. "I'd say a change is in order here, and I'm more than happy to leave that to you." With what she considered a grandmother's privilege, Amanda handed the wet baby to Laura. She continued to sit as Laura took Michael to the changing table.

There was a great deal she'd have liked to say. Amanda was accustomed to voicing her opinions loud and clear—and, if necessary, beating anyone within reach over the head with it. It chafed a bit to hold back, but she'd learned enough in the past few weeks about the Eagletons and about Laura's life with them. Treading carefully, she tried a new tactic.

"Gabe's spending a lot of time at the gallery."

"Yes. I think he's nearly decided to go ahead with a new showing." Almost drowning in love, Laura leaned over to nuzzle Michael's neck.

"Have you been there?"

"The gallery? No, I haven't."

Amanda tapped a rounded, coral-tipped nail on the arm of the rocker. "I'd think you'd be interested in Gabe's work."

"Of course I am." She held Michael over her head, and he began to bubble and smile. "I just haven't thought it wise to take Michael in and interrupt."

It was on the tip of Amanda's tongue to remind Laura that Michael had grandparents who would delight in having him to themselves for a few hours. Again she bit the words back. "I'm sure Gabe wouldn't mind. He's devoted to the boy."

"Yes, he is." Laura retied the ribbons on Michael's pale blue booties. "But I also know he needs some time to organize his work, his career." She handed her son a small cloth bunny, and he stuck it happily in his mouth. "Do you know why Gabe is hesitating about a showing?"

"Have you asked him?"

"No, I—I didn't want to pressure him about it."

"A little pressure might be just what he needs."

Frowning, Laura turned. "Why?"

"It has to do with Michael, my son Michael. I'd prefer it if you asked Gabe the rest."

"They were close?"

"Yes." She smiled. She'd learned it hurt less to remember than to try to forget. "They were very close, though they were very different. He was devastated when Michael was killed. I believe the time in the mountains helped Gabe get back his art. And I believe you and the baby helped him get back his heart."

"If that's true, I'm glad. He's helped me more than I can ever repay."

Amanda gave Laura an even look. "Payments aren't necessary between a husband and wife."

"Perhaps not."

"Are you happy?"

Stalling, Laura laid the baby in the crib and wound the musical mobile so that he could shake his fists and kick at it. "Of course I am. Why wouldn't I be?"

"That was my next question."

"I'm very happy." She went back to folding and storing baby clothes. "It was nice of you to visit, Amanda. I know how busy your schedule is."

"Don't think you can politely show me out the door before I'm ready to go."

Laura turned and saw the faint, amused smile on Amanda's lips. Bad manners were enough out of character for her to make her flush. "I'm sorry."

"Don't be. I don't expect for you to be comfortable with me yet. I'm not entirely sure I'm comfortable with you, either."

A bit more relaxed, Laura smiled back. "I'm sure you're always comfortable. I envy that about you. And I am sorry."

Amanda brushed aside the apology and rose to roam

the room. She liked what her daughter-in-law had done here. It was a bright, cheerful place, not overly fussy, and just traditional enough to make her remember the nursery she had set up herself so many years before. There were the scents of powder and fresh linen.

A loving place, she thought. She knew she wouldn't have wanted any more for her son. It was very obvious to her that Laura had untapped stores of love.

"This is a charming room. I think so every time I step into it." Amanda patted the head of the four-foot lavender teddy bear. "But you can't hide here forever."

"I don't know what you mean." But she did.

"You said you'd never been to San Francisco, and now you're here. Have you gone to a museum, to the theater? Have you strolled down to Fisherman's Wharf, ridden a streetcar, explored Chinatown, any of the things a newcomer would surely do?"

Defensive now, Laura spoke coolly. "No, I haven't. But it's only been a few weeks."

It was time, Amanda decided, to stop circling and get to the point. "Let's deal woman-to-woman a moment, Laura. Forget the fact that I'm Gabe's mother. We're alone. Whatever is said here doesn't have to go any further."

Laura's palms were starting to sweat. She brushed them dry on the thighs of her slacks. "I don't know what you want me to say."

"Whatever needs to be said." When Laura remained silent, Amanda nodded. "All right, I'll begin. You've had some miserable spots in your life, some of them tragic. Gabe gave us the bare essentials, but I learned a good deal more by knowing who and what to ask." Amanda sat down again and crossed her legs. She didn't miss the flash in Laura's eyes. "Wait until I've finished. Then you can be as offended as you like."

"I'm not offended," Laura said stiffly. "But I don't see the purpose in discussing what used to be."

"Until you look what used to be square in the face, you won't be able to go on with what might be." She tried to keep her voice brisk, but even her solid composure wavered. "I know that Tony Eagleton abused you, and that his parents overlooked what was monstrous, even criminal, behavior. My heart breaks for you."

"Please." Her voice was strangled as she shook her head. "Don't."

"No sympathy allowed, Laura, even woman-to-woman?"

Again she shook her head, afraid to accept it and, more, to need it. "I can't bear to think back on it. And I can't stand pity."

"Sympathy and pity are entirely different things."

"All that's behind me. I'm a different person than I was then."

"I have no way of agreeing, as I didn't know you before. But I can say that anyone who stood on her own all these months must have great reserves of strength and determination. Isn't it time you used them, and fought back?"

"I have fought back."

"You've taken sanctuary, a much-needed one. I won't argue that running as you did took courage and stamina. But there comes a time to take a stand."

Hadn't she said that to herself time and time again? Hadn't she hated herself for only saying it? She looked at her son, who gurgled and reached for the colorful birds circling over his head.

"And what? Go to court, to the press, drag the whole ugly mess out for everyone to gawk at?"

"If necessary." Her voice took on a tone of pride that carried to all corners of the room. "The Bradleys aren't afraid of scandal."

"I'm not a—"

"But you are," Amanda told her. "You're a Bradley, and so is that child. It's Michael I'm thinking of in the long run, but I'm also thinking of you. What difference does it make what anyone thinks, what anyone knows? You have nothing to be ashamed of."

"I let it happen," Laura said, with a kind of dull fury. "I'll always be ashamed of that."

"My dear child." Unable to prevent herself, Amanda rose to put her arms around Laura. After the first shock, Laura felt herself being drawn in. Perhaps it was because the comfort came from a woman, but it broke down her defences as nothing else ever had.

Amanda let her weep, even wept with her. The fact that she did, that she could, was more soothing than any words could have been. Cheek-to-cheek, woman-to-woman, they held each other until the storm passed. The bond that Laura had never expected to know was forged in tears. With her arm still around Laura, Amanda led her to the gaily striped daybed.

"That's been coming on for a while, I'd say," Amanda murmured. She drew a lace-edged handkerchief out of her breast pocket and unashamedly wiped her eyes.

"I don't know." Laura used the back of her wrist to

smear away already-drying tears. "I suppose. Crying isn't something I should need, not anymore. It's only when I look back and remember."

"Now listen to me," Amanda said. All the softness had been erased from her voice. "You were young and alone, and you have nothing, nothing, to be ashamed of. One day you'll realize that for yourself, but for now it might be enough to know you're not alone anymore."

"Sometimes I'm so angry, just so angry that I was used as a convenience, or a punching bag, or a status symbol." It was amazing to her that fury could bring calm and wipe out pain. "When I am I know that no matter what it costs I'll never go back to that."

"Then stay angry."

"But…the anger for me, that's personal." She looked across the room at the crib. "It's when I think of Michael and I know they're going to try to take him…then I'm afraid."

"They don't just have to go through you now, do they?"

Laura looked back. Amanda's face was set. Her eyes glittered. So this was where Gabe got his warrior look, Laura thought, and felt a new kind of love stir. It was the most natural thing in the world for Laura to reach out and take her hand. "No, they don't."

They both heard the door open and close on the first floor. Immediately Laura began to brush her hands over her face. "That must be Gabe, home from the gallery. I don't want him to see me like this."

"I'll go down and keep him occupied." On impulse, she glanced at her watch. "Do you have plans for this afternoon?"

"No. Just to—"

"Good. Come down when you're tidied up."

Ten minutes later, Laura came down to find Gabe cornered in the living room, scowling into a glass of club soda.

"Then it's all settled." Amanda fluffed a hand through her hair, well satisfied. "Laura. Good. Are you ready?"

"Ready?"

"Yes. I've explained to Gabe that we're going shopping. He's absolutely delighted with the reception I've planned for the two of you next week." The reception she'd only begun to plan on her way downstairs.

"Resigned," he corrected, but he had to smile at his mother. The smile faded when he glanced over at Laura. "What's wrong?"

"Nothing." It had been foolish to think that a quick wash and fresh makeup could hide anything from him. "Your mother and I were getting sentimental over Michael."

"What your wife needs is an afternoon out." Amanda rose, then leaned over to kiss Gabe. "I'd scold you for keeping her locked up this way, but I love you too much."

"I never—"

"Never once nudged her out of the house," his mother finished for him. "So it's up to me. Get your purse, dear. We have to find you something wonderful for the reception. Gabe, I imagine Laura needs your credit cards."

"My— Oh." Feeling like a tree blowing in a strong wind, he reached for his wallet.

"These should do." Amanda plucked two of them and handed them to Laura. "Ready?"

"Well, I… Yes," she said on impulse. "Michael's just been fed and changed. You shouldn't have any trouble."

"I can handle things," he told her, feeling more than a

little put out. In the first place, he'd have taken her shopping himself if she'd asked. And in the second, though he didn't want to admit it, he wasn't totally sure of himself alone with the baby.

Reading her son perfectly, Amanda kissed him again. "Behave and we may bring you back a present."

He couldn't suppress the grin. "Out," he ordered. Then he caught Laura in turn and kissed her with the same light affection. It surprised him when she returned the embrace so ardently.

"Don't let her talk you into anything with bows," he murmured. "They wouldn't suit you. You should try to find something to match your eyes."

"If you don't let the girl go, we won't buy anything at all," Amanda said dryly, but she was pleased and a bit misty-eyed to see that her son was indeed in love with his wife.

It wasn't anyone's fault that Michael chose that particular afternoon to demand all the time and attention an infant could possibly demand. Gabe walked, rocked, changed, coddled and all but stood on his head. For his part, Michael gurgled, stared owlishly—and wept piteously whenever he was set down. He did everything but sleep.

In the end, Gabe gave up any idea of working for the rest of the day and carted Michael around with him. With the baby nestled in the crook of his arm, he ate a chicken leg and scanned the newspaper. Since no one was around to chuckle at him behind their hands, he discussed world politics and the major-league box scores with Michael while the baby shook a rattle and blew bubbles.

They took a walk in the garden once Gabe located one

of the small knit hats Laura had bought to protect Michael from spring breezes. It gave him enormous pleasure to watch the baby's cheeks turn pink and his eyes look around, alert and interested.

He had Laura's eyes, Gabe thought as he studied them. The same shape, the same color, but without the shadows that made hers both sad and fascinating. Michael's eyes were clear and innocent of sorrow.

Michael whimpered at first, then decided to accept his fate, when Gabe slipped him into the little baby swing. After tucking his blankets in around him, Gabe sat cross-legged in front of him and began to stretch.

The daffodils were up in a glory of white and yellow trumpets. Baby irises poked through, purple and exotic. Lilacs, though still shy of their full bloom, offered their scent. For the first time since his own tragedy, Gabe felt at peace. In the mountains, all through the winter, he'd begun to heal. But here, at home, with spring all around, he could finally see and accept that life did go on.

The baby continued to rock, pink-cheeked and bright-eyed, his hands lifting and falling to the rhythm. His little face was already filling out, taking on his own personal look and shape. Gone was the terrifying fragility of the newborn. He was, Gabe supposed, already growing up.

"I love you, Michael."

And when he spoke he spoke both to the one who was gone and to the one who rocked contentedly in front of him.

She hadn't meant to be gone so long, but the chaotic few hours breezing through the shops had brought back the way she had felt during that brief period when she'd been on her own and eager to test life.

There had been a moment or two of guilt over using Gabe's credit cards so freely. Then it had been almost too easy, with Amanda lending support, to justify the purchases. She was Laura Bradley now.

She had an eye for color and line that came naturally and had been sharpened by her time as a model, so what she had chosen was neither extravagant nor fussy. It had given Laura a great deal of satisfaction to see Amanda nod with approval over her selections.

It was a step, Laura told herself as she carried her bags and boxes through the front door. It might be a step only a woman would understand, but it was definitely a step. She was taking her life in hand again, if only by acknowledging that she needed clothes—clothes that suited her own taste and style—to live it. She was humming when she walked upstairs.

It was there that she found them together, Gabe sprawled over the bed, with Michael snuggled in the curve of his arm. Her husband was sound asleep. Her son had kicked free of his light blanket and was shaking a rattle at the ceiling.

Quietly she set down her bags and crossed to them. It was a purely male scene, the man stretched across the bed, shoes still on, a spy thriller lying facedown on the coverlet, a glass of something that had once been cold leaving a ring on the antique nightstand.

The child, as if he understood that he was a part of this man's world, lay quietly and thought his own thoughts.

She wished she had even a portion of Gabe's skill. If she

had, she would have drawn them together like this. Then the scene, the sweetness of it, would never be lost. For a while she sat on the edge of the bed and watched them.

It was so intimate, she thought, watching a man while he slept. She wanted to brush at the dark blond hair on his forehead, to trace the roughly hewn lines of his face, but she was afraid it would disturb him. Then the vulnerability would be gone, and this look at the private side of him would be over.

He was a beautiful man, though he didn't like to hear it. The compassion in him, which he often coated over with sarcasm or temper, ran deep. When she looked at him now, freely, without his being aware, she could see every reason why she'd fallen in love with him.

When Michael began to fret, she murmured and leaned over him, trying to pick him up without waking Gabe. At the first movement, Gabe's eyes opened. They were drowsy and very close to hers.

"I'm sorry. I didn't want to wake you."

He said nothing. Going with a dream she couldn't see but was very much a part of, he cupped a hand at the back of her head and drew her lips to his. There was a tenderness there that she hadn't felt for a very long time, an offering, a promise.

It was a promise she wanted, if only he would give it. It was a promise she would believe in.

Michael, scenting his mother, decided it was time to eat.

Unsettled and wishing they'd had just a moment more, Laura eased back. When Michael began to root at her breast, she undid two buttons and let him have his way.

"Did he wear you out?"

"We were taking a short break." It never failed to fascinate him how perfectly beautiful she looked when she was nursing the baby. He'd already sketched her like this, but that was for himself. "I didn't realize how much energy you need to handle someone so small."

"It gets worse. When we were shopping I saw a woman with a toddler. She never stopped running. Your mother tells me she used to collapse every afternoon when you'd finally worn down enough to take a nap."

"Lies." He shoved a couple of pillows behind his back and settled comfortably. "I was a perfectly behaved child."

"Then it was some other child who drew with crayon all over the silk wallpaper."

"Artistic expression. I was a prodigy."

"No doubt."

He just lifted a brow. Then he spotted her bags across the room. "I was going to ask if you had a good time with my mother, but the answer's obvious."

She caught herself on the verge of an apology. That had to stop, she reminded herself. "It was wonderful to buy shoes and actually see them when I stood up, and a dress that had a waist in it."

"I suppose that's difficult for a woman, losing her figure during pregnancy."

"I loved every minute of it. The first time I couldn't hook a pair of slacks I was ecstatic." She started to go on, then stopped. That was something he would never be a part of, she realized. The first joys and fears, the first movements. Looking down at Michael, she wished with all her heart that he was Gabe's child in every way. "Still, I'm happy now not to look like an aircraft carrier."

"It was more like a dirigible."

"You give the most charming compliments."

He waited until she shifted Michael to her other breast. There was an urge inside of him to trace his finger there, just above where the baby suckled. It wasn't sexual, or even romantic, it was more a wondering. Instead, he tucked his hands behind his head.

"I tossed some leftovers together. I've no idea if they're edible."

Again there was the urge to apologize. Determined, Laura merely smiled. "I'm hungry enough for marginally edible."

"Good." Now he did lean forward, but only to trace a fingertip over Michael's head. "Come on down when he's settled. After this afternoon, I have a feeling he'll go out like a light when his belly's full."

"I won't be long." She waited until she was alone, then closed her eyes, hoping she had the courage to carry out her plans for the rest of the evening.

She hadn't been just a woman in so long. Laura stood in front of the mirrored wall, fogged now from the steam of her bath. She looked like a woman. Her nightgown was the palest blue, nearly white. She'd chosen it because it had reminded her of the way the snow had looked on the mountains in Colorado. It fell down her body from thin straps and a lacy bodice. She ran her hand down it experimentally. The material was very thin and very soft.

Should she wear her hair up, or wear it down? Did it matter?

What would it be like to be Gabe's wife…really his

wife? She pressed a hand to her stomach, waiting for the nerves to ebb. Memories threatened to surface, and she fought them back. Tonight she would take Amanda's advice. She would think not of what had been, but of what could be.

She loved him so much, but she didn't know how to tell him. Words were so difficult, so irrevocable. Worse, she was afraid that he would take her love with the same discomfort and disregard as he did her gratitude. But tonight…she hoped tonight she could begin to show him.

He was stripping off his shirt when she opened the door to the adjoining bedroom. For a moment the light coming from behind her fell over her hair and ran through the thin fabric of her gown. All movement stopped as though it were a play, just as the curtain rose. He felt the heat and the tightening in his stomach.

Then she switched off the bathroom light. He pulled off his shirt.

"I checked on Michael." Gabe was surprised he could speak at all, but the words sounded normal enough. "He's sleeping. I thought I might work for an hour or two."

"Oh." She caught herself before she could twist her hands together. She was a grown woman. A grown woman should know how to seduce her husband. "I know you lost time this afternoon when I went out."

"I liked taking care of him." She was so slim, so beautifully frail, with her milky white skin and that blue-white gown. The angel again, with a fall of blond curls instead of a halo.

"You're a wonderful father, Gabe." She took a step toward him. She was already beginning to tremble.

"Michael makes it easy."

Should she have known it would be so difficult to simply cross a room? "Do I make it hard, to be a husband?"

"No." He lifted the back of his hand to her cheek. Her eyes were shades upon shades darker than the flow of silk she wore. He drew back, surprised by his own nerves. "You must be tired."

She bit off a sigh as she turned away. "It's obvious I'm not very good at this. Since seducing you isn't working, we'll try the more practical approach."

"Is that what you were doing?" He wanted to be amused, but his muscles were tight with tension. "Seducing me?"

"Badly." Opening her drawer, she drew out a small slip of paper. "This is my doctor's report. It says that I'm a normal, healthy woman. Would you care to read it?"

This time his lips twitched. "Covered all the bases, did you?"

"You said you wanted me." The paper crumpled in her hand. "I thought you meant it."

He had her arms before she could retreat. Her eyes were dry, but he could see, just by looking, her fractured pride. The burden he already felt grew heavier. What they had was still so tenuous. If he made a mistake it might vanish completely.

"I meant it, Laura, started meaning it from the first day you were with me. It hasn't been easy, being with you, needing you, and not being able to touch."

Gingerly she laid a hand on his chest and felt his muscles tighten. "There's no reason you can't now."

He slid his hands up to her shoulders so that his fingers

brushed over the thin straps of her gown. If it was a mistake, he had no choice but to make it. "No physical one any longer. When I take you to bed, there can only be the two of us. No ghosts. No memories." When she dropped her gaze, he drew her closer, challenging her to lift it again. "You won't think of anyone but me."

Whether it was a threat or a promise, he lowered his mouth to hers. Her hands fluttered, then were trapped between their bodies.

It was only the press of lips upon lips, but her blood began to pound. The stirring he could cause so easily started in her stomach and spread, long before his hands moved over her, long before her lips parted.

Her hands were imprisoned, but she didn't feel vulnerable. His mouth wasn't gentle, but she didn't feel afraid. As the kiss deepened, as the intimacy grew, she didn't think of anyone but him.

She tasted as she had the very first time, ripe and fresh. With his tongue he plundered her mouth, greedy for the flavor of her. There would be no turning back now, not when she was caught close in his arms and the lights were dim. He could hear her shuddering breath, and the steady ticking of the pendulum clock in the hallway. It was dark, it was quiet, they were alone. And tonight he would take a wife.

Her heart thudded against his bare chest, adding excitement. He ran his hands over her, feeling the smoothness of her skin, the slickness of her gown, feeling every tremble and every sigh his touch incited.

Greedy, he nipped his teeth into her lip as his hands moved lower. Passion sprung out, from him, from her, mixing together in a sudden, breath-stopping fury. Then he felt her body give against his in the ultimate gift of trust. The emotions that rose up in him tempered his desire. Tenderness, achingly sweet, more precious than diamonds, took its place.

Her hands were free. The paper still crumpled in her palm fluttered to the floor as she slipped her arms around him. Tentatively still. Her bones seemed to liquefy, degree by degree, until she wondered why she didn't simply slide out of his hands. Her mind, which had been swirling with needs, clouded with a pleasure that was softer, truer, than any she had ever imagined.

She stroked her hands over his back, feeling the muscle, the power. Wonder filled her at the discovery that anyone with such strength could be so gentle. His lips brushed over hers, testing, almost teasing, inviting her to set the pace. Or perhaps he was challenging her.

Hunger leaped inside her until she was locked against him, her mouth seeking, avid, impatient. Then she was swept up into his arms. In the dim light she saw his eyes, only his eyes, their clear green darkened by need. Hers remained open and on his as he lowered her onto the bed.

She expected speed, a frenzy of greed and a drive for gratification. She wouldn't have thought less of him for it. Her love wouldn't have diminished. Against hers, his body was taut and straining. Circling her arms around him, she prepared to give him whatever he required.

But it wasn't speed he sought. And the greed was not only to take, but also to give.

When he ranged kisses over her throat, lingering, nibbling, she, too, went taut. She could only whisper his name as he continued the slow journey over her shoulders and down to the curve of her breasts, then up again, in teasing circles. Instinctively she turned her head, seeking his mouth, his jaw, his temple, as her body turned hot and cold with pleasure.

He needed to take care, for her. At the first touch, he'd been terrified. She had been with another man, she had had a child, but he knew the extent of her innocence. He'd seen it, hour after hour, when he'd painted her. He'd felt it each and every time he'd drawn her against him. If he was going to take that innocence, he was going to give her beauty in return.

She was so…responsive. Her body seemed to ebb and flow at the touch of his hands. Wherever he tasted, her skin grew warm. Yet even as she gave, and offered, there was a shyness about her, the slightest of hesitations. He wanted to take her beyond that.

Slowly, with movements that were little more than a whisper along her skin, he drew the gown downward, following the trail of lace with his lips. At her first moan, his blood swam. He hadn't known that a sound, only a sound, could be so alluring. With light, openmouthed kisses he sensitized her skin until she began to shiver beneath him. In the lamplight she was exquisite, her skin like marble, her hair like silver. Her eyes were full of needs and uncertainties.

As he had once used his skill, his insight, to draw her emotions on canvas, he used it now to set them free.

She had never known there could be such sensitivity between a man and a woman. Even through the clouds of pleasure and the steadily rising tide of desire, she sensed his patience. She had never been so driven to touch a man before. With her fingertips and her palms, with her lips and her tongue, she discovered him. The urge came, strong, just to hold him, to wrap tight around him and hold on.

Then, without warning, he was taking her up, making her arch and gasp in shock and indescribable delight. Her mind and body were drained of everything but sensation. For an instant there was a terror of being totally out of control. His name burst out of her as she was carried away by a climax so strong, so intense, that she was left limp and dazed in the aftermath.

"Please, I can't…I've never…"

"I know." Strangely humbled, he lowered his lips to hers. He had wanted to give, had been driven to, but he hadn't known that in giving, so much would be returned to him. "Just relax. There's no hurry."

"But you haven't—"

He laughed against her throat. "I intend to. There's time. I want to touch you," he murmured, and began the slow, seductive journey again.

It wasn't possible. She would have said it couldn't be possible for her body to leap back in response to so gentle, so light, a touch. Yet within moments she was trembling again, aching again, wanting again. His tongue skimmed over her stomach, dipped to the curve of her thigh, until she was writhing, a victim now of her own desire and of the taste of heaven he'd already given her.

Then, impossibly, incredibly, she was tossed up and over again. This time, when she gasped and faltered, he slid into her.

Her moan merged with his.

Damp flesh pressed against damp flesh as they moved

together. She'd never felt so strong, so utterly free, as she did now, joined as closely as was conceivable with Gabe.

She was everything he'd ever wanted, everything he'd ever dreamed of. Indeed, it was like a dream now, with the bursts and shudders of pleasure ripping through him. With his face pressed against her throat, he could smell her lightly provocative fragrance, mixed with the pungent, earthy scent of passion. He would go to the grave remembering that dizzying combination.

Her breath was fast and frenzied in his ear. Her body was just as fast and frenzied beneath his. He could feel her nails as she dug heedlessly into his back.

He would remember all of it.

Then he remembered nothing, and he let himself go.

Chapter 9

There had been a time, a brief time, when Laura had dressed in elegant clothes and gone to elegant parties. She had met people whose names were printed in slick magazines and flashed in bold headlines in tabloids. She'd danced with celebrities and dined with princes of fashion. However much it had seemed like a dream, it had been real.

It was true enough that she had enjoyed her time modeling for Geoffrey. The work might have been hard, but she'd been young enough, untried enough, to have been dazzled by the glamour—even after ten hours on her feet.

He had taught her how to stand, how to walk, even how to look interested when fatigue was all but pouring out of her ears. He'd shown her how to use makeup to enhance subtly or strikingly, how to use her hair to express a mood.

All the things he'd taught her had helped her maintain an image during public events with the Eagletons. She'd been able to appear sophisticated and untroubled. At times, appearances were a great comfort.

She wasn't afraid she would embarrass herself or Gabe at the reception his parents were giving at their Nob Hill estate. But she wasn't certain she wanted to step back into that life again, either.

How might things have been if Gabe had been an ordinary man, a man of ordinary means? They might have found a little house with a little backyard and been swallowed up by anonymity. A part of her yearned for that, for the simplicity of it.

But that was wrong. Laura fastened the earrings she'd bought the week before, starbursts of blue stones. If Gabe had come from a different family and a different life, he wouldn't be the man she loved. The man she was almost ready to believe was beginning to love her.

There was nothing about him she wanted to change, not his looks, not his manner. She might wish occasionally that he would share with her a bit more of his thoughts and feelings, but she continued to hope that someday he would.

She wanted to be a full part of his life—lover, wife and partner. So far, she had come to be the first two.

When the door opened, she turned.

"If you're about ready, we'll—"

And he stopped and stared. This was the woman she'd only told him about, the one who had graced the covers of magazines and modeled silks and sables. Long-limbed and slender, she stood in front of the beveled mirror in a dress of midnight blue. It was very simple, leaving her shoulders and throat bare, then caught like a wish at her breasts to fall ruler-straight to her feet.

She'd wound her hair up, swept it back, so that only a few wheat-colored curls escaped to tease her temples.

She was beautiful, gloriously so, yet even as he was drawn to her, he felt as though he were looking at a stranger.

"You look wonderful." But he kept his hand on the knob and the room between them. "I'll have to paint you like this." *Beauty on Ice*, he thought, cool, aloof and unapproachable.

"I took your advice on the color." She picked up her purse, then clasped and unclasped it as she wondered why he was looking at her as though he'd never seen her before. "And I avoided bows."

"So I see." She should have sapphires, a collar of them, around her throat. "It's still a bit cool. Do you have a wrap?"

"Yes." Irked by his tone, she walked to the bed and snatched up a wide silk scarf in a riot of jewellike colors. It was then that he noticed that the back of the skirt was slit to the thigh.

"I imagine you'll create quite a stir in that little number."

She cringed inwardly, but, falling back on appearances, she managed to keep her face calm. "If you don't like the dress, why don't you just say so?" She swirled the scarf over her shoulders. "It's too late to change, but believe me, I won't wear it again."

"Just a minute." He grabbed her hand as she started through the doorway. He could feel the smooth gold of her plain wedding ring on the index finger of her right hand.

She was still his Laura, he thought as he linked his fingers with hers. He'd only had to look in her eyes to see it.

"I have to get Michael ready," she mumbled, and tried again to move past him.

"Do you expect an apology because I'm human enough to be jealous?"

Her face went still, her eyes blank. "I'm not wearing it to attract other men. I bought it because I liked it and I thought it suited me."

He brought a hand to her face and swore roundly when she jerked. "Look at me. No, damn it, not at him, at me." Her eyes lashed back up to him. "Remember who I am, Laura. And remember this—I won't tolerate having my every mood, my every word, compared with someone else's."

"I'm not trying to do that."

"Maybe you're not trying to, but you do."

"You expect me to turn my life around overnight. I can't."

"No." He ran his thumb over the ring again. "I don't suppose you can. But you can remember that I'm part of your new life, not your old one."

"You're nothing like him." It was becoming easier to let her hand relax in his. "I know that. I guess sometimes it's easier to expect the worst than to hope for the best."

"I can't promise you the best."

No, he wouldn't make promises he couldn't keep. That was the beauty of him. "You could hold me. That's as close as I need to get."

When his arms came around her, he pressed her cheek against the shoulder of his black evening jacket.

It smelled of him, and that made the last twists of tension dissolve.

"I suppose I was jealous, too."

"Oh?"

She smiled as she drew back enough to look into his face. "You look so good tonight."

"Really?" There was both discomfort and amusement in his tone.

"I've never seen you in evening clothes." She ran her finger down the dark lapel, which rested against a crisp white shirt. "Sort of like Heathcliff in a tux."

He laughed and cupped her face in his hands. "What a mind you have, angel. There's no hero in here."

"You're wrong." Her eyes were very solemn, very serious. "You're mine." He shrugged, but she kept him close. "Please, just this once, let me say it without you brushing it aside."

He just flicked a finger down her nose. "Don't expect me to walk around in armor too long. Let's get the baby. My mother knows how to make you miserable if you're late."

He wasn't a hero. He certainly wasn't comfortable being seen as one. Gabe was much more at ease discussing his work or speculating on the Giants' chances during the rest of the baseball season. He preferred arguments to good deeds.

When someone saw you as heroic, you invariably let them down. They expected you to have the right answers, the key to the lock, the light in the dark.

Michael had seen him as a hero. And, of course, he had let his brother down.

Michael had loved parties like this, Gabe thought as he sipped at the champagne that seemed to flow endlessly. He had loved the laughter, the people and the gossip. Michael had been unashamedly fond of rumors and whispers.

People had loved him moments after meeting him. He had been outgoing, funny, and as warm with strangers as with friends. It was Michael who had been the hero, doing favors without tallying the score, always willing to help or simply to be enthusiastic about a project.

Yet he'd had that streak of temper and toughness that had balanced him, prevented him from being overly… overly good, Gabe supposed.

God, he missed him still, at times unbearably.

There were people here who had known Michael, who had raised a glass with him or swapped stories with him. Perhaps that was what made it seem worse tonight, being in their parents' home, where they had grown up and shared so much and knowing that Michael would never walk into that room again.

Somehow you went on. One part of your life closed up, and another opened. Gabe looked across the room to where Laura stood talking to his father.

Sometime between the moment she'd rolled down the window of a wrecked car and the moment she'd placed a newborn child in his arms he'd fallen in love with her. It had come not with trumpets and flares but with quiet, soothing murmurs.

If there were such things as angels, one had sent Laura to him when he'd needed her most.

She was grateful to him, and open enough to give him love and affection in return for what he had given her.

There were days when he believed that would be enough, for today, and for the tomorrows they would have together.

Then there were the other times.

He wanted to grab her, to demand again and again that she look at him, see who he was, what he felt. That she forget what had happened before and trust in what was happening now. He wanted to erase, the way he might have blanked out a canvas, what had gone on before, all the things that had put shadows in her eyes, all the things that made her hesitate just that split second before she smiled.

But he knew better than most that when you painted over part of someone's life you stole something. Bad experience or good, what had happened to Laura had made her what she was, the woman he loved.

But loving as he did, and being a selfish man, he wanted to be loved back, completely, without the strings of gratitude or the shadows of vulnerability. Wanting wouldn't make it so, but time might. He could give her a little more of that.

Someone laughed across the room. Glasses chinked. There was a scent of wine, flowers and women's fragrances. The night had cooperated with a full moon, and its glow shimmered just outside the open terrace doors. The room was ablaze with lamplight. Wanting a few moments away from the crowd and the noise, he slipped upstairs to check on his son.

"The boy looks more like you every time I see him," Cliff was saying.

"Do you think so?" The thought had Laura lighting up. Perhaps she was vain after all.

"Absolutely. Though no one would believe you were a new mother, the way you're looking tonight." He patted her cheek in the way that always made her feel shy and delighted. "My Gabe has excellent taste."

"Shame on you, Cliff, flirting with a beautiful woman when your wife's not looking."

"Marion." Cliff bent down from his rangy height to give the newcomer a kiss. "Late as always."

"Amanda's already scolded me." She turned, sipping at her champagne, to give Laura a thorough study. "So this is the mysterious Laura."

"My new daughter." Cliff gave Laura a quick squeeze around the shoulders. "An old friend, Marion Trussalt. The Trussalt Gallery handles Gabe's paintings."

"Yes, I know. It's nice to meet you." She wasn't a beautiful woman, Laura thought, but she was oddly striking, with her sleek cap of black hair and her dark eyes. She wore a flowing rainbow-colored sheath that managed to be both arty and sophisticated.

"Yes, it is, since we have Gabe in common." Marion tapped a finger on the rim of her glass and smiled, but her eyes didn't warm. Laura recognized carefully polished disdain when she saw it. "You have his heart, and I his soul, you might say."

"Then it would seem we both want the best for him."

"Oh." Marion raised her glass. "Absolutely. Cliff, Amanda told me to remind you that hosts are supposed to mingle."

He grimaced. "Slave driver. Laura, be sure to work your way over to the buffet. You're getting too thin already." With that he went to do his duty.

"Yes, you're amazingly slender for someone who had a child—what was it? A month ago?"

"Almost two." Laura shifted her glass of sparkling water to her other hand. She didn't deal well with subtle attacks.

"Time flies." Marion touched her tongue to her upper lip. "It's odd that in all that time you haven't stirred yourself to come down to the gallery."

"You're right. I'll have to come down and see Gabe's work in a proper setting." She steadied herself. Under no circumstances was she going to allow herself to be intimidated or to fall into the trap of reading between the lines. If Gabe had ever had any kind of romantic involvement with Marion, it had ended. "He relies on you, I know. And I hope you'll be able to persuade him to go through with a new showing."

"I haven't decided that's really a good idea for the time being." Marion turned to smile at someone across the room who had called her name.

"Why? The paintings are wonderful."

"That isn't the only issue." She turned back to give Laura a quick, glittering look. She hadn't been Gabe's lover, nor had there every been any urge on either side to make it so. Her feelings for Gabriel Bradley went far beyond the physical. Gabe was an artist, a great one, and she had been—and intended to go on being—the catalyst for his success.

If he had married within his circle, or chosen someone who could have enhanced or furthered his career, she would have been pleased. But for him to have wasted himself, and her ambitions, on a beautiful face and a smeared reputation was more than Marion could bear.

"Did I mention that I knew your first husband?"

If she had thrown her drink into Laura's face she would have been no less shocked. The cocoon that she had been able to draw around herself and Michael suffered its first crack.

"No. If you'll excuse me—"

"A fascinating man, I always thought. Certainly young, and a bit wild, but fascinating. A tragedy that he died so young, before he ever saw his child." She tilted her glass back until only a sheen of bubbles remained.

"Michael," Laura said evenly, "is Gabe's child."

"So I'm told." She smiled again. "There were the oddest rumors just before and just after Tony died. Some said that he was on the verge of divorcing you, that he'd already removed you from the family home because you were, well, indiscreet." With a shrug, Marion set her glass aside. "But that's all in the past now. Tell me, how are the Eagletons? I haven't spoke with Lorraine for ages."

She was going to be ill, violently and humiliatingly ill, unless she succeeded in fighting back her rolling nausea. "Why are you doing this?" she whispered. "Why should you care?"

"Oh, my dear, I care about anything that has to do with Gabe. I intend to see him reach the very top, and I don't intend to watch him be dragged down. That's a lovely dress," she added. Then she saw Amanda approaching and slipped away.

"Laura, are you all right? You're white as a sheet. Come, let me find you a chair."

"No, I need some air." Turning, she fled through the open glass doors and onto the smooth stone terrace beyond.

"Here, now." Coming up behind her, Amanda took her arm and steered her to a chair. "Sit a minute before Gabe comes along. He'll take one look at you and pounce on me for insisting you come out and socialize too soon."

"It's nothing to do with that."

"And something to do with Marion." Amanda took the water glass out of Laura's tightening grip. "If she led you to believe that there was something—personal—between herself and Gabe, I can only say its totally untrue."

"That wouldn't matter."

With a little laugh, Amanda cast a look back inside. "If you mean that, then you're a better woman than I. I've known one of my husband's former…interests for over thirty-five years. I'd still like to spit in her eye."

With a laugh of her own, Laura drew in the softly scented evening. "I know Gabe's faithful to me."

"And so you should. You should also know that Marion and Gabe were never lovers." She moved her shoulders a bit. "I can't say that I know about all of my son's affairs, but I do know that he and Marion only have art in common. Now, what did she say to upset you?"

"It was nothing." Laura brushed her fingers over her temples, as if to soothe away an ache. "Really, it was my own fault, overreacting. She only mentioned that she'd met my first husband."

"I see." Annoyed, Amanda turned her sharp-eyed glance into the drawing room again. "Well, I have to say I find it very insensitive to bring up the subject at your wedding reception. One would have thought a woman like Marion would have more taste."

"It's over and it's best forgotten." Straightening her

shoulders, Laura prepared to go back in. "I'd appreciate it if you wouldn't mention any of this to Gabe. There's no reason to annoy him."

"No, I agree. I'll speak with Marion myself."

"No." Laura picked up her glass again and sipped slowly. "If there's anything that needs to be said, I'll say it myself."

Amanda's smile spread and she said easily, "If that's what you'd like."

"Yes. Amanda…" A decision made quickly, she thought, was sometimes the best. "Could I leave Michael with you one day next week? I'd like to go into the gallery and see Gabe's paintings."

Laura woke up out of breath and shivering. She struggled her way out of the nightmare to find herself in Gabe's arms.

"Just relax. You're all right."

She drew in a big gulp of air, then let it out slowly. "Sorry," she muttered, dragging a hand through her hair.

"Want anything? Some water?"

"No." As the fear passed, annoyance took its place. The glowing dial of the alarm clock read 4:15. They'd been in bed for only three hours, and now she was wide-awake and restless.

With his arm still around her, Gabe lay back on his pillow. "You haven't had a nightmare since Michael was born. Did something happen at the party tonight?"

She thought of Marion and gritted her teeth. "Why do you ask?"

"I noticed that you seemed upset, and my mother annoyed."

"Did you think that I had an argument with your mother?" That made her smile and settle more comfortably against him. "No, in fact we get along very well."

"You sound surprised."

"I didn't expect to make friends with her. I kept waiting for her to bring out her broom and pointed hat."

He laughed and kissed her shoulder. "Just try criticizing my work."

"I wouldn't dare." Unconsciously she began to stroke her fingers through his hair. When she was here, like this, she believed she could handle anything that threatened her new family. "She showed me the mural in the parlor. The one with all the mythical creatures."

"I was twenty, and romantic." And he'd asked his mother a dozen times to have it painted over.

"I like it."

"No wonder you get along with her."

"I did like it." She shifted so that she could rest her arms on his chest. There was only a little moonlight, but she could see him. She didn't realize that it was her first completely unstudied move toward him, but he did. "What's wrong with unicorns and centaurs and fairies?"

"They have their place, I suppose." But all he was currently interested in was making love with her.

"Good. Then don't you think the side wall in Michael's room is the perfect place for a mural?"

He tugged at a curl that fell over her cheek. "Are you offering me a commission?"

"Well, I've seen a few samples of your work, and it's not bad."

He tugged harder. "Not bad?"

"Shows promise." With a quick laugh, she ducked before he could pull her hair again. "Why don't you submit some sample sketches for consideration?"

"And my fee?"

He was smiling; her skin was warming. Laura began to think the nightmare had been a blessing in disguise. "Negotiable."

"Tell you what. I'll do the mural on one condition."

"Which is?"

"That you let me paint you again, nude."

Her eyes widened. Then she laughed, sure he was joking. "You should at least let me wear a beret."

"You've been watching too many old movies, but you can wear a beret if you like—just nothing else."

"I couldn't."

"All right, then, scratch the beret."

"Gabe, you're not serious."

"Of course I am." To prove it, and to please himself, he ran a hand over her. "You have a beautiful body…long dancer's limbs, smooth white skin, a narrow waist."

"Gabe." She spoke to stop not his roaming hands but his conversation. She stopped neither.

"I've wanted to paint you nude since the first time we made love. I can still see the way you looked when I drew the nightgown away. Capturing that femininity, that subtle sexuality, would be a triumph."

She laid her cheek on his heart. "I'd be embarrassed."

"Why? I know what you look like. Every inch of you." He cupped her breasts, scraping his thumbs lightly over her nipples. Her instant response rippled through him.

"No one else does." Her voice was husky now. Hardly

realizing it, she began to run her hands over him. The journey was long, lazy, thorough.

There was something incredibly exciting about the idea. No one else knew the secrets of her body, the dips and curves. No one else knew how a touch here, a stroke there, could make her shyness melt into passion. He did want to capture that on canvas, the beauty of her, the sweetness of her inhibitions. The fire of passion just discovered. But he could wait.

"I suppose I could just hire a model."

Her head came up at that. "You—" The jealousy rose, so swift and powerful that it left her momentarily speechless.

"It's art, angel," he said, amused and not at all displeased. "Not a centerfold."

"You're trying to blackmail me."

"You're very sharp."

Her eyes narrowed. In deliberate seduction that surprised them both, she shifted so that her body rubbed tantalizingly over his. "Only if I get to choose the model."

His pulse was thudding. As she lowered her head to brush kisses over his chest, he closed his eyes. "Laura."

"No, Mrs. Drumberry. I met her tonight."

He opened his eyes. But when she used her teeth to tug on his nipple he arched beneath her. "Mabel Drumberry is a hundred and five."

"Exactly." She chuckled but continued her explorations, with a growing sense of power and discovery. "I wouldn't trust you closed up in your studio with some sexy young redhead with lush curves."

He started to laugh, but the sound became a moan as

her hand ranged lower. "Don't you think I can resist a sexy young redhead?"

"Of course, but she wouldn't be able to resist you." She rubbed her cheek along his jawline, which was already roughened with morning stubble. "You're so beautiful, Gabe. If I could paint, I'd show you."

"What you're doing is driving me crazy."

"I hope so," she murmured, and lowered her mouth to his.

She'd never had the confidence to take charge, had never been sure enough of her skill or her appeal. Now it seemed right and wonderfully fulfilling to tease and taunt her man in passion.

His hands were in her hair, his fingers tangled and tense, as she dipped her tongue into his mouth and explored. Her moves were instinctive rather than experienced, and all the more seductive for it.

The power came to her not in a wild burst but with quiet certainty. She could be his partner here, his full partner. It was easy to show love, almost as easy as it was to feel it.

As she discovered him, she discovered herself. She wasn't as patient as he, not here. Strangely, in the daylight, the opposite was true. She saw him as a man who needed to move quickly, decisively, and if mistakes were made because of hurry they could be corrected or just as easily ignored. She was more cautious, more prone to think through alternatives before acting.

But in bed, in the role of the seductress, she found little patience in herself.

She was wild and wanton. Gabe found himself reaching for her, then being rocked helplessly by the sensations she brought to him. It was like having a different woman in bed, one who felt like Laura, smelled like Laura, one he wanted as desperately as he wanted Laura.

When her mouth came down on his, it was Laura's taste, yet somehow darker, riper. And her body was like a furnace as she moved over him.

He tried to remember that this was his wife, his shy and still-innocent wife, who required infinite care and gentleness. He had yet to release his full range of passion with her. With Laura he had taken his time, used every drop of his sensitivity.

Now she was stripping him down to the nerve ends.

She could feel the power, and it was glorious. Despite her excitement, her mind was clear as a bell. She could make him weak, she could make him desperate. She could make him tremble. Breathlessly she pressed her lips to pulse points that she found by instinct. His heart was racing. For her. She could feel his body shudder at her touch. When he groaned, it was her own name she heard.

She heard herself laugh, and there was something sultry in the sound. A feminine triumph. The clock in the hallway struck five, and the echo went on and on in her head.

Then his arms were locked around her and the sound that was coming from his throat was long and primitive. His control snapped like a rubber band stretched too far. Needs only half satisfied, so long held in check, flooded free. His mouth covered hers, bruisingly. But it wasn't a skip of fear she felt. It was a leap of victory.

Trapped in madness, they rolled across the bed, seeking, taking, demanding, with a kind of greed that made the mouth go dry and the soul shudder. The modest gown she wore was torn aside, seams ripping, lace shredding. His hands were everywhere, and they were far from gentle.

There was no shame. There was no shyness. This was freedom, a different kind from what he had already shown her. As desperate as he, she opened for him. When he plunged into her, the shock vibrated, wave after wave.

Fast and furious, they locked into their own rhythm, each driving the other.

Endless pleasure, sharp and edgy. Insatiable need spreading like wildfire. As she gave herself to him, as she asked and received more, Laura realized that, for the lucky, time could indeed stop.

Chapter 10

When the sky darkened, Laura was in the garden. It had become her habit to spend her mornings there while the baby slept or sat rocking in his swing in the sunlight. Since her arrival in Gabe's home, she'd found little to do indoors. The house almost took care of itself and, as she had once told him, Gabe was only sloppy when he painted.

More than that, there were too many rooms, too much space that she didn't yet feel a part of. In the nursery, which she'd decorated herself and where, through necessity, she spent many hours during the day and night, she felt at home. The rest of the house, with its heirlooms and its beautiful old rugs, its polished wood and its faded wallpaper, remained aloof to her.

But as spring had taken hold she had discovered an affinity and a talent for gardening, as well as a need for space and air. She liked the sunlight and the smells and the feel of the earth under her hands. She devoured books on plants, much as she had on childbirth, so that she could become familiar with flowers and shrubs and the care they required.

The tulips were beginning to bloom, and the azaleas were already ripe with blossoms. Someone else had planted them, but Laura had no trouble taking them to heart as her own. They flowered afresh every year. Nor did she feel awkward adding her own touches with moss roses and snapdragons.

Already she was planning to plant new bulbs in the fall, daylilies, windflowers, poppies. Then, over the winter, she would root her own spring flowers from seed, starting them in little peat pots that she would set in the sun room on the east side of the house.

"I'll teach you how to plant them next year," she told Michael. She could already imagine him toddling around the garden on short, sturdy legs, patting at the dirt, trying to snatch butterflies off blossoms.

He would laugh. There would be so much for him to laugh about. She would be able to catch him up in her arms and swing him around so that his eyes, which were still as stubbornly blue as hers, glowed and his laughter bounced on the air. Then Gabe would stick his head out of his studio window and demand to know what all the ruckus was about.

But he wouldn't really be annoyed. He'd come down, saying that if there was going to be so much noise he might as well forget about working for the morning. He'd sit on the ground with Michael in his lap and they'd laugh together about nothing anyone else would understand.

Sitting back on her heels, Laura wiped her brow with the back of a gloved hand. Dreaming had always been her escape, her defense, her survival. Now it didn't seem like any of those things, because she was beginning to believe dreams could come true.

"I love your daddy," she told Michael, as she told him at least once every day. "I love him so much that it makes me believe in happy endings."

When the shadow fell over her, Laura glanced up and saw the first dark clouds roll over the sun. She was tempted to ignore them, and she might have if she hadn't known it took more than a quick minute to gather up all her gardening tools, Michael's supplies and the baby himself.

"Well, the rain's good for the flowers, isn't it, sweetie?" She stored the tools and bags of peat moss and fertilizers in the small shed near the back door, then drew Michael out of the swing. With the acquired coordination of motherhood, she carried the baby, his little cache of toys and the folded swing indoors.

She'd barely started upstairs when the first crack of thunder had both her and Michael jumping. As he began to wail, she fought back her own longstanding fear of storms and soothed him.

He calmed down much more quickly than she as she walked and rocked and murmured reassurances. Though the rain held off, she could watch the fury raging in the sky through Michael's windows. Lightning slashed, turning the light from gray to mauve, then back to gray, in the blink of an eye.

Eventually he began to doze, but she continued to hold him, as much for her own comfort as his.

"Silly, isn't it?" she murmured. "A grown woman more afraid of thunder than a tiny baby." As the rain began to lash at the house, she made herself set the sleeping child in his crib so that she could close the windows.

At least that would keep her busy, Laura told herself as she moved from room to room to shut the windows against the pelting rain. Still, each time thunder boomed she jerked back. It wasn't until she started back into the nursery, telling herself she'd curl up on the daybed and read until the storm passed, that she remembered Gabe's studio. Thinking only of his work, she rushed down the hall.

She was grateful that the storm hadn't knocked out the power. The lights flared on at a touch. It seemed that her luck had held. The floor was wet by the ribbon of windows, but none of his paintings were stored there. Laura hurried down the line, shutting each one until the rain was muffled by the glass.

She started to do the practical thing and go for a mop, but then it struck her that this was the first time she had been in Gabe's studio alone. He'd never asked her not to go in, but the lack of privacy she'd lived with most of her life had made her fastidious about respecting that of others. Now, though, with the lights bright overhead and the thunder rolling in the distance, she felt comfortable there, as she did in the nursery. As she had in the cabin in the mountains.

The room smelled of him, she realized. It held that mixture of paint and turpentine, with the powdery addition of chalk, that often clung to his clothes and his hands. It was a scent that invariably put her at ease, even though it was also a scent that invariably aroused her. Like the man, she thought, the scent drew her emotions.

She could love him and be comforted by him, just as she could be excited and confused by him.

What did he want from her? she wondered. And why? She thought she understood part of it. He wanted the solidity of family, an end to his own loneliness and passion in bed. He'd chosen her for those things because she'd been as anxious to give them as he was to take them.

It could be enough, or nearly enough. Her problem was, and continued to be, a quiet longing for more.

Shaking off the mood, she tried to picture him there in that room, alone, working, envisioning.

So much had been done here, she thought, so many hours creating, perfecting, experimenting. What made one man different from another in the way he saw and expressed what he saw? Crossing to his easel, she studied his work in progress.

A painting of Michael. The deep and simple pleasure of it had her hugging herself. There was a rough sketch tacked to the easel, and the portrait on canvas was just beginning to take shape. She could see that even since the sketch, which he'd drawn perhaps a week before, Michael had changed and grown. But because of this she would always be able to look back and see him exactly as he'd been in that one precious moment of time.

With her arms still crossed over her breasts, she turned to study the room. It was different without Gabe in it. Less…dramatic, she thought. Then she laughed a little, knowing he would hate that description.

Without him it was a wide, airy room, largely empty. On the floor were dried drops and smears of paint that could have been there for a week or a year. A small pedestal sink was built into one corner. She saw a towel tossed carelessly over its lip. There were shelves and a worktable with equipment scattered on them. Paints and bottles, jars crammed with brushes, pallet knives, hunks of charcoal and balled-up rags. Unframed canvases were stacked against the walls, much as they had been in Colorado. He hadn't hung anything here.

She wondered why she hadn't thought before to ask Gabe if he had anything she might hang in Michael's room. The posters she'd chosen were colorful, but one of Gabe's paintings would mean more. With that in mind, she knelt down and began to go through canvases.

How easily he drew out emotion. One of his pastel landscapes would make you dreamy. Next an edgy, too-realistic view of a slum would make you shudder. There were portraits, too—an impossibly old man leaning on a cane at a bus stop, three young girls giggling outside a boutique. There was a spectacular nude study of a brunette sprawled on white satin. Instead of jealousy, it raised a feeling of awe in Laura.

She went through more than a dozen, wondering why he'd stacked them so carelessly. Many were unframed, and all were facing the wall. Each one she held left her more astonished that she could be married to a man who could do so much with color and brush. More, each painting gave her a closer look at who he was. She could sense the mood that had held him as he'd worked. Rage for this, humor for that. Sorrow, impatience, desire, delight. Whatever he could feel, he could paint.

These didn't belong here, she thought, frustrated that he would close them up in a room where no one could see them or appreciate them or be touched by them. His signature was dashed in each corner, with the year just below. Everything she found had been painted no more than two years before, and no less than one year.

She turned the last canvas over and was caught immediately. It was another portrait, and this one had been painted with love.

The subject, a young man of no more than thirty, was grinning, a bit recklessly, as though he had all the time in the world to accomplish what he wanted to do. His hair was blond, a few shades lighter than Gabe's, and brushed back from a lean, good-looking face. It was a casual study, full-length, with the subject sprawled in a chair, legs spread out and crossed at the ankle. But, despite the relaxing pose, there was a sense of movement and energy.

She recognized the chair. It sat in the parlor of the Bradley mansion on Nob Hill. And she recognized the subject by the shape of the face, which was so much like her husband's. This was Gabe's brother. This was Michael.

For a long time she sat there, holding the painting in her lap, no longer hearing the storm. The lights flickered once, but she didn't notice.

It was possible, she discovered, to grieve for someone you hadn't even known, to feel the loss and the regret. That Gabe had loved his brother deeply was obvious in each brush stroke. Not only loved, she thought, but respected. Now more than ever she wished he trusted her enough to speak of this Michael, his life and his death. In the sketch of the baby Gabe had tacked on the easel she had seen this same kind of unconditional love.

If he was using the baby to help him get over the loss of

his brother, should she begrudge him that? It didn't mean he loved their Michael any less. Still, it made her sad to think of it. Until he talked to her, opened up his emotions to her as he did in his work, she would never really be his wife and Michael would never really be his son.

Gently she turned the canvas back to the wall and replaced the others.

When the rain stopped, Laura decided to call Amanda and follow through with her decision to visit the gallery. If she wanted Gabe to take another step toward her, she would have to take another toward him. She'd avoided going to the gallery, not for all the reasons she had given, but because she hadn't felt comfortable in her role as wife to the public person, the well-known artist. Insecurity, she knew, could only be overcome by taking a confident step forward, even if that step took all the courage you could muster.

She'd grown, Laura told herself. In the past year she'd learned not just to be strong but to be as strong as she needed to be. She might not have reached the peak, but she was no longer scrambling for a foothold at the bottom of the hill.

It was as easy as asking. After her thanks were brushed aside Laura hung up the phone and glanced at her watch. If Michael stuck to his usual schedule, he would wake within the hour and demand to be fed. She could take him to Amanda—the first big step—then drive to the gallery. She glanced down at the dirt-stained knees of her jeans. First she had to change.

The doorbell caught her halfway up the stairs. Feeling too optimistic to be annoyed by the interruption, she went to answer it.

And the world crashed silently at her feet.

"Laura." Lorraine Eagleton gave a brisk nod, then strode into the hall. She stood and glanced idly around as she drew off her gloves. "My, my, you've certainly landed on your feet, haven't you?" She tucked her gloves tidily in a buff-colored alligator bag. "Where is the child?"

She couldn't speak. Both words and air were trapped in her lungs, crowding there so that her chest ached. Her hand, still gripping the doorknob, was ice-cold, though the panicked rhythm of her heart vibrated in each fingertip. She had a sudden, horrible flash of the last time she had seen this woman face-to-face. As if they had just been spoken, she remembered the threats, the demand and the humiliation. She found her voice.

"Michael's asleep."

"Just as well. We have business to discuss."

The rain had cooled the air and left its taste in it. Watery sunlight crept through the door, which Laura still hadn't closed. Birds were beginning to chirp optimistically again. Normal things. Such normal things. Life, she reminded herself, didn't bother to stop for personal crises.

Though she couldn't make her fingers relax on the doorknob, she did keep her eyes and her voice level. "You're in my home now, Mrs. Eagleton."

"Women like you always manage to find rich, gullible husbands." She arched a brow, pleased that Laura was still standing by the door, tense and pale. "That doesn't change who you are, what you are. Nor will your being clever enough to get Gabriel Bradley to marry you stop me from taking what's mine."

"I have nothing that belongs to you. I'd like you to leave."

"I'm sure you would," Lorraine said, smiling. She was a tall, striking woman with dark, sculpted hair and an unlined face. "Believe me, I have neither the desire nor the intention to stay long. I intend to have the child."

Laura had a vision of herself standing in the mist, holding an empty blanket. "No."

Lorraine brushed the refusal aside as she might have brushed a speck of lint from her lapel. "I'll simply get a court order."

The cold fear was replaced by heat, and she managed to move then, though it was only to stiffen. "Then do it. Until you do, leave us alone."

Still the same, Lorraine thought as she watched Laura's face. She spit a bit now when she was backed into a corner, but she was still easily maneuvered. It infuriated her now, as it always had, that her son had settled for so little when he could have had so much. Even in fury she never raised her voice. Lorraine had always considered derision a better weapon than volume.

"You should have taken the offer my husband and I made to you. It was generous, and it won't be made again."

"You can't buy my baby, any more than you can buy back Tony."

Pain flashed across Lorraine's face, pain that was real enough, sharp enough, to make Laura form words of sympathy. They could talk, had to be able to talk now, as one mother to another. "Mrs. Eagleton—"

"I won't speak of my son with you," Lorraine said, and the pain vanished into bitterness. "If you had been what he needed, he'd still be alive. I'll never forgive you for that."

There had been a time when she would have crumbled

at those words, ready to take the blame. But Lorraine had been wrong. Laura was no longer the same. "Do you want to take my baby to punish me or to bind your wounds? Either reason is wrong. You have to know that."

"I know I can and will prove that you're unfit to care for the child. I'll produce documentation that you made yourself available to other men before and after your marriage to my son."

"You know that's not true."

Lorraine continued as if Laura hadn't spoken. "Added to that will be the record of your unstable family background. If the child proves to be Tony's, there'll be a custody hearing, and the outcome is without question."

"You won't take Michael, not with money, not with lies." Her voice rose, and she fought to bring it back down. Losing her temper would get her nowhere. Laura knew all too well how easily Lorraine could bat aside emotion with one cold, withering look. She believed, she had to believe, there was still a way of reasoning with her. "If you ever loved Tony, then you'll know just how far I'll go to keep my son."

"And you should know just how far I'll go to see to it that you have no part in raising an Eagleton."

"That's all he is to you, a name, just a symbol of immortality." Despite her efforts, her voice was growing desperate and her knees were beginning to shake. "He's just a baby. You don't love him."

"Feelings have nothing to do with it. I'm staying at the Fairmont. You have two days to decide whether or not you want a public scandal." Lorraine drew out her gloves again. The terror on Laura's face assured her that there was no risk of that. "I'm sure the Bradleys would be displeased, at the least, to learn of your past indiscretions. Therefore, I have no doubt you'll be sensible, Laura, and not risk what you've so conveniently acquired." She walked out the door and down the steps to where a gray limo waited.

Without waiting for it to drive away, Laura slammed the door and bolted it. She was panting as though she'd been running. And it was running that occurred to her first. Dashing up the stairs, she raced into the nursery and began to toss Michael's things into his carryall.

They'd travel light. She'd only pack what was absolutely necessary. Before sundown they could be miles away. Headed north, she thought quickly. Maybe into Canada. There was still enough money left to help them get away, to buy them enough time to disappear. A rattle slipped out of her hand and landed with a clatter. Giving in to despair, she sunk onto the daybed and buried her face in her hands.

They couldn't run. Even if they had enough funds to keep them for a lifetime, they couldn't run. It was wrong, wrong for Michael, for Gabe, even for herself. They had a life here, the kind she'd always wanted, the kind she needed to give her son.

But what could she do to protect it?

Take a stand. Ride out the attack. Not cave in. But caving in was what she'd always done best. Lifting her head, she waited until her breathing had calmed. That was the old Laura's thinking, and that was exactly what Lorraine was counting on. The Eagletons knew how easily manipulated she had been. They expected her to run, and they would use that impulsive, erratic behavior to take her baby. They thought that if she was too tired to run she would sacrifice her child to protect her position with the Bradleys.

But they didn't know her. They had never taken the time or effort to really know her. She wouldn't cave in. She wouldn't run with her son. She was damn well going to fight for him.

The anger came then, and it felt wonderful. Anger was a hot, animate emotion, so unlike the icy numbness of fear. She'd stay angry, as Amanda had advised, because angry she would not only fight but fight rough and dirty. The Eagletons were in for a surprise.

By the time she reached the gallery she was in control again. Michael was safe with Amanda, and Laura was taking the first step of the route she'd already mapped out to see that he stayed safe.

The Trussalt Gallery was in a gracefully refurbished old building. Flowers, neatly trimmed and still wet from the recent rain, were grouped near the main entrance. Laura could smell roses and damp leaves as she pulled the door open.

Inside, skylights offered an open view of the still-cloudy sky, but the gallery itself was brilliant with recessed and track lighting. It was as quiet as a church. Indeed, as Laura paused to look, she could see that this was a place designed for the worship of art. Sculptures in marble and wood, in iron and bronze, were placed lovingly. Rather than competing with each other, they harmonized. As did the paintings aligned stylishly on the walls.

She recognized one of Gabe's, a particularly solemn

view of a garden going to seed. It wasn't pretty; it certainly wasn't joyful. Looking at it, she thought of the mural he'd painted for his mother. The same man who believed enough in fantasies to bring them to life also saw reality, perhaps a bit too clearly. They had that in common, as well.

There were only a few patrons here on this rainy weekday afternoon. They had time to browse, Laura reminded herself. She didn't. Spotting a guard, she moved toward him.

"Excuse me, I'm looking for Gabriel Bradley."

"I'm sorry, miss. He wouldn't be available. If you have a question about one of his paintings, you may want to see Ms. Trussalt."

"No. You see, I'm—"

"Laura." Marion breezed out of an alcove. She was wearing pastels today, a long, slim skirt in baby blue that reached to her ankles, with a hip-skimming sweater in soft pink. The quiet colors only accentuated her exotic looks. "So you decided to pay us a visit after all."

"I'd like to see Gabe."

"What a pity." Without so much as a glance, Marion motioned the guard aside. "He's not here at the moment."

Laura curled her fingers tighter around the clasp of her purse. Intimidation from this quarter meant less than nothing now. "Do you expect him back?"

"As a matter of fact, he should be back before too long. We're booked for drinks in, oh—" she glanced at her watch "—half an hour."

Both the glance and the tone were designed to dismiss her, but Laura was far beyond worrying about games. "Then I'll wait."

"You're welcome to, of course, but I'm afraid Gabe and I have business to discuss. So boring for you."

Weariness was a dull throb at the base of her skull. She had no desire to cross swords now. Her energy had to remain focused for a much more vital fight. "I appreciate your concern, but nothing about Gabe's art is boring for me."

"Spoken like a little Trojan." Marion tilted her head. There was a smile that had nothing to do with friendship in her eyes. "You're looking a bit pale. Trouble in paradise?"

And she knew. As clearly as if Marion had said it out loud, she knew how Lorraine had found her. "Nothing that can't be dealt with. Why did you call her, Marion?"

The smile remained in place, cool and confident. "I beg your pardon?"

"She was already paying good money for detectives. I only had a week or two longer at most."

Marion considered a moment, then turned to fuss with the alignment of a painting. "I've always thought time was better saved than wasted. The sooner Lorraine deals with you, the sooner I can get Gabe back on track. Let me show you something."

Marion moved across the gallery in a separate room, where the walls and floors were white. A sweeping spiral staircase, again in white, rose up in one corner. Above, balconies ran in a circle. A trio of ornamental trees grew under the staircase, fronted by a towering ebony sculpture of a man and a woman in a passionate, yet somehow despairing, embrace.

But it was the portrait that caught her attention, that drew it and demanded it. It was her own face that looked serenely back at Laura, from the portrait Gabe had painted during those long, quiet days in Colorado.

"Yes, it's stunning." Marion rubbed a finger over her lip as she studied it. She'd been tempted to take a knife to the canvas when Gabe had first unpacked it, but the temptation had faded quickly. She was too much a patron of the arts to let personal feelings interfere. "It's one of his best and most romantic pieces. It's been hanging only three weeks and I've already had six serious offers for it."

"I've already seen the painting, Marion."

"Yes, but I doubt you understand it. He calls it *Gabriel's Angel*. That should tell you something."

"Gabriel's Angel," Laura repeated in a murmur. The warmth spread through her as she took a step closer. "What should that tell me?"

"That he, like Pygmalion, fell a bit in love with his subject. That's expected now and again, even encouraged, as it often inspires great work such as this." She tapped a finger against the frame. "But Gabe's much too practical a man to string out the fantasy for long. The portrait's finished, Laura. He doesn't need you any longer."

Laura turned her head so that she could look directly at Marion. What was being said had run through her mind countless times. She told Marion what she had already told herself. "Then he'll have to tell me that."

"He's an honorable man. That's part of his charm. But once things come to a head, once he realizes his mistake, he'll cut his losses. A man only believes in an image," she said, with a gesture toward the portrait, "as long as the image is unsmeared. From what Lorraine tells me, you don't have much time."

Laura fought back the urge to turn and run. Oddly, she discovered it didn't take as much effort this time. "If you believe that, why are you taking so much trouble to move me along?"

"No trouble." She smiled again and let her hand fall away from the painting. "I consider it part of my job to encourage Gabe to concentrate on his career and avoid the kind of controversies that can only detract from it. As I've already explained, his involvement with you isn't acceptable. He'll realize that soon enough himself."

No wonder she had called Lorraine, Laura thought. They were two of a kind. "You're forgetting something, Marion. Michael. No matter what Gabe feels or doesn't feel for me, he loves Michael."

"It takes a particularly pitiful woman to use a child."

"You're right." Laura met her eyes levelly. "You couldn't be more right." When Laura saw that retort had hit home, she continued calmly, "I'll wait here for Gabe. I'd appreciate it if you'd tell him when he gets back."

"So you can run and hide behind him?"

"I can't see that Laura's reasons for coming to see me are your concern."

Gabe spoke from the entranceway. Both women turned toward him. He could read fury on Marion's face and distress on Laura's. Even as he watched, both women composed themselves in their own way. Marion lifted her brow and smiled. Laura folded her hands and raised her chin.

"Darling. You know it's part of my job to protect my artists from panicky spouses and lovers." Crossing to him, Marion laid a hand on his arm. "We're going to be meeting with the Bridgetons in a few minutes about the three paintings. I don't want you distracted and out of sorts."

He spared her only the briefest of glances, but in it Marion saw that he had heard too much. "I'll worry about my moods. If you'll excuse us now?"

"The Bridgetons—"

"Can buy the paintings or go to hell. Leave us alone, Marion."

She aimed a vicious glare at Laura, then stormed out of the room. Her heels echoed on the tile. "I'm sorry," Laura said after a long breath. "I didn't come here to make waves."

"Why, then? From the look of you, you didn't come to spend an afternoon in art appreciation." Before she could answer, he was striding to her. "Damn it, Laura, I don't like having the two of you standing here discussing me as though I were some prize to be awarded to the highest bidder. Marion's a business associate, you're my wife. The two of you are going to have to resolve that."

"I understand that completely." Her voice had changed, hardened to match his. "And you should understand that if I believed you were involved with her in any way I would already have left you."

Whatever he'd been about to say slipped completely away from him. Because he recognized the unshakable resolve in the statement, he could only stare at her. "Just like that?"

"Just like that. I've already lived through one marriage where fidelity meant nothing. I won't live through another."

"I see." Comparisons again, he thought. He wanted to shout at her. Instead, he spoke softly, too softly. "Then I've been warned."

She turned away so that she could close her eyes for a moment. Her head was pounding ruthlessly. If she didn't take the time to draw herself in, she would throw herself into his arms and beg for help. "I didn't come here to discuss the terms of our marriage."

"Maybe you should have. It might be time for us to go back to square one and spell it out."

She shook her head and made herself turn to face him again. "I wanted to tell you that I'm going to see a lawyer in the morning."

He felt the life drain out of him in one swift flood. She wanted a divorce. Then, as quickly as he'd been left limp, the fury came. Unlike Laura, he had never had to prime himself for a fight. "What the hell are you talking about?"

"It can't be put off any longer. I can't keep pretending it's not necessary." Again she wanted to step into his arms, to feel them close around her, make her safe. She kept an arm's length away and stood on her own. "I didn't want to start what will be a difficult and ugly period without letting you know."

"That's big of you." Spinning away, he dragged a hand through his hair. Above him, her portrait smiled gently down. As he stood between them, he felt as though he were caught between two women, between two needs. "What in the hell brought this on? Do you think you can kiss me goodbye at the door, then talk about lawyers a few hours later? If you haven't been happy, why haven't you said so?"

"I don't know what you're talking about, Gabe. We knew this would probably happen eventually. You were the one who told me there'd come a time when I'd have to face it. Now I'm ready to. I just want to give you the option of backing off before it's too late to turn back."

He started to snap at her, then stopped himself. It occurred to him that what he had thought they were talking about, and what was actually being discussed were two different things. "Why do you need to see a lawyer in the morning?"

"Lorraine Eagleton came to the house this afternoon. She wants Michael."

No relief came at the realization that they weren't speaking of divorce. There was no room for it. He recognized a flash of panic before fury replaced it. "She may as well want the moon, because she won't have that, either." He reached out to touch a hand to her cheek. "Are you all right?"

She nodded. "I wasn't, but I am now. She's threatening a custody suit."

"On what grounds?"

She pressed her lips together, but her gaze didn't waver. "On the grounds that I'm not fit to care for him. She told me she'll prove that I was…that there were other men before and during my marriage to Tony."

"How can she prove what isn't true?"

So he believed in her. It was just that easy. Laura reached for his hand. "You can get people to do or say a great many things if you pay them enough. I've seen the Eagletons do that kind of thing before."

"Did she tell you where she was staying?"

"Yes."

"Then it's time I talked with her."

"No." She had his hand before he could stride from

the room. "Please, I don't want you to see her yet. I need to talk with a lawyer first, make certain what can and can't be done. We can't afford the luxury of making a mistake in anger."

"I don't need a lawyer to tell me she can't walk into my house and threaten to take Michael."

"Gabe, please." Again she had to stop him. When her fingers curled around his arms, she felt the fury vibrating in him. "Listen to me. You're angry. So was I, and frightened, too. My first impulse was to run again. I'd even started to pack."

He thought of what it would have done to him to have come home to find the house empty. The score he had to settle with the Eagletons was getting bigger. "Why didn't you?"

"Because it wouldn't have been right, not for Michael, not for you or for me. Because I love both of you too much."

He stopped and cupped her face in his hands, trying to read what was behind her eyes. "You wouldn't have gotten very far."

The smile came slowly as she wrapped her fingers around his wrists. "I hope not. Gabe, I know what I have to do, and I also know that I can do it."

He paused, taking it in. She spoke of love one moment, then of what she would do, not of what they would do. "Alone?"

"If necessary. I know you've taken Michael as your own, but I want you to understand that if she pursues the suit it's going to get ugly, and what's said about me will affect you and your family." There was a moment's hesitation as she worked up the courage to give him a choice.

"If you'd rather not be involved in what's going to happen now, I understand."

His choices had narrowed from the moment he'd seen her. They'd disappeared completely when she'd first put Michael in his arms. Because he didn't know how to explain, he cut through to the bottom line.

"Where's Michael?"

Relief made her giddy. "He's with your mother."

"Then let's pick him up and take him home."

Chapter 11

She couldn't sleep. Both memory and imagination worked against Laura as her mind insisted on racing over what had happened, and what might happen the next day. It was almost a year since she had fled Boston. Now, thousands of miles away, she had chosen to take her stand. But she was no longer alone.

Gabe hadn't waited to make an appointment with his lawyer during regular business hours. He had made a phone call and requested—demanded—a meeting that evening.

Her life, her child, her marriage and her future had been discussed over coffee and crumb cake in the parlor while a low, wispy fog had rolled in from the bay. Her initial embarrassment about speaking with a stranger about her life, her first marriage and her mistakes had sharpened painfully, then vanished. It had seemed as though they were talking about someone else's experiences. The more openly it was discussed, with details meticulously examined and noted, the less shame she'd felt.

Matthew Quartermain had been the Bradleys' attorney for forty years. He was crusty and shrewd and, despite his stuffy exterior, not easily shocked. He'd nodded and made notes and asked questions until Laura's mouth had dried up from answering.

Because he hadn't sympathized or condemned, it had become easier to talk plainly. The truth, spoken in simple, unemotional terms, had been easier to face than it had to keep hidden. In the end she hadn't spared herself or Tony. And in the end she'd felt a powerful sense of having been cleansed.

At last she'd said it all, put all the misery and pain into words. She'd purged her heart and her mind in a way that her lingering sense of shame had never permitted before. Now that it was done, she understood what it was to wipe the slate clean and begin again.

Quartermain hadn't been happy with her final decision, but she'd been firm. Before papers of any kind were served or answered, she would see Lorraine again, face-to-face.

Beside Laura, Gabe lay sleepless. Like her, he was thinking back over the scene in the parlor. With every word that played back in his head his fury inched higher. She had spoken of things there that she had never told him, going into detail she had glossed over before. He'd thought he understood what she'd been through, and he'd thought his feelings about it had already peaked. He'd been wrong.

She hadn't told him about the black eye that had prevented her from leaving the house for nearly a week, or about Lorraine explaining away Laura's split lip by speaking of her daughter-in-law's clumsiness. She hadn't told him about the drunken attacks in the middle of the night, the jealous rages if she'd spoken with another man at a social function, the threats of revenge and violence when she'd finally found the courage to leave.

They'd come out tonight, in excruciating detail.

He hadn't touched her when they'd prepared for bed. He wondered how she could bear to be touched at all.

What she had been through was all too clear now. How could he expect her to put it aside, when he was no longer certain he could? No matter how gentle he was, how much care he took with her, the shadow of another man and another time was between them.

She'd said she loved him. As much as he wanted to believe it, he couldn't understand how anyone who had lived through that kind of hell could ever trust a man again, much less love him.

Gratitude, devotion, with Michael as the common ground. That he could understand. And that, Gabe thought as he lay in the dark, was more than many people were ever given.

He'd wanted more for them, had been on the verge of believing they could have more. That had been before all those words had been spoken downstairs while the quiet spring breeze had ruffled the curtains.

Then she turned toward him, her body brushing his. He stiffened.

"I'm sorry. Did I wake you?"

"No." He started to shift so that they were no longer

touching, but she moved again until her head rested on his shoulder.

The gesture, the easy, uncomplicated movement toward him, tore him in two. The one who needed, and the one who was afraid to ask.

"I can't sleep, either. I feel as though I've run an obstacle course, and my body's exhausted from it. But my mind keeps circling."

"You should stop thinking about tomorrow."

"I know." Laura brushed her hair aside, then settled more comfortably. She felt the slight drawing away, the pulling back. With her eyes shut tight, she wondered if he thought less of her now that he knew everything.

"There's no need for you to worry. It's going to be all right."

Was it? Taking a chance, she reached through the dark for his hand. "The trouble is, different scenes keep popping into my head. What I'll say, what she'll say. If I don't…" Her words trailed off when the baby started crying. "Sounds like someone else is restless."

"I'll get him."

Though she'd already tossed the covers aside, Laura nodded. "All right. I'll nurse him in here if he's hungry."

She sat up and hugged her knees to her chest as Gabe tossed on a robe and strode to the nursery. A moment later the crying stopped, then started again. Under it, she could hear Gabe's voice, murmuring and soothing.

It was so easy for him, so natural. Sensitivity, tenderness, were as much a part of him as temper and arrogance. Wasn't that why she'd finally been able to admit that she loved him? There would be no cycle of despair, submission and terror with Gabe, as there had been with Tony. She could love him without giving up the pieces of herself that she'd so recently discovered.

No, he didn't think less of her. She couldn't be sure of all of his feelings, but she could be sure of that. It was just that he was as worried as she and felt obligated to pretend otherwise.

The light from the nursery slanted into the hallway. In it she could see Gabe's shadow as he moved. The crying became muffled, then rose in a wail. Recognizing the tone of the crying, Laura leaned back and shut her eyes. It was going to be a long night.

"Teething," she murmured when Gabe brought a sobbing Michael into the bedroom. Switching on the bedside lamp she smiled at him. All of them needed support tonight. "I'll nurse him and see if that helps any."

"There you go, old man. Best seat in the house." Gabe settled him in Laura's arms. The crying faded to a whimper, then disappeared completely as he suckled. "I'm going down for a brandy. Do you want anything?"

"No. Yes, some juice. Whatever's in there."

Alone, she held Michael with one arm and arranged her pillows behind her back with the other. It seemed so normal, so usual, just like any other night. Though there were nights when Michael was restless when her body craved sleep, there were others when she prized these hours in the middle of the night. These were the times she and Gabe would remember years down the road, when Michael took his first steps, when he started school, when he rode a two-wheeler for the first time. They'd look back and remember how they'd walked the floor, half dozing themselves. Nothing could change that.

They needed this, needed the normalcy of it. And, if only for a few hours, they would have it.

When Gabe came back in, he set her glass on the table beside her. Smiling, she lifted a hand to his arm. "Can I smell your brandy?"

Amused, he tilted the snifter for her and let her draw in the scent. "Enough?"

"Thanks. I always loved the taste of brandy late at night." Lifting her juice glass, she clinked it against his snifter. "Cheers." He didn't join her in bed, as she'd hoped he would, but turned to stand by the window. "Gabe?"

"Yes?"

"I'd like to make a deal with you. You tell me what's on your mind, ask any question you need to ask, and I'll tell you the absolute truth. Then, in return, I'll ask you and you'll do the same."

"Haven't you answered enough questions for one night?"

So that was it. Laura set her glass aside before she gently shifted Michael to her other breast. "You're upset because of the things I told Mr. Quartermain."

"Did you expect I would take them with a shrug?" When he whirled, the brandy sloshed dangerously close to the lip of the snifter. Laura said nothing as he tossed back half the contents and began to pace.

"I'm sorry it had to be brought up. I'd have preferred another way myself."

"It's not a matter of its being brought up." The words lashed out. He drank more brandy, but it did nothing to soothe him. "My God, it's killing me to think of it, to imagine it. I'm afraid to touch you, because it might bring it back."

"Gabe, you've been telling me all along that it's over, that things are different now. I know they are. You were right when you said I compared you with Tony, but maybe you don't understand that by doing that I helped myself realize that things could change."

He looked at her then, only for a moment, but long enough for her to see that her words weren't enough, not yet. "Things are different now, but I wonder why you don't hate any man who puts his hands on you."

"There was a time when I wouldn't have let any man within ten feet of me, but I was able to start putting things in perspective, through therapy, listening to other women who'd pulled themselves out of the spin." She watched him as he stood in the shadow, his hands thrust in the pockets of his robe and clenched into fists. "When you touch me, when you hold me, it doesn't bring any of that back. It makes me feel the way I've always wanted to feel about myself, about my husband."

"If he were alive," Gabe said evenly, "I'd want to kill him. I find myself resenting the fact that he's already dead."

"Don't do that to yourself." She reached out a hand to him, but he shook his head and walked back to the window. "He was ill. I didn't know that then, not really. And I prolonged it all by not walking away."

"You were afraid. You had nowhere to go."

"That's not enough. I could have gone to Geoffrey. I knew he would have helped me, but I didn't go, because I was pinned there by my own shame and insecurities. When

I finally did leave, it was because of the baby. That's when I began to get well myself. Finding you was the best medicine of all, because you made me feel like a woman again."

He remained silent while she searched for the right words. "Gabe, there's nothing either of us can do to change things that have already happened. Don't let it change what we have now."

Calmer now, he swirled his brandy and continued to look out of the window. "When you talked of lawyers in the gallery today, I thought you wanted a divorce. It scared me to death."

"But I wouldn't have— Did it?"

"There you were, standing under the portrait, and I couldn't imagine what I would do if you walked away. I may have changed your life, angel, but no more than you've changed mine."

Pygmalion, she thought. If he loved the image, he might eventually love the woman. "I won't walk away. I love you, Gabe. You and Michael are my whole life."

He came to her then, to sit on the edge of the bed and take her hand. "I won't let anyone hurt either one of you."

Her fingers tightened on his. "I need to know that whatever we have to do we'll do it together."

"We've been in this together right from the start." Leaning forward, he kissed her, while the baby dozed between them. "I need you, Laura, maybe too much."

"It can't be too much."

"Let me go put him down," Gabe murmured. "Then maybe we can continue that."

He took the baby, but the moment he eased off the bed Michael began to cry.

They took turns walking, rocking, rubbing tender gums. Each time Michael was laid back in his crib he woke with a wail. Dizzy with fatigue, Laura leaned over the rail, patting and rubbing his back. Each time she moved her hand away he cried again.

"I guess we're spoiling him," she murmured.

Gabe sat heavy-eyed in the rocking chair and watched her. "We're entitled. Besides, he sleeps like a rock most of the time."

"I know. This teething's got him down. Why don't you go to bed? There's no sense in both of us being up."

"It's my shift." He rose and discovered that at 5:00 a.m. the body could feel decades older than it was. "You go on to bed."

"No—" Her own yawn cut her off. "We're in this together, remember?"

"Or until one of us passes out."

She would have laughed if she had had the energy. "Maybe I'll just sit down."

"You know, I've been known to watch the sun come up after a night of drinking, card playing or…other forms of entertainment." He began to pat Michael's back as Laura collapsed in the rocker. "And I can't remember ever feeling as though someone had run over me with a truck."

"This is one of the joys of parenting," she told him as she curled her legs under her and shut her eyes. "We're actually having the time of our lives."

"I'm glad you let me know. I think he's giving in."

"That's because you have such a wonderful touch," she murmured as she drifted off. "Such a wonderful touch."

Inch by cautious inch, Gabe drew his hand away. A

man backing away from a tiger couldn't have taken more care. When he was a full two feet from the crib, he nearly let out a breath of relief. Afraid to push his luck, he held it and turned to Laura.

She was sound asleep, in an impossibly uncomfortable position. Hoping his energy held out for five minutes longer, Gabe walked over to pick her up. She shifted and cuddled against him instinctively. As he carried her from the room, she roused enough to murmur. "Michael?"

"Down for the count." He walked into their room, but rather than taking her to bed he moved to the window. "Look, the sun's coming up."

Laura stirred and opened her eyes. Through the window she could see the curve of the eastern sky. If she looked hard enough she could see the water of the bay, like a mist in the distance. The sun seemed to vibrate as it rose. And the echoes brought colors: pinks, mauves, golds. Softly at first, with the darker night sky still dominating above, the colors spread, then deepened. Pinks became reds, vibrant and glowing.

"Sometimes your paintings are like that," she thought aloud. "Changing, shifting angles, with the colors intensifying from the core to the edges." She nestled her head against his shoulder as they watched the new day dawn. "I don't think I've ever seen a more beautiful sunrise."

His skin was warm beneath her cheek, his arms strong, firm with muscle, as they held her to him. She could feel the light, steady beating of his heart. She turned her face toward his as the first birds woke and began to sing. When love was so easily reached, only a fool questioned it.

"I want you, Gabe." She laid her hand on his cheek,

her lips on his lips. "I've never wanted anyone the way I want you."

There was a moment's hesitation. She felt it, understood it, then coaxed him past it. This wasn't the time to think of yesterdays or tomorrows. Her lips softened and parted against his and her hand slipped back to brush through his hair.

"You were right," she murmured.

"About what?"

"I don't think of anyone but you when we make love."

He hadn't meant to ask her for anything. He found there was nothing he couldn't ask.

She was so beautifully open. It made it possible, even easy, to put that part of her life that left him angry and bitter aside. That had nothing to do with where they could take each other. With his mouth still on hers, he moved to the bed. She wrapped her arms around him as he lay beside her. For a moment that was enough.

Morning embraces, sunrise kisses, after a long, sleepless night. Her face was pale with fatigue, but still she trembled for him. The sigh that passed from her lips to his was soft and drowsy. Her body arched, lazy, limber, at the stroke of his hands.

The dawn air was balmy as it fluttered through the window and over their skin. She parted his robe, pushed it back from his shoulders, so that she could warm his skin herself. Just as slowly, he drew off her nightgown. Naked, they lay on the rumpled sheets and made long, luxurious love.

Neither of them set the pace. It wasn't necessary. Here they were in tune, without words or requests. Demands were for other moments, night moments, when passion was hot and urgent. As the light turned gray with morning, desire was deliciously cool.

Perhaps the love she felt for him was best displayed this way, with ease and affection that lasted so much longer than the flare of a flame. She moved with him and he with her, and they brought pleasure to each other that came in sighs and murmurs instead of gasps and shudders.

She felt the roughness of his cheek when she stroked her hand there. This was real. Marriage was more than the band she wore on her finger or the coming together full of need and excitement in the dark. Marriage was holding on at daybreak.

He would have scaled mountains for her. Until now, somehow, the full extent of his feelings for her had escaped him. He'd recognized the need first, the love later, but now he understood the devotion. She was his in a way no other woman could ever be. For the first time in his life, he wanted to be a hero.

When they came together, full light was pouring over the bed. Later, still entwined, they slept.

"I know I'm doing the right thing." Still, Laura hesitated when they stepped off the elevator in Lorraine's hotel. "And, no matter what happens, I'm not going to back down." She caught Gabe's hand in hers and held it tight. Lack of sleep had left her feeling light-headed and primed for action. "I'm awfully glad you're here."

"I told you before, I don't like the idea of you having to see her again, to deal with her on any level. I can easily handle this on my own."

"I know you could. But I told you, I need to. Gabe..."

"What?"

"Please don't lose your temper." She laughed a little at the way his brows rose. The tension rising inside her eased. "There's no need to look like that. I'm only trying to say that shouting at Lorraine won't accomplish anything."

"I never shout. I do occasionally raise my voice to get a point across."

"Since we've gotten that straightened out, I guess the only thing left to do is knock." She felt the familiar flutter of panic and fought it back as she knocked on the door. Lorraine answered, looking regal and poised in a navy suit.

"Laura." After the briefest of nods, she turned to Gabe. "Mr. Bradley. It's nice to meet you. Laura didn't mention that you were coming with her this afternoon."

"Everything that concerns Laura and Michael concerns me, Mrs. Eagleton." He entered, as Laura could never have done, without an invitation.

"I'm sure that's very conscientious of you." Lorraine closed the door with a quick click. "However, some of the things Laura and I may discuss are private family matters. I'm sure you understand."

"I understand perfectly." He met her level gaze with one of his own. "My wife and son are my family."

The war of wills was silent and unpleasant. Lorraine ended it with another nod. "If you insist. Please, sit. I'll order coffee. The service here is tolerable."

"Don't bother on our account." Laura spoke with only the slightest trace of nerves as she chose a seat. "I don't think this should take very long."

"As you like." Lorraine sat across from them. "My

husband would have been here, but business prevented him from making the trip. I do, however, speak for both of us." That said, she laid her hands on the arms of her chair. "I'll simply repeat what has already been discussed. I intend to take Tony's son back to Boston and raise him properly."

"And I'll repeat, you can't have him." She would try reason one last time, Laura thought, leaning forward. "He's a baby, not an heirloom, Mrs. Eagleton. He has a good home and two parents who love him. He's a healthy, beautiful child. You should be grateful for that. If you want to discuss reasonable visitation rights—"

"We'll discuss visitation rights," Lorraine said, interrupting her. "Yours. And if I have anything to say about it, they will be short and spare. Mr. Bradley," she continued, turning away from Laura. "Surely you don't want to raise another man's child as your own. He hasn't your blood, and he only has your name because, for whatever reason, you married his mother."

Gabe drew out a cigarette and lit it slowly. Laura had asked him not to lose his temper. Though he wouldn't be able to accommodate her, it wouldn't do to let it snap so quickly. "You're very wrong" was all he said.

She sighed, almost indulgently. "I understand you have feelings for Laura. My son had them, too."

The first chain on his temper broke clean in half. The rage could be seen in his eyes and heard in each precise, bitten-off word. "Don't you ever compare my feelings for Laura with your son's."

Lorraine paled a little, but went on evenly. "I have no idea what she may have been telling you—"

"I told him the truth." Before Gabe could speak, or move, Laura put a hand on his arm. "I told him what you know is the truth, that Tony was ill, emotionally unstable."

Now it was Lorraine who moved, rising deliberately from her chair. Her face was flushed and pinched, but her voice was held at the same even pitch. "I will not sit here and listen to you defame my son."

"You will listen." Laura's fingers dug hard into Gabe's arm, but she didn't give way. "You'll listen now the way you never listened when I was desperate for help. The way you never listened when Tony was screaming for it in the only way he knew. He was an alcoholic, an emotional wreck who abused someone weaker than he. You knew he hurt me, you saw the marks and ignored them or made excuses. You knew there were other women. By your silence, you gave him approval."

"What was between you and Tony was none of my concern."

"That's for you to live with. But I warn you, Lorraine, if you open the lid, you won't be able to handle what comes out."

Lorraine sat again, if for no other reason than the tone of Laura's voice and the fact that for the first time Laura had called her by her first name. That one change made them equals. This wasn't the same frightened, easily pressured woman she had known only a year before.

"Threats from someone like you don't worry me. The courts will decide if some loose-moraled young tramp will have custody of an Eagleton or if he'll be placed with those who can give him the proper upbringing."

"If you refer to my wife in that way again you'll have

more than threats to deal with." Gabe blew out a long, narrow stream of smoke. "Mrs. Eagleton."

"It doesn't matter." Laura squeezed his hand. She knew he was on the verge of losing control. "You can't make me cringe anymore, Lorraine, and you won't make me beg. You know very well that I was faithful to Tony."

"I know that Tony didn't believe that."

"Then how do you know the child is his?"

Absolute silence fell the moment Gabe spoke. Laura started to speak but was held off by the look in Gabe's eyes. Color flooded into Lorraine's face again when she found her voice.

"She wouldn't have dared—"

"Wouldn't she? That's odd. You intend to prove that Laura was unfaithful to your son, and now you claim she wasn't. Either way, you have a problem. If she had had an affair with anyone. Me, for example." He smiled again as he crushed out his cigarette. "Or haven't you wondered why we were married so quickly, why, as you've already asked, I accept the child as my own?" He let that thought take hold before he continued. "If she had been unfaithful, the child could be anyone's. If she wasn't unfaithful, you haven't got a case."

Lorraine clenched and unclenched her fingers on the arm of the chair. "My husband and I have every intention of determining the child's paternity. I would hardly take someone's bastard into my home."

"Be careful," Laura said, so quietly that the words seemed to vibrate in the air. "Be very careful, Lorraine. I know you have no concern for Michael as a person."

Fighting for control she so rarely lost, Lorraine settled again. "I have nothing but the gravest concern for Tony's son."

"You've never asked about him, what he looks like, if he's well. You've never demanded to see him, even a picture or a doctor's report. You've never once called him by name. If you had, if I'd seen in you one ounce of love or affection for the baby, I'd feel differently about what I'm about to say." The courage came without the need to muster it. "You're free to draw up the papers and initiate a custody suit. Gabe and I have already notified our attorney. We'll fight you, and we'll win. And in the meantime, I'll go to the press with the story of what my life was like with the Eagletons of Boston."

Lorraine's nails dug into the material on the arm of the chair. "You wouldn't have the nerve."

"I have that and more when it comes to protecting my son."

She could see it, the calm, unshakable determination in Laura's eyes. "Even if you did, no one would believe you."

"But they would," Laura told her. "People have a way of recognizing the truth."

Lorraine's face was set when she turned to Gabe. "Do you have any conception of what this kind of gossip could do to your family name? Do you want to risk your reputation, your parents' reputation, over this woman and a child who isn't even of your blood?"

"My reputation can handle it, and, to be frank, my parents are looking forward to a fight." There was a challenge in his voice now that didn't have to be feigned. "Michael may not be of my blood, but he's mine."

"Lorraine." Laura waited until they were face-to-face

again. "You lost your son, and I'm sorry for you, but you won't replace him with mine. Whatever the cost to protect Michael's welfare, I'll pay. And so will you."

Putting a hand under her arm, Gabe rose, keeping Laura beside him. "Your attorney can contact us once you've made your decision. Remember, Mrs. Eagleton, you're not pitting yourself against a lone pregnant woman. You're up against the Bradleys now."

The moment they were in the hall, Gabe pulled Laura against him. He could feel the tremors coursing through her, so he held her a moment longer. "You were wonderful." He kissed her hair before he drew her away from him. "In fact, angel, you were amazing. Lorraine still doesn't know what hit her."

The flush of pride was as warm and satisfying as anything she'd ever felt. "It wasn't as bad as I thought," she said with a sigh, but she kept her hand in his as they walked to the elevator. "I used to be so terrified of her, afraid to speak two words. Now I can see her for what she really is, a lonely woman trapped by her own strict sense of family honor."

Gabe gave a quick, humorless laugh as the elevators doors opened. "Honor has nothing to do with it."

"No, but that's how she sees it."

"Tell you what." He pressed the button for the lobby. "We're going to forget about Lorraine Eagleton for the rest of the day. In fact, we're going to forget about her completely before long, but for now there's a little restaurant a few blocks away. Not too quiet, and very expensive."

"It's too early for dinner."

"Who said anything about dinner?" He slipped an arm

around her waist as they walked out into the lobby. "We're going to sit at a table over the water, and I'm going to watch everyone stare at my gorgeous wife while we drink a bottle of champagne."

She loved him for that. Then her heart skipped a beat when he brought her fingers to his lips. "Don't you think we should wait to celebrate until Lorraine gives us her decision?"

"We'll celebrate then, too. Right now I want to celebrate being witness to an angel breathing fire."

She laughed and walked outside with him. "I could do it again. In fact…"

"What?"

She swept her gaze up to his. "I'd like to."

"Sounds as though I'm going to have to watch my step."

"Probably." She was giddy with success, but she was still practical. "I really shouldn't have champagne. Michael—"

Gabe kissed her, and signaled for his car.

Chapter 12

"You look exhausted." Amanda gave a quick shake of her head as she stepped into the house.

"Michael's teething." The excuse was valid enough, but more than a fretful baby was keeping Laura from sleeping at night. "He's been down all of ten minutes. With luck, he might make an entire hour straight."

"Then why aren't you napping?"

Since Amanda was already stepping into the parlor, Laura followed her in. "Because you called and said you were coming over."

"Oh." With a faint smile, Amanda took a seat, then tossed her purse on the table. "So I did. Well, I won't keep you long. Gabe's not home?"

"No. He said he had something to see to." Laura sat in the chair facing her and let her head fall back. Sometimes small luxuries felt like heaven. "Can I get you some coffee, or something cold?"

"You don't look as though you can get yourself out of that chair. And, no, I don't need a thing. How is Gabe?"

"He hasn't been getting a great deal of rest, either."

"I'm not surprised. No word from Lorraine Eagleton or her attorney?"

"Nothing."

"I don't suppose that you're able to take the attitude that no news is good news?"

Laura managed a smile. "Afraid not. The longer this goes on, the easier it gets to imagine the worst."

"And if she takes this to court?"

"Then we'll fight." Despite her fatigue, her newly discovered power came through. "I meant everything I said to her."

"That's really all I wanted to hear." Sitting back, Amanda adjusted the pin on her lapel. A little too thin, a little too pale, she thought as she studied Laura. But, all in all, she thought her daughter-in-law was holding up well. "When this is over, you and Gabe should be able to tie up a few loose ends."

Laura caught herself before she dozed off. "Loose ends?"

"Yes, little things. Such as what you intend to do with the rest of your lives."

"I don't know what you mean."

"Gabe has his art, and you both have Michael, and however many other children you choose to bring into the world."

That was something that made Laura sit up straighter.

More children. They'd never discussed the possibility of more. As she began to, she wondered if Gabe even wanted any. Did she? She passed a hand over her now flat stomach and imagined it filled with another child—Gabe's child this time, from the very first moment. Yes, she wanted that. Glancing over, she saw Amanda studying her quietly and with complete understanding.

"It's difficult to make decisions with so much hanging over us."

"Exactly. But it will pass. When it does, what are you going to look for? Since I spent more than two decades under the same roof as Gabe, I know that he can, when the muse in on him, lock himself in his studio for hours and days on end."

"I don't mind. How could I, when I see what he can accomplish?"

"A woman needs a solid sense of accomplishment, as well. Children can be the best of that, but…" She reached for her purse, opened it and took out a business card. "There's an abuse clinic downtown. It's rather small, and unfortunately not well funded. Yet." She intended to correct that. "They need volunteers, women who understand, who know there can be normal life after hell."

"I'm not a therapist."

"You don't need a degree to give support."

"No." She looked at the card on the table as the idea took root. "I don't know. I…"

"Just think about it."

"Amanda, did you go to the clinic?"

"Yes, Cliff and I went there yesterday. We were very impressed."

"Why did you go?"

Amanda lifted a brow in a gesture Laura knew Gabe had inherited. "Because there's someone we both care about who we wanted to understand better. Don't get up," she said as she rose. "I'll let myself out. Give Gabe my love and tell him his father wants to know if they're ever going to play poker again. The man thrives on losing money."

"Amanda." Laura pushed off her shoes before she curled her legs up in the chair. "I never had a mother, and the one I always imagined for myself was nothing like you." She smiled as her eyes began to close. "I'm not at all disappointed."

"You're coming along," Amanda said, and left Laura sleeping in the chair.

She was still there when Gabe came in. He tilted the bulky package against the wall. When she didn't stir at the rattle of the paper, he walked over to the couch. He didn't even have the energy to wish for his sketchpad as he stretched out his legs and almost instantly fell asleep.

The baby woke both of them. Gabe merely groaned and pulled a throw pillow over his face. Disoriented, Laura pulled herself up, blinked groggily at Gabe, then put one foot in front of the other to get upstairs.

A short time later, he went up after her.

"My timing's good," he decided when he saw that Laura was fastening a fresh diaper.

"I'm beginning to wonder about your timing." But she was smiling as she lifted Michael over her head to make him laugh. "How long have you been home?"

"Long enough to see that my wife has nothing better to do than lounge around all day." He plucked Michael from her while she pretended to glare at him. "Do you think if we kept him awake and exhausted him with attention he'd sleep tonight?"

"I'm willing to try anything."

At that, Gabe sat on the floor and began to play nonsense games. Bouncing the Baby, Flying the Baby, Tickling the Baby.

"You're so good with him." Finding her second wind, Laura sat on the floor with them. "It's hard to believe you're new at this."

"I never thought about parenthood. It certainly has its compensations." He set Michael on his knee and jiggled him.

"Like walking the ten-minute mile at 2:00 a.m."

"That, too."

"Gabe, your mother came by."

"Should I be surprised?"

She smiled a little as she leaned over to let Michael tug at her hair. "She left a card—from an abuse clinic."

"I see." He reached over himself to untangle her hair from Michael's grip. "Do you want to go back into therapy?"

"No…at least I don't think so." She looked over at him. Michael was chewing madly at his chin. All the therapy she needed was sitting across from her. "She suggested I might like to volunteer there."

He frowned as he let Michael gnaw on his knuckle. "And be reminded day after day?"

"Yes—of what I was able to change."

"I thought you'd want to go back to modeling eventually."

"No, I haven't any desire to go back to modeling. I think I could do this, and I know I'd like to try."

"If you're asking for my approval, you don't need to."

"I'd still like to have it."

"Then you do, unless I see this wearing you down."

She had to smile. He still saw her as more fragile than she was or could ever have afforded to be. "You know, I've been thinking…with everything that's happened, and everything we've had to think and worry about, we haven't had much time to really get to know a lot about each other."

"I know you take entirely too long in the bathtub and like to sleep with the window open."

She took the stuffed rabbit Michael liked to chew on and passed it from hand to hand. "There are other things."

"Such as?"

"The other night, I said that you could ask me anything and I'd tell you the truth, and then I'd ask you something. Do you remember?"

"I remember."

"I never had my turn."

He shifted so that he could rest his back against the daybed. They were avoiding speaking of the phone call they were both waiting for. And they both knew it. Perhaps that was best, Gabe mused as the baby continued to rub his sore gums against his knuckles.

"Do you want to hear about my misspent youth?"

Though she was plucking nervously at the rabbit's ears, she smiled. "Is there time?"

"You flatter me."

"Actually, I'd like to ask you about something else. A

few days ago, when it rained, I went into your studio to close the windows. I looked through some of your paintings. Perhaps I shouldn't have."

"It doesn't matter."

"There was one in particular. The one of Michael. Your brother. I'd like you to tell me about him."

He was silent for so long that she had to fight back the urge to tell him that it didn't matter. But it mattered too much. She was certain it was his brother's death that had sent him to Colorado, that was preventing him, even after all these months, from having a showing of his work.

"Gabe." She laid a tentative hand on his arm. "You asked me to marry you so that you could take on my problems. You wanted me to trust you, and I have. Until you can do the same, we're still strangers."

"We haven't been strangers since the first time we laid eyes on each other, Laura. I would have asked you to marry me with or without your problems."

Now she fell silent, as surprise ran through her, chased frantically by hope. "Do you mean that?"

He shifted the baby onto his shoulder. "I don't always say everything I mean, but I do mean what I say." When Michael began to whimper, Gabe stood to walk him. "You needed someone, I wanted to be that someone. And I, though I didn't know it until you were already part of my life, needed someone, too."

She wanted to ask him how he needed her, and why, and if love—the kind she'd always hoped for—was somehow mixed up with that need. But they needed to go back further than that if they were ever to move forward.

"Please tell me about him."

He wasn't certain he could, that he wouldn't trip over the pain, and then the words. It had been so long since he'd spoken of Michael. "He was three years younger than I," he began. "We got along fairly well growing up because Michael tended to be even-tempered unless backed into a corner. We didn't have many of the same interests. Baseball was about it. It used to infuriate me that I couldn't outhit him. As we grew older, I turned to art, and Michael to law. The law fascinated him."

"I remember," she murmured, as some vague recollection stirred. "There was something about him in an article I read about you. He was working in Washington."

"As a public defender. He set a lot of tongues clucking over that decision. He wasn't interested in corporate law or big fees. Of course, a lot of people said he didn't need the money, anyway. What they didn't understand was that he would have done the same thing with or without his stock portfolio behind him. He wasn't a saint." Gabe set Michael in the crib and wound up the mobile. "But he was the best of us. The best and the brightest, my father used to say."

She had risen, but she wasn't certain he wanted her to go to him. "I could see that in the portrait. You must have loved him very much."

"It's not something you think about, one brother loving another. Either it's there or it isn't. It isn't something you say, because you don't think it needs to be said. Then all you have is time to regret."

"He had to know you loved him. He only had to see the portrait."

With his hands in his pockets, Gabe walked to the window. It was easier than he could have imagined to talk to her about it. "I'd badgered him to sit for me off and on for years. It became a family joke. I won five sittings from him in a poker game. A heart flush to his three of a kind." The pain clawed at him, no longer fresh, but still sharp. "That was the last time we played."

"What happened to him?"

"An accident. I've never believed in accidents. Luck, fate, destiny, but they called it an accident. He was researching a case in Virginia and took a small commuter plane to New York. Minutes after takeoff it went down. He was coming to New York because I was having a showing."

Her heart broke for him. This time there was no hesitation as she went to him and put her arms around him. "You've blamed yourself all this time. You can't."

"He was coming to New York for me, to be there for me. I watched my mother fall apart for the first and only time in her life. I saw my father walk through his own home as if he'd never seen it before, and I didn't know what to say or do."

She stroked his back, aching for him. There was no use telling him that being there was sometimes all that could be done. "I've never lost anyone I've loved, but having you and Michael now, I can imagine how devastating it would be. Sometimes things happen and there's no one to blame. Whether that's an accident or fate, I don't know."

He rested his cheek on her hair and looked out at the flowers she'd planted. "I went to Colorado to get away for a while, to be alone and see if I could paint again. I hadn't been able to here. When I found you, I'd begun to pull myself back. I could work again, I could think about coming home and picking up my life. But there was still something missing." He drew back and cupped her face in his hand. "You filled in those last pieces for me."

She curled her fingers around his wrist. "I'm glad."

When he held her, she closed her eyes. They would make it, Laura told herself. Whatever happened, they would make it. Sometimes need was enough.

"Gabe." She slid her hands down until they gripped his. "The paintings in your studio. They don't belong there." She squeezed his fingers with hers before he could speak or turn away. "It's wrong to keep them there, facing the wall and pretending they don't exist. If your brother was proud enough of you to want to be there for one of your showings, it's time you had one. Dedicate it to him. Maybe you didn't say the words, but there can't be any better way to show that you loved him."

He had started to brush it aside, to make excuses, but her last words hit home. "He would have liked you."

Her lips curved. "Will you do it?"

"Yes." He kissed her while she was still smiling. "Yes, it's time. I've known that, but I haven't been able to take the last step. I'll have Marion start the arrangements." She stiffened, and though the change was only slight he drew her away to study her face. "Problem?"

"No, of course not."

"You do a lot of things well, angel. Lying isn't one of them."

"Gabe, nothing could please me more than you going ahead with this. That's the truth."

"But?"

"Nothing. All of this has really put me behind schedule. I need to give Michael his bath."

"He'll hold a minute." He kept her with him by doing no more than running his hands down her arms. "I know there's some tension between you and Marion. I've already told you there's nothing between us but business."

"I understand that. I've told you what I would have done if I thought otherwise."

"Yes, you did." Amusement moved over his face. She would have packed her bags and headed for the door, but she would have gotten no more than five feet. "So what's the problem?"

"There is no problem."

"I'd prefer not going to Marion with this."

"So would I." Her chin came up. "Don't push this, Gabe. And don't push me."

"Well, well." He brought his hands to her shoulders as he nodded. "It's a rare thing for you to get that look on your face. Whenever you do, I have this deep-seated urge to drag you down on the floor and let loose." When color flooded her face, he laughed and drew her closer.

"Don't laugh at me." She would have twisted away, but his hands were firm.

"Sorry. I wasn't, really, more at the situation." He thought that perhaps delicacy was called for, but then he rejected the idea. "Want to fight?"

"Not at the moment."

"If you can't lie better than that, we'll have to keep you out of poker games," he murmured, and watched her eyes cool. "I overheard your discussion with Marion at the gallery."

"Then you obviously don't need me to spell things out for you. She believes I'm going to hold you back, prevent you from reaching your full potential, and she took steps to stop it. I realize that the Eagletons would have found us, probably in a matter of days, but I won't forgive her for calling them. The fact that you're associated with her gallery means I have to be polite to her in public, but that's the extent of it."

His hands had tightened on her shoulders, and all amusement had been wiped from his face. "You're telling me that Marion called the Eagletons?"

"You just said you'd heard us, so—"

"I hadn't heard that much." Deliberately he relaxed his hands, then took a step back. "Why didn't you explain this to me before so that we could have told her to go to hell?"

"I didn't think that you—" She stopped and stared at him. "Would you have?"

"Damn it, Laura, what more do I have to do to convince you that I'm committed totally to you and Michael?"

"But she said—"

"What difference does it make what she said? It's what I say, isn't it?"

"Yes." She folded her hands but didn't lower her gaze. It was what he said. And not once had he ever said he loved her. "I didn't want to interfere when it came to your work."

"And I won't tolerate Marion interfering in my life. I'll handle it."

"How?"

Exasperated, he tugged his hand through his hair. "One minute you talk of my work as though I had an obligation to mankind to share it, and the next you act as though I'd have to go begging to find another gallery."

"I didn't mean... You'll take your paintings out of Marion's gallery?"

"Good God," he muttered, and took another turn around the room. "Obviously we need to talk—or maybe talking's not what's called for." He took a step toward her, then swore when the phone rang. "Stay here." With that he turned on his heel and strode out.

Laura let out a long breath. He'd said something about dragging her to the floor and letting loose. That was what had been in his eyes a moment before. And what would that have proved?

She moved to the crib to hand a fretful Michael his favorite rabbit. It would only have proved that he wanted and needed her. She had no doubts about that. Why shouldn't she be surprised that he would cut himself off from Marion for her? But not for her, really, Laura thought as she leaned over to nuzzle the baby. For himself. Marion had made the mistake of interfering.

Reasons didn't matter, she told herself. Results did. A great deal had been accomplished here this afternoon. He'd finally trusted her with his feelings about his brother. She'd been able to say the right things to convince him to show his work, and Marion was out of their lives.

"That should be enough for one day," she murmured to Michael. But there was still an ache in her heart.

She wouldn't think about the Eagletons.

"He needs us, Michael." That, too, should have been enough. Perhaps they were a replacement for someone he had loved and lost, but he had already given the baby unconditional love. He had given her a promise of his fidelity. That was more than she'd ever had, more than she had come to believe she would ever have. And yet it wasn't enough.

"Laura."

She turned, annoyed because she was feeling weepy and dejected. "What is it?"

"That was Quartermain on the phone." He saw the fear come first, then saw it vanish to be replaced by determination. "It's over," he told her before she could ask. "The Eagletons' attorney contacted him a few minutes ago."

"Over?" She could only whisper. The strength she'd built up, layer by layer, began to slip.

"They've pulled back. There'll be no custody suit. Not now, not ever. They don't want anything to do with the baby."

"Oh, God." She covered her face with her hands. The tears came, but she wasn't ashamed of them, not even when Gabe gathered her close. "Is he sure? If they change their minds—"

"He's sure. Listen to me." He drew her back, just a little. He wasn't entirely certain how she would feel about the rest. "They're going to file papers claiming that Tony wasn't Michael's biological father. They want him cut off legally from any future claim to the Eagleton estate."

"But she doesn't believe that."

"She wants to believe that."

She closed her eyes while relief and regret poured through her. "I would have tried to be fair, to let them see Michael. At least I want to believe I would have tried."

"He'll lose his heritage."

"The money?" When she opened her eyes, they were dark and damp. "I don't think that will matter to him. It doesn't to me. As far as family goes, he already has one. Gabe, I don't know how to thank you."

"Then don't. You were the one who stood up to her."

"I did." She brushed the tears away, and then there was laughter as she threw her arms around him. "Yes, I did. No one's ever going to take him away from us. I want to celebrate. To go dancing, have a party." She laughed again and squeezed him hard. "After I sleep for a week."

"It's a date." He found her lips with his, then held them there as she melted into him. Another beginning, he thought, and this time they'd take the first step properly. "I want to call my parents and let them know."

"Yes, right away." She pressed against him for a moment longer. "I'll give Michael his bath, and then we'll be down."

It was nearly an hour before she came downstairs, bringing a more contented Michael with her. The baby, fresh from his bath, was awake and ready to be entertained. Because her jeans had gotten wet, she'd changed into a pale lavender shirt and slacks. Her hair was loose around her shoulders, and both she and Michael smelled of soap and soft talc. Gabe met her at the foot of the stairs.

"Here, let me have him." He curled his arm around the baby and tickled his belly. "Looks like you're ready to go field a few grounders."

"So do you." Envious, Laura muffled a yawn. "You haven't had any more sleep than I have. How do you manage it?"

"Three decades of clean living—and a body accustomed to all-night poker games."

"Your father wants to play. Maybe Michael could sit in."

"Maybe." He tipped her chin up with his finger. "You really are ready to drop, aren't you?"

"I've never felt better in my life."

"And you can barely keep you eyes open."

"That's nothing five straight hours of sleep wouldn't fix."

"I've got something to show you. Afterward, why don't you go up and take a nap? Michael and I can entertain ourselves." His thumb traced along her jawline. Until Laura, he hadn't known that the scent of soap and powder could be arousing. "Once you've rested, we can have our private celebration."

"I'll go now."

He laughed and caught her arm before she could start back up. "Come see first."

"Okay, I'm too weak to argue."

"I'll keep that in mind for later." With the baby in one arm and the other around Laura, he walked into the parlor.

She'd seen the painting before, from the first brush strokes to the last. Yet it seemed different now, here, hung over the mantel. In the gallery, she had seen it as a beautiful piece of work, something to to be studied by art students and patrons, a thing to be commented on and discussed, dissected and critiqued. Here, in the parlor, in the late afternoon, it was a personal statement, a part of all three of them.

She hadn't realized just how much she'd resented seeing it in Marion's gallery. Nor had she known that seeing it here would make her feel, as nothing else had, that she had finally come home.

"It's beautiful," she murmured.

He understood. It wasn't vanity or self-importance.

"I've never done anything in my life that compares to this. I doubt I will again. Sit down, will you?"

Something in his tone had her glancing over at him before she settled on the couch. "I didn't know you intended to bring it home. I know you've had offers."

"I never had any intention of selling it. I always meant it for here." Resting the baby on his hip, he walked over to the portrait. "As long as I've lived here, I haven't done anything, or found anything, that I wanted to hang in that spot. It goes back to fate again. If I hadn't been in Colorado, if it hadn't been snowing, if you hadn't been running. It took what had happened to you, and what had happened to me, to bring us together and make this."

"When you were painting it, I wondered why you seemed so driven. I understand now."

"Do you?" With a half smile, he turned back to her. "I wonder just what you understand, angel. It wasn't until a little while ago that I realized you have no idea what I feel for you."

"I know you need me, me and Michael. Because of what happened to all of us, we're able to make things better."

"And that's it?" He wondered if he was pushing too far, but he thought that if he didn't push now it might be too late. "You said you loved me. I know gratitude's a big part of that, but I want to know if there's anything more."

"I don't know what you want me to say."

"I want you to look." He held out a hand. When she didn't move, he walked over to her and drew her to her feet. "Look at the portrait and tell me what you see."

"Myself."

It seemed to be the day for showdowns, Gabe thought.

He quickly carried the sleeping Michael upstairs to the nursery and put him in the crib. Going back down to Laura, he took her by the shoulders and, holding her in front of him, made her face the portrait. "Tell me what you see."

"I see myself as you saw me then." Why was her heart hammering? "I seem a little too vulnerable, a little too sad."

Impatience had him giving her a quick shake. "You don't see enough."

"I want to see strength," she blurted out. "I think I do. And I see a woman alone who's ready to protect what's hers."

"When you look at her eyes. Look at them, Laura, and tell me what you see."

"A woman falling in love." She shut her own. "You must have known."

"No." He didn't turn her toward him. Instead, he wrapped his arms around her so that they both continued to face the portrait. "No, I didn't know, because I kept telling myself I was painting what I wanted to see. And what I was feeling myself."

Her heart leaped into her throat and throbbed there. Whatever he could feel, he could paint. That had been her own conclusion. "What are you feeling?"

"Can't you see it?"

"I don't want to see it there." She turned to grip the front of his shirt. "I want to hear it."

He wasn't sure he had the words. Words came so much less easily than emotion. He could paint his moods, and he could shout them, but it was difficult to speak them quietly when they mattered so much.

He touched her face, her hair, then her hand. "Almost

from the first you pulled at me in a way no one ever had before and no one ever will again. I thought I was crazy. You were pregnant, totally dependent on me, grateful for my help."

"I was grateful. I'll always be grateful."

"Damn it" was all he could manage as he turned away.

"I'm sorry you feel that way." She was calm now, absolutely, beautifully calm, as he glared at her. She'd remember him like this always, she thought, with his hair tousled from his hands, a gray shirt with the sleeves shoved up to the elbows and his face full of impatience. "Because I intend to be grateful for the rest of my life. And that has nothing to do with my intending to love you for the rest of my life."

"I want to be sure of that."

"Be sure. You didn't paint what you wanted to see, you never do. You paint the truth." She took one step toward him, the most important step she'd ever taken. "I've given you the truth, Gabe. Now I have to ask for it. Are your feelings for me tied up in that portrait, in that image, are they an effect of your love for Michael, or are they for me?"

"Yes." He caught her hands in his. "I'm in love with the woman I painted, with the mother of my child, and with you. Separately and together. We could have met anywhere, under any circumstances, and I would still have fallen in love with you. Maybe it wouldn't have happened as quickly, maybe it wouldn't have been as complicated, but it would have happened." She started to move into his arms, but he held her back. "When I married you, it was for purely selfish reasons. I wasn't doing you any favors."

She smiled. "Then I won't be grateful."

"Thank you." He lifted her hands to his lips, the one that wore the old wedding band, then the one that wore the new. "I want to paint you again."

She was laughing as his lips came down to her. "Now?"

"Soon."

Then his hands were in her hair, and the kiss became urgent and seeking. It was met equally as her arms went around him. Love, fully opened, added its own desperation.

There was a murmur of pleasure, then a murmur of protest as he drew her to the floor. Her laugh turned to a moan when he unbuttoned her blouse.

"Michael—"

"Is asleep." He dragged her hair back, leaving her face unframed. Everything he'd wanted to see was there. "Until he wakes up, you're mine. I love you, Laura. Every time you look at the painting, you'll see it. You were mine from the first moment I touched you."

Yours, she thought as she drew him back to her. Gabriel's angel was more than a portrait. And she finally belonged.

* * * * *

"Thank you." He lifted her hands to his lips, the [illegible] that wore the ruby Claddagh ring, then the one that wore [illegible] ing ring. "I want to paint you again."

She was [illegible] to her. "Now?"

"Soon."

Then this [illegible] and the [illegible] upon and sealing. It was not enough [illegible] [illegible]

There was a [illegible] then a [illegible] of [illegible]

"Michael—"

"It's here." [illegible]

[illegible] the Lord [illegible]

[illegible]

First Impressions

To Georgeann,
neighbour and friend

Chapter 1

The morning sun shot shafts of light over the mountains. It picked up the hints of red and gold among the deep green leaves and had them glowing. From somewhere in the woods came a rustling as a rabbit darted back to its burrow, while overhead a bird chirped with an insistent cheerfulness. Clinging to the line of fences along the road were clumps of honeysuckle. The light scent from the few lingering blossoms wafted in the air. In a distant field a farmer and his son harvested the last of the summer hay. The rumble of the bailer was steady and distinct.

Over the mile trek to town only one car passed. Its driver lifted his hand in a salute. Shane waved back. It was good to be home.

Walking on the grassy shoulder of the road, she

plucked a blossom of honeysuckle and, as she had as a child, drew in the fleetingly sweet aroma. When she crushed the flower between her fingers, its fragrance briefly intensified. It was a scent she associated with summer, like barbecue smoke and new grass. But this was summer's end.

Shane looked forward to fall eagerly, when the mountains would be at their best. Then the colors were breathtaking and the air was clean and crisp. When the wind came, the world would be full of sound and flying leaves. It was the time of woodsmoke and fallen acorns.

Curiously, she felt as though she'd never been away. She might still have been twenty-one, walking from her grandmother's to Sharpsburg to buy a gallon of milk or a loaf of bread. The busy Baltimore streets, the sidewalks and crowds of the last four years might have been a dream. She might never have spent those four years teaching in an inner-city school, correcting exams and attending faculty meetings.

Yet four years had passed. Her grandmother's narrow two-story house was now Shane's. The uneven, wooded three acres of land were hers as well. And while the mountains and woods were the same, Shane was not.

Physically, she looked almost as she had when she had left western Maryland for the job in a Baltimore high school. She was small in height and frame, with a slender figure that had never developed the curves and roundness she'd hoped for. Her face was subtly triangular with its creamy skin touched with warm color. It had been called peaches and cream often enough to make Shane wince. There were dimples that flashed when she smiled, rather than the elegant cheekbones she had wished for. Her nose was small, dusted with freckles, tilted up at the end. Pert. Shane had suffered the word throughout her life.

Under thin arched brows, her eyes were large and dark. Whatever emotion she felt was mirrored in them. They were rarely cool. Habitually, she wore her hair short, and it curled naturally to frame her face in a deep honey blond. As her temperament was almost invariably happy, her face was usually animated, her small, sculpted mouth tilted up. The adjective used most to describe her was *cute.* Shane had grown to detest the word, but lived with it. Nothing could be done to alter sharp, vital attractiveness into sultry beauty.

As she rounded the last curve in the road before coming into town, she had a sudden flash of having done so before—as a child, as a teenager, as a girl on the brink of womanhood. It gave her a sense of security and belonging. Nothing in the city had ever given her the simple pleasure of being part of the whole.

Laughing, she took the final yards at a run, then burst through the door of the general store. The bells jingled fiercely before it slammed shut.

"Hi!"

"Hi, yourself." The woman behind the counter grinned at her. "You're out early this morning."

"When I woke up, I discovered I was out of coffee." Spotting the box of fresh doughnuts on the counter, Shane rolled her eyes and headed for them. "Oh, Donna, cream filled?"

"Yeah." Donna watched with an envious sigh as

Shane chose one and bit into it. For the better part of twenty years, she'd seen Shane eat like a linebacker without gaining an ounce of fat.

Though they had grown up together, they were as different as night and day. Where Shane was fair, Donna was dark. Shane was small; Donna was tall and well rounded. For most of their lives, Donna had been content to play follower to Shane's leader. Shane was the adventurer. Donna had liked nothing better than to point out all the flaws in whatever plans she was hatching, then wholeheartedly fall in with it.

"So, how are you settling in?"

"Pretty well," Shane answered with her mouth full.

"You've hardly been in since you got back in town."

"There's been so much to do. Gran couldn't keep the place up the last few years." Both affection and grief came through in her voice. "She was always more interested in her gardening than a leaky roof. Maybe if I had stayed—"

"Oh, now don't start blaming yourself again." Donna cut her off, drawing her straight dark brows together. "You know she wanted you to take that teaching job. Faye Abbott lived to be ninety-four; that's more than a lot of people can hope for. And she was a feisty old devil right to the end."

Shane laughed. "You're absolutely right. Sometimes I'm sure she's sitting in her kitchen rocker making certain I wash up my dishes at night." The thought made her want to sigh for the childhood that was gone, but she pushed the mood away. "I saw Amos Messner out in the field with his son haying." After finishing off the doughnut, Shane dusted her hands on the seat of her pants. "I thought Bob was in the army."

"Got discharged last week. He's going to marry a girl he met in North Carolina."

"No kidding?"

Donna smiled smugly. It always pleased her, as proprietor of the general store, to be the ears and eyes of the town. "She's coming to visit next month. She's a legal secretary."

"How old is she?" Shane demanded, testing.

"Twenty-two."

Throwing back her head, Shane laughed in delight. "Oh, Donna, you're terrific. I feel as though I've never been away."

The familiar unrestricted laugh made Donna grin. "I'm glad you're back. We missed you."

Shane settled a hip against the counter. "Where's Benji?"

"Dave's got him upstairs." Donna preened a bit, thinking of her husband and son. "Letting that little devil loose down here's only asking for trouble. We'll switch off after lunch."

"That's the beauty of living on top of your business."

Finding the opening she had hoped for, Donna pounced on it. "Shane, are you still thinking about converting the house?"

"Not thinking," Shane corrected. "I'm going to do it." She hurried on, knowing what was about to follow. "There's always room for another small antique shop, and with the museum attached, it'll be distinctive."

"But it's such a risk," Donna pointed out. The excited gleam in Shane's eyes had her worrying all the more. She'd seen the same gleam before the beginning of any number of outrageous and wonderful plots. "The expense—"

"I have enough to set things up." Shane shrugged off the pessimism. "And most of my stock can come straight out of the house for now. I want to do it, Donna," she went on as her friend frowned at her. "My own place, my own business." She glanced around the compact, well-stocked store. "You should know what I mean."

"Yes, but I have Dave to help out, to lean on. I don't think I could face starting or managing a business all on my own."

"It's going to work." Her eyes drifted beyond Donna, fixed on their own vision. "I can already see how it's going to look when I'm finished."

"All the remodeling."

"The basic structure of the house will stay the same," Shane countered. "Modifications, repairs." She brushed them away with the back of her hand. "A great deal of it would have to be done if I were simply going to live there."

"Licenses, permits."

"I've applied for everything."

"Taxes."

"I've already seen an accountant." She grinned as Donna sighed. "I have a good location, a solid knowledge of antiques, and I can recreate every battle of the Civil War."

"And do at the least provocation."

"Be careful," Shane warned her, "or I'll give you another rundown on the Battle of Antietam."

When the bells on the door jingled again, Donna heaved an exaggerated sigh of relief. "Hi, Stu."

The next ten minutes were spent in light gossiping as Donna rang up and bagged dry goods. It would take little time to catch up on the news Shane had missed over the last four years.

Shane was accepted as an oddity—the hometown girl who had gone to the city and come back with big ideas. She knew that to the older residents of the town and countryside she would always be Faye Abbott's granddaughter. They were a proprietary people, and she was one of their own. She hadn't settled down and married Cy Trainer's boy as predicted, but she was back now.

"Stu never changes," Donna said when she was alone with Shane again. "Remember in high school when we were sophomores and he was a senior, captain of the football team and the best-looking hunk in a sweaty jersey?"

"And nothing much upstairs," Shane added dryly.

"You always did go for the intellectual type. Hey," she continued before Shane could retort, "I might just have one for you."

"Have one what?"

"An intellectual. At least that's how he strikes me. He's your neighbor too," she added with a growing smile.

"*My* neighbor?"

"He bought the old Farley place. Moved in early last week."

"The Farley place?" Shane's brows arched, giving Donna the satisfaction of knowing she was announcing fresh news. "The house was all but gutted by the fire. Who'd be fool enough to buy that ramshackle barn of a place?"

"Vance Banning," Donna told her. "He's from Washington, D.C."

After considering the implications of this, Shane shrugged. "Well, I suppose it's a choice piece of land even if the house should be condemned." Wandering to a shelf, she selected a pound can of coffee then set it on the counter without checking the price. "I guess he bought it for a tax shelter or something."

"I don't think so." Donna rang up the coffee and waited while Shane dug bills out of her back pocket. "He's fixing it up."

"The courageous type." Absently, she pocketed the loose change.

"All by himself too," Donna added, fussing with the display of candy bars on the counter. "I don't think he has a lot of money to spare. No job."

"Oh." Shane's sympathies were immediately aroused. The spreading problem of unemployment could hit anyone, she knew. Just the year before, the teaching staff at her school had been cut by 3 percent.

"I heard he's pretty handy though," Donna went on. "Archie Moler went by there a few days ago to take him some lumber. He said he's already replaced the old porch. But the guy's got practically no furniture. Boxes of books, but not much else." Shane was already wondering what she could spare from her own collection.

She had a few extra chairs… "And," Donna added warmly, "he's wonderful to look at."

"You're a married woman," Shane reminded her, clucking her tongue.

"I still like to look. He's tall." Donna sighed. At five foot eight, she appreciated tall men. "And dark with a sort of lived-in face. You know, creases, lots of bone. And shoulders."

"You always did go for shoulders."

Donna only grinned. "He's a little lean for my taste, but the face makes up for it. He keeps to himself, hardly says a word."

"It's hard being a stranger." She spoke from her own experience. "And being out of work too. What do you think—"

Her question was cut off by the jingle of bells. Glancing over, Shane forgot what she had been about to ask.

He was tall, as Donna had said. In the few seconds they stared at each other, Shane absorbed every aspect of his physical appearance. Lean, yes, but his shoulders were broad, and the arms exposed by the rolled-up shirt sleeves were corded with muscle. His face was tanned, and it narrowed down to a trim, clipped jaw. Thick and straight, his black hair fell carelessly over a high forehead.

His mouth was beautiful. It was full and sharply sculpted, but she knew instinctively it could be cruel. And his eyes, a clear deep blue, were cool. She was certain they could turn to ice. She wouldn't have called it a lived-in face, but a remote one. There was an air of arrogant distance about him. Aloofness seemed to vie with an inner charge of energy.

The spontaneous physical pull was unexpected. In the past, Shane had been attracted to easygoing, good-natured men. This man was neither, she knew, but what she felt was undeniable. For a flash, all that was inside her leaned toward him in a knowledge that was as basic as chemistry and as insubstantial as dreams. Five seconds, it could have been no longer. It didn't need to be.

Shane smiled. He gave her the briefest of acknowledging nods, then walked to the back of the store.

"So, how soon do you think you'll have the place ready to open?" Donna asked Shane brightly with one eye trained toward the rear of the store.

"What?" Shane's mind was still on the man.

"Your place," Donna said meaningfully.

"Oh, three months, I suppose." She glanced blankly around the store as if she had just come in. "There's a lot of work to do."

He came back with a quart of milk and set it on the counter, then reached for his wallet. Donna rang it up, shooting Shane a look from under her lashes before she gave him his change. He left the store without having spoken a word.

"That," Donna announced grandly, "was Vance Banning."

"Yes." Shane exhaled. "So I gathered."

"You see what I mean. Great to look at, but not exactly the friendly sort."

"No." Shane walked toward the door. "I'll see you later, Donna."

"Shane!" With a half laugh, Donna called after her. "You forgot your coffee."

"Hmm? Oh, no thanks," she murmured absently. "I'll have a cup later."

When the door swung shut, Donna stared at it, then at the can of coffee in her hand. "Now what got into her?" she wondered aloud.

As she walked home, Shane felt confused. Though emotional by nature, she could, when necessary, be very analytical. At the moment, she was dealing with the shock of what had happened to her in a few fleeting seconds. It had been much more than a feminine response to an attractive man.

She had felt, inexplicably, as though her whole life had been a waiting period for that quick, silent meeting. Recognition. The word came to her out of nowhere. She had recognized him, not from Donna's description, but from some deep inner knowledge of her own needs. *This was the man.*

Ridiculous, she told herself. Idiotic. She didn't know him, hadn't even heard him speak. No sensible person felt so strongly about a total stranger. More likely, her response had stemmed from the fact that she and Donna had been speaking of him as he had walked in.

Turning off the main road, she began to climb the steep lane that led to her house. He certainly hadn't been friendly, she thought. He hadn't answered her smile or made the slightest attempt at common courtesy. Something in the cool blue eyes had demanded distance. Shane didn't think he was the kind of man she usually liked. Then again, her reaction had been far removed from the calm emotion of liking.

As always when she saw the house, Shane felt a rush

of pleasure. This was hers. The woods, thick and touched with the first breath of autumn; the narrow struggling creek; the rocks that worked their way through the ground everywhere—they were all hers.

Shane stood on the wooden bridge over the creek and looked at the house. It did need work. Some of the boards on the porch needed replacing, and the roof was a big problem. Still, it was a lovely little place, nestled comfortably before woods, rolling hills and distant blue mountains. It was more than a century old, fashioned from local stone. In the rain, the colors would burst out of the old rock and gleam like new. Now, in the sunlight, it was comfortably gray.

The architecture was simple—straight lines for durability rather than style. The walkway ran to the porch, where the first step sagged a bit. Shane's problem wouldn't be with the stone but with the wood. She overlooked the rough edges to take in the beauty of the familiar.

The last of the summer flowers were fading. The roses were brown and withered, while the first fall blooms were coming to life. Shane could hear the hiss of water traveling over rocks, the faint whisper of wind through leaves, and the lazy drone of bees.

Her grandmother had guarded her privacy. Shane could turn a full circle without seeing a sign of another house. She had only to walk a quarter mile if she wanted company, or stay at home if she didn't. After four years of crowded classrooms and daily confinement, Shane was ready for solitude.

And with luck, she thought as she continued walking, she could have her shop open and ready for business before Christmas. Antietam Antiques and Museum. Very dignified and to the point, she decided. Once the outside repairs were accomplished, work could start on the interior. The picture was clear in her mind.

The first floor would be structured in two informal sections. The museum would be free, an inducement to lure people into the antique shop. Shane had enough from her family collection to begin stocking the museum, and six rooms of antique furniture to sort and list. She would have to go to a few auctions and estate sales to increase her inventory, but she felt her inheritance and savings would hold her for a while.

The house and land were hers free and clear, with only the yearly taxes to pay. Her car, for what it was worth, was paid for. Every spare penny could go into her projected business. She was going to be successful and independent—and the last was more important than the first.

As she walked toward the house, Shane paused and glanced down the overgrown logging trail, which led to the Farley property. She was curious to see what this Vance Banning was doing with the old place. And, she admitted, she wanted to see him again when she was prepared.

After all, they were going to be neighbors, she told herself as she hesitated. The least she could do was to introduce herself and start things off on the right foot. Shane set off into the woods.

She knew the trees intimately. Since childhood she had raced or walked among them. Some had fallen and lay aging and rotting on the ground among layers of old leaves. Overhead, branches arched together to form an intermittent roof pierced by streams of morning sunlight. Confidently she followed the narrow, winding path. She was still yards from the house when she heard the muffled echo of hammering.

Though it disturbed the stillness of the woods, Shane liked the sound. It meant work and progress. Quickening her pace, she headed toward it.

She was still in the cover of the trees when she saw him. He stood on the newly built porch of the old Farley place, hammering the supports for the railing. He'd stripped off his shirt, and his brown skin glistened with a light film of sweat. The dark hair on his chest tapered down, then disappeared into the waistband of worn, snug jeans.

As he lifted the heavy top rail into place, the muscles of his back and shoulders rippled. Totally intent on his work, Vance was unaware of the woman who stood at the edge of the woods and watched. For all his physical exertion, he was relaxed. There was no hardness around his mouth now or frost in his eyes.

When she stepped into the clearing, Vance's head shot up. His eyes instantly filled with annoyance and suspicion. Overlooking it, Shane went to him.

"Hi." Her quick friendly smile had her dimples flashing. "I'm Shane Abbott. I own the house at the other end of the path."

His brow lifted in acknowledgment as he watched her. What the hell does she want? he wondered, and set his hammer on the rail.

Shane smiled again, then took a long, thorough look at the house. "You've got your work cut out for you," she commented amiably, sticking her hands into the back pockets of her jeans. "Such a big place. They say it was beautiful once. I think there used to be a balcony around the second story."

She glanced up. "It's a shame the fire did so much damage to the inside—and then all the years of neglect." She looked at him then with dark, interested eyes. "Are you a carpenter?"

Vance hesitated briefly, then shrugged. It was close to the truth. "Yes."

"That's handy then." Shane accepted the answer, attributing his hesitation to embarrassment at being out of work. "After D.C. you must find the mountains a change." His mobile brow lifted again and Shane grinned. "I'm sorry. It's the curse of small towns. Word gets around quickly, especially when a flatlander moves in."

"Flatlander?" Vance leaned against the post of the railing.

"You're from the city, so that's what you are." She laughed, a quick bubbling sound. "If you stay for twenty years, you'll still be a flatlander, and this will always be the old Farley place."

"It hardly matters what it's called," he said coldly.

The faintest of frowns shadowed her eyes at his response. Looking at the proud, set face, Shane decided he would never accept open charity. "I'm doing some work on my place too," she began. "My grandmother loved clutter. I don't suppose you could use a couple of chairs? I'm going to have to haul them up to the attic unless someone takes them off my hands."

His eyes stayed level on hers with no change of expression. "I have all I need for now."

Because it was the answer she had expected, Shane treated it lightly. "If you change your mind, they'll be gathering dust in the attic. You've got a good piece of land," she commented, gazing over at the section of pasture in the distance. There were several outbuildings, though most were in desperate need of repair. She wondered if he would see to them before winter set in. "Are you going to have livestock?"

Vance frowned, watching her eyes roam over his property. "Why?"

The question was cold and unfriendly. Shane tried to overlook that. "I can remember when I was a kid, before the fire. I used to lie in bed at night in the summer with the windows open. I could hear the Farley cows as clearly as if they were in my grandmother's garden. It was nice."

"I don't have any plans for livestock," he told her shortly, and picked up his hammer again. The gesture of dismissal was crystal clear.

Puzzled, Shane studied him. Not shy, she concluded. Rude. He was plainly and simply rude. "I'm sorry I disturbed your work," she said coolly. "Since you're a flatlander, I'll give you some advice. You should post your property lines if you don't want trespassers."

Indignantly, Shane strode back to the path to disappear among the trees.

Chapter 2

Little snit, Vance thought as he gently tapped the hammer against his palm. He knew he'd been rude, but felt no particular regret. He hadn't bought an isolated plot of land on the outskirts of a dot on the map because he wanted to entertain. Company he could do without, particularly the blond cheerleader type with big brown eyes and dimples.

What the hell had she been after? he wondered as he drew a nail from the pouch on his hip. A cozy chat? A tour of the house? He gave a quick, mirthless laugh. Very neighborly. Vance pounded the nail through the wood in three sure strokes. He didn't want neighbors. What he wanted, what he intended to have, was time to himself. It had been too may years since he had taken that luxury.

Drawing another nail out of the pouch, he moved down the rail. He set it, then hammered it swiftly into place. In particular, he hadn't cared for the one moment of attraction he had felt when he had seen her in the general store. Women, he thought grimly, had an uncanny habit of taking advantage of a weakness like that. He didn't intend for it to happen to him again. He had plenty of scars to remind him what went on behind big, guileless eyes.

So now I'm a carpenter, he mused. With a sardonic grin, Vance turned his hands palms up and examined them. They were hard and calloused. For too many years, he mused, they had been smooth, used to signing contracts or writing checks. Now for a time, he was back where he had started—with wood. Yes, until he was ready to sit behind a desk again, he was a carpenter.

The house, and the very fact that it was falling to pieces, gave him the sense of purpose that had slipped from him over the last couple of years. He understood pressure, success, duty, but the meaning of simple enjoyment had become lost somewhere beneath the rest.

Let the vice-president of Riverton Construction, Inc., run the show for a few months, he mused. He was on vacation. And let the little blonde with her puppy-dog eyes keep on her own land, he added, pounding in another nail. He didn't want any part of the good-neighbor policy.

When he heard leaves rustling underfoot, Vance turned. Seeing Shane striding back up the path, he muttered a long stream of curses in a low voice. With the exaggerated care of a man greatly aggravated, he set down his hammer.

"Well?" He aimed cold blue eyes and waited.

Shane didn't pause until she had reached the foot of the steps. She was through being intimidated. "I realize you're *extremely* busy," she began, matching his coolness ice for ice, "but I thought you might be interested in knowing there's a nest of copperheads very close to the footpath. On *your* edge of the property," she added.

Vance gave her a narrowed glance, weighing the possibility of her fabricating the snakes to annoy him. She didn't budge under the scrutiny, but paused just long enough to let the silence hang before she turned. She'd gone no more than two more yards when Vance let out an impatient breath and called her back.

"Just a minute. You'll have to show me."

"I don't *have* to do anything," Shane began, but found herself impotently talking to the swinging screen door. Briefly, she wished that she'd never seen the nest, or had simply ignored it and continued down the path to her own home. Then, of course, if he'd been bitten, she would have blamed herself.

Well, you'll do your good deed, she told herself, and that will be that. She kicked a rock with the toe of her shoe and thought how simple it would have been if she'd stayed home that morning.

The screen door shut with a bang. Looking up, Shane watched Vance come down the steps with a well-oiled rifle in his hands. The sleek, elegant weapon suited him. "Let's go," he said shortly, starting off without her. Gritting her teeth, Shane followed.

The light dappled over them once they moved under

the cover of trees. The scent of earth and sun-warmed leaves warred with the gun oil. Without a word, Shane skirted around him to take the lead. Pausing, she pointed to a pile of rocks and brown, dried leaves.

"There."

After taking a step closer, Vance spotted the hour-glass-shaped crossbands on the snakes. If she hadn't shown him the exact spot, he never would have noticed the nest…unless, of course, he'd stepped right on it. An unpleasant thought, he mused, calculating its proximity to the footpath. Shane said nothing, watching as he found a thick stick and overturned the rocks. Immediately the hissing sounded.

With her eyes trained on the angry snakes, she didn't see Vance heft the rifle to his shoulder. The first shot jolted her. Her heart hammered during the ensuing four, her eyes riveted to the scene.

"That should do it," Vance muttered, lowering the gun. After switching on the safety, he turned to Shane. She'd turned a light shade of green. "What's the matter?"

"You might have warned me," she said shakily. "I wish I'd looked away."

Vance glanced back to the gruesome mess on the side of the path. That, he told himself grimly, had been incredibly stupid. Silently, he cursed her, then himself, before he took her arm.

"Come back and sit down."

"I'll be all right in a minute." Embarrassed and annoyed, Shane tried to pull away. "I don't want your gracious hospitality."

"I don't want you fainting on my lane," he returned,

drawing her into the clearing. “You didn’t have to stay once you’d shown me the nest.”

“Oh, you’re very welcome,” she managed as she placed a hand on her rolling stomach. “You are the most ill-mannered, unfriendly man I’ve ever met.”

“And I thought I was on my best behavior,” he murmured, opening the screen door. After pulling Shane inside, Vance led her through the huge empty room toward the kitchen.

After a glance at the dingy walls and uncovered floor, Shane sent him what passed as a smile. “You must give me the name of your decorator.”

She thought he laughed, but could have been mistaken.

The kitchen, in direct contrast to the rest of the house, was bright and clean. The walls had been papered, the counters and cabinets refinished.

“Well, this is nice,” she said as he nudged her into a chair. “You do good work.”

Without responding, Vance set a kettle on the stove. “I’ll fix you some coffee.”

“Thank you.”

Shane concentrated on the kitchen, determined to forget what she’d just seen. The windows had been reframed, the wood stained and lacquered to match the grooved trim along the floor and ceiling. He had left the beams exposed and polished the wood to a dull gleam. The original oak floor had been sanded and sealed and waxed. Vance Banning knew how to use wood, Shane decided. The porch was basic mechanics, but the kitchen showed a sense of style and an appreciation for fine detail.

It seemed unfair to her that a man with such talent

should be out of work. Shane concluded that he had used his savings to put a down payment on the property. Even if the house had sold cheaply, the land was prime. Remembering the barrenness of the rest of the first floor, she couldn't prevent her sympathies from being aroused again. Her eyes wandered to his.

"This really is a lovely room," she said, smiling. The faintest hint of color had seeped back into her cheeks. Vance turned his back to her to take a mug from a hook.

"You'll have to settle for instant," he told her.

Shane sighed. "Mr. Banning… Vance," she decided, and waited for him to turn. "Maybe we got off on the wrong foot. I'm not a nosy, prying neighbor—at least not obnoxiously so. I was curious to see what you were doing to the house and what you were like. I know everyone within three miles of here." With a shrug, she rose. "I didn't mean to bother you."

As she started to brush by him, Vance took her arm. Her skin was still chilled. "Sit down…Shane," he said.

For a moment, she studied his face. It was cool and unyielding, but she sensed some glimmer of suppressed kindness. In response to it, her eyes warmed. "I disguise my coffee with milk and sugar," she warned. "Three spoonsful."

A reluctant smile tugged at his mouth. "That's disgusting."

"Yes, I know. Do you have any?"

"On the counter."

Vance poured the boiling water, and after a moment's hesitation, took down a second mug for himself. Carrying them both, he joined Shane at the drop-leaf table.

"This really is a lovely piece." Before reaching for the milk, she ran her fingers over the table's surface. "Once it's refinished, you'll have a real gem." Shane added three generous spoons of sugar to her mug. Wincing a little, Vance sipped his own black coffee. "Do you know anything about antiques?"

"Not really."

"They're a passion of mine. In fact, I'm planning on opening a shop." Shane brushed absently at the hair that fell over her forehead, then leaned back. "As it turns out, we're both settling in at the same time. I've been living in Baltimore for the last four years, teaching U.S. history."

"You're giving up teaching?" Her hands, Vance noted, were small like the rest of her. The light trail of blue veins under the pale skin made her seem very delicate. Her wrists were narrow, her fingers slender.

"Too many rules and regulations," Shane claimed, gesturing with the hands that had captured his attention.

"You don't like rules and regulations?"

"Only when they're mine." Laughing, she shook her head. "I was a pretty good teacher, really; my problem was discipline." She gave him a rueful grin as she reached for her coffee. "I'm the worst disciplinarian on record."

"And your students took advantage of that?"

Shane rolled her eyes. "Whenever possible."

"But you stuck with it for four years?"

"I had to give it my best shot." Leaning her elbow on the table, Shane rested her chin on her palm. "Like a lot of people who grow up in a small, rural town, I thought the city was my pot of gold. Bright lights, crowds, hustle-bustle. I wanted excitement with a capital E. I had four years of it; that was enough." She picked up her coffee again. "Then there are people from the city who think their answer is to move to the country and raise a few goats and can some tomatoes." She laughed into her cup. "The grass is always greener."

"I've heard it said," he murmured, watching her. There were tiny gold flecks in her eyes. How had he missed them before?

"Why did you choose Sharpsburg?"

Vance shrugged negligently. Questions about himself were to be evaded. "I've done some work in Hagerstown. I like the area."

"Living this far back from the main road can be inconvenient, especially in the winter, but I've never minded being snowed in. We lost power once for thirty-two hours. Gran and I kept the wood-stove going, taking shifts, and we cooked soup on top of it. The phone lines were down too. We might have been the only two people in the world."

"You enjoyed that?"

"For thirty-two hours," she told him with a friendly grin. "I'm not a hermit. Some people are city people, some are beach people."

"And you're a mountain person."

Shane brought her eyes back to him. "Yes."

The smile she had started to give him never formed. Something in the meeting of their eyes was reminiscent of the moment in the store. It was only an echo, but somehow more disturbing. Shane understood it was bound to happen again and again. She needed time to decide just what she was going to do about it. Rising, she walked to the sink to rinse out her mug.

Intrigued by her reaction, Vance decided to test her. "You're a very attractive woman." He knew how to make his voice softly flattering.

Laughing, Shane turned back to him. "The perfect face for advertising granola bars, right?" Her smile was devilish and appealing. "I'd rather be sexy, but I settled for wholesome." She gave the word a pained emphasis as she came back to the table.

There was no guile in her manner or her expression. What, Vance wondered again, was her angle? Shane was involved in studying the details of the kitchen and didn't see him frown at her.

"I do admire your work." Inspired, she turned back to him. "Hey listen, I've got a lot of remodeling and renovating to do before I can open. I can paint and do some of the minor stuff myself, but there's a lot of carpentry work."

Here it is, Vance reflected coolly. What she wanted was some free labor. She would pull the helpless-female routine and count on his ego to take over.

"I have my own house to renovate," he reminded her coolly as he stood and turned toward the sink.

"Oh, I know you wouldn't be able to give me a lot of time, but we might be able to work something out." Excited by the idea, she followed him. Her thoughts were already racing ahead. "I wouldn't be able to pay what you could make in the city," she continued. "Maybe five dollars an hour. If you could manage ten or fifteen hours a week…" She chewed on her bottom lip. It seemed a paltry amount to offer, but it was all she could spare at the moment.

Incredulous, Vance turned off the water he had been running, then faced her. "Are you offering me a job?"

Shane flushed a bit, afraid she'd embarrassed him. "Well, only part-time, if you're interested. I know you can make more somewhere else, and if you find something, I wouldn't expect you to keep on, but in the meantime…" She trailed off, not certain how he would react to her knowing he was out of work.

"You're serious?" Vance demanded after a moment.

"Well…yes."

"Why?"

"I need a carpenter; you're a carpenter. There's a lot of work. You might decide you don't want any part of it. But why don't you think about it, drop by tomorrow and take a look?" She turned to leave, but paused for an instant with her hand on the knob. "Thanks for the coffee."

For several minutes, Vance stared at the door she had closed behind her. Abruptly, he burst into deep, appreciative laughter. This, he thought, was one for the books.

Shane rose early the next morning. She had plans and was determined to begin systematically. Organization didn't come naturally to her. It was one more reason why teaching hadn't suited her. If she was to plan a business, however, Shane knew an inventory was a primary factor—what she had, what she could bear to sell, what she should pack away for the museum.

Having decided to start downstairs and work her way up, Shane stood in the center of the living room and took stock of the situation. There was a good Chippendale fireplace seat in mahogany and a gateleg table that needed no refinishing, a ladderback chair that needed new caning in the seat, a pair of Aladdin lamps, and a tufted sofa that would require upholstering. On a Sheridan coffee table was a porcelain pitcher, circa 1830, that held a spray of flowers Shane's grandmother had dried. She touched them once briefly before she picked up her clipboard. There was too much of her childhood there to allow herself the luxury of thinking of any of it. If her grandmother had been alive, she would have told Shane to be certain what she did was right, then do it. Shane was certain she was right.

Systematically, she listed items in two columns: one for items that would need repairs; one for stock she could sell as it was. Everything would have to be priced, which would be a huge job in itself. Already she was spending her evenings poring through catalogs and making notations. There wasn't an antique shop within a radius of thirty miles she hadn't visited. Shane had taken careful account of pricing and procedure. She would incorporate what appealed to her and disregard what didn't. Whatever else her shop would be, she was determined it would be her own.

On one wall of the living room was a catchall shelf that had been built before she'd been born. Moving to it, Shane began a fresh sheet of items she designated for the museum.

An ancestor's Civil War cap and belt buckle, a glass jar filled with spent shells, a dented bugle, a cavalry officer's sabre, a canteen with the initials JDA scratched into the metal—these were only a few pieces of the memorabilia that had been passed down to her. Shane knew there was a trunk in the attic filled with uniforms and old dresses. There was a scrawled journal that had been kept by one of her great-great-uncles during the three years he fought for the South, and letters written to an ancestral aunt by her father, who had served the North. Every item would be listed, dated, then put behind glass.

Shane might have inherited her grandmother's fascination for the relics of history, but not her casualness. It was time the old photos and objects came down from the shelf. But as always when she examined or handled the pieces, Shane became caught up in them.

What had the man been like who had first blown that bugle? It would have been shiny then, and undented. A boy, she thought, with peach fuzz on his face. Had he been frightened? Exhilarated? Fresh off the farm, she imagined, and sure his cause was the right one. Whichever side he had fought for, he had blown the bugle into battle.

With a sigh, she took it down and set it in a packing box. Carefully, Shane wrapped and packed until the shelves were clear, but for the highest one. Standing back, she calculated how she would reach the pieces that sat several feet above her head. Not bothering to move the heavy ladder from across the room, she dragged over a nearby chair. As she stood on the seat, a knock sounded at the back door.

"Yes, come in," she called, stretching one arm up while balancing herself with a hand on one of the lower shelves. She swore and muttered as her reach still fell short. Just as she stood on tiptoe, teetering, someone grabbed her arm. Gasping as she overbalanced, Shane found herself gripped firmly by Vance Banning. "You scared me to death!" she accused.

"Don't you know better than to use a chair like that?" He kept his hands firmly at her waist as he lifted her down. Then, though he'd had every intention of doing so, he didn't release her. There was a smudge of dust on her cheek, and her hair was tousled. Her small, narrow hands rested on his arms while she smiled up at him. Without thinking, Vance lowered his mouth to hers.

Shane didn't struggle, but felt a jolt of surprise. Then she relaxed. Though she hadn't expected the kiss then, she had known the time would come. She let the first stream of pure pleasure run its course.

His mouth was hard on hers, with no gentleness, no trace of what kissing meant to her—a gesture of affection, love or comfort. Yet instinct told her he was capable of tenderness. Lifting a hand to his cheek, Shane sought to soothe the turbulence she sensed. Immediately, he released her. The touch of her hand had been too intimate.

Something told Shane to treat it lightly no matter how her body ached to be held again. Tilting her head, she gave him a mischievous smile. "Good morning."

"Good morning," he said carefully.

"I'm taking inventory," she told him with a sweeping gesture of the room. "I want to list everything before I haul it upstairs for storage. I plan to use this room for the museum and the rest of the first floor for the shop. Could you get those things off the top shelf for me?" she asked, looking around for her clipboard.

In silence, Vance moved the ladder and complied. The fact that she'd made no mention of the turbulent kiss disconcerted him.

"Most of the work will be gutting the kitchen and

putting one in upstairs," Shane went on, giving her lists another glance. She knew Vance was watching her for some sort of reaction. She was just as determined to give him none. "Of course, some walls will have to be taken out, doorways widened. But I don't want to lose the flavor of the house in the remodeling."

"You seem to have it all plotted out." Was she really so cool? he wondered.

"I hope so." Shane pressed the clipboard to her breasts as she looked around the room. "I've applied for all the necessary permits. What a headache. I don't have any natural business sense, so I'll have to work twice as hard learning. It's a big chance." Then her voice changed, became firm and determined. "I'm going to make it work."

"When do you plan to open?"

"I'm shooting for the first part of December, but…" Shane shrugged. "It depends on how the work goes and how soon I can beef up my inventory. I'll show you the rest of the place; then you can decide if you want to take it on."

Without waiting for his consent, Shane walked to the rear of the house. "The kitchen's a fairly good size, particularly if you include the pantry." Opening a door, she revealed a large shelved closet. "Taking out the counters and appliances should give me plenty of room. Then if this doorway is widened," she continued as she pushed open a swinging door, "and left as an archway, it would give more space in the main showroom."

They entered the dining room with its long diamond-paned windows. She moved quickly, he noted, and knew precisely what she wanted.

"The fireplace hasn't been used in years. I don't know whether it still works." Walking over, Shane ran a finger down the surface of the dining table. "This was my grandmother's prize. It was brought over from England more than a hundred years ago." The cherrywood stroked by sunlight, gleamed under her fingers. "The chairs are from the original set. Hepplewhite." Shane caressed the heart-shaped back of one of the remaining six chairs. "I hate to sell this, she loved it so, but..." Her voice was wistful as she unnecessarily straightened a chair. "I won't have anywhere to keep it, and I can't afford the luxury of storing it for myself." Shane turned away. "The china cabinet is from the same period," she continued.

"You could keep this and leave the house as it is if you took a job in the local high school," Vance interrupted. There was something valiant and touching in the way she kept her shoulders straight while her voice trembled.

"No." Shane shook her head, then turned back to him. "I haven't the character for it. It wouldn't take long before I'd be cutting classes just like my students. They deserve a better example than that. I love history." Her face brightened again. "*This* kind of history," she said as she walked back to the table. "Who first sat in this chair? What did she talk about over dinner? What kind of dress did she wear? Did they discuss politics and the upstart colonies? Maybe one of them knew Ben Franklin and was a secret sympathizer of the Revolution." She broke off laughing. "That's not the sort of thing you're supposed to teach in second-period eleventh-grade history."

"It sounds more interesting than reciting names and dates."

"Maybe. Anyway, I'm not going back to that." Pausing, Shane watched Vance steadily. "Did you ever find yourself caught up in something you were good at, something you'd been certain was the right thing for you, then woke up one morning with the feeling you were locked in a cage?"

The words hit home, and he nodded affirmatively.

"Then you know why I have to choose between something I love and my sanity." She touched the table again. After a deep breath, Shane took a circle around the room. "I don't want to change the architecture of this room except for the doorways. My great-grandfather built the chair rail." She watched Vance walk over to examine it. "He was a mason by trade," she told him, "but he must have been handy with wood as well."

"It's a beautiful job," Vance agreed, admiring the workmanship and detail. "I'd have a hard time duplicating this quality with modern tools. You wouldn't want to touch this, or any of the woodwork in this room."

In spite of himself he was becoming interested in the project. It would be a challenge—a different sort than the house he had chosen to test himself on. Sensing his change of attitude, Shane pressed her advantage.

"There's a small summer parlor through there." Indicating another door, she took Vance's arm to draw him with her. "It adjoins the living room, so I plan to make it the entrance to the shop, with the dining room as the main showroom."

The parlor was no more than twelve by twelve with

faded wallpaper and a scarred wooden floor. Still, Vance recognized a few good pieces of Duncan Phyfe and a Morris chair. On the brief tour, he had seen no furniture less than a hundred years old, and unless they were excellent copies, a few pieces of Wedgwood. The furniture's worth a small fortune, he mused, and the back door's coming off the hinges.

"There's a lot of work here," Shane commented, moving over to open a window and dispel the faint mustiness. "This room's taken a beating over the years. I suppose you'd have a better idea than I would exactly what it needs to whip it into shape."

She watched his frowning survey of chipped floorboards and cracked trim. It was obvious to her that his professional eye missed little. It was also obvious the state of disrepair annoyed him. And, she thought, faintly amused, he hadn't seen anything yet.

"Maybe I shouldn't press my luck and take you upstairs just yet," she commented.

A quizzical brow shot up as he turned to her. "Why?"

"Because the second floor needs twice the attention this does, and I really want you to take the job."

"You sure as hell need somebody to do it," he muttered. His own place needed a major overhaul. Heavy physical work and a lot of time. This, on the other hand, needed a shrewd craftsman who could work with what was already there. Again, he felt the pull of the challenge.

"Vance..." After a moment's hesitation, Shane decided to take a chance. "I could make it six dollars an hour, throw in your lunches and all the coffee you can drink. The people who come in here will see the quality of your work. It could lead to bigger jobs."

He surprised her by grinning. Her heart leaped into her throat. More than the tempestuous kiss, the quick boyish grin drew her to him.

"All right, Shane," Vance agreed on impulse. "You've got a deal."

Chapter 3

Pleased with herself and Vance's abrupt good humor, Shane decided to show him the second floor. Taking his hand, she led him up the straight, steep stairway. Though she had no notion of what had prompted the amused gleam or sudden grin, Shane wanted to keep him with her while his mood lasted.

Against his work-hardened hand, her palm was baby soft. It made Vance wonder how the rest of her would feel—the slope of her shoulder, the length of her thigh, the underside of her breast. She wasn't his type, he reminded himself, and glanced at the hairline crack in the wall to his left.

"There are three bedrooms," Shane told him as they came to the top landing. "I want to keep my own room, and turn the master into a sitting room and the third into my kitchen. I can handle the painting and papering after the initial work is done." With her hand on the knob of the master bedroom door, she turned to him. "Do you know anything about drywall?"

"A bit." Without thinking, Vance lifted a finger and ran it down her nose. Their eyes met in mutual surprise. "You've dust on your face," he mumbled.

"Oh." Laughing, Shane brushed at it herself.

"Here." Vance traced the rough skin of his thumb down her cheekbone. Her skin felt as it looked: soft, creamy. It would taste the same, he mused, allowing his thumb to linger. "And here," he said, caught up in his own imagination. Lightly he ran a fingertip along her jawline. He felt her slight tremor as his gaze swept over her lips.

Her eyes were wide and fixed unblinkingly on his. Abruptly, Vance dropped his hand, shattering the mood but not the tension. Clearing her throat, Shane pushed open the door.

"This—umm..." Frantically, Shane gathered her scattered thoughts. "This is the master," she continued, combing nervous fingers through her hair. "I know the floor's in bad shape, and I'd like to skin whoever painted that oak trim." She let out a long breath as her pulse began to level. "I'm going to see if it can be refinished." Idly, she touched a section of peeling wallpaper. "My grandmother didn't like changes. This room hasn't altered one bit in thirty years. That's when her husband died," she added softly. "The windows stick, the roof leeks, the fireplace smokes. Basically, the house, except for the dining room, is in a general state of disrepair. She never had the inclination to do more than a patch job here and there."

"When did she die?"

"Three months ago." Shane lifted a corner of the patchwork coverlet, then let it fall. "She just didn't wake up one morning. I was committed to teaching a summer course and couldn't move back permanently until last week."

Clearly, he heard the sting of guilt in her words. "Could you have changed anything if you had?" he asked.

"No." Shane wandered to a window. "But she wouldn't have died alone."

Vance opened his mouth, then closed it again. It wasn't wise to offer personal advice to strangers. Framed against the window, she looked very small and defenseless.

"What about the walls in here?" he asked.

"What?" Years and miles away, Shane turned back to him.

"The walls," he repeated. "Do you want any of them taken down?"

For a moment, she stared blankly at the faded roses on the wallpaper. "No…No," she repeated more firmly. "I'd thought to take out the door and enlarge the entrance." Vance nodded, noting she had won what must be a continuing battle with her emotions. "If the woodwork cleans off well," she continued, "the entrance could be framed in oak to match."

Vance walked over to examine it. "Is this a bearing wall?"

Shane made a face at him. "I haven't the slightest idea. How do—" She broke off, hearing a knock at the front door. "Damn. Well, can you look around up here for a few minutes? You'll probably get the lay of things just as well without me." With this, Shane was dashing down the steps. Shrugging, Vance took a rule out of his back pocket and began to take measurements.

Shane's instinctively friendly smile faded instantly when she opened the door.

"Shane."

"Cy."

His expression became faintly censorious. "Aren't you going to ask me in?"

"Of course." With a restraint unnatural to her, Shane stepped back. Very carefully, she shut the door behind him, but moved no farther into the room. "How are you, Cy?"

"Fine, just fine."

Of course he was, Shane thought, annoyed. Cy Trainer, Jr., was always fine—permanent-pressed and groomed. And prosperous now, she added, giving his smart-but-discreet suit a glance.

"And you, Shane?"

"Fine, just fine," she said, knowing the sarcasm was both petty and wasted. He'd never notice.

"I'm sorry I didn't get by last week; things have been hectic."

"Business is good?" she asked without any intonation of interest. He failed to notice that too.

"Money's loosening up." He straightened his tie unnecessarily. "People are buying houses. Country property's always good investment." He gave her a quick nod. "The real estate business is solid."

Money was still first, Shane noticed with irony. "And your father?"

"Doing well. Semiretired now, you know."

"No," she said mildly. "I didn't." If Cy Trainer, Sr., relinquished the reins to Trainer Real Estate six months after he was dead, it would have surprised Shane. The old man would always run the show, no matter what his son liked to think.

"He likes to keep busy," Cy told her. "He'd love to see you though. You'll have to drop by the office." Shane said nothing to that. "So…" Cy paused as he was wont to do before a big statement. "You're settling in."

Shane lifted a brow as she watched him glance around at her packing cases. "Slowly," she agreed. Though she knew it was deliberately rude, she didn't ask him to sit. They remained standing, just inside the door.

"You know, Shane, this house isn't in the best of shape, but it is a prime location." He gave her a light, condescending smile that set her teeth on edge. "I'm sure I could get you a good price for it."

"I'm not interested in selling, Cy. Is that why you came by? To do an appraisal?"

He looked suitably shocked. "Shane!"

"Was there something else?" she asked evenly.

"I just dropped by to see how you were." The distress in both his voice and eyes had an apology forming on her lips. "I heard some crazy story about your trying to start an antique shop."

The apology slipped away. "It's not a story, crazy or otherwise, Cy. I am going to start one."

He sighed and gave her what she termed his paternal look. She gritted her teeth. "Shane, have you any idea how difficult, how risky it is to start a business in today's economy?"

"I'm sure you'll tell me," she muttered.

"My dear," he said in calm tones, making her blood pressure rise alarmingly. "You're a certified teacher with four years' experience. It's just nonsense to toss away a good career for a fanciful little fling."

"I've always been good at nonsense, haven't I, Cy?" Her eyes chilled. "You never hesitated to point it out to me even when we were supposed to be madly in love."

"Now, Shane, it was because I cared that I tried to curb your…impulses."

"Curb my impulses!" More astonished than angry, Shane ran her fingers through her hair. Later, she told herself, later she would be able to laugh. Now she wanted to scream. "You haven't changed. You haven't changed a whit. I bet you still roll your socks into those neat little balls and carry an extra handkerchief."

He stiffened a bit. "If you'd ever learned the value of practicality—" he began.

"You wouldn't have dumped me two months before the wedding?" she finished furiously.

"Really, Shane, you can hardly call it that. You know I was only thinking of what was best for you."

"Best for me," she muttered between clenched teeth. "Well, let me tell you something." She poked a dusty finger at his muted striped tie. "You can stuff your practicality, Cy, right along with your balanced checkbook and shoe trees. I might have thought you hurt me at the time, but you did me a big favor. I *hate* practicality and rooms that smell like pine and toothpaste tubes that are rolled up from the bottom."

"I hardly see what that has to do with this discussion."

"It has *everything* to do with this discussion," she flared back. "You don't see anything unless it's listed in neat columns and balanced. And I'll tell you something else," she continued when he would have spoken. "I'm going to have my shop, and even if it doesn't make me a fortune, it's going to be fun."

"Fun?" Cy shook his head hopelessly. "That's a poor basis for starting a business."

"It's mine," she retorted. "I don't need a six-digit income to be happy."

He gave her a small, deprecating smile. "You haven't changed."

Flinging open the door, Shane glared at him. "Go sell a house," she suggested. With a dignity she envied and despised, Cy walked through the door. She slammed it after him, then gave in to temper and slammed her hand against the wall.

"Damn!" Putting her wounded knuckles to her mouth, she whirled. It was then she spotted Vance at the foot of the stairs. His face was still and serious as their eyes met. With angry embarrassment, Shane's cheeks flamed. "Enjoy the show?" she demanded, then stormed back to the kitchen.

She gave vent to her frustration by banging through the cupboards. She didn't hear Vance follow her. When he touched her shoulder, she spun around, ready to rage.

"Let me see your hand," he said quietly. Ignoring her jerk of protest, he took it in both of his.

"It's nothing."

Gently, he flexed it, then pressed down on her knuckles with his fingers. Involuntarily, she caught her breath at the quick pain. "You didn't manage to break it," he murmured, "but you'll have a bruise." He was forced to control a sudden rage that she had damaged that small, soft hand.

"Just don't say anything," she ordered through gritted teeth. "I'm not stupid. I *know* when I've made a fool of myself."

He took a moment to bend and straighten her fingers again. "I apologize," he said. "I should have let you know I was there."

After letting out a deep breath, Shane drew her hand from his slackened hold. The light throbbing gave her a perverse pleasure. "It doesn't matter," she muttered as she turned to make tea.

He frowned at her averted face. "I don't enjoy embarrassing you."

"If you live here for any amount of time, you'll hear about Cy and me anyway." She tried to make a casual shrug, but the quick jerkiness of the movement showed only more agitation. "This way you just got the picture quicker."

But he didn't have the full picture. Vance realized, with some discomfort, that he wanted to know. Before he could speak, Shane slammed the lid onto the kettle.

"He always makes me feel like a fool!"

"Why?"

"He always dots his *i*'s and crosses his *t*'s." With an angry tug, she pulled open a cabinet. "He carries an umbrella in the trunk of his car," she said wrathfully.

"That should do it," Vance murmured, watching her quick, jerky movements.

"He never, never, *never* makes a mistake. He's always reasonable," she added witheringly as she slammed two cups down on the counter. "Did he shout at me just now?" she demanded as she whirled on Vance. "Did he swear or lose his temper? He doesn't *have* a temper!" she shouted in frustration. "I swear, the man doesn't even sweat."

"Did you love him?"

For a moment, Shane merely stared; then she let out a small broken sigh. "Yes. Yes, I really did. I was sixteen when we started dating." As she went to the refrigerator, Vance turned the gas on under the kettle, which she had forgotten to do. "He was so perfect, so smart and, oh…so articulate." Pulling out the milk, Shane smiled a little. "Cy's a born salesman; he can talk about anything."

Vance felt a quick, unreasonable dislike for him. As Shane set a large ceramic sugar bowl on the table, sunlight shot into her hair. The curls and waves of her hair shimmered briefly in the brilliance before she moved away. With an odd tingling at the base of his spine, Vance found himself staring after her.

"I was crazy about him," Shane continued, and Vance had to shake himself mentally to concentrate on her words. The subtle movements of her body beneath the snug T-shirt had begun to distract him. "When I turned eighteen, he asked me to marry him. We were both going to college, and Cy thought a year's engagement was proper. He's very proper," she added ruefully.

Or a cold-blooded fool, Vance thought, glancing at the faint outline of her nipples against the thin cotton.

Annoyed, he brought his eyes back to her face. But the warmth in his own blood remained.

"I wanted to get married right away, but he told me, as always, that I was too impulsive. Marriage was a big step; things had to be planned out. When I suggested we live together for a while, he was shocked." Shane set the milk on the table with a little bang. "I was young and in love, and I wanted him. He felt it his duty to control my more…primitive urges."

"He's a damn fool," Vance muttered under the hissing of the kettle.

"Through that last year, he molded me, and I tried to be what he wanted: dignified, sensible. I was a complete failure." Shane shook her head at the memory of that long, frustrating year. "If I wanted to go out for pizza with a bunch of other students, he'd remind me we had to watch our pennies. He already had his eye on this little house outside of Boonsboro. His father said it was a good investment."

"And you hated it," Vance commented.

Surprised, Shane looked back at him. "I despised it. It was the perfect little rancher with white aluminum siding and a hedge. When I told Cy I'd smother there, he laughed and patted my head."

"Why didn't you tell him to get lost?" he demanded.

Shane shot him a brief look. "Haven't you ever been in love?" she murmured. It was her answer, not a question, and Vance remained silent. "We were constantly at odds that year," she went on. "I kept thinking it was just the jitters of a long engagement, but more and more, the basic personality conflicts came up. He'd always say I'd feel differently once we were settled. Usually, I'd believe him."

"He sounds like a boring jackass."

Though the icy contempt in Vance's voice surprised her, Shane smiled. "Maybe, but he could be gentle and sweet." When Vance gave a derisive snort, she only shrugged. "I'd forget how rigid he was; then he'd get more critical. I'd get angry, but I could never win a fight because he never lost control. The final break came over the plans for the honeymoon. I wanted to go to Fiji."

"Fiji?" Vance repeated.

"Yes," she said defiantly. "It's different, exotic, romantic. I was barely nineteen." On a fresh wave of fury, Shane slammed down her spoon. "He had plans for this—this plastic little resort hotel in Pennsylvania. The kind of place where they plan your activities, have contests and an indoor pool. Shuffleboard." She rolled her eyes before she gulped down tea. "It was a package deal—three days, two nights, meals included. He'd inherited a substantial sum from his mother, and I had some savings, but he didn't want to waste money. He'd already outlined a retirement plan. I couldn't stand it!"

Vance sipped his own tea where he stood and studied her. "So you called off the wedding." He wondered if she would take the opportunity he was giving her to claim the break had been her idea.

"No." Shane pushed her cup aside. "We had a terrible fight, and I stormed off to spend the rest of the evening with friends at this little club near the college. I had told Cy I wouldn't spend my first night as a married woman watching a tacky floor show or playing bingo."

Vance's lips twitched but he managed to control his grin. "That sounds remarkably sensible," he murmured.

On a weak laugh, Shane shook her head. "After I'd calmed down, I decided where we went wasn't important, but that we'd finally be together. I told myself Cy was right. I was immature and irresponsible. We needed to save money. I still had two more years of college and he was just starting in his father's firm. I was being frivolous. That was one of his favorite adjectives for me."

Shane frowned down at her cup but didn't drink. "I went by his house ready to apologize. That's when he very reasonably, very calmly jilted me."

There was a long moment of silence before Vance came to the table to join her. "I thought you told me he never made mistakes."

Shane stared at him a moment, then laughed. It was a quick, pure sound of appreciation. "I needed that." Impulsively, she leaned her head against his shoulder. The anger had vanished in the telling, the self-pity with the laugh.

The tenderness that invaded him made Vance cautious. Still, he didn't resist the urge to stroke his hand down her disordered cap of hair. The texture of her hair was thick and unruly. And incredibly soft. He wasn't even aware that he twisted a curl around his finger.

"Do you still love him?" he heard himself ask.

"No," Shane answered before he could retract the question. "But he still makes me feel like an irresponsible romantic."

"Are you?"

She shrugged. "Most of the time."

"What you said to him out there was right, you

know." Forgetting caution in simple wanting, he drew her closer.

"I said a lot of things."

"That he'd done you a favor," Vance murmured as his fingers roamed to the back of her neck. Shane sighed, but he couldn't tell if the sound came from pleasure or agreement. "You'd have gone crazy rolling up his socks in those little balls."

Shane was laughing as she tilted her head back to look at his face. She kissed him lightly in gratitude, then again for herself.

Her mouth was small and very tempting. Wanting his fill, Vance cupped his hand firmly on the back of her neck to keep her there. There was nothing shy or hesitant in her response to the increased pressure. She parted her lips and invited.

On a tiny moan of pleasure, her tongue met his. Suddenly hot, suddenly urgent, his mouth moved over hers. He needed her sweetness, her uncomplicated generosity. He wanted to saturate himself with the fresh, clean passion she offered so willingly. When his mouth crushed down harder, she only yielded; when his teeth nipped painfully at her lip, she only drew him closer.

"Vance," she murmured, leaning toward him.

He rose quickly, leaving her blinking in surprise. "I've got work to do," he said shortly. "I'll make a list of the materials I'll need to start. I'll be in touch." He was out the back door before Shane could form any response.

For several moments, she stared at the screen door. What had she done to cause that anger in his eyes? How was it possible that he could passionately kiss her one second and turn his back on her the next? Miserably, she looked down at her clenched hands. She had always made too much of things, she reminded herself. A romantic? Yes, and a dreamer, her grandmother had called her. For too long she'd been waiting for the right man to come into her life, to complete it. She wanted to be cherished, respected, adored.

Perhaps, she mused, she was looking for the impossible—to keep her independence and to share her dreams, to stand on her own and have a strong hand to hold. Over and over she had warned herself to stop looking for that one perfect love. But her spirit defied her mind.

From the first instant, she had sensed something different about Vance. For the flash of a second when their eyes had first held, her heart had opened and shouted. *Here he is!* But that was nonsense, Shane reminded herself. Love meant understanding, knowledge. She neither knew nor understood Vance Banning.

With a jolt, she realized she might have offended him. She was going to be his employer, and the way she had kissed him…he might think she wanted more than carpentry for her money. He might think she intended to seduce him while dangling a few much-needed dollars under his nose.

Abruptly, she burst into laughter. As her mirth grew, she threw back her head and pounded both fists on the table. Shane Abbott, seductress. Oh Lord! she thought, wiping tears of hilarity from her eyes. That was rich. After all, what red-blooded man could withstand a woman with dirt on her face who tries to punch holes in walls?

She sighed with the effort of laughing. Her imagination, she decided, needed a rest. Shane went back to her inventory.

Chapter 4

Vance couldn't sleep. He had worked until late in the evening, sweating off anger and frustrated desire. The anger didn't worry him. He knew that emotion too well to lose sleep over it. Neither was he a stranger to desire, but having to acknowledge he felt it for a snippy little history buff infuriated him…and made him restless.

He should never have agreed to take the job, he told himself yet again. What devil had provoked him into doing it? Annoyed with himself, Vance wandered outside to stand on the porch.

The air had cooled considerably with nightfall. Overhead, the stars were spread in a wide, brilliant pattern around a white half-moon. Venus was as clear as he'd ever seen it. An army of crickets sent out their high, monotonous signal while fireflies danced, tiny yellow lights, over the fallow field to his right. When he looked straight ahead, he could see to the edge of the trees but no farther. The woods were dark, mysterious, secret. Shane slept on the other side in a room with faded wallpaper and a Jenny Lind bed.

He imagined her cuddled under the wedding-ring quilt he'd seen on the bed. Her window would be open to let in the sounds and scents of night. Did she sleep in one of those fussy cotton nightgowns that would cover her from neck to feet, he wondered, or would she slip under the quilt in solitary nakedness?

Furious with the direction of his thoughts, Vance cursed himself. No, he should never have taken the damn job. It had appealed to his ego and his humor. Six dollars an hour. He laughed shortly, startling an owl in a nearby tree. Leaning on a post, he continued to stare into the woods, seeing nothing but silhouettes and shadows.

When was the last time he'd worked for an hourly wage? To answer his own question, Vance looked back, trying to remember. Fifteen years? Good God, he thought with a shake of his head. Had so much time passed?

He'd been a teenager starting out at the bottom of his mother's highly successful construction firm. "Learn the ropes," she had told him, and he'd eagerly agreed. Vance had wanted nothing more than to work with his hands, and with wood. He'd had his share of youthful confidence—and youthful arrogance. Administration was for old men in business suits who wouldn't know how to miter a corner. He'd wanted no part of their stuffy business meetings or complicated contract negotiations. Shuffle papers? No, he was too clever to fall into that trap.

How long had it taken before he had been pulled in—chained behind a desk? Five years? he thought. Six? With a shrug, he decided it didn't matter. He'd gone beyond the time when a year made much difference.

Sighing, Vance walked the length of the porch. Under his hand, the rail he had built himself was rough and sturdy. What choice had there been? he asked himself. There had been his mother's sudden stroke and long painful recovery. She had begged him to take over as president of Riverton. As a widow with only one child, she had been desperate not to see her business run by strangers. It had mattered to her, perhaps too much, that the firm she had inherited, had struggled to keep during the lean years, stay in the family. Vance knew that she had fought prejudices, taken chances and worked nearly half her life to turn a mediocre firm into an exemplary one. Then she had been all but helpless, and asking him.

If he had been a failure at it, he could have delegated the responsibilities and stayed a figurehead without a qualm. He could have picked up his tools again. But he hadn't been a failure—there was too much of his mother in him.

Riverton Construction had thrived and expanded under his leadership. It had grown beyond the prestigious Washington concern into a national conglomerate. It was his own misfortune that he had the same knack with administration that he had with a hammer. He had bolted the lock on his own cage.

Then there had been Amelia. Vance's mouth tightened into a cynical smile. Soft, sexy Amelia, he mused, with hair like a sunset and a quiet Virginia drawl. She had kept him yapping at her heels for months, drawing him in, holding him off, until he had been mad to have her. Mad, Vance thought again. A very apt word. If he had been sane, he would have seen through that beautiful, cultured mask to the calculating scrambler she had been—before he had put the ring on her finger.

Not for the first time, he wondered how many men had envied him his lovely, dignified wife. But they hadn't seen the face unmasked—the perfect face with a rotted shell beneath. Cold. In all of his experience, Vance had known no one as cold as Amelia Ryce Banning.

The owl in the oak to his left set up a steady hooting: two short calls then a long—two short, then a long. Vance listened to the monotonous sound as he thought over the years of his marriage.

Amelia had spent his money lavishly those first months—clothes, furs, cars. That had mattered little to him as he had felt her unearthly beauty demanded the finest. And he had loved her—or the woman he had thought she'd been. He had thought she was a woman made for diamonds, for soft, exotic furs and silks. It had pleased him to surround her with them, to see her sulky beauty glow. For the most part, he had ignored the excessive bills, paying them without a murmur. Once or twice he had commented on her extravagance and had received her sweet distress and apologies. He'd hardly noticed that the bills had continued to flow in.

Then he had discovered she was draining his bank account to feed her brother's teetering construction firm in Richmond. Amelia had been tearful and helpless when confronted with it. She had pleaded prettily for her brother. She had claimed she couldn't bear to have him almost facing bankruptcy while she lived so well.

Because he'd believed her familial concern, Vance had agreed to a personal loan, but he'd refused to siphon money from Riverton into an unstable and mishandled company. Amelia had been far from satisfied, had pouted and cajoled. Then when he'd remained adamant, she had attacked him like a crazed tigress, raking his face with her well-manicured nails, spewing out obscenities through her tinted cupid's-bow mouth. Her anger had driven her to strike out and tell him why she had married him—for his money and position, and what both could do for her and her own family business. Then Vance had looked beneath the beauty and the careful charm to see what she was. It had been only the first of many shocks and disillusionments.

Her warm passion had become frigidity; her adoring smiles had become sneers. She had refused to consider having children. It would have spoiled her figure and restricted her freedom. For more than two years Vance had struggled to save his failing marriage, to salvage something of the life he had planned to have with Amelia. But he had come to know that the woman he thought he had married was an illusion.

Ultimately, he'd demanded a divorce and Amelia had laughed and agreed. She would happily give him his freedom for half of everything he owned—including his share of Riverton. She had promised him an ugly court battle and plenty of publicity. After pointing out that she would be the injured party, Amelia had vowed to play her part of the cast-off wife to the hilt.

Trapped, Vance had lived with her for another year, keeping up the pretense of marriage in public, avoiding her privately. When he had discovered Amelia was taking lovers, he'd seen the first ray of hope.

He had felt no pain on being betrayed, for there had been no emotion in him for her. Slowly, discreetly, Vance had begun to compile the evidence that would give him his freedom. He was willing to face the humiliation and publicity of a messy court battle to free himself and his company. Then there had been no more need. One of Amelia's discarded lovers put a bullet through her heart and ended it.

It had been due to Vance's wealth and influence that the publicity hadn't been worse than it had been. Still, the whispers and speculation had been ugly enough. Yet there had been a staggering relief in him rather than grief. The guilt this had brought had caused him to bury himself even more in his work. There were condominiums to be built in Florida, a large medical complex in Minnesota, an addition to a university in Texas. But there had been no peace for him.

Determined to find Vance Banning again, he'd bought the dilapidated house in the mountains and had taken an extended leave of absence. Time, solitude, and the work he loved had been his prescription. Then, just when he had thought he had found the answer, he had met Shane Abbott.

She was no smoldering hothouse beauty as Amelia had been, no poised sophisticate as were the women he had taken to his bed over the last two years. She was fresh and vital. Instinctively, he was attracted to her good-natured generosity. But his wife's legacy to him had been cynicism and distrust. Vance knew that only a fool fell for the innocent act twice. And he was no fool.

He had taken the job with Shane on impulse, and now he would see it through. It would be a challenge to learn if he was still capable of the fine precision work she required. And he knew how to be cautious with a woman now. It was true her fresh looks and artless charm had appealed to him. He admired her way of dealing with her former fiancé. She'd been hurt, yet she had held her own and booted Cy out the door.

It might be interesting, he decided, to spend his vacation remodeling Shane's house and learning what she hid under her mask. Everyone wore masks, he thought grimly. Life was one long masquerade. It wouldn't take long to discover what went on behind her big brown eyes and bubbling laugh.

With a sound of disgust, Vance hurled himself back into the house. He wasn't going to lose any sleep over a woman. Nevertheless, he tossed and turned much of the night.

It was a perfect morning. In the west, the mountains rose into a paintbrush blue sky. Birds chattered in noisy jubilation as Shane tossed open the windows. The air that rushed in was warm, laced with the scent of zinnias. It was all but impossible for one of her nature to remain inside on such a day, cooped up with dust and a clipboard. But there were ways, Shane decided as she leaned on the windowsill, of doing her duty *and* having fun.

After dressing in an old T-shirt and faded red shorts,

she rummaged through the basement storage closet and unearthed a can of white paint and a roller. The front porch, she knew, needed more repair than her meager talents could provide, but the back was still sturdy enough. All it required was a coat or two of paint to make it bright and cheerful again.

Picking up a portable radio on her way, Shane headed outside. She fiddled with the tuner until she found a station that matched her mood; then, after turning the volume up, she went to work.

In thirty minutes, the porch was swept clean and hosed down. In the bright sun, it dried quickly while Shane pried the lid off the paint can. She stirred it, enjoying the day and the prospect of work. Once or twice, she glanced toward the old logging path, wondering when Vance would "keep in touch." She would have liked to have seen him coming down the path toward her. He had a long, loose-limbed stride she admired, and a way of looking as though he were in complete command of himself and anything that might get in his way. Shane liked that—the confidence, the hint of controlled power.

She had always admired people of strength. Her grandmother, through all her hardships and disappointments, had remained a strong woman right to the end. Shane would have admitted, for all their disagreements, that Cy was a strong man. What he lacked, in her opinion, was the underlying kindness that balanced strength and kept it from being hard. She sensed there was kindness in Vance, though he was far from easy with it. But the fact that the trait existed at all made the difference for Shane.

Turning away from the path, she took her bucket, roller and pan to the end of the porch. She poured, knelt, then took a deep breath and began to paint.

When Vance came to the end of the path, he stopped to watch her. She had nearly a third of the porch done. Her arms were splattered with tiny specks of white. The radio blared, and she sang exuberantly along with it. Her hips kept the beat. As she moved, the thin, faded material of her shorts strained over her bottom. That she was having a marvelous time with the homey chore was as obvious as her lack of skill. A smile tugged at his mouth when Shane leaned over for the bucket and rested her palm on the wet paint. Cheerfully, she swore, then wiped her hand haphazardly on the back of her shorts.

"I thought you said you could paint," Vance commented.

Shane started, nearly upsetting the contents of the bucket as she turned. Still on all fours, she smiled at him. "I said I could paint; I didn't say I was neat." Lifting her hand, she shielded her eyes against the sun and watched him walk to her. "Did you come to supervise?"

He looked down at her and shook his head. "No, I think it's already too late for that."

Shane lifted a brow. "It's going to be just fine when I've finished."

Vance made a noncommittal sound. "I've got a list of materials for you, but I need to make a few more measurements."

"That was quick." Shane sat back on her haunches. Vance shrugged, not wanting to admit he'd written it out in the middle of the night when sleep had eluded him.

"There was something else," she continued, stretching her back muscles. Leaning over, she turned down the volume on the radio so that it was only a soft murmur. "The front porch."

Vance glanced down at her handiwork. "Have you painted that too?"

Correctly reading his impression of her talents, Shane made a face. "No, I didn't paint that too."

"That's a blessing. What stopped you?"

"It's falling apart. Maybe you can suggest what I should do about it. Oh, look!" Shane grabbed his hand, forgetting the paint as she spotted a family of quail bobbing single file across the path behind them. "They're the first I've seen since I've been home." Captivated, she watched them until they were out of sight. "There's deer, too. I've seen the signs, but I haven't been able to catch sight of any yet." She gave a contented sigh as the quail rustled in the woods. All at once, she remembered the condition of her hand.

"Oh, Vance, I'm sorry!" Releasing him, she jumped to her feet. "Did I get any on you?"

For an answer, he turned his palm up, studying the white smear ironically.

"I really am sorry," she managed, choking on a giggle. He shot her a look as she struggled to swallow the irrepressible laughter. "No, really I am. Here." Taking the hem of her T-shirt, Shane lifted it to rub unsuccessfully at his palm. Her stab at assistance exposed the pale, smooth skin of her midriff.

"You're rubbing it in," Vance said mildly, trying not to be affected by the flash of skin or the glimpse of her narrow waist.

"It'll come off," she assured him while she fought a desperate battle with laughter. "I must have some turpentine or something." Though Shane pressed the back of her hand against her mouth, the giggle escaped. "I *am* sorry," she claimed, then dropped her forehead on his chest. "And I wouldn't laugh if you'd stop looking at me that way."

"What way?"

"Patiently."

"Does patience usually send you into uncontrollable laughter?" he asked. Her hair carried the scent of her shampoo, a faint tang of lemon. It was odd that he would think just then of the honey-sweetness of her mouth.

"Too many things do," she admitted in a strangled voice. "It's a curse." She drew a deep breath, but left her hand on his chest as she tried to compose herself. "One of my students drew a deadly caricature of his biology teacher. When I saw it, I had to leave the room for fifteen minutes before I could pretend I disapproved."

Vance drew her away, unnerved by his unwanted, unreasonable response to her. "Didn't you?"

"Disapprove?" Grinning, Shane shook her head. "I wanted to, but it was so good. I took it home and framed it."

Suddenly, she became aware that he was holding her arms, that his thumbs were caressing her bare skin while his eyes watched her in the deep, guarded way he had. Looking at him, Shane was certain he was unaware of the gentle, intimate gesture. There was nothing gentle in his eyes. If she had followed her first instinct, she would have risen to her toes and kissed him. It was what she wanted—what she sensed he wanted as well.

Something warned her against making the move. Instead, she stood still. Her eyes met his calmly, with no secrets to be seen in them. All of the secrets were his, and at that moment, they both knew it.

Vance would have been more comfortable with secrets than candor. When he realized that he was holding her, that he wanted to go on holding her, he released her.

"You'd better get back to your painting," he said. "I'll take those measurements."

"All right." Shane watched him walk to the door. "There's hot water in the kitchen if you want some tea."

What a strange man, she thought, frowning after him. Unconsciously, she lifted a finger to the warm spot on her arm where his flesh had touched hers. What had he been looking for, she wondered, when he had searched her eyes so deeply? What did he expect to find? It would be so much simpler if he would only ask her the questions he had. Shrugging, Shane went back to her painting.

Vance paused by the foot of the stairs and glanced at the living room. Surprised, he walked in for a closer look. It was clean as a whistle, with every vase, lamp and knickknack packed away in labeled boxes.

She must have really worked, he thought. That compact little body stored a heavyweight energy. She had ambition, he concluded, and the guts to carry it through. Whatever her former fiancé termed her, Vance would hardly characterize Shane Abbott as frivolous. Not from what he had seen so far, he reminded himself. He felt another flash of admiration for her as he mounted the stairs.

She'd been at work on the second floor as well, Vance discovered. She must move like a whirlwind, he concluded as he looked at the labeled boxes in the master bedroom. After taking his measurements and notations, he moved into Shane's room.

It was a beehive of activity, with none of the meticulous organization he had found in the other rooms. Papers, lists, notes, scrawled tablets and bills sat heaped on the open slant top of a Governor Winthrop desk. They fluttered a bit from the breeze through the opened windows. On the floor beside it were dozens of catalogs on antiques. A nightgown—not the one he had envisioned her in, but a thigh-length chemise—was tossed inside out over a chair. A pair of worn sneakers sat propped against the closet as if they had been kicked there then forgotten.

In the center of the room was a large box of books which he remembered seeing the day before. Then they had been in the third bedroom. Obviously, Shane had dragged them into her own room the night before to sort through them. Several were piled precariously on the floor; others littered her nightstand. It was apparent that her style of working and style of living were completely at variance.

Oddly, Vance thought of Amelia and the elegant order of her private rooms. They had been decorated in pinks and ivories, without the barest trace of dust or clutter. Even the army of bottles of creams and scents on her vanity had been carefully arranged. Shane had no vanity at all, and the bureau top held only a small enameled box, a framed photo and a single bottle of scent. He noted the photo was a color snapshot of a teenaged Shane beside a very erect, white-haired woman.

So this is the grandmother, Vance mused. She had a prim, proper smile on her face, but he was certain her eyes were laughing out of the lined face. He observed none of the softness of old age about her, but a rather leathery toughness that contrasted well with the girl beside her.

They stood on the summer grass, their backs to the creek. The grandmother wore a flowered housedress, the girl a yellow T-shirt and cut-off jeans. This Shane was hardly different from the woman outside. Her hair was longer, her frame thinner, but the look of unbridled amusement was there. Though her arm was hooked through the old woman's, the impression was of camaraderie, not of support.

She was more attractive with her hair short, Vance decided as he studied her. The way it curled and clung to the shape of her face accented the smoothness of her skin, and the way her jaw tapered…

He found himself wondering if Cy had taken the picture and was immediately annoyed with the idea. He disliked Cy on principle, though he'd certainly employed a good many men like him over the years. They plotted their way through life as though it were a tax return.

What the hell had she seen in him? Vance thought in disgust as he turned away to take more measurements. If she had tied herself up with him, she would be living in some stuffy house in the suburbs with 2.3 children, the Ladies Auxiliary on Wednesdays, and a two-week vacation in a rented beach cottage every year. Fine for some, he thought, but not for a woman who liked to paint porches and wanted to see Fiji.

That buttoned-down jerk would have picked on her for the rest of her life, Vance concluded before he headed back downstairs. She'd had a lucky escape. Vance thought it was a pity he hadn't had one himself. Instead he had spent an intolerable four years wishing his wife out of existence and another two dealing with the guilt of having his wish come true.

Shaking off the mood, Vance walked outside to take a look at Shane's front porch.

Later, when he was measuring and muttering, Shane came out with a mug of tea in each hand. "Pretty bad, huh?"

Vance looked up with an expression of disgust. "It's a wonder someone hasn't broken a leg on this thing."

"No one uses it much." Shane shrugged as she worked her way expertly around the uncertain boards. "Gran always used the back door. So does anyone who comes to visit."

"Your boyfriend didn't."

Shane shot him a dry look. "Cy wouldn't use the back door, and he's not my boyfriend. What do you think I should do about it?"

"I thought you'd already done it," he returned, and pocketed his rule. "And very well."

Shane eyed him a moment, then laughed. "No, not about Cy, about the porch."

"Tear the damn thing down."

"Oh." Gingerly, Shane sat on the top step. "All of it? I was hoping to replace the worst boards, and—"

"The whole thing's going to collapse if three people stand on it at the same time," Vance cut in, frowning at the sagging wood. "I can't understand how anyone could let something get into this condition."

"All right, don't get riled up," she advised as she held out a mug of tea. "How much do you think it'll cost me?"

Vance calculated a moment, then named a price. He saw the flicker of dismay before Shane sighed.

"Okay." It killed her last hope of holding on to her grandmother's dining-room set. "If it has to be done. I suppose it's first priority. The weather might turn cold anytime." She managed a halfhearted smile. "I wouldn't want my first customer to fall through the porch and sue me."

"Shane." Vance stood in front of her. As she sat on the top step, their faces were almost level. Her look was direct and open, yet still he hesitated before speaking. "How much do you have? Money," he added bluntly when she gave him a blank look.

She drew her brows together at the question. "Enough to get by," she said, then made a sound of annoyance as he continued to stare at her. "Barely," she admitted. "But it'll hold until my business makes a few dollars. I've got so much budgeted for the house, so much for buying stock. Gran left me a nest egg, and I had my own savings."

Vance hesitated again. He had promised himself not to become involved, yet he was being drawn in every time he saw her. "I hate to sound like your boyfriend," he began.

"Then don't," Shane said quickly. "And he's not."

"All right." Vance frowned down at his mug. It was

one thing to take on a job as a lark, and another to take money from a woman who was obviously counting her pennies. He sipped, trying to find a reasonable way out of his hourly wage. "Shane, about my salary—"

"Oh, Vance, I can't make it any more right now." Distress flew into her eyes. "Later, after I've gotten started…"

"No." Embarrassed and annoyed, he put a hand on hers to stop her. "No, I wasn't going to ask you to raise it."

"But—" Shane stopped. Realization filled her eyes. Tears followed it. Swiftly, she set down the mug and rose. Shaking her head, she descended the stairs. "No, no, that's very kind of you," she managed as she walked away from him. "I—I appreciate it, really, but it's not necessary. I didn't mean to make it sound as though—" Breaking off, she stared at the surrounding mountains. For a moment there was only the sound of the creek bubbling on its way behind them.

Cursing himself, Vance went to her. After a brief hesitation, he put his hands on her shoulders. "Shane, listen—"

"No, please." Swiftly, she turned to face him. Though the tears hadn't brimmed over, her eyes still swam with them. When she lifted her hands to his forearms, he found her fingers surprisingly strong. "It's very kind of you to offer."

"No, it's not," Vance snapped. Frustration, guilt and something more ran through him. He resented all of it. "Damn it, Shane, you don't understand. The money isn't—"

"I understand you're a very sweet man," she interrupted. Vance felt himself become tangled deeper when she put her arms around him, pressing her cheek to his chest.

"No, I'm not," he muttered. Intending to push her away and find a way out of the mess he'd gotten himself into, Vance put his hands back on her shoulders. The last thing he wanted was misplaced gratitude. But his hands found their way into her hair.

He didn't want to pull her away, he realized. No, by God, he didn't. Not when her small firm breasts were pressed against him. Not when her hair curled riotously around his fingers. It was soft, so soft, and the color of wild honey. Her mouth was soft, he remembered, aching. Surrendering to need, Vance buried his face in her hair, murmuring her name.

Something in the tone, the hint of desperation, made Shane long to comfort him. She didn't yet sense his desire for her, only his trouble. She pressed closer, wanting to ease it while she ran soothing hands over his back. At her touch, his blood leaped. In a swift, almost brutal move, Vance pulled her head back to savage her mouth with his.

Shane's instinctive cry of alarm was silenced. Her struggles went unnoticed. A fire consumed him—so great, so unbearably hot, he had no thought but to quench it. She felt fear, then, greater than fear, passion. The fire spread, engulfing her until her mouth answered his wildly.

No one, nothing had ever brought her to this—this madness of need, terror of desire. She moaned in panicked excitement as his teeth nipped into her bottom lip. Along her skin, quick thrills raced to confuse and inflame. There was never a thought to deny him. She knew she was already his.

He thought he would go mad if he didn't touch her, learn just one of the secrets of her small, slim body. For countless hours the night before, his imagination had tormented him. Now, he had to satisfy it. Never stopping his assault on her mouth, he reached beneath her shirt to find her breast. Her heart pounded beneath his hand. She was firm and small. His appetite only increased, making him groan while his thumb and finger worked the already erect peak.

Colors exploded inside her head like a blinding, brilliant rainbow. Shane clutched at him, afraid, enthralled, while her lips and tongue continued with a demand equal to his. Against her smooth skin his palm was rough and callused. His thumb scraped her, lifting her to a delirium of excitement. There was no smoothness, no softness in him. His mouth was hard and hot with the stormy taste of anger. Crushed to hers, his body was taut and tense. Some raw, turbulent passion seemed to pour out of him to dare her to match it.

She felt his arms tighten around her convulsively; then she was free so quickly she staggered, grabbing his arm to steady herself.

In her eyes, Vance saw the clouds of passion, the lights of fear. Her mouth was bruised and swollen from the fierceness of his. He frowned at it. Never before had he been rough with a woman. For the most part, he was a considerate lover, perhaps indifferent at times but never ungentle. He took a step back from her. "I'm sorry," he said stiffly.

Shane lifted her fingers to her still-tender lips in a nervous gesture. Her reaction, much more than Vance's technique, had left her shaken. Where had all that fire and feeling been hiding all this time? she wondered. "I don't..." Shane had to clear her throat to manage more than a whisper. "I don't want you to be sorry."

Vance studied her steadily for a moment. "It would be better all around if you did." Reaching in his back pocket, he drew out a list. "Here are the materials you'll need. Let me know when they're delivered."

"All right." Shane accepted the list. When he started to walk away, she drew up all of her courage. "Vance..." He paused and turned back to her. "I'm not sorry," she told him quietly.

He didn't answer, but walked around the side of the house and disappeared.

Chapter 5

Shane decided she had worked harder over the following three days than she had ever worked in her life. The spare bedroom and dining room were loaded with packing boxes, labeled and listed and sealed. The house had been scrubbed and swept and dusted from top to bottom. She had pored through catalogs on antiques until the words ran together. Every item she owned was listed systematically. The dating and pricing was more grueling for her than the manual work and often kept her up until the early hours of the morning. She would be up to start again the moment the sunlight woke her. Yet her energy never flagged. With each step of progress she made, the excitement grew, pushing her to make more.

As the time passed, she became more convinced, and more confident, that what she was doing was right. It *felt* right. She needed to find her own way—the sacrifices and the financial risk were necessary. She didn't intend to fail.

For her, the shop would be not only a business but an adventure. Though Shane was impatient for the adventure to begin, as always, the planning and anticipation were just as stimulating to her. She had contracted with a roofer and a plumber, and had chosen her paints and stains. Just that afternoon, in a torrent of rain, the materials she had ordered from Vance's list had been delivered. The mundane, practical occurrences had given her a thrill of accomplishment. Somehow, the lumber, nails and bolts had been tangible evidence that she was on her way. Shane told herself that Antietam Antiques and Museum became a reality when the first board was set in place.

Excited, she had phoned Vance, and if he were true to his word, he would begin work the next morning.

Over a solitary cup of cocoa in the kitchen, Shane listened to the constant drumming rain and thought of him. He had been brief and businesslike on the phone. She hadn't been offended. She had come to realize that moodiness was part of his character. This made him only more attractive.

The windows were dark as she stared out, with a ghostly reflection of the kitchen light on the wet panes. She thought idly about starting a fire to chase away the damp chill, but she had little inclination to move. Instead, she rubbed the bottom of one bare foot over the top of the other and decided it was too bad her socks were all the way upstairs.

Sluggishly, a drip fell from the ceiling into a pot on the floor. It gave a surprising ping now and again. There were several other pots set at strategic places throughout the house. Shane didn't mind the rain or the isolation. The sensation of true loneliness was almost foreign to her. Content with her own company, the activity of her own mind, she craved no companionship at that moment, nor would she have shunned it. Yet she thought of Vance, wondering if he sat watching the rain through a darkened window.

Yes, she admitted, she was very much attracted to him. And it was more than a physical response when he held her, when he kissed her in that sudden, terrifyingly exciting way. Just being in his presence was stimulating—sensing the storm beneath the calm. There was an amazing drive in him. The drive of a man uncomfortable, even impatient, with idleness. The lack of a job, she thought with a sympathetic sigh, must frustrate him terribly.

Shane understood his need to produce, to be active, although her own spurts of frantic energy were patchworked with periods of unapologetic laziness. She moved fast but didn't rush. She could work for hours without tiring, or sleep until noon without the least blush of guilt. Whichever she did, she did wholeheartedly. It was vital to her to find some way to enjoy the most menial or exhausting task. She concluded that while Vance would work tirelessly, he would find the enjoyment unnecessary.

The basic difference in their temperaments didn't trouble her. Her interest in history, plus her teaching experience, had given her insight into the variety of human nature. It wasn't necessary to her that Vance's thoughts and moods flow along the same stream as hers. Such comfortable compatibility would offer little excitement and no surprises at all. Absolute harmony, she mused, could be lovely, rather sweet, and very bland. There were more… interesting things.

She'd seen a spark of humor in him, perhaps an almost forgotten sense of the ridiculous. And he was far from cold. While she accepted his faults and their differences, these qualities caused her to accept her own attraction to him.

What she had felt from the first meeting had only intensified. There was no logic in it, no sense, but her heart had known instantly that he was the man she'd waited for. Though she'd told herself it was impossible, Shane knew the impossible had an uncanny habit of happening just the same. Love at first sight? Ridiculous. But…

Impossible or not, ridiculous or not, Shane's heart was set. It was true she gave her affections easily, but she didn't give them lightly. The love she had felt for Cy had been a young, impressionable love, but it had been very real. It had taken her a long time to get over it.

Shane had no illusions about Vance Banning. He was a difficult man. Even with spurts of kindness and humor, he would never be anything else. There was too much anger in him, too much drive. And while Shane could accept the phenomenon of love at first sight on her part, she was practical enough to know it wasn't being reciprocated.

He desired her. She might puzzle over this, never having thought of herself as a woman to attract desire, but she recognized it. Yet, though he wanted her, he kept his distance. This was the reserve in him, she decided, the studied caution that warred with the passion.

Idly, she sipped her drink and stared out into the rain. The problem as Shane saw it was to work her way through the barrier. She had loved before and faced pain and emptiness. She could accept pain again, but she was determined not to face emptiness a second time. She wanted Vance Banning. Now all she had to do was to make him want her. Smiling a little, Shane set down her cup. She'd been raised to succeed.

The glare of headlights against the window surprised her. Rising, Shane went to the back door to see who'd come visiting in the rain. Cupping her hands on either side of her face, she peered through the wet glass. She recognized the car and immediately threw open the door. Cold rain hurled itself into her face, but she laughed, watching Donna scramble around puddles with her head lowered.

"Hi!" Still laughing, Shane stepped back as her friend dashed through the door. "You got a little wet," she observed.

"Very funny." Donna stripped off her raincoat to hang it over a peg near the back door. With the casualness of an old friend, she stepped out of her wet loafers. "I figured you were hibernating. Here." She handed Shane a pound can of coffee.

"A welcome home present?" Shane asked, turning the can over curiously. "Or a hint that you'd like some?"

"Neither." Shaking her head, Donna ran her fingers through her wet hair. "You bought it the other day, then left it at the store."

"I did?" Shane thought about it a moment, then

laughed. "Oh, that's right. Thanks. Who's minding the store while you're out making deliveries?" Turning, she popped the can into a cupboard.

"Dave." With a sigh, Donna plopped onto a kitchen chair. "His sister's baby-sitting, so he kicked me out."

"Aw, out in the storm."

"He knew I was restless." She glanced out the window. "It doesn't seem as though this rain's ever going to let up." With a shiver, she frowned at Shane's bare feet. "Aren't you cold?"

"I thought about starting a fire," she said absently, then grinned. "It seemed like an awful lot of trouble."

"So's the flu."

"The cocoa's still warm," Shane told her, automatically reaching for another cup. "Want some?"

"Yes, thanks." Donna ran her fingers through her hair again, then folded her hands, but she couldn't keep them still. Suddenly, she gave Shane a glowing smile. "I have to tell you before I burst."

Mildly curious, Shane looked over her shoulder. "Tell me what?"

"I'm having another baby."

"Oh, Donna, that's wonderful!" Shane felt a twinge of envy. Hurriedly dismissing it, she went to hug her friend. "When?"

"Not for another seven months." Laughing, Donna wiped the rain from her face. "I'm just as excited as I was the first time. Dave is too, though he's trying to be very nonchalant." She sent Shane a beaming look. "He's managed to mention it, very casually, to everyone who came into the store this afternoon."

Shane gave her another quick hug. "You know how lucky you are?"

"Yes, I do." A little sheepishly, she grinned. "I've spent all day thinking up names. What do you think of Charlotte and Samuel?"

"Very distinguished." Shane moved back to the stove. After pouring cocoa, she brought two cups to the table. "Here's to little Charlotte or Samuel."

"Or Andrew or Justine," Donna said as they touched rims.

"How many kids are you planning to have?" Shane asked wryly.

"Just one at a time." Donna gave her stomach a proud little pat.

The gesture made Shane smile. "Did you say Dave's sister was watching Benji? Isn't she still in school?"

"No, she graduated this summer. Right now she's hunting for a new job." With a contented sigh, Donna sat back. "She was planning to go to college part-time, but money's tight and the hours she's working right now make it next to impossible." Her brow creased in sympathy. "The best she can manage this term is a couple of night classes twice a week. At that rate it's going to take her a long time to earn a degree."

"Hmm." Shane stared into her cocoa. "Pat was a very bright girl as I remember."

"Bright and pretty as a picture."

Shane nodded. "Tell her to come see me."

"You?"

"After the shop's set up, I'm going to need some part-time help." She glanced over absently as the wind hurled rain at the windows. "I wouldn't be able to do anything for her for a month or so, but if she's still interested, we should be able to work something out."

"Shane, she'll be thrilled; but are you sure you can afford to hire someone?"

With a toss of her head, Shane lifted her drink. "I'll know within the first six months if I'm going to make it." As she considered, she twisted a curl around her finger—a gesture Donna recognized as nerves. She drew her brows together but said nothing. "I want to keep the place open seven days a week," Shane continued. "Weekends are bound to be the busiest time if I manage to lure in any tourists. Between sales and bookkeeping, inventory and the buying I have to do, I won't be able to manage alone. If I'm going down," she murmured, "I'm going down big."

"I've never known you to do anything halfway," Donna observed with a trace of admiration vying with concern. "I'd be scared to death."

"I am a little scared," Shane admitted. "Sometimes I imagine this place the way it's going to look, and I see customers coming in to handle merchandise. I see all the rooms and records I'm going to have to keep…" She rolled her eyes to the ceiling. "What makes me think I can handle all that?"

"As long as I can remember, you've handled everything that came your way." Donna paused a moment as she considered Shane carefully. "You're going to try this no matter how many pitfalls I point out?"

A grin had Shane's dimples deepening. "Yes."

"Then I won't point out any," Donna said with a wry

smile. "What I will say is that if anyone can make it work, you can."

After frowning into her cocoa, Shane raised her eyes to Donna's. "Why?"

"Because you'll give it everything you've got."

The simplicity of the answer made Shane laugh. "You're sure that'll be enough?"

"Yes," Donna said so seriously that Shane sobered.

"I hope you're right," Shane murmured, then shook off the doubts. "It's a little late in the game to start worrying about it now. So," she continued in a lighter tone, "what's new besides Justine or Samuel?"

After a moment's hesitation, Donna plunged ahead. "Shane, I saw Cy the other day."

"Did you?" Shane lifted a brow as she sipped. "So did I."

Donna moistened her lips. "He seemed very…ah, concerned about your plans."

"Critical and concerned are entirely different things," Shane pointed out, then smiled as the color in Donna's cheeks deepened. "Oh, don't worry about it, Donna. Cy's never approved of any of my ideas. It doesn't bother me anymore. In fact, the less he approves," she continued slowly, "the more I'm sure it's the right thing to do. I don't think he's ever taken a chance in his entire life." Noting that Donna was busy gnawing on her bottom lip, Shane fixed her with a straight look. "Okay, what else?"

"Shane." Donna paused, then began running her fingertip around and around the rim of her cup. Shane recognized the stalling gesture and kept silent. "I think I should tell you before—well, before you hear it from someone else. Cy…"

Shane waited patiently for a few seconds. "Cy what?" she demanded. Miserably, Donna looked up.

"He's been seeing quite a lot of Laurie MacAfee." Seeing Shane's eyes widen, Donna continued in a rush. "I'm sorry, Shane, so sorry, but I did think you should know. And I figured it might be easier hearing it from me. I think…well, I'm afraid it's serious."

"Laurie…" Shane broke off and seemed to stare, fascinated, at the water dripping into the pot. *"Laurie MacAfee?"* she managed after a strangled moment.

"Yes," Donna said quietly, and she stared down at the table. "Rumor is they'll be married next summer." Donna waited, unhappily, for Shane's reaction. When she heard the burst of wild laughter, she looked up, fearing hysterics.

"Laurie MacAfee!" Shane pounded her palms on the table and laughed until she thought she would burst. "Oh, it's wonderful, it's perfect! Oh God. Oh God, what an *admirable* couple!"

"Shane…" Concerned with the damp eyes and rollicking laughter, Donna searched for the right thing to say.

"Oh, I wish I had known before so I could have congratulated him." Almost beside herself with delight, Shane laid her forehead on the table. Taking this as a sign of a broken heart, Donna put a comforting hand on her hair.

"Shane, you mustn't take on so." Her own eyes filled as she gently stroked Shane's hair. "Cy isn't for you. You deserve better."

The statement sent Shane into a fresh peal of laughter.

"*Oh, Donna!* Oh, Donna, do you remember how she always wore those neat little coordinates to school? And she got straight A's in home economics." Shane was forced to take deep breaths before she could continue. "She did a term paper on planning household budgets."

"Please, darling, don't think about it." Donna cast her eyes around the kitchen, wondering if there were any medicinal brandy in the house.

"She'll have her own shoe trees," Shane said weakly. "I just know it. And she'll label them so they don't get them mixed up. Oh, Cy!" On a new round of giggles, she pounded a fist on the table. "Laurie. Laurie MacAfee!"

Almost frantic with concern, Donna gently lifted Shane's face. "Shane, I..." With a jolt she saw that rather than being devastated, her friend was simply overcome with amusement. For a moment, Donna stared into round dancing eyes. "Well," she said dryly, "I knew you'd be upset."

Shane howled with laughter. "I'm going to give them a Victorian whatnot as a wedding present. Donna," she added with grinning gratitude, "you've made my day. Absolutely made it."

"I knew you'd take it badly," Donna said with a baffled smile. "Just try not to weep in public."

"I'll keep my chin up," Shane promised, then smiled. "You're sweet. Did you really think I was carrying a torch for Cy?"

"I wasn't sure," Donna admitted. "You were...well, an item for so long, and I knew how crushed you were when the two of you broke up. You'd never talk about it after that."

"I needed some time to lick my wounds," Shane told her. "They've been healed over for a long while. I was in love with him, but I got over it. He put a large dent in my pride; I survived."

"I could have killed him at the time," Donna muttered darkly. "Two months before the wedding."

"Better than two months after," Shane pointed out logically. "We would never have made a go of it. But now, Cy and Laurie MacAfee…"

This time they both broke out into laughter.

"Shane." Donna gave her a sudden sober look. "A lot of people are going to be thinking you still care for Cy."

Shane shrugged it off. "You can't do anything about what people think."

"Or what they say," Donna murmured.

"They'll find something more interesting to talk about before long," Shane returned carelessly. "Besides, I have too much to do to be worried about it."

"So I noticed from the pile of stuff on the porch. What's under that tarp?"

"Lumber and materials."

"Just what are you going to do with it?"

"Nothing. Vance Banning's going to do it. Want some more cocoa."

"Vance Banning!" Stunned, then fascinated, Donna leaned forward. "Tell me."

"There's not much to tell. You didn't answer me," Shane reminded her.

"What? No, no, I don't want any more." Impatiently, she brushed the offer away. "Shane, what is Vance Banning going to do with your lumber and materials?"

"The carpentry work."

"Why?"

"I hired him to do it."

Donna gritted her teeth. "Why?"

"Because he's a carpenter."

"Shane!"

Valiantly, Shane controlled a grin. "Look, he's out of work, he's talented, I needed someone who'd work under union scale, so…" She spread her hands.

"What have you found out about him?" Donna demanded the right to fresh news.

"Not much." Shane wrinkled her nose. "Nothing, really. He doesn't say much."

Donna gave her a knowing smirk. "I already knew that."

A quick grin was Shane's response. "Well, he can be downright rude when he wants to. He has a lot of pride and a marvelous smile that he doesn't use nearly enough. Strong hands," she murmured, then brought herself back. "And a streak of reluctant kindness. I think he can laugh at himself but he's forgotten how. I know he's a workhorse because when the wind's right I can hear him hammering and sawing at all hours." She glanced out the window in the direction of the path. "I'm in love with him."

"Yes, but what—" Donna caught her breath and choked on it. *"What!"*

"I'm in love with him," Shane repeated with an amused smile. "Would you like some water?"

For nearly a full minute, Donna only stared at her. *She's joking,* she told herself. But by Shane's expression, she saw her friend was perfectly serious. It was her duty, Donna decided, as a married woman starting on her second child, to point out the dangers of this kind of thinking.

"Shane," she began in a patient, maternal tone, "you only just met the man. Now—"

"I knew it the minute I set my eyes on him," Shane interrupted calmly. "I'm going to marry him."

"Marry him!" Beyond words, Donna could only come up with sputters. Indulgently, Shane rose to pour her some water. "He—he asked you to marry him?"

"No, of course not." Shane chuckled at the idea as she handed Donna a glass. "He only just met me."

In an attempt to understand Shane's logic, Donna closed her eyes and concentrated. "I'm confused," she said at length.

"I said I was going to marry him," Shane explained, taking her seat again. "He doesn't know it yet. First I have to wait for him to fall in love with me."

After setting the untouched water aside, Donna gave her a stern look. "Shane, I think you're under more strain than you realize."

"I've been giving this a lot of thought," Shane answered, ignoring Donna's comment. "Number one, why would I have fallen in love with him in the blink of an eye if it wasn't right? It must be right, so number two, sooner or later he's going to fall in love with me."

Donna followed the pattern of thought and found it filled with snags. "And how are you going to make him do that?"

"Oh, I can't make him," Shane said reasonably. Her voice was both serene and confident. "He'll have to fall in love with me just as I am and in his own time—the same way I fell in love with him."

"Well, you've had some nutty ideas before, Shane Abbott, but this is the top." Donna folded her arms over her chest. "You're planning on marrying a man you've known barely a week who doesn't know he's going to marry you, and you're just going to sit patiently by until he gets the idea."

Shane thought for a moment, then nodded. "That's about it."

"It's the most ridiculous thing I've ever heard," Donna stated, then let out a surprised laugh. "And knowing you, it'll probably work."

"I'm counting on it."

Leaning forward, Donna took Shane's hands in hers. "Why do you love him, Shane?"

"I don't know," she answered immediately. "That's another reason I'm sure it's right. I know almost nothing about him except he's not a comfortable man. He'll hurt me and make me cry."

"Then why—"

"He'll make me laugh too," Shane interrupted. "And make me furious." She smiled a little, but her eyes were very serious. "I don't think he'll ever make me feel—inadequate. And when I'm near him, I *know*. That's enough for me."

"Yes." Donna nodded, giving Shane's hands a squeeze. "It would be. You're the most loving person I've ever known. And the most trusting. Those are wonderful traits, Shane, and—well, dangerous. I only wish we knew more about him," she added in a mutter.

"He has secrets," Shane murmured, and Donna's eyes sharpened. "They're his until he's ready to tell me about them."

"Shane…" Donna's fingers tightened on hers. "Be careful, please."

A little surprised by the tone, Shane smiled. "I will. Don't worry. Maybe I am more trusting than most, but I have my defenses. I'm not going to make a fool of myself." Unconsciously, she glanced out the window again, seeing the path to his house in her mind's eye. "He's not a simple man, Donna, but he is a good one. That much I'm sure of."

"All right," Donna agreed. Silently, she vowed to keep a close eye on Vance Banning.

For a long time after Donna left, Shane sat in the kitchen. The rain continued to pound. The steady drip from the ceiling plopped musically into the pan. She was aware of how reckless her words to Donna had been, yet she felt better having said them out loud.

No, she wasn't as blindly confident as she appeared. Inside, she was terrified by the knowledge that she loved so irrationally. She was trusting, yes, but not naive. She understood there was a price to pay for trust, and that often it was a dear one. Yet she knew her choice had already been made—or perhaps she'd never had one.

Rising, Shane switched off the lights and began to wander through the darkened house. She knew its every twist and turn, every board that creaked. It was everything familiar and comforting to her. She loved it. She knew none of Vance's twists and turns, none of his secret corners. He was everything strange and disturbing. She loved him.

If it had been a quiet, gentle love, she could have accepted it easily. But there was nothing quiet in the storm churning inside her. For all her energy and love of adventure, Shane had grown up in a slow, peaceful world where excitement was a run through the woods or a ride on the back of a tractor at haymaking. To fall suddenly in love with a stranger might seem romantic and wonderful in a story, but when it happened in real life, it was simply terrifying.

Shane walked upstairs, habitually avoiding the steps that creaked or groaned. The rain was a hollow, drumming sound all around her, whipped up occasionally by the wind to fly at the windows. Her bare feet met bare wood with a quiet patter. A small bucket caught the drip in the center of the hall. Expertly, she skirted around it.

Who was she to think all she had to do was to sit patiently by until Vance fell in love with her? she asked herself. After flipping on the light in her room, she went to stare at herself in the mirror. Was she beautiful? Shane asked her reflection. Alluring? With a half laugh, she rested her elbows on the dresser to look closer.

She saw the dash of freckles, the large dark eyes and cap of hair. She didn't see the stunning vitality, the temptingly smooth skin, the surprisingly sensual mouth.

Was that a face to send a man into raptures? she asked herself. The thought amused her so, that the reflection grinned back with quick good humor. Hardly, Shane decided, but she wouldn't want a man who looked only for a perfect face. No, she hadn't the face or figure to lure a man into love had she wanted to. She had only herself and the love in her heart.

Shane flashed the mirror a smile before she turned away to prepare for bed. She'd always thought love the ultimate adventure.

Chapter 6

Weak sunlight filtered through the bad-tempered clouds. The creek was swollen from the rainfall so that it ran its course noisily, hissing and complaining as it rounded the bend at the side of Shane's house. Shane was doing some complaining of her own.

The day before, she had moved her car out of the narrow driveway so that the delivery truck could have easy access to the back porch. Not wanting to ruin the grass, she had parked in the small square of dirt her grandmother had used as a vegetable garden. Once the car had been moved, Shane had become involved with the unloading of lumber and had promptly forgotten it. Now, it was sunk deep in mud, firmly resisting all efforts to get it out.

She pressed the gas lightly, tried forward, then

reverse. She gunned the engine and swore. Slamming out of the driver's side, Shane sloshed ankle-deep in mire as she stomped back to the rear tire. She gave it an accusing stare, then kicked it.

"That's not going to help," Vance commented. He had been watching her for the last few minutes, torn somewhere between amusement and exasperation. And pleasure. There was a simple pleasure in just seeing her. He'd stopped counting the times over the last few days that he'd thought of her.

Out of patience, Shane turned to him, hands on hips. Her predicament was annoying enough without the added benefit of an audience. "You might have let me know you were there."

"You were…involved," he said, glancing pointedly at her mired car.

She sent him a cool look. "You've got a better idea, I suppose."

"A few," he agreed, moving across the lawn to join her. Her eyes snapped with temper while her mouth pouted. Her boots were caked with mud past the ankle. Her jeans, rolled up to the calf, had fared little better. She looked ready to boil over at the first wrong word. A cautious man would have said nothing.

"Who the hell parked it in this mud hole?" Vance demanded.

"*I* parked it in this mud hole." Shane gave the tire another fierce kick. "And it wasn't a mud hole when I did."

He lifted a brow. "I suppose you noticed it rained all night."

"Oh, get out of my way." Incensed, Shane pushed

him aside and stomped back to the driver's seat. She turned on the ignition, shoved the shift into first, then stepped heavily on the gas. Mud flew like rain. The car groaned and sank deeper.

For a moment, Shane could only pound on the steering wheel in enraged impotence. She would have dearly loved to tell Vance that she didn't require any assistance. There was nothing more infuriating than an amused, superior male…especially when you needed one. Forcing herself to take a deep breath, she climbed back out of the car to meet Vance's grin with icy composure. "What's the first of your few ideas?" she asked coolly.

"Got a couple of planks?"

Even more annoyed that she hadn't thought of it herself, Shane went to the shed and found two long, thin boards. Without fuss or conversation, Vance took them and secured them just under the front wheels. Shane folded her arms and tapped one muddy boot as she watched him.

"I'd have thought of that in a minute," she muttered.

"Maybe." Vance stood again to walk to the rear of the car. "But you wouldn't get anywhere the way your back wheels are stuck."

Shane waited for him to make some comment on feminine stupidity. Then she would have an excuse to give him the full force of her temper. He merely studied her flushed face and furious eyes. "So?" she said at length.

Something suspiciously like a smile tugged at his mouth. Shane's eyes narrowed. "So, get back in and I'll push," he said, then put a restraining hand on her arm. "Gentle on the gas this time, hot rod. Just put it in drive and easy does it."

"It's a four-speed," she told him with dignity.

"I beg your pardon." Vance waited until she had waded her way back to the front of the car. For the first time in months, perhaps years, he had to make a concentrated effort to control laughter. "Let the clutch out slow," he instructed after clearing his throat.

"I know how to drive," she snapped, and slammed the door smartly. Frowning into the rearview mirror, Shane watched him until he gave her a nod. With meticulous care, she engaged the clutch and gently pressed on the gas. The front wheels crept slowly onto the planks. The back tires slid, then stuck, then ponderously moved again. Shane kept the speed slow and even. It was humiliating, she thought, glaring straight ahead, absolutely humiliating that he was going to get her out without a hitch.

"Just a little more," Vance called to her, shifting his weight. "Keep it slow."

"What?" Shane rolled down the window, then stuck her head out to hear his answer. As she did, her foot slipped and fell heavily on the gas. The car shot out of the mud like a banana squeezed from its peel. With a gasp, Shane hit the brake, rocking to an abrupt halt.

Closing her eyes, she sat for a moment and considered making a run for it. She didn't dare glance in the rearview mirror now. It wouldn't be difficult, she reflected, to make a U-turn, then keep right on going. But cowardice wasn't her way. She swallowed, bit her lip, then climbed out of the car to face the music.

Vance was kneeling in the mud. He was thoroughly splattered and hopping mad. *"You idiot!"* he shouted before Shane could say a word. Even as she started to agree with him, he continued. "What the hell did you think you were doing? Pea-brained little twit, I told you to take it *slow.*"

He didn't stop there. He swore at length, and fluently, but Shane lost track of the content. It was enough to know he was in a justifiable high rage, while she was fighting a desperate battle with laughter. She did her best, her very best, to keep her face composed and penitent. Feeling it would be unwise, as well as useless to interrupt with apologies, she folded her lips, bit the bottom one and swallowed repeatedly.

At first she concentrated on keeping her eyes directly on his, hoping the fury there would kill the urge to giggle. But the sight of his mud-splattered face had her sides aching with restrained mirth. She hung her head, ostensibly from shame.

"I'd like to know who the hell told you you could drive," Vance went on furiously. "And what person with a brain cell working would have parked the car in a swamp to begin with?"

"It was my grandmother's garden," Shane managed in a strangled voice. "But you're right. You're absolutely right. I'm so sorry, really…" She broke off here as a gurgle of laughter rose dangerously. Clearing her throat, she hurried on. "Sorry, Vance. It was very"—she had to look over his head in order to compose herself—" careless of me."

"Careless!"

"Stupid," she amended quickly, thinking that might placate him. "Absolutely stupid. I'm really sorry." Helplessly, she pressed both hands to her mouth, but the giggles came through. "I *am* sorry," she insisted, giving up as he glared at her. "I don't mean to laugh. It's terrible." Dizzy with the effort of trying to hold back, Shane bent over double. "Really awful," she added on a howl of laughter.

"Since you think it looks like fun..." he muttered grimly, and grabbed her hand. Shane landed on her seat with a gentle splash and kept on laughing.

"I didn't—I didn't thank you," she said on a peal of giggles, "for getting my car out."

"Think nothing of it." Most women, he mused, would have been infuriated to find themselves sitting in a pile of mud. Shane was laughing just as hard at herself as she had at him. His grin was completely unexpected and spontaneous. "Brat," he accused, but Shane shook her head.

"Oh no, no I'm not, really." She pressed the back of her hand to her mouth. "It's just this terrible habit of laughing at the wrong time. Because I really am sorry." The last word was drowned in a flood of laughter.

"I can see you are."

"Anyway, I didn't get it *all* over you." Scooping up some mud, she wiped it across his cheek. "I missed that part right there." She made a little choking sound in her throat. "That's much better," she approved.

"You aren't wearing nearly enough," Vance returned. He trailed both muddy palms down her face. Trying to avoid him, Shane slid, ending up flat on her back. Vance's boom of laughter broke into her shriek. "Much better," he agreed, then spotting the handful of mud she was about to heave, he made a grab for her arm. "Oh, no, you don't!"

As he laughed, she shifted. Vance landed half on his chest, half on his side. With a muttered curse, he propped himself up, studying her out of narrowed eyes.

"City boy," she mocked on a whoop of appreciation. "Probably never been in a mud fight in your life." She was too pleased with her maneuver to see the next one coming.

In a flash, Vance had her by the shoulders. Rolling her over, he straddled her, holding a hand to the back of her head. Lying full length, Shane looked wide-eyed at the mud inches away from her face.

"Oh, Vance, you *wouldn't!*" The helpless laughter bubbled still as she struggled.

"The hell I wouldn't." He pushed her face an inch closer.

"Vance!" Though she was slippery as an eel by this time, Vance held her firmly, clamping his knees around her while his hand urged her down. As the distance between revenge and her nose lessened, Shane closed her eyes and held her breath.

"Give?" he demanded.

Cautiously, Shane opened one eye. She hesitated a moment, torn between the desire to win and the image of having her face pushed into the mud. She didn't doubt he'd do it. "Give," she said reluctantly.

Abruptly, Vance rolled her over so that she lay in his lap. "City boy, huh?"

"You wouldn't have won if I weren't out of practice," she told him. "It was just beginner's luck."

Her eyes were mocking him. Her face was streaked with mud from his own fingers. The hands pressed against his chest were slippery with it. The grip on the back of her neck lightened until it was a caress. The hand at her hip roamed absently down her thigh as he lowered his eyes to her mouth. Slowly, without any conscious thought of doing so, Vance began to draw her closer.

Shane saw the change in his eyes and was suddenly afraid. Did she really have the defenses she had bragged to Donna about? Now that she was certain she loved him, could there be any defense? It was too fast, she thought frantically. It was all happening too fast. Breathless from the race of her heart, she scrambled up.

"I'll beat you to the creek," she challenged, then was off in a flash.

Pondering on her abrupt retreat, Vance watched her run around the side of the house. Normally, he would have considered it a ploy, but he found it didn't fit this time. Nothing about her fit, he concluded as he rose. Oddly, he realized he didn't seem to fit either. He hadn't realized he could find anything amusing or enjoyable about wrestling in the mud. Nor had he realized he could find a woman like Shane Abbott both intriguing and desirable. Trying to organize his thoughts, Vance walked around the side of the house to find her.

She had stripped off her boots and was wading knee-deep in the rushing creek water. "It's freezing!" she called out, then lowered herself to her waist. At the shock of cold, she sucked in her breath. "If it was warmer, we could walk down to Molly's Hole and take a quick swim."

"Molly's Hole?" Watching her, Vance sat on the grass to pull off his own boots.

"Right around the bend." She pointed vaguely in the

direction of the main road. "Great swimming hole. Fishing too." Shivering a bit, she rubbed at the front of her shirt to help the water take off the worst of the mud. "We're lucky it rained, or else the creek wouldn't be high enough to do any good."

"If it hadn't rained, your car wouldn't have been stuck in the mud."

Shane shot him a grin. "That's beside the point." She watched him step into the water. "Cold?" she said sweetly when he winced.

"I should have pushed your face in," he decided. Stripping off his shirt, Vance tossed it on the grassy bank before scrubbing at his hands and arms.

"You'd have felt really bad if you had." Shane rubbed her face with creek water.

"No, I wouldn't have."

Glancing up, Shane laughed. "I like you, Vance. Gran would have called you a scoundrel."

He lifted a brow. "Is that praise?"

"Her highest," Shane agreed, rising to rub at the thighs of her jeans. They were plastered against her, molding her legs while her shirt clung wetly to her breasts. The cold had her nipples taut, straining against the thin cotton. Involved with cleaning off her clothes, she chattered, sublimely unaware they left her as good as naked.

"She loved scoundrels," Shane continued. "I suppose that's why she put up with me. I was always getting into one scrape or another."

"What kind?" Vance's torso was wet, cleaned of mud now, but he stayed where he was. Her body was exquisitely formed. He wondered how he hadn't noted before how perfectly scaled it was—small round breasts, wasp-thin waist, narrow hips, lean thighs.

"I don't like to brag." Shane worked the mud from the slippery sleeves of her shirt. "But I can show you the best way into old man Trippet's orchard if you want to snitch a few green apples. And I used to have a great time riding Mr. Poffenburger's dairy cows." Shane sloshed over to him. "Here, you haven't got it all off your face." Cupping some water in her hand, she lifted it and began to clean his face herself. "I tore my britches on every farmer's fence for three miles," she went on. "Gran would patch them up saying she despaired of my being any more than a hooligan."

With one small, smooth hand, she methodically scrubbed Vance's face. The other she held balanced against his naked chest. He made no protest, but stood still, watching her.

"'That Abbot girl,' they'd say," Shane told him, rubbing at a spot on his jawline. "Now I have to convince them I'm an upstanding citizen so they'll forget I filched their apples and buy my antiques. No one takes a hooligan very seriously. There, that's better." Satisfied, Shane started to lower her hand. Vance caught it in his. Her eyes didn't waver from his, but she became very still.

Without speaking, he began to wash the few lingering traces of mud from her face. He worked in very slow, very deliberate circles, his eyes fixed on hers. Though his palm was rough, his touch was gentle. Shane's lips trembled apart. With something like curiosity, Vance took a damp finger to trace their shape. He felt her quick, convulsive shudder. Still slow, still inquisitive, he ran his fingertip along the inside of her bottom lip. Under his thumb, the pulse in her wrist began to hammer. The sun broke briefly through the clouds, so that the light shifted and brightened before it dimmed again. He watched it play over her face.

"You won't run away this time, Shane," he murmured, as if to himself.

She said nothing, afraid to speak while his finger lingered on her lips. Slowly, he traced it down, over her chin, over the throbbing pulse in her throat. He paused there a moment, as if gauging and enjoying her response to him. Then he allowed his fingertip to sweep up over the swell of her breast and lie lightly on the erect peak covered only by the thin wet shirt.

Heat and cold shot through her; her skin was chilled from the water, her blood flamed at his touch. Vance watched the color drain from her face while her eyes grew impossibly large and dark. Yet she didn't draw away or protest the intimacy. He heard the sharp intake of her breath, then the slow, ragged expulsion.

"Are you afraid of me?" he asked, bringing his hand up to cup the back of her neck.

"No," she whispered. "Of me."

Puzzled, he drew his brows together. For a moment he looked hard and very fierce. Though his eyes weren't cold, they were piercing—full of questions, full of suspicion. Still Shane felt no fear of him, only of the needs and longing running through her. "An odd answer, Shane," he murmured thoughtfully. "You're an odd woman." With his fingers, he kneaded the back of her neck while he searched her face for answers. "Is that why you excite me?"

"I don't know," she said, struggling for breath. "I don't want to know. Just kiss me."

He lowered his lips, but only tested hers with the same lightness as his fingertip. "I wonder," he said softly against her mouth, "what it is about you I can't quite shake. Your taste?" He dug his teeth almost experimentally into her bottom lip. A low moan of pleasure was wrenched from her. "Fresh as rain one minute and honey soaked the next." Lightly, languidly, he traced her lips with his tongue. "Is it the way you feel? That skin of yours…like the underside of a rose petal." He ran his hands down her arms, then up again, gradually bringing her to him until she was caught close. The thud of her heart sounded like thunder in her ears.

"Why do you have to know?" The question was low and shaky. "Feeling's enough." They might have been naked, pressed body to body with only wet clinging clothes between them. "Kiss me, Vance, just kiss me. It's enough."

"You smell like rain now," he murmured, telling himself to resist her but knowing he wouldn't. "Pure and honest. When I look in your eyes, I'd swear there isn't a lie in you. Is there?" he demanded, but he crushed his mouth to hers before she could answer.

Shane reeled from the impact. Even as she gasped, his tongue was probing and exploring. The anger she had sensed in him before was now pure passion. Hunger, the rawness of his hunger, thrilled her. The water ran swiftly, grumbling as it hurried on its way to the river, but Shane heard only her own heartbeat. She no longer felt the stinging cold, only the warmth of his hand as it ran up her spine and down again.

He wasn't content with only her lips now, but took his own wild journey of her face. It was still wet, tasting of the cold freshness of the creek. But wherever his kisses wandered, he was drawn back again to the soft sweet taste of her mouth. It seemed always to be waiting for him, ready to open, invite, demand. Beneath the pliancy, beneath the willingness was a passion as great as his own and a strength he was just beginning to measure.

Vance told himself he needed a woman. That was why he was so desperate for Shane. He needed a woman's softness and flavor, and she was here. There was no exclusivity to it. How could there be? Yet there was something about her slight body, her fascinatingly different taste that drove every other woman to some dark corner of his mind, leaving only Shane in the light.

He could take her now, on the bank of the creek, in the dim daylight on the rain-damp grass. As her mouth moved, moist and warm under his, Vance could imagine how it would be to take full possession of her body. Her energy and hunger would match his own. There would be no false, foolish pretense of seduction, but an honest meeting of desires.

Her small round breasts pressed into his naked chest. Vance thought he could feel the aching need in them—or was it his own need? It raged in him, drove at him, until she was all he craved. Her mouth was small too, but avid, never retreating from the savageness of his.

Instead, she matched it, propelling him further and further, pulling him closer and closer. All women or one woman, he was no longer certain, but she was overpowering him.

Somehow he knew that if he took her, he would never walk away easily. The reasons might not be fully clear yet, but she wasn't like the other women he had known and bedded. He was afraid her eager hands and mouth could hold him—and he wasn't yet ready to chance it.

Vance drew her away, but Shane dropped her head on his chest. There was something vulnerable in the gesture though the arms around his waist were strong. The contrast aroused him, as did the lightning fast beat of her heart. For a moment, he stood holding her while the water ran cold and fast around their legs and hazy sunlight drifted through the trees.

She'd once told him that a snowfall had made her feel a complete isolation. Vance felt it now. There might have been nothing, no one beyond the rushing creek and fringe of trees. And to his own confusion, he felt a need for none. He wanted only her. Perhaps they were alone… The thought both excited and disturbed him. Perhaps there was nothing beyond that forgotten little spot, and no reason not to take what he wanted.

Shane shivered, making him realize she must be chilled to the bone. It brought him back to reality in a rush. His arms dropped away from her.

"Come on," he muttered. "You should get inside." Vance pulled her up the slippery bank.

Shane bent over to pick up her boots. When she was

certain she could do so calmly, she met his eyes. "You're not coming in." It wasn't a question. She had sensed all too well his change of attitude.

"No." His tone was cool again though his blood still throbbed for her. "I'll go change, then come back and get started on the porch."

Shane had known he would bring her pain, but she hadn't thought it would be so soon. The old wounds of rejection opened again. "All right. If I'm not here, just do whatever you have to do."

Vance could feel the hurt, yet she met his eyes and her voice was steady. Recriminations he could have dealt with easily. Anger he would have welcomed. For the first time in years, he was completely baffled by a woman.

"You know what would happen if I came in now." The words were rough with impatience. Vance found himself wanting to shake her.

"Yes."

"Is that what you want?"

Shane said nothing for a moment. When she smiled, the light didn't reach her eyes. "It's not what you want," she said quietly. Turning, she started back to the house, but Vance caught her arm, spinning her around. He was furious now, all the more furious when he saw the effort her composure was costing her.

"Damn it, Shane, you're a fool if you think I don't want you."

"You don't want to want me," she returned evenly. "That's more important to me."

"What difference does it make?" he ground out impatiently. Frustrated by the calmness of her answer, he did shake her. How could she look at him with those big quiet eyes when she'd driven him to the wall only moments before? "You know how close I came to taking you right here on the ground. Isn't it enough to know you can push me to that? What more do you want?"

She gave him a long searching look. "Push you to it," she repeated quietly. "Is that really how you see it?"

The conflict raged in him. He wanted badly to get away from her. "Yes," he said bitterly. "How else?"

"How else," she agreed with a shaky laugh that started a new ache moving in him. "I suppose for some that might be a compliment of sorts."

"If you like," he said curtly as he picked up his shirt.

"I don't," she murmured. "But then, you said I was odd." With a sigh, she stared into his eyes. "You've cut yourself off from your feelings, Vance, and it eats at you."

"You don't know a damn thing," he tossed back, only more enraged to hear her speak the truth.

As he glared at her, Shane heard a bird set up a strident song in the woods behind her. The high, piercing notes suited the air of tension and anger. "You're not nearly as hard or cold as you'd like to think," she said calmly.

"You don't know anything about me," he countered furiously, grabbing her arms again.

"And it infuriates you when the guard slips," Shane continued without breaking rhythm. "It infuriates you even more that you might actually feel something for me." His fingers loosened on her arms, and Shane drew away. "I don't push you, but something else certainly does. No, I don't know what it is, but you do." She took a long steadying breath as she studied him. "You've got to fight your own tug-of-war, Vance."

Turning, she walked to the house, leaving him staring after her.

Chapter 7

He couldn't stop thinking of her. In the weeks that passed, the mountains became a riot of color. The air took on the nip of fall. Twice, Vance spotted deer through his own kitchen window. And he couldn't stop thinking of her.

He split his time between the two houses. His own was taking shape slowly. Vance calculated he would be ready to start the more detailed inside work by winter.

Shane's was progressing more quickly. Between roofers and plumbers, the house had been bedlam for more than a week. The old kitchen had been gutted and stood waiting for new paint and trim. Shane had waited patiently for rain after the roof had been repaired. Then she had checked all the familiar spots for signs of leaks. Oddly, she found herself a trifle sad that she didn't have to set out a single pan or bucket.

The museum area was completely finished. While Vance worked elsewhere, Shane busied herself arranging and filling the display cases that had been delivered.

At times she would be gone for hours, hunting up treasures at auctions and estate sales. He always knew the moment she returned because the house would spring to life again. In the basement, she'd set up a workroom where she refinished certain pieces or stored others. He saw her dash out, or dash in. He saw her carting tables, dragging packing boxes, climbing ladders. He never saw her idle.

Her attitude toward him was just as it had been from the first—friendly and open. Not once did she mention what had happened between them. It took all of his strength of will not to touch her. She laughed, brought him coffee and gave him amusing accounts of her adventures at auctions. He wanted her more every time he looked at her.

Now, as he finished up the trim on what had been the summer parlor, Vance knew she was downstairs. He went over his work critically, checking for flaws, while the simple awareness of her played havoc with his concentration. It might be wise, he thought, to take a trip back to Washington. So far, he had handled everything pertaining to his company by phone or mail. There was nothing urgent that required his attention, but he wondered if it wouldn't be wise to have a week of distance. She was haunting him. Plaguing him, Vance corrected. On a wave of frustration he packed his tools. The woman was trouble, he decided. Nothing but trouble.

Still, as he got ready to leave, Vance detoured to the

basement steps. He hesitated, cursed himself, then started down.

Dressed in baggy cord jeans and a hip-length sweater, she was working on a tilt-top table. Vance had seen the table when Shane had first brought it in. It had been scarred and scratched and dull. Flushed with excitement, she had claimed to have bought it for a song, then had hustled it off to the basement. Now, the grain of mahogany gleamed through the thin coats of clear lacquer she had applied. She was industriously buffing it with paste wax. The basement smelled of tung oil and lemon.

Vance would have turned to go back upstairs, but Shane raised her head and saw him. "Hi!" Her smile welcomed him before she gestured him over. "Come take a look. You're the expert on wood." As he crossed the room, Shane stood back to survey her work. "The hardest thing now," she muttered as she twisted a curl around her finger, "is going to be parting with it. I'll make a nice profit; I only paid a fraction of its worth."

Vance ran a fingertip over the surface. It was baby smooth and flawless. His mother had a similar piece in the drawing room of her Washington estate. Since he had purchased it for her himself, he knew the value. He also knew the difference between an amateur job of refinishing and an expert one. This hadn't been done haphazardly. "Your time's worth something," he commented. "And your talent. It would have cost a good deal to have this done."

"Yes, but I enjoy it, so it doesn't count."

Vance lifted his eyes. "You're in business to make money, aren't you?"

"Yes, of course." Shane snapped the lid back on the can of paste wax. "I love the smell of this stuff."

"You won't make a lot of money if you don't consider your own time and labor."

"I don't need to make a lot of money." She placed the can on a shelf, then examined the ladder-back chair, which needed recaning. "I need to pay bills and stock my shop and have a bit left over to play with." Turning the chair upside down, she frowned at the frayed hole in the center of the seat. "I wouldn't know what to do with a lot of money."

"You'd find something," Vance said dryly. "Clothes, furs."

Shane glanced up, saw he was serious, then burst out laughing. "Furs? Oh, yes, I can see myself waltzing into the general store to buy milk in a mink. Vance, you're a riot."

"I've never known a woman who didn't appreciate a mink," he countered.

"Then you've known the wrong women," she said lightly as she set the chair upright again. "I know this man in Boonsboro who does caning and rushing. I'll have to give him a call. Even if I had the time, I wouldn't know where to begin on this."

"What kind of woman are you?"

Shane's thoughts came back from her ladder-back chair. When she looked at him again, she noted that Vance's expression was cynical. She sighed. "Vance, why do you always look for complications?"

"Because they're always there," he returned.

She shook her head, keeping her hands on the top rung

of the chair's back. "I'm exactly the kind of woman I seem to be. Perhaps that's too simple for you, but it's true."

"The kind who's content to work twelve hours a day just for enough money to get by on?" Vance demanded. "The kind who's willing to slave away hour after hour—"

"I don't slave," Shane interrupted testily.

"The hell you don't. I've watched you. Dragging furniture, lugging boxes, scrubbing on your hands and knees." Remembering only made him angrier. She was too small to labor the way he had seen over the past weeks. The fact that he wanted to insist she stop only infuriated him further. "Damn it, Shane, it's too much for you to handle by yourself."

"I know what I'm capable of," she tossed back, springing to her own defense. "I'm not a child."

"No, you're a woman who doesn't crave furs or all the niceties an attractive female can have if she plays her cards right." The words were cool with sarcasm.

Temper sprang into Shane's eyes. Struggling not to explode, she turned away from him. "Do you think everyone has a game to play, Vance?"

"And some play better than others" was his response.

"Oh, I feel sorry for you," she said tightly. "Really very sorry."

"Why?" he demanded. "Because I know that grabbing all they can get is what motivates people? Only a fool settles for less."

"I wonder if you really believe that," she murmured. "I wonder if you really could."

"I wonder why you pretend to believe otherwise," he retorted.

"I'm going to tell you a little story." When she turned back, her eyes were dark with anger. "A man like you will probably find it corny and a bit boring, but you'll just have to listen anyway." Stuffing her hands into her pockets, she paced the low-ceilinged room until she was certain she could continue.

"Do you see these?" Shane demanded, indicating a row of shelves that held filled mason jars. "My grandmother—technically, she was my great-grandmother—canned these. Putting by, she always called it. She'd dig and hoe and plant and weed, then spend hours in a hot, steamy kitchen canning. Putting by," Shane repeated more quietly as she studied the colorful glass jars. "When she was sixteen, she lived in a mansion in southern Maryland. Her family was very wealthy. They still are," Shane added with a shrug. "The Bristols. The Leonardtown Bristols. You might have heard of them."

He had, and though his eyes registered surprise, he said nothing. Bristols Department Stores were scattered strategically all over the country. It was a very old, very prestigious firm that catered to the wealthy and the prominent. Even now, Vance's firm was contracted to build another branch in Chicago.

"In any case," Shane continued, "she was a young, beautiful, pampered girl who could have had anything. She'd been educated in Europe, and there were plans for her to be finished in Paris before a London debut. If she had followed her parents' plans, she would have married well, had her own mansion and her own staff of servants.

The closest she would have come to planting would have been watching her gardener prune a rose bush."

Shane gave a little laugh as though the thought both amused and baffled her. "She didn't follow the plan, though. She fell in love with William Abbott, an apprentice mason who had been hired to do some stone work on the estate. Of course, her family would have none of it. They were already planning the groundwork for a marriage between Gran and the heir to some steel company. The moment they got wind of what was happening, they fired him. To keep it brief, Gran made her choice and married him. They disowned her. Very dramatic and Victorian. The I-have-no-daughter sort of thing you read in a standard Gothic."

Vance said nothing as she stared at him, almost daring him to comment. "They moved here, back with his family," Shane continued. "They had to share this house with his parents because there wasn't enough money for one of their own. When his father died, they cared for his mother. Gran never regretted giving up all the *niceties.* She had such tiny hands," she murmured, looking down at her own. "You wouldn't have thought they could be so strong." She shook off the mood and turned away. "They were poor by the standards she had grown up with. What horses they had were for pulling a plow. Some of your land was hers at one time, but with the taxes and no one to work it…" She trailed off, lifting down a mason jar, then setting it back. "The only gesture her parents ever made was when her mother left Gran the dining-room set and a few pieces of china. Even that was done through lawyers after her mother had died."

Shane plucked up her polishing cloth and began to run it through her hands.

"Gran had five children, lost two in childhood, another in the war. One daughter moved to Oklahoma and died childless about forty years ago. Her youngest son settled here, married and had one daughter. Both he and his wife were killed when the daughter was five." She paused a moment, brooding up at the small window set near the ceiling. Light poured through it to lie in a patch on the concrete floor. "I wonder if you can appreciate how a mother feels when she outlives every one of her children."

Vance said nothing, only continued to watch as Shane moved agitatedly around the room. "She raised her granddaughter, Anne. Gran loved her. Maybe part of the love was grief, I don't know. My mother was a beautiful child—there are pictures of her upstairs—but she was never content. The stories I've heard came mostly from people in town, though once or twice Gran talked to me. Anne hated living here, hated not having enough. She wanted to be an actress. When she was seventeen, she got pregnant."

Shane's voice altered subtly, but he heard the change. It was flat now, devoid of emotion. He'd never heard that tone from her before. "She didn't know—or wouldn't admit—who the father was," she said simply. "As soon as I was born, she took off and left me with Gran. From time to time, she came back, spent a few days and talked Gran out of more money. At last count she's been married three times. I've seen her in furs. They don't seem to make her happy. She's still beautiful, still selfish, still discontented."

Shane turned and looked at Vance for the first time since she had begun. "My grandmother only grabbed for one thing in her life, and that was love. She spoke French beautifully, read Shakespeare and tilled a garden. And she was happy. The only thing my mother ever taught me was that *things* meant nothing. Once you have a *thing,* you're too busy looking for the next one to be happy with it. You're too worried that someone might have a better one to be able to enjoy it. All the games my mother played never brought anything but pain to the people who loved her. I don't have the time or the skill for those games."

As she started to walk to the stairs, Vance stepped in front of her to bar her way. She lifted her chin to stare with eyes that glittered with anger and tears. "You should have told me to go to hell," he said quietly.

Shane swallowed. "Go to hell then," she muttered, and tried to move past him again.

Vance took her shoulders, holding her firmly at arm's length. "Are you angry with me, Shane, or with yourself for telling me something that was none of my business?" he asked.

After taking a deep breath, Shane stared at him, dry-eyed. "I'm angry because you're cynical, and I've never been able to understand cynicism."

"Any more than I understand an idealist."

"I'm not an idealist," she countered. "I simply don't automatically assume there's someone waiting to take advantage of me." She felt calmer suddenly, and sadder. "I think you miss a lot more by not trusting people than you risk by trusting them."

"What happens when the trust is violated?"

"Then you pick up and go on," she told him simply. "You're only a victim if you choose to be."

His brows drew together. Is that what he considered himself? A victim? Was he continuing to allow Amelia to blight his life two years after she'd died? And how much longer would he look over his shoulder for the next betrayal?

Shane felt his fingers relax, saw the puzzled consideration on his face. She lifted a hand to touch his shoulder. "Were you hurt very badly?" she asked him.

Vance focused on her again, then released her. "I was…disillusioned."

"That's the worst kind of hurt, I think." In compassion, she laid a hand on his arm. "When someone you love or care for turns out to be dishonest, or an ideal turns to glass, it's difficult to accept. I always set my ideals high. If they're going to crumble, I'd just as soon take the long fall." She smiled, slipping her hand down so it linked with his. "Let's go for a drive."

His thoughts were so bound up in her words, it took him a moment to understand the suggestion. "A drive?" he repeated.

"We've been cooped up for weeks," Shane stated as she pulled him toward the stairs. "I don't know about you, but I haven't done anything but work until I tumbled into bed. It's a beautiful day, maybe the last of Indian summer." She shut the basement door behind them. "And I bet you haven't had a tour of the battlefield yet. Certainly not with an expert guide."

"Are you," he asked with the beginnings of a smile, "an expert guide?"

"The best," she said without modesty. As she had hoped, the tension went out of the fingers that were laced with hers. "There's nothing about the battle I can't tell you, or as some of my critics would claim, won't tell you."

"As long as I don't have to take a quiz afterward," Vance agreed as she pulled him out the back door.

"I'm retired," she reminded him primly.

"The Battle of Antietam," Shane began as she drove down a narrow, winding road lined with monuments, "though claimed as a clear victory for neither side, resulted in the repulse of Lee's first effort to invade the North." Vance gave a quick grin at her faintly lecturing tone, but didn't interrupt. "Near Antietam Creek here in Sharpsburg," she continued, "on September 17, 1862, Lee and McClellan engaged in the bloodiest single day of the Civil War. That's Dunker Church." Shane pointed to a tiny white building set off the road. "Some of the heaviest fighting went on there. I have some pretty good prints for the museum."

Vance glanced back at the peaceful little spot as Shane drove by. "Looks quiet enough now," he commented, and earned a mild look.

"Lee divided his forces," she went on, ignoring him, "sending Jackson to capture Harper's Ferry. A Union soldier picked up a copy of Lee's orders, giving McClellan an advantage, but he didn't move fast enough. Even when he engaged Lee's much smaller army in Sharpsburg, he failed to smash through the line before Jackson returned with support. Lee lost a quarter of his army and withdrew. McClellan still didn't capitalize on his advantage. Even so, twenty-six thousand men were lost."

"For a retired schoolteacher, you don't seem to have forgotten the facts," Vance remarked.

Shane laughed, taking a bend in the road competently. "My ancestors fought here. Gran didn't let me forget it."

"For which side?"

"Both." She gave a small shrug. "Wasn't that the worst of it really? The choosing sides, the disintegration of families. This is a border state. Though it went for the North, sympathies this far south leaned heavily toward the Confederacy as well. It isn't difficult to imagine a number of people from this area cheering secretly or openly for the Stars and Bars."

"And with this section being caught between Virginia and West Virginia—"

"Exactly," she said, very much like a teacher approving of a bright student. Vance chuckled but she didn't seem to notice. Shane pulled off the side of the road into a small parking area. "Come on, let's walk. It's beautiful here."

Around them mountains circled in the full glory of fall. A few leaves whipped by—orange, scarlet, amber—to be caught by the wind and carried off. There were rolling hills, gold in the slanting sunlight, and fields with dried, withering stalks of corn. The air was cooler now as the sun dropped toward the peaks of the western mountains. Without thinking, Vance linked his hand with hers.

"Bloody Lane," Shane said, bringing his attention to a long, narrow trench. "Gruesome name, but apt. They came at each other from across the fields. Rebs from the north; Yanks from the south. Artillery set up there—" she pointed "—and there. This trench is where most of them lay after it was over. Of course, there were engagements all around—at the Burnside Bridge, the Dunker Church—but this…"

Vance shot her a curious look. "War really fascinates you, doesn't it?"

Shane looked out over the field. "It's the only true obscenity. The only time killing's glorified rather than condemned. Men become statistics. I wonder if there's anything more dehumanizing." Her voice became more thoughtful. "Haven't you ever found it odd that to kill one to one is considered man's ultimate crime, but the more a man kills during war, the more he's honored? So many of these were farm boys," she continued before Vance could form an answer. "Children who'd never shot at anything more than a weasel in the henhouse. They put on a uniform, blue or gray, and marched into battle. I doubt if a fraction of them had any idea what it was really going to be like. I'll tell you what fascinates me." Shane looked back at Vance, too wrapped up in her own thoughts to note how intensely he watched her. "Who were they really? The sixteen-year-old Pennsylvania farm boy who rushed across this field to kill a sixteen-year-old boy from a Georgia plantation—did they start out looking for adventure? Were they on a quest? How many pictured themselves sitting around a camp fire like men and raising some hell away from their mothers?"

"A great many, I imagine," Vance murmured.

Affected by the image she projected, he slipped an arm around her shoulders as he looked out over the field. "Too many."

"Even the ones who got back whole would never be boys again."

"Then why history, Shane, when it's riddled with wars?"

"For the people." She tossed back her head to look at him. The lowering sun shining on her eyes seemed to accentuate the tiny gold flecks that he sometimes couldn't see at all. "For the boy I can imagine who came across that field in September more than a hundred and twenty years ago. He was seventeen." She turned back to the field as if she could indeed see him. "He'd had his first whiskey, but not his first woman. He came running across that field full of terror and glory. The bugles were blaring, the shells exploding, so that the noise was so huge, he never heard his own fear. He killed an enemy that was so obscure to him it had no face. And when the battle was over, when the war was over, he went home a man, tired and aching for his own land."

"What happened to him?" Vance murmured.

"He married his childhood sweetheart, raised ten kids and told his grandchildren about his charge to Bloody Lane in 1862."

Vance drew her closer, not in passion, but in camaraderie. "You must have been a hell of a teacher," he said quietly.

That made Shane laugh. "I was a hell of a storyteller," she corrected.

"Why do you do that?" he demanded. "Why do you underrate yourself?"

She shook her head. "No, I know my capabilities and my limitations. And," she added, "I'm willing to stretch them both a bit to get what I want. It's much smarter than thinking you're something you're not." Before he could speak, she laughed, giving him a friendly hug. "No, no more philosophizing. I've done my share for the day. Come on, let's go up in the tower. The view's wonderful from there." She was off in a sprint, pulling Vance with her. "You can see for miles," she told him as they climbed the narrow iron steps.

The light was dim though the sun shot through the small slits set in the sides of the stone tower. It grew brighter as they climbed, then poured through the opening at the top. "This is the part I like best," she told him, while a few annoyed pigeons fluttered away from their roost in the roof. She leaned over the wide stone, pleased to let the wind buffet her face. "Oh, it's beautiful, the perfect day for it. Look at those colors!" She drew Vance beside her, wanting to share. "Do you see? That's our mountain."

Our mountain. Vance smiled as he followed the direction of her hand. The way she said it, it might have belonged to the two of them exclusively. Beyond the tree-thick hills, the more distant mountains were cast in blue from the falling afternoon light. Farmhouses and barns were set here and there, with the more closely structured surrounding towns quiet in the early evening hush. Just barely, he could hear the whiz of a car on the highway. As he looked over a cornfield, he saw three enormous crows take flight. They argued, taunting each other as they glided across the sky. The air was very still after they passed, so quiet he could hear the breeze whisper in the dry stalks of corn.

Then he saw the buck. It stood poised no more than ten yards from where Shane had parked her car. It was still as a statue, head up, ears pricked. Vance turned to Shane and pointed.

In silence, hands linked, they watched. Vance felt something move inside him, a sudden sense of belonging. He wouldn't have been amused now if Shane had said "our mountain." Remnants of bitterness washed from him as he realized his answer had been staring him in the face. He'd kept himself a victim, just as Shane had said, because it was easier to be angry than to let go.

The buck moved quickly, bounding over the grassy hill, taking a low stone fence with a graceful leap before he darted out of sight. Vance felt rather than heard Shane's long, slow sigh.

"I never get used to it," she murmured. "Every time I see one, I'm struck dumb."

Shane turned her face up to his. It seemed natural to kiss her here, with the mountains and fields around them, with the feeling of something shared still on both of them. Above their heads a pigeon cooed softly, content now that the intruders were quiet.

Here was the tenderness Shane had sensed but had not been sure of. His mouth was firm but not demanding, his hands strong but not bruising. Her heart seemed to flutter to her throat. Everything warm and sweet poured through her until she was limp and pliant in his arms. She had been waiting for this—this final assurance of what she knew he held trapped inside him: a gentle goodness she would respect as much as his strength and confidence. Her sigh was not of surrender but of joy in knowing she could admire what she already loved.

Vance drew her closer, changing the angle of the kiss, reluctant to break the moment. Emotions seeped into him, through the cracks in the wall he had built so long ago. He felt the soft give of her mouth, tasted its moist generosity. With care, he let his fingertips reacquaint themselves with the texture of her skin.

Could she have been there all along, he wondered, waiting for him to stumble onto her through a curtain of bitterness and suspicion?

Vance drew her against his chest, holding her tightly with both arms as if she might vanish. Was it too late for him to fall in love? he wondered. Or to win a woman who already knew the worst of him and had no notion of his material advantages? Closing his eyes, he rested his cheek on her hair. If it wasn't too late, should he take the chance and tell her who and what he was? If he told her now, he might never be fully certain, if she came to him, that she came only to him. He needed that—to be taken for himself without the Riverton-Banning fortune or power. He hesitated, torn and indecisive. That alone shook him. Vance was a man who ruled a multimillion-dollar company by being decisive. Now a slip of a woman whose hair curled chaotically under his cheek was changing the order of his life.

"Shane." Vance drew her away to kiss her brow.

"Vance." Laughing, she kissed him soundly, more like a friend than a lover. "You look so serious."

"Have dinner with me." It came out too swiftly and he cursed himself. What had become of his finesse with women?

Shane pushed at her windblown hair. "All right. I can fix us something at the house."

"No, I want to take you out."

"Out?" Shane frowned, thinking of the expense.

"Nothing fancy," he told her, thinking she was worried about her bulky sweater and jeans. "As you said, neither of us has done anything but work in weeks." He brushed his knuckles over the back of her cheek. "Come with me."

She smiled, pleasing him. "I know a nice little place just over the border in West Virginia."

Shane chose the tiny, out-of-the-way restaurant because it was inexpensive and she had some fond memories of an abbreviated career as a waitress there. She'd worked the summer after her high school graduation in order to earn extra money for college.

After they had settled into a cramped booth with a sputtering candle between them, she shot him a grin. "I knew you'd love it."

Vance glanced around at the painted landscapes in vivid colors and plastic frames. The air smelled ever so faintly of onion. "Next time, I choose."

"They used to serve a great spaghetti here. It was Thursday's special, all you can eat for—"

"It's not Thursday," Vance pointed out, dubiously opening the plastic-coated menu. "Wine?"

"I think they probably have it." Shane smiled at him when he peered over the top of the menu. "We could go next door and get a whole bottle for two ninety-seven."

"Good vintage?"

"Just last week," she assured him.

"We'll take our chances here." He decided next time he would take her somewhere he could buy her champagne.

"I'll have the chili," Shane announced, bringing his thoughts back.

"Chili?" Vance frowned at the menu again. "Is it any good?"

"Oh, no!"

"Then why are you—" He broke off as he lowered his menu and saw Shane buried behind her own. "Shane, what—"

"They just came in," she hissed, turning her menu toward the entrance and peeping around the side of it.

Curiously, he glanced over. Vance spotted Cy Trainer with a trim brunette in a severely tailored tan suit and sensible pumps. His first reaction was annoyance; then, looking the woman over again and noting the way her hand rested on Cy's arm, he turned back to Shane. She was fully hidden behind the menu.

"Shane, I know it must upset you, but you're bound to run into him from time to time and…" He heard a muffled sound from behind the plastic-coated cardboard. Instinctively, Vance reached for her hand. "We could go somewhere else, but we can't leave now without his seeing you."

"It's Laurie MacAfee." She squeezed Vance's fingers

convulsively. He returned the pressure, furious that she still had feelings for the man who had hurt her.

"Shane, you've got to face this and not let him see you make a fool of yourself."

"I know, but it's so hard." Cautiously, she tilted the menu to the side. With a jolt, Vance saw she was convulsed not with tears but with laughter. "As soon as he sees us," she began confidentially, "he's going to come over and be polite."

"I can see that's going to cause you a lot of pain."

"Oh, it is," she agreed. "Because you've got to promise to kick me under the table or stomp on my foot the minute you see I'm going to laugh."

"My pleasure," he assured her.

"Laurie used to keep her dolls lined up according to height and she sewed little name tags on all their clothes," Shane explained, taking deep breaths to prepare herself.

"That certainly clears everything up."

"Okay, now I'm going to put the menu down." She swallowed, lowering her voice a bit more. "Whatever you do, don't look at them."

"I wouldn't dream of it."

After a final cleansing breath, Shane set the menu on the table. "Chili?" she said in a normal tone. "Yes, it's always been good here. I believe I'll have it too."

"You're an idiot."

"Oh yes, I agree." Smiling, she picked up her water glass. Out the corner of her eye, she spotted Cy and Laurie crossing the room toward them. To kill the first bubble of laughter, she cleared her throat violently.

"Shane, how nice to see you."

Looking up, Shane managed to feign surprise. "Hello, Cy. Hello, Laurie. How've you been?"

"Very well," Laurie answered in her carefully modulated voice. She's really very pretty, Shane thought. Even if her eyes are just a fraction too close together.

"I don't think you know Vance," she continued. "Vance, this is Cy Trainer and Laurie MacAfee, old school friends of mine. Vance is my neighbor."

"Ah, of course, the old Farley place." Cy extended his hand. Vance found it soft. The grip was correctly firm and brief. "I hear you're fixing the place up."

"A bit." Vance allowed himself to study Cy's face. He was passable, Vance decided, considering he had a weak jaw.

"You must be the carpenter who's helping Shane set up her little shop," Laurie put in. Her glance slipped over his work clothes before it shifted to Shane's sweater. "I must say, I was surprised when Cy told me your plans."

Seeing Shane's lip quiver, Vance set his foot firmly on top of hers. "Were you?" Shane said as she reached for her water again. Her eyes danced with suppressed amusement as they met Vance's over the rim. "Well, I've always liked to surprise people."

"We couldn't imagine you with your own business, could we, Cy?" Laurie went on without giving him a chance to answer. "Of course, we wish you the very best of luck, Shane, and you can count on both of us to buy something to help you get started."

The laughter was a pain in her stomach. Shane had

to press a hand against it while Vance increased the pressure on her foot. "Thank you, Laurie. I can't tell you what that means to me…I really can't."

"Anything for an old friend, right, Cy? You know we wish you every success, Shane. I'll be sure to tell everyone I know about your little shop. That should help bring a few people in. Though of course," she sighed apologetically, "the selling's up to you."

"Y-yes. Thank you."

"We'll just be running along now. We want to order before it gets too crowded. So nice meeting you." Laurie sent Vance a brief smile and drew Cy away.

"Oh, God, I think I'm going to burst!" Shane drank down the whole glass of water without a breath.

"Your boyfriend got just what he deserved," Vance murmured, glancing after them. "She'll regiment everything right down to their sex life." Thoughtfully, he looked after them. "Do you think they have one yet?"

"Oh, stop," Shane begged, savaging her lip in defense. "I'll be hysterical in a minute."

"Do you suppose she picked out that tie he's wearing?" Vance asked.

Giving up, Shane burst in to laughter. "Oh, damn you, Vance," she whispered when Laurie turned her head. "I was doing so well too."

"Want to give them something to talk about over dinner?" Before she could answer, Vance pulled her across the narrow booth and planted a long, lingering kiss on her lips. To keep Shane from ending it too soon, he caught her chin in his hand and held her still. He drew her away for only seconds, tilting her head, then pressing his mouth to hers again at a fresh angle. He heard her give a tiny moan of distress. Though she lifted a hand to his shoulder to push him away, when he deepened the kiss, she allowed it to lie unresisting until he took his lips from hers.

"Now you've done it," she said when she gathered her wits again. "By noon tomorrow it'll be all over Sharpsburg that we're lovers."

"Will it?" Smiling, he lifted her hand to his lips, then slowly kissed her fingers one by one. It satisfied him to feel the faint tremor of arousal.

"Yes," Shane answered breathlessly, "and I don't…" she trailed off when he turned her palm up to press another long kiss in its center.

"Don't what?" he asked softly, taking his lips to the inside of her wrist. Her pulse pounded against the light trace of his tongue.

"Think it's—it's wise," she managed, forgetting the restaurant and Cy and Laurie and everything else.

"That we're lovers or that it's all over Sharpsburg?" Vance enjoyed the confusion in her eyes and the knowledge that he had put it there.

Her pulse beat jerkily. He was different. Reckless? she thought, and felt a fresh thrill race down her spine. Smooth? How could he be both at once? Yet he was. The recklessness was in his eyes, but the romantic moves were smooth with experience.

She hadn't been afraid of the hard, angry man she had met, but she felt a skip of fear for the one who even now traced his thumb over the speeding pulse at her wrist.

"I'm going to have to give that some thought," she murmured.

"Do that," he said agreeably.

Chapter 8

Shane opened the doors of Antietam Antiques and Museum the first week of December. As she had expected, for the first few days the shop and museum were crowded, for the most part with people she knew. They had come to buy or browse out of curiosity or affection. Others came to see what "that Abbott girl" had up her sleeve this time. It amused Shane to hear her past crimes discussed as though they had taken place the day before. Cy's name was dropped a time or two, causing her to force back a chuckle and change the subject. Still, after the initial novelty had worn off, she had a steady trickle of customers. That was enough to satisfy her.

As planned, she hired Donna's sister-in-law, Pat, on a part-time basis. The girl was eager and willing, and not opposed to giving Shane weekend hours. Shane considered the additional expense well worth it when Pat, flushed with triumph, rang up her first sale. With her coaching, and Pat's own enthusiastic studying, Shane's assistant had learned enough to classify certain articles in the shop and to handle questions in the museum section.

Shane found herself busier than ever, managing the shop, watching for ads for estate sales and overseeing the remodeling still under way on the second floor. The long, chaotic hours stimulated her, and helped her deal with the slow but steady loss of her grandmother's treasures. It was business, Shane reminded herself again and again as she sold a corner cabinet or candle holder. It was necessary. The bills in her desk had mounted over the weeks of preparation, and they had to be paid.

She saw Vance almost daily as he came to hammer and saw and trim on the second floor. Though he wasn't as withdrawn as he once had been, the intimacy they had shared for an afternoon and evening had faded. He treated her as a casual friend, not a woman whose palm he would kiss in a restaurant.

Shane concluded that he had taken on a loverlike aspect for Cy's benefit, and now it was back to business as usual. She wasn't discouraged. In fact, the man she had dined with had made her nervous and uncertain. She was more confident with Vance's temper than with soft words and tender caresses. Knowing herself well, Shane was aware it would be difficult not to make a fool of herself over him if he continued to treat her with gentleness. She had little defense against romance.

Daily, her love for him grew. It only made her more

certain than ever that he was the only man for her. It would only be a matter of time, she decided, before he realized she was the woman for him.

It was late afternoon when Shane carried her latest acquisition up the new front steps and into the shop. She was flushed with cold and highly pleased with herself. She was learning to be ruthless when bargaining. After pushing the door open with her bottom, she carried the table through the entrance sideways.

"Just look what I've got!" she said to Pat before she closed the door behind her. "It's a Sheridan; not a scratch on it either."

Pat stopped washing the glass on the display case. "Shane, you were supposed to take the afternoon off." Automatically she polished off a lingering smear before giving Shane her full attention. "You've got to take some time for yourself," she reminded her with a hint of exasperation. "That's why you hired me."

"Yes, of course," Shane said distractedly. "There's a mantel clock in the car and a complete set of cut-glass saltcellars." Pat sighed, smart enough to know when she was being ignored, and followed Shane into the main showroom.

"Don't you ever quit?" she demanded.

"Uh-uh." After setting the table beside a Hitchcock chair, Shane stepped back to view the results. "I don't know," she said slowly. "It might look better in the front room, right under the window. Well, I want to polish it first anyway." She darted to the work counter, rummaging for the furniture polish. "How'd we do today?"

Pat shook her head. The first thing she had learned

on the job was that Shane Abbott was a powerhouse. "I'll do that," she said, taking the polish and rag from Shane's hands. Shane grinned at Pat's weighty sigh but said nothing. "You had seven people come through the museum," Pat told her as she began to polish the Sheridan. "I sold some postcards and a print of the Burnside Bridge. A woman from Hagerstown bought the little table with the fluted edges."

Shane stopped unbuttoning her coat. "The rosewood piecrust?" It had sat in the summer parlor for as long as she could remember.

"Yes. And she was interested in the bentwood rocker." Pat tucked a strand of hair behind her ear while Shane struggled to be pleased. "I think she'll be back."

"Good."

"Oh, and you had a nibble on Uncle Festus."

"Really?" Shane grinned, thinking of the portrait of a dour Victorian man she'd been unable to resist. She had bought it because it amused her, though she had had little hope of selling it. "Well, I'll be sorry to lose him. He gives the place dignity."

"He gives me the creeps," Pat said baldly as Shane headed for the front door to fetch the rest of her new stock. "Oh, I nearly forgot. You didn't tell me you'd sold the dining-room set."

"What?" Puzzled, Shane stopped with her hand on the knob.

"The dining-room set with the heart-shaped chairs," Pat explained. "The Hepplewhite," she added, pleased that she was beginning to remember makes and periods. "I nearly sold it again."

"Again?" Shane released the knob and faced Pat fully. "What are you talking about?"

"There were some people in here a few hours ago who wanted it. It seems their daughter's getting married, and they were going to buy it as a wedding gift. They must be rich," she added with feeling. "The reception's going to be at a Baltimore country club… with an orchestra." She began to daydream about this a bit, but then she noted Shane's hard look. "Anyway," she continued quickly, "I'd nearly finalized the sale when Vance came downstairs and explained it was taken already."

Shane's eyes narrowed. "Vance? Vance said it was already sold?"

"Well, yes," Pat agreed, puzzled by the tone. If she had known Shane better, she would have recognized the beginnings of rage. Innocently, she continued. "It was a lucky thing too, or else they'd have bought it and arranged for the shipping right then and there. I guess you'd have been in a fix."

"A fix," Shane repeated between set teeth. "Yeah, somebody's in a fix all right." Abruptly, she turned to stride toward the rear of the shop while Pat looked after her, wide-eyed.

"Shane? Shane, what's wrong?" Confused, she trotted after her. "Where are you going?"

"To settle some business," she said tightly. "Get the rest of the stuff out of my car, will you?" she called back without slackening her pace. "And lock up; this might take a while."

"Sure, but…" Pat trailed off when she heard the back

door slam. She puzzled a moment, shrugged, then went to follow orders.

"A fix," Shane muttered as she crushed dead leaves underfoot. "Lucky thing he came down." Furiously, she kicked at a fallen branch and sent it skidding ahead of her, waiting to be kicked again. Grinding her teeth, she stormed purposefully down the path between denuded trees. "Already taken!" Enraged, she made a dangerous sound in her throat. A hapless squirrel started across the path, then dashed in the other direction.

Through the bare trees, she could see his house, with smoke puffing from the chimney to struggle up into a hard blue sky. Shane set her jaw and increased her pace. Into the quiet came a steady thump, pause, thump. Without hesitation, she skirted around to the back of the house.

Vance put another log on the tree stump he used as a chopping block, then bore down with his axe to split it neatly in two. Without a pause in rhythm, he set a new log. Shane took no time to admire the precision or grace of the movement.

"You!" she spat, and stuck her fists on her hips.

Vance checked his next swing. Glancing over, he saw Shane glaring at him with glittering eyes and a flushed face. He thought idly that she looked her best when in a temper, then followed through. The next log split to fall in two pieces on either side of the stump. The generous pile was evidence that he had been working for some time.

"Hello, Shane."

"Don't you 'hello Shane' me," she snapped, closing the distance between them in three quick strides. "How dare you?"

"Most people consider it an acceptable greeting," he countered as he bent down for another log. Shane knocked it off the stump with a sweep of her hand.

"You had no right to interfere, no right to cost me a sale. An important sale," she added furiously. Her breath puffed out visibly in the frigid air. "Just who the hell do you think you are, telling my customers something's already taken? Even if it had been, which it wasn't, it's hardly your place to add your two cents."

Calmly, Vance picked up the log again. He had been expecting her—and her anger. He had acted on impulse but didn't regret it. Very clearly, he could recall the look on her face when she had first shown him her grandmother's pride and joy. There was no way he was going to stand by and do nothing while she watched it being carted out the door.

"You don't want to sell it, Shane."

Her eyes only became more furious. "It's none of your business what I want to do. I have to sell it. I'm *going* to sell it. If you hadn't opened your big mouth, I *would* have sold it."

"And spent several hours hating yourself and crying over the invoice," he tossed back, slamming the blade of the axe into the stump before he faced her. "The money isn't worth it."

"Don't you tell me what it's worth," she retorted, and poked a finger into his chest. "You don't know how I feel. You don't know what I have to do. *I* do. I need the money, damn it."

With strained calm, he curled his hand around the finger that dug into his chest, held it aloft a moment, then let it drop. "You don't need it enough to give up something that's important to you."

"Sentiment doesn't pay bills." The color in her cheeks heightened. "I've got a desk full of them."

"Sell something else," he shouted back at her. Her face was lifted to his, her eyes glowing with anger. He felt conflicting urges to protect her and to throttle her. "You've got the damn place packed with junk as it is."

"Junk!" He had just declared war. *"Junk!"* Her voice rose.

"Unload some of the other stuff you've got piled in there," he advised with a coolness that would have rattled his business associates. A dangerous hissing sound escaped through Shane's teeth.

"You don't know the first thing about it," she fumed, poking him again so that he stepped back. "I stock the very best pieces I can find, and *you*"—she poked again—"you don't know a Hepplewhite from a—a piece of pressboard. You keep your city nose out of my affairs, Vance Banning, and play with your planes and drill bits. I don't need some flatlander to hand out empty advice."

"That's it," he said grimly. In one swift move, he swept Shane off her feet and dumped her over his shoulder.

"What the hell do you think you're doing?" she screamed, thrashing and pounding him with her fists.

"I'm taking you inside to make love to you," he stated between his teeth. "I've had enough."

In absolute astonishment, Shane stopped thrashing. "You're *what?*"

"You heard me."

"You're crazy!" More furious than frantic, she

renewed her efforts to inflict pain wherever she could land a hit. Vance continued through the back door. "You're not taking me inside," she raged, even as he carted her through the kitchen. "I'm not going with you."

"You're going exactly where I take you," he countered.

"Oh, you're going to pay for this, Vance," she promised as she pounded against his back.

"I don't doubt that," he muttered, starting up the stairs.

"You put me down this minute. I'm not putting up with this."

Weary of being kicked, he pulled off her shoes, tossed them over the banister, then tightened an arm around the back of her knees. "You're going to put up with a hell of a lot more in a few minutes."

With her legs effectively pinned, she wiggled uselessly as he continued up the stairs. "I'm telling you, you're in big trouble. I'll get you for this," she warned, beating furiously against him as he strode down the hall and into a bedroom. "If you don't put me down this minute, *right this minute,* you're fired!" Shane let out a shriek as she tumbled through the air, then a whoosh as she thudded heavily on the bed. Breathless and infuriated, she scrambled to her knees. "You idiot!" she raged, puffing a bit. "Just what do you think you're doing?"

"I told you what I was doing." Vance stripped off his jacket and tossed it aside.

"If you think for one minute you can toss me over your shoulder like a bale of hay and get away with it, you're sadly mistaken." Shane watched with mounting fury as he unbuttoned his shirt. "And you stop that right now. You can't *make* me make love with you."

"Watch me." Vance peeled off his shirt.

"Oh no, you don't." Though she stuck her hands on her hips, the indignant pose lost something as she knelt on the bed. "Just put that right back on."

Watching her coolly, Vance dropped it to the floor, then bent to pull off his boots.

Shane glared at him. "You think you can just dump me on the bed and that's all there is to it?"

"I haven't even started yet," he informed her as the second boot dropped with a clatter.

"You simpleminded clod," she returned, heaving a pillow at him. "I wouldn't let you touch me if—" She searched for something original and scathing but settled on the standby. "If you were the last man on earth!"

Vance sent her a long, glittering look before he unbuckled his belt.

"I told you to stop that." Shane pointed a warning finger. "I mean it. Don't you dare take another thing off. Vance!" she added threateningly as he reached for the snap of his jeans. "I'm serious." The word ended on a giggle. His hands paused; his eyes narrowed. "Put your clothes back on this minute," she ordered, but pressed the back of her hand to her mouth. Over it, her eyes were wide and brilliant with amusement.

"What the hell's so funny?" he demanded.

"Nothing, not a thing." With this, Shane collapsed on her back, helpless with laughter. "Funny? No, no, this is a very grave situation." Convulsed with giggles, she pounded her fists on the bed. "The man is standing there, pulling off his clothes and looking fit for murder. Nothing could be more serious."

Shane glanced over at him, then covered her mouth with both hands. "*That* is the face of a man overcome by lust and desire." She laughed until tears came to her eyes.

Damn her, Vance thought as a grin tugged at his mouth. He crossed to the bed; then, sitting beside her, he planted his hands on either side of her head. The harder she tried to control her amusement, the more her eyes laughed at him. "Glad you're having a good time," he commented.

She swallowed a chuckle. "Oh no, I'm furious, absolutely furious, but it was *so* romantic."

"Was it?" His grin widened as he considered her.

"Oh yes, why you just swept me off my feet." Her laughter rang through the room. "I don't know when I've been more *aroused,*" she managed.

"Is that so?" Vance murmured as Shane gave herself wholly to mirth. Very deliberately, he lowered his lips to brush her chin.

"Yes, unless it was when Billy Huffman pushed me into the briars in second grade. Obviously I inflame males into violent seizures of passion."

"Obviously," Vance agreed, tucking her hair behind her ear. "I've had several since I tangled with you." Her fit of giggles ceased abruptly when he caught her earlobe between his teeth. "I think I'm bound to have several more," he murmured, moving down to her neck.

"Vance—"

"Soon," he added against her throat. "Any minute."

"I have to get back," she began breathlessly. As she attempted to sit up, he pressed a hand to her shoulder to keep her still.

"I wonder what else might arouse you." He nibbled at the cord of her neck. "This?"

"No, I…"

"No?" He gave a deep, quiet laugh, feeling her pulse hammer against his lips. "Something else then." Her coat was unzipped, and deftly he loosened the range of buttons on her blouse. "This?" Very gently, he touched the tip of her breast with his tongue.

On a gasp, Shane arched against him. Vance drew her nipple into his mouth to let her taste seep through him. He savored it a moment as Shane dug her nails into his bare shoulders. But when the heat shot into him, he knew he had to pull back before he took her too quickly. He'd been careful since the night they had dined together to keep some space between them. He hadn't wanted to rush her. Now that he had her in his bed, he intended to savor every moment.

Vance lifted his head and looked down at her. Her eyes were wide and fixed on his. For a moment, they both looked for answers. Very slowly, Shane smiled. "This," she whispered, and drew his mouth down to hers.

She hadn't been prepared for the sweetness of the kiss. His lips moved gently over hers. Their breath merged and matched rhythm. With light kisses he roamed her face, only to return over and over to her waiting mouth. To linger, to savor, to make each moment, each taste last; that was his only thought. The fiery needs were banked by the simple knowledge that she was his to touch, to kiss, to love. For the first time in his memory, he wanted to bring a woman pleasure much more than he wanted to take his own. He could give her that with the slow kisses that made his own blood thunder. Until he sensed she craved more, he used only his lips and tongue to arouse her.

Hardly touching her, Vance drew her jacket over her shoulders and arms, lifting her slightly to slip it from under her. His touch was so sure, so gentle, she remained unaware of his inner conflict between passion and tenderness. Without hurry, he drew off her shirt, following its progress over her shoulders with his lips. Shane sighed as his kisses ranged down her arm to nibble at the inside of her elbow. Fighting the growing need to rush, Vance trailed his lips down to her wrist.

If the wind still blew outside the windows, if leaves still rustled along the ground, Shane was unaware. There was only the play of Vance's fingertips, only the warm trace of his mouth. Content, almost sleepy, she ran her fingers through his thick mane of hair as his teeth tugged lightly at the cord of her neck. The lazy friction of his skin against hers had her pulse beating thickly. She felt she could stay forever, floating in a world halfway between passion and serenity.

He began the downward journey slowly, hardly seeming to move at all. With kisses and light love bites, he circled her breast, moving inward until he captured the peak. It grew hot and hard in his mouth while she began to move under him. He suckled, using his tongue to bring them both to the edge of delirium. Her breathing was as raspy as his. Now he could feel the energy flowing from her, pouring out in passion and urgency. Moaning his name, she pressed him closer to her.

But there was so much more to give, so much more

to take. With deliberate care, Vance repeated the same aching journey around her other breast, feeling her shudders, listening to the storm of her heartbeat under his hungry, seeking lips.

"So soft," he murmured. "So beautiful." For a moment he merely buried his face against her breast, struggling to hang on to his control. On a moan of need, Shane reached for him as if to bring his mouth back to hers, but he slipped lower.

Taking her arching hips in his hands, Vance traced his tongue down her quivering skin. Shane felt her jeans loosen at the waist and shifted to help him. But he only pressed his mouth deep into the vee of exposed flesh. Again she shifted, curving her back to offer herself, but he lingered, tracing lazy circles with his tongue.

When he worked the jeans over her hips, she felt each searing brush of his fingers. Down her thighs he journeyed, pausing to caress their soft inner flesh, over her calves to nibble gently at the taut muscles, then to her ankles, sending a devastating flush of heat up her body with a quick flick of his tongue.

He found points of pleasure she had been unaware existed. Then he was at the core of her, his tongue stabbing inside her to catapult her beyond all bounds of reason. She moaned his name, moving with him, moving for him, with mind and body tormented by dark, pulsing delights.

Vance heard his name come huskily through her lips and thrilled to it. Her energy, her wellspring of passion inflamed him, driving him to take her deeper before he took all. The sweet, sweet taste of her made him greedy.

Somewhere in the back of his clouded mind he knew he was no longer gentle with her, but needs whipped at him.

Madness overcame him. His mouth roamed wildly over her body as his fingers took her from peak to staggering peak. Her breath was heaving when he found her breast. If she had been capable of words, Shane would have pleaded with him to take her. Her world was spinning at a terrifying speed, a speed far beyond the scope of her imagination. When his mouth crushed hers, she answered blindly. He thrust into her.

The flow of energy came from nowhere—a power, a strength that hurled her beyond the reasonable and into the impossible. One fed the other, driving higher and faster until they found the apex. Together, they clung to it, shuddering.

How long he lay still, Vance was unsure. Perhaps he even dozed. When his mind began to clear, he found his mouth nuzzled against Shane's throat, her arms wrapped around him. He was still inside her and could feel the light pulses of lingering passion deep within her. For a moment longer he kept his eyes closed, wondering how it was possible to be both sated and exhilarated. When he started to move, thinking of her comfort, Shane tightened her hold to keep him close.

"No," she murmured. "Just a little longer."

He laughed as his lips grazed her ear. "Can you breathe?"

"I'll breathe later."

Content, he snuggled back into the curve of her neck. "I like the way you taste. I've had a problem with that since the first time I kissed you."

"A problem?" she said lazily, running experimental fingers over the muscles of his back. "That doesn't sound much like a compliment to me."

"Would you like one?" He pressed his mouth to her skin. "You're the most exquisite creature I've ever seen."

Shane received this news with a snort of laughter. "Your first compliment was a bit more credible."

Vance lifted his head and looked down at her. Though her eyes were still sleepy with passion, they were amused. "You really don't see it, do you?" he said thoughtfully. Did she really have no notion what big velvet eyes and satin skin could do to a man when combined with her kind of vivacity? Didn't she realize the kind of power there was in striking innocence when it was offset by a sensual mouth and an open, honest sexuality? "You might lose it if you did," he said half to himself. "What if I said I liked your nose?"

She eyed him warily for a moment. "If you say I'm cute, I'll hit you."

He chuckled, then kissed both dimpled cheeks. "Do you know how long I've wanted you like this?"

"From the first moment in the general store." She smiled when he lifted his head to stare down at her. "I felt it too. It was as though I'd been expecting you."

Vance laid his forehead on hers. "I was furious."

"I was stunned. I forgot my coffee."

They laughed before their mouths met. "You were terribly rude that day," she remembered.

"I meant to be." He lured her lips back to his. "I wanted to get rid of you."

"Did you really think you could?" Chuckling, she

nipped at his bottom lip. "Don't you know a determined woman when you see one?"

"I *would* have gotten rid of you if I'd been able to close my eyes at night without seeing you."

"Did you really? Poor Vance." She gave him a sympathetic kiss.

"I'm sure you're very sorry I lost sleep over you."

She made a suspicious sound. Vance lifted his head again to see her bottom lip caught firmly between her teeth. "I would be sorry," she assured him, "if I didn't think it was wonderful."

"I often wanted to strangle you at three o'clock in the morning."

"I'm sure you did," she returned soberly. "Why don't you kiss me instead?"

He did, roughly, as banked passions began to smolder again. "That day when you sat in the mud, laughing like a fool, I wanted you so badly I hurt. Damn you, Shane, I haven't been able to think straight for weeks." His mouth crushed down on hers again with a touch of the anger she remembered. She soothed the back of his neck with her fingers.

When he lifted his head, their eyes met in a long, deep look. Shane lifted her palm to his cheek.

So much turbulence, she thought. So many secrets.

So much sweetness, he thought. So much honesty.

"I love you," they said together, then stared at each other in amazement. For a moment, they neither moved nor spoke. It seemed even their breathing had halted at the same instant. Then, as one, they reached out, clinging heart to heart, mouth to mouth. What started as a desperate meeting of lips softened, then sweetened, then promised.

Vance closed his eyes on waves of relief and towering pleasure. When he felt Shane's shudders he drew his arms tighter around her. "You're trembling. Why?"

"It's too perfect," she said in a voice that shook. "It frightens me. If I were to lose you now—"

"Shh." He cut her off with a kiss. "It *is* perfect."

"Oh, Vance, I love you so much. I've been waiting all these weeks for you to love me back, and now..." She took his face in her hands and shook her head. "Now that you do, I'm scared."

Looking down at her, he felt a surge of passion and possession. She was his now; nothing was going to change it. No more mistakes, no more disillusionments. He heard her breath catch then shudder.

"I love you," he said fiercely. "I'm going to keep you, do you understand? We belong together. We both know it. Nothing, by God, nothing's going to interfere with that."

He took her on a wild surge of need and desperation, ignoring the shadow of trepidation that watched over his shoulder.

Chapter 9

It was dark when Shane woke. She had no idea of time or place, only of deep inner contentment and security. The weight of an arm around her waist meant love; the quiet breathing near her ear meant her lover slept beside her. She needed nothing more.

Idly, she wondered how long they had slept. The sun had been setting when she had closed her eyes. The moon was up now. Its cool white light filtered in through the windows to slant across the bed. Shifting slightly, Shane tilted her head back to look at Vance's face. In the dim light, she could make out the sweep of cheek-bone and outline of jaw, the strong straight nose. With a fingertip, she traced his mouth gently, not wanting to wake him. As long as he slept, she could look her fill.

It was a strong face, even a hard one, she mused, with

its sharp angles and dark coloring. His mouth could be cruel, his eyes cold. Even in his loving there was a ruthless sort of power in him. While a woman might feel safe in his arms, she would never be completely comfortable. A life with him would be full of constant demands, arguments, passion.

And he loves me, Shane thought in a kind of terrified wonder.

In sleep, Vance shifted, drawing her closer. As their naked bodies pressed intimately close, a dull throb of need moved through her. Her skin heated against his, tingling with the contact. Against the slow, steady beat of his heart, hers began to thud erratically. Desire had never seemed more demanding, yet he did nothing more than lie quietly beside her, deep in his own dreams.

It would always be like this, she realized as she settled her head in the crook of his shoulder. He would give her very little peace. Though she was a woman who had always taken peace for granted, Shane would now forfeit it cheerfully. He was her fate; she had known it from the first instant. Now, she felt as bound to him as if she had been his wife for decades.

For a long time she lay awake, listening to him sleep, feeling the steady rise and fall of his chest against her breasts. This would never change, she told herself. This need to hold each other. She burrowed against him for a moment, filling herself with his scent. As long as she lived, Shane knew she would remember every second, every word spoken during their first time together. She would need no diary to remind her of young, churning fires when she was old. No passage of time would dull her memory or her feelings.

With a sigh, she brushed a whisper of a kiss over his lips. He didn't stir, but she wondered if he dreamed of her. She wanted him to, and closing her eyes, she willed him to. Carefully, she drew away from him, then moving lightly, slipped from the bed. Their clothes were in scattered heaps. Finding Vance's shirt, Shane slipped it on before she left the room.

Her scent lingered on the pillowcase. It was the first thing to penetrate Vance's senses as he drifted awake. It suited her so, the fresh, clean fragrance with a suggestion of lemon. Lazily, he allowed it to seep into him. Even in sleep, his mind was full of her. There was a slight stiffness in his shoulder where her head had rested. Vance flexed it before reaching out to bring her back to him. He found himself alone. Opening his eyes, Vance whispered her name.

He experienced the same sense of time disorientation that Shane had. The room was dim with moonlight, so that for a moment he thought he must have dreamed it all. But the sheets were still warm from her, and her scent still lingered. No dream. The relief he felt overwhelmed him. Softly, he called her name. It was then he smelled the bacon. In the dark, he grinned foolishly and settled back. As he lay quietly, he could just hear Shane's voice as she sang some silly popular song.

She was in the kitchen, he thought. Vance stayed where he was, listening. She was rooting through the cupboards, clattering something. Water was running. The scent of bacon grew stronger. How long, he wondered, had he waited to feel this way? *Complete.* He hadn't known he had been waiting, but he did know what he had found. She filled the emptiness that had nagged at him for years, healed an old, festering wound. She was all the answers to all the questions.

And what would he bring her? his conscience demanded. Vance closed his eyes. He knew himself too well to pretend he would give her a smooth, serene life. His temper was too volatile, his responsibilities too intrusive. Even with adjustments to both, he could paint her no soft pastoral scene. His life, past, present and future, had too many complications. Even this, their first night together, would have to be marred by one of his ghosts. He had to tell her about Amelia. There was a burst of rage followed by a prickle of fear.

No, he wouldn't accept the fear, he told himself as he rose quickly from the bed. Nothing, no one was going to interfere with him. No shadow of a dead wife or demands of a hungry business were going to take her from him. She was strong, he reminded himself, trying to override the apprehension. He could make her see his past as it was—something that had happened before her. It might shock her to learn he was president of a multimillion-dollar firm, but she could hardly be displeased once it was out in the open. He would tell Shane everything and wipe the slate clean. When it was done, he could ask her to marry him. If he had to make professional adjustments, he'd make them. He had sacrificed his own youthful dream for the good of the company, but he wouldn't sacrifice Shane.

As he pulled on his jeans, Vance tried to work out the

best way to tell her and, perhaps more important, to explain why he had yet to tell her.

Shane added a dash of thyme to the canned soup she was heating. She rose on her bare toes to reach for a bowl on the shelf, the hem of Vance's shirt skimming her naked thighs. Her hair was tousled, her cheeks flushed. Vance stood for a moment in the doorway watching her.

Then in three strides, he was behind her, wrapping his arms around her waist and burying his face in the curve of her neck. "I love you," he murmured in a low, fierce whisper. "God, how I love you."

Before she could answer, he spun her around to take her mouth with his. Both stunned and aroused, Shane clung to him as her knees buckled. But she met the kiss with equal passion with soft, willing lips until he slowly drew her away. As the flame mellowed to a glow, Vance looked down at her and smiled.

"Any time you want to drive me crazy, just put on one of my shirts."

"If I'd known the kind of results I'd get, I'd have done it weeks ago." Returning his smile, Shane clasped her hands around his neck. "I thought you'd be hungry; it's after eight."

"I smelled food," he said with a grin. "That's why I came down."

"Oh." Shane lifted a brow. "Is that the only reason?"

"What else?"

Her retort ended on a laugh as he nuzzled her neck. "You could make something up," she suggested.

"If it makes you feel better, I could pretend it was because I couldn't keep away from you." He kissed her until she was limp and breathless. "That I woke up reaching for you, then lay listening to your clattering in the kitchen and knew I'd never been happier in my life. Will that do?"

"Yes, I..." She sighed as his hands slid down to caress beneath the loose shirt. Behind her, bacon popped and hissed. "If you don't stop, the food's going to burn."

"What food?" He chuckled, pleased that she was flushed and breathing unsteadily when she struggled away from him.

"My own specially doctored tomato soup and prize-winning BLTs."

He pulled her back to nuzzle her neck another moment. "Mmm, it does smell pretty good. So do you."

"It's your shirt," she claimed as she wiggled out of his arms again. "It smells like wood chips." Deftly, Shane took the sizzling bacon from the frying pan to let it drain. "If you want coffee, the water's still hot."

Vance watched her finish preparing the simple meal. She did more than fill the kitchen with the scents and sounds of cooking. He'd done that himself often enough in the past weeks. Shane filled it with life. He may have repaired and renovated and remodeled, but the house had always been empty. Vance realized now that without her, it would have always been unfinished.

There would be no living there without her—no living anywhere. Fleetingly, he thought of the large white house in an exclusive Washington suburb—the house he had bought for Amelia. There was an oval swimming pool sheltered by a white brick wall, a formal rose garden with flagstone paths, a clay tennis court. Two maids, a gardener and a cook. When Amelia had been alive there had been yet another maid to tend to her personally. Her dressing room alone had been larger than the kitchen where Shane was now fixing soup and sandwiches. There was a parlor with a rosewood cabinet Shane would adore, and heavy damask drapes she would detest.

No, Vance thought, he wouldn't go back there now, nor would he ask Shane to share his ghosts. He had no right to ask her to cope with something he was only beginning to resolve himself. But he would have to tell her something of his former marriage, and of his work, before yesterday could be buried.

"Shane…"

"Sit down," she ordered, busily pouring soup into bowls. "I'm starving. I skipped lunch this afternoon bargaining for this wonderful Sheridan table. I paid a bit more for the clock than I should have, but made it up on the table and the saltcellars."

"Shane, I have to talk to you."

Deftly, she sliced a sandwich in half. "Okay, I can talk and eat at the same time. I'm going to have some milk. Even I can tell that instant coffee's dreadful."

She was bustling here and there, putting bowls and plates on the table, poking into the refrigerator. Vance was suddenly struck with the picture of his life before she had come into it—the rush, the demands, the work that had ultimately added up to nothing. If he lost her… He couldn't bear thinking about it.

"Shane." He stopped her abruptly, taking both of her arms in a strong grip. Looking up, she was surprised by the fierceness in his eyes. "I love you. Do you believe it?" His grip tightened painfully on the question, but she made no protest.

"Yes, I believe it."

"Will you take me just as I am?" he demanded.

"Yes." There was no hesitation in her, no wavering. Vance pulled her toward him.

A few hours, he thought, squeezing his eyes tight. Just a few hours with no questions, no past. It's not too much to ask.

"There are things I have to tell you, Shane, but not tonight." As the tension drained, he loosened his hold to a caress. "Tonight, I only want to tell you that I love you."

Sensing turmoil and wanting to soothe it, Shane tilted her face back to his. "Tonight it's all I need to know. I love you, Vance; nothing you tell me will change that." She pressed her lips to his cheek and felt some of the tightness in his body loosen. Part of her wanted to coax him to tell her what caused the storm inside him, but she was conscious of the same need for isolation that Vance had. This was their night. Problems were for the practical, for the daytime. "Come on," she said lightly, "the food's getting cold." The fierce hug she gave him made him laugh. "When I fix a gourmet meal, I expect it to be properly appreciated."

"I do," he assured her, kissing her nose.

"Do what?"

"Appreciate it. And you." He dropped a second kiss on her mouth. "Let's go into the living room."

"Living room?" Her brow creased, then cleared. "Oh, I suppose it would be warmer."

"Exactly what I had in mind," he murmured.

"I tossed a couple of logs onto the fire when I came downstairs."

"You're a clever soul, Shane," Vance said admiringly as he took her arm and steered her from the room.

"Vance, we have to take the food."

"What food?"

Shane laughed and started to turn back, but he propelled her into the sparsely furnished, firelit room. "Vance, the soup'll have to be reheated in a minute."

"It'll be terrific," he told her as he began to unbutton the oversize shirt she wore.

"Vance!" Shane brushed his fingers away. "Be serious."

"I am," he said reasonably, even as he pulled her down on the oval braided rug. "Deadly."

"Well, *I'm* not going to reheat it," she promised huffily while he leaned on an elbow to undo the rest of the buttons.

"No one would blame you," he told her as he parted the shirt. "It'll be fine cold."

She gave a snort. "It'll be dreadful cold."

"Hungry?" he asked lightly, cupping her breast.

Shane looked up at him. He saw the dimples flash. "Yes!" In a quick move, she was lying across his chest, her mouth fixed greedily on his.

The verve and speed of her passion stunned him. He had meant to tease her, to stroke her desires slowly, but she was suddenly and completely in command. Her mouth was avid, demanding, with her small teeth nibbling, her quick tongue arousing him so quickly he would have rolled her over and taken her at once had his limbs not been so strangely weak. Her weight was nothing, yet he couldn't move her when she shifted to do clever, torturous things to his ear. Her hands were busy too, stroking through his hair, skimming over his shoulders and chest to find and exploit small, devastating points of pleasure.

He reached to pull off her shirt, too dazed to realize his fingers shook, but he fumbled, dragging at it. High on her own power, Shane gave a quick, almost nervous laugh. "Too soon," she whispered into his ear. "Much too soon."

He swore, but the curse ended on a groan when she pressed her lips to his throat. She burned even as he did, but she was driven to heighten his pleasure to the fullest. It spun through her mind until she was giddy that her touch, her kisses were enough to make him weak and vulnerable. Under her roaming mouth, his skin grew hot and damp. He stroked her where he could reach, but there was something dreamlike in the touch, as though he had passed the first feeling of desperation. For all his strength and power, he had surrendered to hers.

The light shifted and jumped with the crackling of the fire. A log broke apart, crumbling in a shower of sparks. The wind picked up, pushing a sluggish puff of smoke back down the chimney so that it struggled half-heartedly into the room to vie with the lingering scent of fried bacon. Neither of them was aware.

Shane heard the thunderous beat of his heart under her ear, the shallow, ragged sound of his breathing. Taking his mouth again, she kissed him deeply, filling herself on him, knowing she drained him. She luxuriated in him, experimenting with angles, allowing her tongue to twine with his. Then she began the journey down his throat.

Once, he murmured her name as though he were dreaming. She grew bolder. With firm, quick kisses, she ranged down his chest to the taut flat stomach. Vance jolted as though he had been scorched. Shane pressed her lips to the heated skin, wrenching a moan from him, then circled almost lazily with her tongue.

Her excitement was almost unbearable. He was hers, and she was learning his secrets. Her body felt weightless and capable of anything. The gnawing hunger in the pit of her stomach was growing, but the need to learn, to explore was greater. With a kind of greedy wonder, she took her hands and lips over him, reveling in a man's taste—*her* man's taste. The hair on his chest tapered down. Shane followed it.

Slowly, with a light touch, she loosened his jeans and began to draw them over his hips. Curious, Shane moved her lips over his hipbone and down to his thigh.

She heard him call out to her, hoarse, desperate, but she found the corded muscles of his thighs fascinating. So strong, she thought as her heart began to thud painfully. She ran fingers down his leg, aroused by the lean firmness and straining sinews. Testing, she replaced her fingers with her tongue, then her teeth. Vance shifted under her, murmurming something between his short, ragged breaths. His taste was everything male and mysterious. Shane felt she would never get her fill of him.

But he was on the point of madness. Her slender

fingers, her curious tongue had him plunging down and rocketing up so that each breath he drew was an agony of effort. His body was alive with pleasure and pain, his blood swimming with passion that was both tantalized and frustrated. He wanted her to go on touching him, driving him mad. He wanted to take her quickly before he lost his mind. Then slowly, her small avid mouth roamed back up over his stomach, so that his skin quivered with fresh dampness. The heat was unbearable and more wonderful than anything he had ever known. Her breasts with their hard, erect points brushed over him, making him long to taste them. She gave him her mouth instead. Lying full length on his, her body was furnace hot and agile.

"Shane, in the name of God," he breathed, groping for her. Then she slid down, taking him inside her with a shuddering sigh of triumph.

His sanity shattered. Not knowing what he did, Vance seized her shoulders, rolling her over roughly, driving inside her with all the fierce, desperate strength that was pent up in him. Passion hammered through his core. Need was delirium.

She cried out as her hips arched to meet him, but he was far beyond any control. Harder and faster he took her, never feeling the bite of her nails on his flesh, barely hearing her harsh, quick breathing. She dragged him closer when he could get no closer. He drove her, drove himself to a crest that was dangerously high. Even the plummet was a shattering thrill.

She was shuddering beneath him, dazed, weak, powerful. Experimentally, Vance ran a hand over her arm, then linked his fingers around it. His thumb and forefinger met. "You're so small," he murmured. "I didn't mean to be rough."

Shane brushed a hand through his hair. "Were you?"

His sigh ended on a chuckle. "Shane, you make me crazy. I don't usually toss women around."

"I don't think this is a good time to go into that," she said dryly.

Shifting, he supported himself on his elbow so he could look down at her. "Would it be better to tell you that you inflame me into violent seizures of passion?"

"Infinitely."

"It appears to be true," he murmured.

She smiled at him, running her hand down his shoulder to the arm taut with muscle. "Would you rather I didn't?"

"No," he said definitely, then covered her laughing lips with his.

"Actually," she began in a considering tone, "since you do the same to me, it's only fair."

He liked seeing her with the sleepy, just-loved look on her face. Her eyes were soft and heavy, her mouth slightly swollen. With shifting shadows and a red glow, firelight danced over her skin. "I like your logic." Gently, he traced the shape of her face with a fingertip, imagining what it would be like to wake beside her every morning. Shane captured his hand, pressing his palm to her lips.

"I love you," she said softly. "Will you get tired of hearing that?"

"No." He kissed her brow, then her temple. Slipping an arm under her, he drew her close. "No," he said again on a sigh.

Shane snuggled, running a casual hand over his chest. "The fire's getting low," she murmured.

"Mmm."

"We should put some more wood on."

"Mmm-hmm."

"Vance." She tilted her face to look up at him. His eyes were closed. "Don't you dare go to sleep. I'm hungry."

"God, the woman's insatiable." After a long sigh, he cupped her breast. "I might find the energy with the right incentive."

"I want my dinner," she said firmly, but made no move to stop his caressing hand. "*You're* going to reheat the soup."

"Oh." Vance considered that a moment, running a lazy finger over the peak of her breast. "Aren't you afraid I might interfere with that special touch you have?"

"No," she told him flatly. "I have every confidence in you."

"I thought you might," he said as he sat up to tug on his jeans. Leaning over, he planted a quick kiss on her mouth. "*You* can toss some logs in the fire."

But after he had gone to the kitchen, Shane lay dreaming a moment. The hiss of the fire was comforting. She drew the soft flannel of Vance's shirt closer around her, smiling as his scent stayed with her. Could it really be true that he needed her so much? she wondered sleepily. Love, yes, and desire, but she had a deep, innate knowledge that he very simply needed her. Not just for lovemaking, for holding, but to *be* there. Though she was unsure what it was, Shane knew there was something she had—or something she was—that

Vance needed. Whatever she brought to him, it was enough to balance his anger, his mistrust. Fleetingly, she wondered again what had caused him to retreat behind cynicism. Disillusioned, he had said. Who or what had disillusioned him? A woman, a friend, an ideal?

Shane watched the sizzling red coals in the fire and wondered. The anger was still there. She had sensed it when he had demanded to know if she would take him just as he was. Patience, she told herself. She had to be patient until he was ready to share his secrets with her. But it was difficult for Shane to love and not try to help. Shaking her head, she sat up to rebutton her shirt. She'd promised him that love was enough for tonight; she had to abide by it. Tomorrow would be soon enough for problems. Expertly, she arranged more wood on the coals before she went to the kitchen.

"About time," Vance said coolly as she walked in. "There's nothing I hate more than having food get cold."

Shane shot him a look. "How inconsiderate of me."

After setting the bowls back on the table, Vance shrugged. "Well, no harm done," he told her in a forgiving tone. His eyes brimmed with amusement as Shane sat. "Coffee?"

"Not yours," she said witheringly. "It's terrible."

"I suppose if someone really cared, they'd see to it that I had decent coffee in the morning."

"You're right." Shane lifted her spoon. "I'll buy you a percolater." Grinning, she began to eat. The soup was hot and tangy, causing her to close her eyes in appreciation. "Good grief, I'm starving!"

"You should know better than to miss meals," Vance

commented before applying himself to the meal. He quickly discovered he was famished.

"It was worth it." Shane shot him another grin. "The Sheridan I bought is fabulous." When he only lifted a brow, she chuckled. "Then I had intended to have an early dinner…but I was distracted."

Vance reached over to take her hand. Gently, he lifted it to his lips, then bit her knuckle. "Ow!" Shane snatched her hand away as he picked up his sandwich. "I didn't say it wasn't an enjoyable distraction," she added after a moment. "Even if you did make me furious."

"The feeling was mutual," he assured her mildly.

"At least I control my temper," she said primly. She eyed him coolly as he choked over his soup. "I *wanted* to punch you," she explained. "Hard."

"Again the feeling was mutual."

"You're not a gentleman," she accused with her mouth full.

"Good God, no," he agreed. For a moment, he hesitated, wanting to choose his words carefully. "Shane, will you hold off for a little while on that dining-room set?"

"Vance," she began, but he took her hand again.

"Don't tell me I shouldn't have interfered. I love you."

Shane stirred her soup, frowning down at it. She didn't want to tell him how pressing her bills were. In the first place, she had every confidence that between her current stock and the small amount of capital she had left, she could straighten out her finances. And more, she simply didn't want to heap her problems on him.

"I know you did what you did because you cared,"

she began slowly. "I appreciate that, really. But it's important to me to make the shop work." She lifted her eyes now to meet the frown in his. "I didn't fail as a teacher, but I didn't succeed either. I have to make a go of this."

"By selling the one tangible thing you have left of your grandmother's?" Immediately, he saw he had hit a nerve. He tightened his fingers around hers. "Shane…"

"No. It is hard for me, I won't pretend it isn't." Wearily, she let out a long breath. "I'm not basically a practical person, but in this case I have to be. I have no place to keep that set and it's very valuable. The money it'll bring into the shop will keep me going for quite a while. And more than that…" She broke off with a little shake of her head. "If you can understand, it's more difficult for me having it there, knowing it has to be sold, than if it were already done."

"Let me buy it. I could—"

"No!"

"Shane, listen to me."

"No!" Pulling her hand from his, she rose to lean against the sink. For a moment she stared hard out the window at the trees splattered with moonlight. "Please, it's very sweet of you, but I couldn't allow it."

Frustrated, Vance rose, taking her shoulders, he drew Shane back against him. And how, he wondered, was he going to begin to explain? "Shane, you don't understand. I can't bear watching you hurting, watching you work so hard when I could—"

"Please, Vance." Shane turned to him. Though her eyes were dry, they were eloquent. "I'm doing what I have to do, and what I want." She took his hands tightly in hers. "It's not that I don't love you even more for wanting to help. I do."

"Then let me help," he began. "If it's just a matter of the money right now—"

"It wouldn't make any difference if you were a millionaire," she said, giving him a little shake. "I'd still say no."

Not knowing whether to laugh or swear, Vance pulled her against him. "Stubborn little twit, I could make it easier for you. Let me try to explain."

"I don't want anyone, not even you, to make it easier." She gave him a fierce squeeze. "Please understand. All of my life I've been cute little Shane Abbott, Faye's sweet, slightly odd granddaughter. I need to prove something."

Remembering how frustrating it had been to be known as Miriam Riverton Banning's son, Vance sighed. Yes, he understood. And the understanding made him keep his silence on how simple it would be for him to help. "Well," he said, wanting to hear her laugh, "you are kind of cute."

"Oh, Vance," she moaned.

"And sweet," he added, tilting her face up for a kiss. "And slightly odd."

"That's no way to endear yourself to me," she warned. "I'll wash, you dry."

"Wash what?"

"The dishes."

He pulled her closer, wrapping his arms firmly around her waist. "I don't see any dishes. You have wonderful eyes, just like a cocker spaniel."

"Watch it, Vance," she said threateningly.

"I like your freckles." He placed a light kiss on the bridge of her nose. "I've always thought that Becky Thatcher had freckles."

"You're heading for trouble," she told him, narrowing her eyes.

"And your dimples," he continued blithely. "She probably had dimples too, don't you think?"

Shane bit her lips to hold back a smile. "Shut up, Vance."

"Yes," he continued, beaming down at her, "I'd say that's definitely a cute little face."

"Okay, that does it." Putting a good deal of effort into it, Shane tried to wiggle out of his hold.

"Going somewhere?"

"Home," she told him grandly. "You can do your own dishes."

He sighed. "I guess I have to get tough again."

Anticipating him, Shane began to struggle in earnest. "If you throw me over your shoulder again, you really are fired!"

Hooking an arm behind her knees, Vance swept her up. "How's this?"

She circled his neck. "Better," she said grudgingly. The smile was becoming impossible to control.

"And this?" Softly, he placed his lips on hers, letting the kiss deepen until he heard her sigh.

"Much better," she murmured as he carried her from the room. "Where are we going?"

"Upstairs," he told her. "I want my shirt back."

Chapter 10

"Yes, of course you could convert it," Shane agreed, passing her fingertip over the porcelain base of a delicate oil lamp.

"That's just what I thought." Mrs. Trip, her potential customer, nodded her carefully groomed white head. "And my husband's very handy with electrical things too."

Shane managed a smile for Mr. Trip's prowess. It broke her heart to think that the sweet little lamp would be tampered with. "You know," she began, trying another tactic, "an oil lamp is a smart thing to have around in case of power failure. I keep a couple myself."

"Well yes, dear," Mrs. Trip said placidly, "but I have candles for that. This lamp's going to go right next to my rocker. That's where I do my crocheting."

Though she knew the value of a sale, Shane couldn't

stop herself from adding, "If you really want an electric lamp, Mrs. Trip, you could buy a good reproduction much cheaper."

Mrs. Trip sent her a vague smile. "But it wouldn't be a real antique then, would it? Do you have a box I can carry it in?"

"Yes, of course," Shane murmured, seeing it was useless to repeat that converting the lamp would decrease both its value and its charm. Resigned, she wrote out the sales slip, comforting herself with the thought that the profit from the lamp would help pay her own electric bill.

"Oh my, I didn't see this!"

Glancing up, Shane noted that Mrs. Trip was admiring a tea set in cobalt blue. The sun slanting in the windows fell generously on the dark, rich glass. There was a contrast of delicate gold leaf painted around the rim of each cup and the edge of each saucer.

"It's lovely, isn't it," Shane agreed, though she bit the underside of her lip as the lady began to handle the sugar bowl. When she found the discreet price tag, she lifted a brow. "It goes as a complete set," Shane began, knowing the price would seem staggering to someone unacquainted with valuable glass. "It's late nineteenth century and..."

"I must have it," Mrs. Trip said decisively, cutting off Shane's explanation. "It's just the thing for my corner cabinet." She sent a surprised Shane a grin. "I'll tell my husband he's just bought me a Christmas present."

"I'll wrap it for you," Shane decided, as pleased as Mrs. Trip with the idea.

"You have a lovely shop," the woman told her as Shane began to box the glass. "I must say, I only stopped in because the sign at the bottom of the hill intrigued me. I wondered what in the world I would find. But it wasn't a big barn of a place with nonsense packed around like a yard sale." She pursed her lips, glancing around again. "You've done very well." Shane laughed at the description and thanked her. "And it's so nice to have the little museum too," she went on. "A very clever idea, and so tidy. I believe I'll bring my nephew by the next time I'm in the area. Are you married, dear?"

Shane sent her a look of wary amusement. "No, ma'am."

"He's a doctor," Mrs. Trip disclosed. "Internal medicine."

Clearing her throat, Shane sealed the box. "That's very nice."

"A good boy," Mrs. Trip assured her as Shane adjusted the sales ticket to include the tea set. "Dedicated." She dug out her checkbook, pulling her wallet along with it. "I have a picture of him right here."

Politely, Shane examined the snapshot of a young, attractive man with serious eyes. "He's very good-looking," she told his aunt. "You must be proud of him."

"Yes," she said wistfully, tucking the wallet back into her purse. "Such a pity he hasn't found the right girl yet. I'm going to be sure to bring him by." Without a blink for the amount, Mrs. Trip wrote out a check.

It wasn't easy, but Shane maintained her composure until the door shut behind her customer. With a shout of laughter, she dropped into a button-back chair.

Though she was uncertain if the nephew should be congratulated or pitied for having such a dedicated aunt, she did know what appealed to her sense of humor. Her next thought was how Vance would try not to grin when she told him of the lady's matchmaking attempts.

He'd lift a brow, Shane thought, and make some dry comment about her charming the old ladies so that they'd dangle their nephews under her nose. She was beginning to know him very well. Most of him, Shane corrected with a considering smile. The rest would come.

She checked her watch, finding herself impatient that two hours remained before he would be with her. She'd promised him dinner—a more elaborate dinner than the soup and sandwiches they had eaten the night before. Even now, the small rib roast was cooking gently in the oven upstairs. She considered closing early, calculating she had just about enough time to whip up some outrageous, elaborate dessert before he arrived. As the thought passed through her head, the door opened again.

Laurie MacAfee stepped in, buttoned to the neck in a long tan coat. "Shane," she said, observing her casual posture in the chair. "Not busy I see."

Though she smiled in greeting, some demon kept her seated. "Not at the moment. How are you, Laurie?"

"Just fine. I took off work early to go to the dentist, so I thought I'd drop by afterward."

Shane waited, half expecting Laurie to comment on her good checkup. "I'm glad you did," she said at length. "Would you like a tour?"

"I'd love to browse," Laurie told her, glancing around. "What sweet things you have."

Shane swallowed a retort and rose. "Thank you," she said with a humility Laurie never noticed. Shane thought again how well suited she was to Cy.

"I must say, the place looks so much different." In her slow, measured step, Laurie began to wander the old summer parlor. Though she hadn't expected to approve, she could find nothing to condemn in Shane's taste. The room was small, but light and airy with its ivory-toned walls, and the gleaming natural wood floor was scattered with hand-hooked rugs. Furniture was set to advantage, with accessories carefully arranged to give the appearance of a tidy, rather comfortable room instead of a store. Loosening the first few buttons of her coat, she roamed to the main showroom, then stood perusing it from the doorway.

"Why, you've hardly changed this at all?" she exclaimed. "Not even the wallpaper."

"No," Shane agreed, unable to keep her eyes from skimming over the dining-room set. "I didn't want to. Of course, I had to set more stock in here, and widen the doorways, but I loved the room as it was."

"Well, I'll confess I'm surprised," Laurie commented as she wandered through to what had been the kitchen. "It's so organized, not jumbled up at all. Your bedroom was always a disaster."

"It still is," Shane replied dryly.

Laurie gave what passed for a laugh before continuing into the museum. "Yes, this I might have expected." She gave a quick nod. "You always were a whiz at this sort of thing. I could never understand it."

"Because I wasn't a whiz at anything else?"

"Oh, Shane." Laurie flushed, revealing how close Shane's words had been to her thoughts.

"I'm sorry." Immediately contrite, Shane patted her arm. "I was only teasing you. I'd show you the upstairs, Laurie, but it's not quite finished, and I shouldn't leave the shop in any case. Pat has classes this afternoon."

Mollified, Laurie strolled back into the shop. "I'd heard she was working for you. It was very kind of you to give her the job."

"She's been a big help. I couldn't manage it seven days a week all alone." Shane felt a twinge of impatience as Laurie began to browse again. There wasn't going to be time to whip up anything more than instant chocolate pudding at this rate.

"Oh well, this is very nice." Laurie's voice held the first true ring of admiration as she studied the Sheridan table Shane had bought the day before. "It doesn't look old at all."

That was too much for Shane. She gave a burst of appreciative laughter. "No, I'm sorry," she assured Laurie when she turned to frown at her. "You'd be surprised how many people think antiques should look moldy or dented. It's quite old, really, and it is lovely."

"And expensive," Laurie added, squinting at the price. "Still, it would look rather nice with the chair Cy and I just bought. Oh…" Turning, she gave Shane a quick, guilty look. "I wonder if you'd heard—that is, I'd been meaning to have a talk with you."

"About Cy?" Shane controlled the smile, noting Laurie was truly uncomfortable. "I know you're seeing quite a lot of each other."

"Yes." Hesitating, Laurie brushed some fictitious lint from her coat. "It's a bit more than that really. You see, we're—actually…" She cleared her throat. "Shane, we're planning to be married next June."

"Congratulations," Shane said so simply that Laurie's eyes widened.

"I hope you're not upset." Laurie began to twist the strap of her purse. "I know that you and Cy…well, it was quite a few years ago, but still, you were…"

"Very young," Shane said kindly. "I really do wish you the best, Laurie." But a demon of mischief had her adding, "You suit him much better than I ever could."

"I appreciate your saying that, Shane. I was afraid you might…" She flushed again. "Well, Cy's such a wonderful man."

She means it, Shane noted with some surprise. She really loves him. She felt simultaneous tugs of shame and amusement. "I hope you're happy, Laurie, both of you."

"We will be." Laurie gave her a beaming smile. "And I'm going to buy this table," she added recklessly.

"No," Shane corrected her. "You're going to take the table as an early wedding present."

Comically, Laurie's mouth dropped open. "Oh, I couldn't! It's so expensive."

"Laurie, we've known each other a long time, and Cy was a very important part of my" —she searched for the proper phrase—"growing up years. I'd like to give it to both of you."

"Well, I—thank you." Such uncomplicated generosity baffled her. "Cy will be so pleased."

"You're welcome." Laurie's flustered appreciation made her smile. "Can I help you out to the car with it?"

"No, no, I can manage." Laurie lifted the small table, then paused. "Shane, I really hope you have a tremendous success here. I really do." She stood awkwardly at the door a moment. "Goodbye."

"Bye, Laurie."

Shane closed the door with a smile, then immediately put Laurie and Cy out of her mind. After a glance at her watch, she noted that she had barely more than an hour now before Vance would be there. She hurried around to lock up the museum entrance. If she moved fast, she would have time to… The sound of an approaching car had her swearing.

Business is business, she reminded herself, and unlocked the door again. If Vance wanted dessert, he'd have to settle for a bag of store-bought cookies. Hearing the sound of footsteps on the porch, she opened the door with a ready smile. It faded instantly, as did her color.

"Anne," she managed in a voice unlike her own.

"Darling!" Anne bent down for a quick brush of cheeks. "What a greeting. Anyone would think you weren't glad to see me."

It took only a few seconds to see that her mother was as lovely as ever. Her pale, heart-shaped face was unlined, her eyes the same deep china blue, her hair a glorious sweeping blond. She wore a casual, expensive blue fox stroller belted at the waist with black leather, and silk slacks unsuitable for an Eastern winter. Her beauty, as always, sent the same surges of love and resentment through her daughter.

"You look lovely, Anne."

"Oh, thank you, though I know I must look a wreck after that dreadful drive from the airport. This place is in the middle of nowhere. Shane, dear, when are you going to do something about your hair?" She cast a critical eye over it before breezing past. "I'll never understand why… Oh, my Lord, what *have* you done!"

Stunned, she gazed around the room, taking in the display cases, the shelves, the racks of postcards. With a trill of laughter, she set down her exquisite leather bag. "Don't tell me you've opened a Civil War museum right in the living room. I don't believe it!"

Shane folded her hands in front of her, feeling foolish. "Didn't you see the sign?"

"Sign? No—or perhaps I did but didn't pay any attention." Her eyes slid, sharp and amused around the room. "Shane, what *have* you been up to?"

Determined not to be intimidated, she straightened her shoulders. "I've started a business," she said boldly.

"You?" Delighted, Anne laughed again. "But, darling, surely you're joking."

Stabbed by the utter incredulity in Anne's voice, Shane angled her chin. "No."

"Well, for heaven's sake." She gave a pretty chuckle and eyed Shane's dented bugle. "But what happened to your teaching job?"

"I resigned."

"Well, I can hardly blame you for that; it must have been a terrible bore." She brushed away Shane's former career as a matter of indifference. "But why in God's name did you come back here and bury yourself in Hicksville?"

"It's my home."

With a mild *hmm* for the temper in Shane's eyes, Anne spun the rack of postcards. "Everyone to his own taste. Well, what have you done with the rest of the place?" Before Shane could answer, Anne swept through the doorway and into the shop. "Oh, no, don't tell me, an antique shop! Very quaint and tasteful. Shane, how clever of you." Her eye was sharp enough to recognize a few very good pieces. She began to wonder if her daughter wasn't quite the fool she'd always considered her. "Well…" Anne unbelted her fur and dropped it carelessly over a chair. "How long has this been going on?"

"Not long." Shane stood rigid, knowing part of herself was drawn, as it always was, to the strange, beautiful woman who was her mother. Knowing, too, that Anne was deadly.

"And?" Anne prompted.

"And what?"

"Shane, don't be difficult." Masking quick annoyance, Anne gave her a charming smile. She was an actress. Though she had never made the splash she had hoped for, she wrangled a bit part now and again. She felt she knew her trade well enough to handle Shane with a friendly smile. "Naturally I'm concerned, darling. I only want to know how you're doing?"

Uncomfortable with her own manners, Shane unbent. "Well enough, though I haven't been open long. I wasn't happy with teaching. Not bored," she explained, "just not suited for it. I am happy with this."

"Darling, that's wonderful." She crossed her nylon-clad legs and looked around again. It occurred to her that

Shane might be useful after all. It had taken brains and determination to set up this kind of establishment. Perhaps it was time she started to take a little more interest in the daughter she had always thought of as a mild annoyance. "It helps to know you're settling your life, especially since mine's such a mess at the moment." Noting the wariness in Shane's eyes, she sent her a sad smile. If memory served her, the girl was very susceptible to an unhappy story. "I divorced Leslie."

"Oh?" Shane only lifted a brow.

Momentarily set back by Shane's coolness, Anne continued. "I can't tell you how mistaken I was in him, how foolish it feels to know I was deceived into thinking he was a kind, charming man." She didn't add that he had failed, again and again, to get her the kind of parts that would lead to the fame she craved—or that she'd already begun to cultivate a certain producer she felt would be more successful. In any event, Leslie had begun to bore her to distraction. "There's nothing more devastating than to have failed in love."

You've had practice, Shane thought, but held her tongue.

"These past few months," Anne added on a sigh, "haven't been easy."

"For any of us," Shane agreed, understanding Anne too well. "Gran died six months ago. You didn't even bother to come to the funeral."

She'd been ready for this. With a tiny sigh, she dropped her eyes to her soft, pampered hands. "You must know how badly I felt, Shane. I was finishing a film. I couldn't be spared."

"You couldn't find the time for a card, a phone call?" Shane asked. "You never even bothered to answer my letter."

As if on cue, Anne's lovely eyes filled with tears. "Darling, don't be cruel. I couldn't—I just couldn't put the words down on a piece of paper." She drew a delicate swatch of silk from her breast pocket. "Even though she was old, somehow I felt she would just live forever, always be here." Mindful of her mascara, she dabbed at the tears. "When I got your letter telling me she was…I was so devastated." She lifted beautifully drenched eyes to Shane's, waiting while a single tear trickled gently down her cheek. "You of all people must know how I feel. She raised me." A little sob caught in her throat. "I still can't believe she's not in the kitchen, fussing over the stove."

Because the image tore at her own grief, Shane knelt at her mother's feet. She'd had no family to mourn with her, no one to help her through the wrenching, aching hours after the numbness had passed. If she had been unable to share anything else with her mother throughout her life, perhaps they could share this. "I know," she managed in a thick voice. "I still miss her terribly."

Anne began to think the little scene had a great deal of possibility. "Shane, please forgive me." Anne gripped her hands, concentrating on adding a tremor to her voice. "I know it was wrong of me not to come, wrong to make excuses. I just wasn't strong enough to face it. Even now, when I thought I could…" She trailed off, bringing Shane's hand to her damp cheek.

"I understand. Gran would have understood too."

"She was so good to me always. If I could only see her one more time."

"You mustn't dwell on it." Those very thoughts had haunted Shane's mind a dozen times after the funeral. "I felt the same way, but it's better to remember all the good times. She was so happy here in this house, doing her gardening, her canning."

"She did love the house," Anne murmured, casting a nostalgic eye around the old summer parlor. "And I imagine she'd have been pleased with what you're doing here."

"Do you think so?" Earnestly, Shane looked up into her mother's damp eyes. "I was so sure, but still sometimes..." Trailing off, she glanced at the freshly painted walls.

"Of course she would." Anne said briskly. "I suppose she left the house to you?"

"Yes." Shane was looking around the room, remembering how it had been.

"There was a will then?"

"A will?" Distracted, Shane glanced back at her. "Yes, Gran had a will drawn up years ago. She had Floyd Arnette's son do it after he passed the bar. She was his first client." Shane smiled, thinking how proud Gran had been of the fancy legal terms that "sassy Arnette boy" had come up with.

"And the rest of the estate?" Anne prompted, attempting to curb her impatience.

"There was the house and land of course," Shane answered, still looking back. "Some stocks I sold to pay the taxes and the funeral expenses."

"She left everything to you?"

The tightness in Anne's voice didn't penetrate. "Yes. There was enough cash in her savings to handle most of the repairs on the place, and—"

"You're lying!" Anne shoved at her as she sprung to her feet. Shane grabbed the arm of the chair to keep from toppling; then, too stunned to move, she stayed on the floor. "She wouldn't have cut me off without a penny!" Anne exploded, glaring down at her.

The blue eyes were hard and glittery now, the lovely face white with fury. Once or twice before, Shane had seen her mother in this sort of rage—when her grandmother hadn't given her precisely what she had wanted. Slowly, she rose to face her. Anne's tantrums, she knew, had to be handled carefully before they turned violent.

"Gran would never have thought of it as cutting you off, Anne," Shane said with a calm she was far from feeling. "She knew you'd have no interest in the house or land, and there weren't that many extra pennies after taxes."

"What kind of fool do you think I am?" Anne demanded in a harsh, bitter voice. It was her temper more than a lack of talent that had snagged her career. Too often, she had let it rake over directors and other actors. Even now, when patience and the right words would have insured success, she lashed out. "I know damn well she had money socked away, molding in some bank. I had to pry every penny I got out of her when she was alive. I'm going to have my share."

"She gave you what she could," Shane began.

"What the hell do you know? Do you think I'm so stupid I don't know this property is worth a tidy sum on the market?" She glanced around once in disgust. "You want the place, keep it. Just give me the cash."

"There isn't any to give. She didn't—"

"Don't hand me that." Anne shoved her aside and strode toward the stairs.

For a moment, Shane stood still, caught in a turmoil of disbelief. How was it possible anyone could be so unfeeling? And how, she asked herself, was it possible for her to be taken in again and again? Well, she would end it this time, once and for all. On her own wave of fury, she raced after her mother.

She found Anne in her bedroom, pulling papers out of her desk. Without hesitation, Shane dashed across the room and slammed the desk lid shut. "Don't you touch my things," she said in a dangerous voice. "Don't you ever touch what belongs to me."

"I want to see the bankbooks, and this so-called will." Anne turned to leave the room, but Shane grabbed her arm in a surprisingly strong grip.

"You'll see nothing in this house. This is mine."

"There *is* money," Anne said furiously, then jerked away. "You're trying to hide it."

"I don't have to hide anything from you." Rage raced through Shane, fed by years of cast-aside love. "If you want to see the will and the status of the estate, get yourself a lawyer. But I own this house, and everything in it. I won't have you going through my papers."

"Well…" Anne's blue eyes became slits. "Not such a sweet simpleton after all, are you?"

"You've never known what I am," Shane said evenly. "You've never cared enough to find out. It didn't matter, because I had Gran. I don't need you." Though saying the words was a relief, they didn't bank her fury. "There were times I thought I did, when you came sweeping in, so beautiful I hardly believed you were real. That was closer to the truth than I knew, because there's nothing real about you. You never cared about her. She knew that and she loved you anyway. But I don't." Her breathing was coming quickly, but she was unaware of how close it was to sobbing. "I can't even work up a hate. I just want to be rid of you."

Turning, she pulled open the desk and drew out her checkbook. Quickly, she wrote out a check for half of the capital she had left. "Here." She held it out to Anne. "Take it; consider it from Gran. You'll never get anything from me."

After snatching the check, Anne scanned the amount with a smirk. "If you think I'll be satisfied with this, you're wrong." Still, she folded the check neatly, then slipped it into her pocket. She knew better than to press her luck, and her own financial status was far from solid. "I'll get that lawyer," she promised, though she had no intention of wasting her money on the slim chance of getting more. "And I'll contest the will. We'll just see how much I get from you, Shane."

"Do what you like," Shane said wearily. "Just stay away from me."

Anne tossed back her hair with a harsh laugh. "Don't think I'll spend any more time in this ridiculous house than I have to. I've always wondered how the hell you could possibly be my daughter."

Shane pressed a hand to her throbbing temple. "So have I," she murmured.

"You'll hear from my lawyer," Anne told her. Turning on her heel, she glided from the room, exiting gracefully.

Shane stood beside the desk until she heard the slam of the front door. Bursting into tears, she crumpled into a chair.

Chapter 11

Vance sat in the one decent chair he had in the living room. Impatiently, he checked his watch. He should have been with Shane ten minutes ago. And would have been, he thought with a glance at the front door, if the phone hadn't caught him as he'd been leaving the house. Resigned, he listened to the problems listed by the manager of his Washington branch. Though it wasn't said in words, Vance was aware there was some grumbling in the ranks that the boss had taken a sabbatical.

"...and with the union dispute, the construction on the Wolfe project is three weeks behind schedule," the manager continued. "I've been informed that there will be a delay in delivery of the steel on the Rheinstone site—possibly a lengthy one. I'm sorry to bother you with this, Mr. Banning, but as these two projects are of paramount importance to the firm, particularly with the bids going out on the shopping mall Rheinstone is planning, I felt…"

"Yes, I understand." Vance cut off what promised to be a detailed explanation. "Put a double shift on the Wolfe project until we're back on schedule."

"A double shift? But—"

"We contracted for completion by April first," Vance said mildly. "The increase in payroll will be less than the payment of the penalty clause, or the damage to the firm's reputation."

"Yes, sir."

"And have Liebewitz check into the steel delivery. If it's not taken care of satisfactorily by Monday, I'll handle it from here." Picking up a pencil, Vance made a scrawled note on a pad. "As to the Rheinstone bid, I looked it over myself last week. I see no problem." He scowled at the floor a moment. "Set up a meeting with the department heads for the end of next week. I'll be in. In the meantime," he added slowly, "send someone…Masterson," he decided, "up here to scout out locations for a new branch."

"New branch? Up there, Mr. Banning?"

The tone had a smile tugging at his mouth. "Have him concentrate on the Hagerstown area and give me a report. I want a list of viable locations in two weeks." He checked his watch again. "Is there anything else?"

"No, sir."

"Good. I'll be in next week." Without waiting for a reply, Vance broke the connection.

His last orders, he thought ruefully, would put them

into quite a stir. Well, he reflected, Riverton had expanded before; it was going to expand again. For the first time in years, the company was going to bring him some personal happiness. He would be able to settle down with the woman he loved, where he chose to settle down, and still keep a firm rein on his business. If he had to justify the new branch to the board, which he would certainly have to do, he would point out that Hagerstown was the largest city in Maryland. There was also its proximity to Pennsylvania to consider…and to West Virginia. Yes, he mused, the expansion could be justified to the board easily enough. His track record would go a long way toward swaying them.

Rising, Vance shrugged back into his coat. All he had left to do now was to talk to Shane. Not for the first time, he speculated on her reaction. She was bound to be a bit stunned when he told her he wasn't precisely the unemployed carpenter she had taken him for. And he hadn't discounted the possibility that she might be angry with him for allowing her to go on believing him to be one. Vance felt a slight tug of apprehension as he stepped out into the cold, clear night.

There was a stiff breeze whipping in from the west. It sent stiff, dead leaves scattering and smelled faintly of snow. With his mind fully occupied, Vance never noticed the old stag fifty yards to his right, scenting the air and watching him.

He'd never set out to deceive her, he reminded himself. When they had first met, it had been none of Shane's business who he was. More, he added thoughtfully, he had simply wanted to shake loose of his company title for a while and be exactly what she had perceived him to be. Had there been any way of knowing she would become more important to him than anything else in his life? Could he have guessed that weeks after he met her he would be planning to ask her to marry him, finding himself ready to toss his company into a frenzy of rush and preparation so that she wouldn't have to give up her home or the life she had chosen for herself?

Once he'd explained the circumstances, Vance told himself as he crunched through frosted leaves, she'd understand. One of Shane's most endearing qualities was understanding. And she loved him. If he was sure of nothing else, he was sure of that. She loved him without questions, without demands. No one had ever given him so much for so little. He intended to spend the rest of his life showing her just what that meant to him.

He imagined that once the surprise of what he had to tell her had worn off, she would laugh. The money, the position he could offer her would mean nothing. She would probably find it funny that the president of Riverton had cut and hammered the trim in her kitchen.

Telling her about Amelia would be more difficult, but it would be done—completely. He wouldn't pass over his first marriage, but would tell her everything and rely on her to understand. He wanted to tell her that she had been responsible for softening his guilt, lightening his bitterness. Loving her was the only genuine emotion he'd felt in years. Tonight, he would open up his past long enough to let the air in; then he would ask Shane to share his future.

Still, Vance felt a twinge of apprehension as he approached her house. He might have ignored it if it hadn't been for the sudden realization that all the windows were dark. It was odd, he thought, unconsciously increasing his pace. She was certainly home, not only because her car was there, but because he knew she was expecting him. But why in God's name, he wondered, wasn't there a single light on? Vance tried to push away a flood of pure anxiety as he reached the back door.

It was unlocked. Though he entered without knocking, he called her name immediately. The house remained dark and silent. Hitting a switch, Vance flooded the rear showroom with light. A quick glance showed him nothing amiss before he continued through the first floor.

"Shane?"

The quiet was beginning to disturb him even more than the darkness. After making a quick circle of the lower floor, he went upstairs. At once he caught the scent of cooking. But the kitchen was empty. Absently turning off the oven, Vance went back into the hall. The thought struck him that she might have lain down after closing the shop and had simply fallen asleep. Amused more than concerned now, he walked quietly into her bedroom. All the amusement fled when he saw her curled up in the chair.

Though the room was in darkness, there was enough moonlight to make her out clearly. She wasn't asleep, but was curled up tightly with her head resting on the arm of the chair. He'd never seen her like that. His first thought was that she looked lost; then he corrected himself. Stricken. There was no innate vivacity in her eyes, and her face glowed palely in the silvery light of the moon. He might have thought her ill, but something told him that even in illness Shane wouldn't lose all of her spark. The thought ran through his mind in only seconds before he crossed the room to her. She made no sign that she saw him, nor was there any response when he spoke her name again. Vance knelt in front of her and took her chilled hands.

"Shane."

For a moment, she stared at him blankly. Then, as though a dam had burst, desperate emotion flooded her eyes. "Vance," she said brokenly, throwing her arms around his neck. "Oh, Vance."

She trembled violently, but didn't weep. The tears were dry as stone inside her. With her face pressed into his shoulder, she clung to him, breaking out of the numbed shock which had followed her earlier bout of tears. It was the warmth of him that made her realize how cold she had been. Without questions, with both strength and sweetness he held her to him.

"Vance, I'm so glad you're here. I need you."

The words struck him more forcibly than even her declaration of love. Up to that moment he had been almost uncomfortably aware that his needs far outweighed hers. Now it seemed there was something he could do for her, if it was only to listen.

"What happened, Shane?" Gently he drew her away only far enough to look into her eyes. "Can you tell me?"

She drew a raw breath, making him eloquently aware of the effort it cost her to speak. "My mother."

With his fingertips, he brushed the tousled hair from her cheeks. "Is she ill?"

"No!" It was a quick, furious explosion. The violence of the denial surprised him, but he took her agitated hands in his.

"Tell me what happened."

"She came," Shane managed, then fought to compose herself.

"Your mother came here?" he prompted.

"Near closing time. I didn't expect… She didn't come for the funeral or answer my letter." Her hands twisted in his, but Vance kept them in a gentle grip.

"This is the first time you've seen her since your grandmother died?" he asked. His voice was calm and quiet. Shane's eyes were still for a moment as she met his eyes directly.

"I haven't seen Anne in over two years," she said flatly. "Since she married her publicity agent. They're divorced now, so she came back." Shaking her head, Shane drew in a breath. "She almost made me believe she cared. I thought we could talk to each other. Really talk." She squeezed her eyes shut. "It was all an act, all the tears and grief. She sat there begging me to understand, and I believed—" Breaking off again, she shuddered with the effort of continuing. "She didn't come because of Gran or because of me." When she opened her eyes again Vance saw they were dull with pain. With a savage effort he kept his voice calm.

"Why did she come, Shane?"

Because her breathing was jerky again, she took a moment to answer. "Money," she said flatly. "She thought there would be money. She was furious that Gran left everything to me, and she wouldn't believe me when I told her how little there had been. I should have known!" she said in a quick rage, which then almost immediately subsided. "I did know." Her shoulders slumped as though she bore an intolerable weight. "I've always known. She's never cared about anyone. I'd hoped there might be some feeling in her for Gran, but... When she came running up here to paw through my papers, I said horrible things. I can't be sorry that I did." Tears sprang to her eyes, only to be swiftly controlled. "I gave her half of what's left and made her leave."

"You gave her money?" Vance demanded, incredulous enough to interrupt.

Shane gave him a weary look. "Gran would have given it to her. She's still my mother."

Disgust and rage rose in his throat. It took all the willpower he had not to give in to it. His anger wouldn't help Shane. "She's not your mother, Shane," he said matter-of-factly. When she opened her mouth to speak, he shook his head and continued. "Biologically, yes, but you're too smart to think that means anything. Cats have kittens too, Shane." He tightened his grip when he saw the flicker of pain on her face. "I'm sorry, I don't want to hurt you."

"No. No, you're right." Her hands went limp again as she let out a sigh. "The truth is, I very rarely think of her. Whatever feelings I have for her are mostly because Gran loved her. And yet..."

"And yet," he finished, "you make yourself sick with guilt."

"How can it be natural to want her to stay away?" Shane demanded in a rush. "Gran—"

"Your grandmother might have felt differently, might have given her money out of a sense of obligation. But think, who did she leave everything to? Everything important to her?"

"Yes, yes, I know, but…"

"When you think of the meaning of 'mother,' Shane, who comes to your mind?"

She stared at him. This time when the tears gathered, they brimmed over. Without a word, she dropped her head back onto his shoulder. "I told her I didn't love her. I meant it, but…"

"You don't owe her anything." He drew her closer. "I know something about guilt, Shane, about letting it tear at you. I won't let you do that to yourself."

"I told her to stay away from me." She gave a long, weary sigh. "I don't think she will."

Vance remained silent for a moment. "Is that what you want?"

"Oh God, yes."

He pressed his lips to her temple before lifting her into his arms. "Come on, you're exhausted. Lie down for a while and sleep."

"No, I'm not tired," she lied as her lids fluttered down. "I just have a headache. And dinner's—"

"I turned off the oven," he told her as he carried her to the bed. "We'll eat later." After flipping down the quilt, he bent to lay Shane between the cool sheets. "I'll go get you some aspirin." He slipped off her shoes, but as he started to pull the quilt over her, Shane took his hand.

"Vance, would you just…stay with me?"

Touching the back of his hand to her cheek, he smiled at her. "Sure." As soon as he had pulled off his boots, he slipped into bed beside her. "Try to sleep," he murmured, gathering her close. "I'll be right here."

He heard her long, quiet sigh, then felt the feather-brush of her lashes against his shoulder as her eyes shut.

How long they lay still, he had no idea. Though the grandfather clock which stood in Shane's sitting room struck the hour once, Vance paid no attention. She wasn't trembling anymore, nor was her skin chilled. Her breathing was slow and even. The fingers that absently soothed at her temple were gentle, but his thoughts were not.

No one, nothing, was ever going to put that look on Shane's face again. He would see to it. He lay staring at the ceiling as he thought out the best way to deal with Anne Abbott. He'd let the money go, because that's the way Shane wanted it. But he couldn't resign himself to allowing her to deal with a constant emotional drain. Nothing had ever wrenched at him like the sight of her pale, shocked face or pain-filled eyes.

He should have known that anyone with as open a heart as Shane's could be hurt just as deeply as she could be made happy. And how, he wondered, could anyone who had dealt with that kind of pain since childhood be so generous and full of joy? The trial of a careless mother, the embarrassment and hurt of a broken engagement, the loss of the one constant family member she had known—none of it had broken her spirit, or her simple kindness.

But tonight she needed an arm around her. It would be his tonight—and whenever she needed him. Unconsciously he drew her closer as if to shield her from anything and everything that could hurt.

"Vance."

He thought she spoke his name in sleep and brushed a light kiss over her hair.

"Vance," Shane said again, so that he looked down to see the glint of her eyes against the darkness. "Make love with me."

It was a quiet, simple request that asked for comfort rather than passion. The love he already thought infinite tripled. So did his concern that he might not be gentle enough. Very softly, cupping the shape of her face in one hand, he touched his lips to hers.

Shane let herself float. She was too physically and emotionally drained to feel stinging desire, but he seemed to know what she asked for. Never had she felt such tenderness from him. His mouth was warm, and softer than she had thought possible. Minute after minute, he kissed her—and only kissed her. His fingers stroked soothingly over her face, then moved to the base of her neck as if he knew the dull, throbbing ache that centered there. Lovingly, patiently, he drew the quiet response from her, never asking for more than she could give. She relaxed and let him guide her.

With slow care, he roamed her face with kisses, touching his lips lightly to her closed lids as he shifted the gentle massage to her shoulders. There was a concentrated sweetness in his touch that was more kind than loverlike. When his mouth came back to hers, he used only the softest pressure, taking the kiss deep without fire or fury. With a sigh, she answered it, letting her needs pour out.

Passively, she let him undress her. His hands were deft and slow and undemanding. With a sensitivity neither of them had been aware he possessed, he made no attempt to arouse. Even when they were naked, he did nothing more than kiss her and hold her close. She knew she was taking without giving any in return, and murmuring, reached for him.

"Shh." He kissed her palm before turning her gently onto her stomach. With his fingertips only at first, he stroked and soothed, running them down her back, over her shoulders. She hadn't known love could be so compassionate or unselfish. With a sigh, she closed her eyes again and let her mind empty.

He was drawing out the pain, bringing back the warmth. As she lay quietly, Shane felt herself settle and balance. There was no need to think, and no need to feel anything but Vance's strong, sure hands. All of her trust was his. Knowing this, he took even more care not to abuse it.

The old bed swayed slightly as he bent to kiss the back of her neck. Shane felt the first stir of desire. It was mild and wonderfully easy. Content, she remained still to allow herself the full enjoyment of being treasured. He was treating her like something fragile and precious. She wallowed in the new experience as he ranged soft kisses down her spine. Tension and tears were a world away from the Jenny Lind bed with a sagging mattress and worn linen sheets. The only reality now was Vance's sweet loving and the growing response of her pampered body.

He heard the subtle change in her breathing, the faint quickening, which meant relaxation was becoming desire. Still, he kept his hands easy, not wanting to rush her. The clock in the sitting room struck the hour again with low, ponderous bongs. Creakily the house settled around them with moans and groans. Vance heard little but Shane's deepening breathing.

The moonlight shivered over her skin, seeming to chase after his roaming hands. It only made him see more clearly how slender her back was, how slight the flare of her hips. Pressing his lips to her shoulder, he could smell the familiar lemon tang of her hair mixed with the lavender sachet lingering on the sheets. The room was washed in shadows.

Her cheek rested on the pillow, giving him a clear view of her profile. She might have been sleeping had it not been for the breath hurrying between her lips and the subtle movements her body was beginning to make. Still gentle, he turned her onto her back to press his mouth to hers.

Shane moaned, so lost in him she noticed no sound, no scent that didn't come from him. But his pace never altered, remaining slow and unhurried. He wanted her, God, yes, but felt no fierce, consuming drive. Love, much more than desire, pulled him to her. When he lowered his mouth to her breast, it was with such infinite tenderness that she felt a warmth, half glow, half ache, pour into her. His tongue began to turn the warmth into heat. She rose up, but seemed to take the journey on a cloud.

With the same infinite care, he took his lips and hands over her. Her skin hummed at his touch, but softly.

There was no sweet pain in the passion he brought her, but such pleasure, such comfort, she desired him all the more. Her thoughts became wholly centered on her own body and the quiet delights he had awakened.

Though his lips might stray from hers to taste her neck or her cheek, they returned again and again. Her mindless answer, the husky breath that trembled into his mouth, had the fires roaring inside him. But he banked them. Tonight, she was porcelain. She was as fragile as the moonlight. He wouldn't allow his own passion and needs to overtake him, then find he had treated her roughly. Tonight he would forget her energy and strength and only think of her frailty.

And when he took her, the tenderness made her weep.

Chapter 12

In a thick, steady curtain, the snow fell. Already the road surface was slick. Trees had been quickly transformed from dark and stark to glittery. Vance's windshield wipers swept back and forth with the monotonous swish of rubber on glass. The snow brought him neither annoyance nor pleasure. He barely noticed it.

With a few phone calls and casual inquiries, he had learned enough about Anne Abbott—or Anna Cross, as she called herself professionally—to make his anger of the night before intensify. Shane's description had been too kind.

Anne had been through three turbulent marriages. Each had been a contact in the film industry. She had coolly bled each husband for as much as she could get before jumping into the next relationship. Her latest, Leslie Stuart, had proven a bit too clever for her—or his attorney had. She'd come out of her last marriage with nothing more than she had gone into it. And, as she had a penchant for the finer things, she was already badly in debt.

She worked sporadically—bit parts, walk-ons, an occasional commercial. Her talent was nominal, but her face had earned her a few lines in a couple of legitimate films. It might have earned her more had her temper and self-importance not interfered. She was tolerated more than liked by Hollywood society. Even the tolerance, it seemed, was due more to her various husbands and intermittent lovers than to herself. Vance's contacts had painted a picture of a beautiful, scheming woman with a streak of viciousness. He felt he already knew her.

As he drove through the rapidly falling snow, his thoughts centered on Shane. He'd held her through the night, soothing her when she became restless, listening when she needed to talk. The shattered expression in her eyes would remain with him for a long time to come. Even that morning, though she had tried to be cheerful, there'd been an underlying listlessness. And he sensed her unspoken fear that Anne would come back and put her through another emotional storm. Vance couldn't change what had happened, but he could take steps to protect her in the future. That was precisely what he intended to do.

Vance turned into the lot of the roadside motel and parked. For a moment, he only sat, watching the snow accumulate on the windshield. He had considered telling Shane he intended to see her mother, then had rejected the idea. She'd been so pale that morning. In any case, he didn't doubt she would have been against it—even violently opposed to it. She was a woman who insisted on solving her own problems. Vance respected that, even admired it, but in this instance he was going to ignore it.

Stepping out of the car, he walked across the slippery parking lot to find the office and the information he needed. Ten minutes later, he knocked on Anne Abbott's door.

The crease of annoyance between her brows altered into an expression of consideration when she saw Vance. He was certainly a very pleasant surprise. Vance eyed her coolly, discovering that Shane's description hadn't been exaggerated. She was lovely. Her face had a delicacy of bone and complexion complemented by the very deep blue eyes and mane of blond hair. Her body, clad in a clinging pink dressing gown, was ripe and rounded. Though her glittery fairness was the direct opposite of Amelia's sultry beauty, Vance knew instantly they were women of the same mold.

"Well, hello." Her voice was languid and sulky, her eyes amused and appraising. Though he looked for it, Vance found not the slightest resemblance to her daughter. Overcoming a wave of disgust, he smiled in return. He had to get in the door.

"Hello, Ms. Cross."

He saw instantly that the use of her stage name had been a wise move. She flashed him the full-power smile that was one of her best tools. "Do I know you?" She touched the pink tip of her tongue to her top lip. "There is something familiar about you, but I can't believe I'd forget your face."

"Vance Banning, Ms. Cross," he said, keeping his eyes on hers. "We have some mutual friends, the Hourbacks."

"Oh, Tod and Sheila!" Though she couldn't abide them, Anne infused her voice with rich pleasure. "Isn't that marvelous! Oh, but you must come in; it's freezing out there. Appalling Eastern weather." She closed the door behind him, then stood leaning back against it a moment. Perhaps, she mused, the hometown visit wouldn't be so boring after all. This was the best-looking thing to knock at her door for quite some time. And, if he knew the stuffy Hourbacks, chances were he'd have a few dollars as well. "Well, well, isn't it a small world," she murmured, gently tucking a strand of delicate blond behind her ear. "How are Tod and Sheila? I haven't seen them for an age."

"Fine when I last spoke to them." Well aware where her thoughts were traveling, Vance smiled again, this time with cold amusement. "They mentioned that you were in town. I couldn't resist looking you up, Ms. Cross."

"Oh, Anna, please," she said graciously. With a sigh, she gave the room a despairing glance. "I must apologize for my accommodations, but I have some business nearby, and…" She gave a tiny shrug. "I'm forced to make do. I can offer you a drink, however, if you'll take bourbon."

It was barely eleven, but Vance answered smoothly, "If it's not too much trouble."

"None at all." Anne glided to a small table. She felt particularly grateful that she had packed the silk dressing gown and hadn't yet drummed up the energy to change. It was, she knew, both becoming and alluring. A quick glance in the mirror as she poured assured her she looked perfect. Thank God she'd just finished putting on her makeup. "But tell me, Vance," she continued, "what in the world are you doing in this dull little place? You're not a hometown boy, are you?"

"Business," he said simply, nodding his thanks as she handed him a neat bourbon.

Anne's eyes narrowed a moment, then widened. "Oh, of course. How could I be so foolish!" She beamed at him as the wheels began to spin in her head. "I've heard Tod speak of you. Riverton Construction, right?"

"Right."

"My, my, I am impressed." Her tongue ran lightly over her teeth as she considered. "It's about the biggest in the country."

"So I'm told," he answered mildly, watching her eye him over the rim of her glass. Without much interest, he wondered how much bait she would toss out before she tried to reel him in. If it hadn't been for Shane, he might have enjoyed letting her make a fool of herself.

With her carefully languid grace, Anne sat on the edge of the bed. As she sipped again, she wondered how soon he would try to sleep with her and how much resistance she should feign before she obliged him. "Well, Vance, what can I do for you?"

Vance swirled the bourbon without drinking. He sent her a cool, direct stare. "Leave Shane alone."

The change in her expression might have been comical under any other circumstances. She forgot herself long enough to gape at him. "What are you talking about?"

"Shane," he repeated. "Your daughter."

"I know who Shane is," Anne said sharply. "What has she to do with you?"

"I'm going to marry her."

Shock covered her face, then dissolved with her burst of laughter. "Little Shane? Oh, that's too funny. Don't tell me my cute little daughter caught herself a live one! I've underestimated her." Tossing her head, she sent Vance a shrewed glance. "Or I overestimated you."

Though his fingers tightened on the glass, he controlled his temper. When he spoke, his voice was dangerously mild. "Be careful, Anne."

The look in his eye checked her laughter. "Well," she continued with an unconcerned shrug, "so you want to marry Shane. What's that to me?"

"Not a damn thing."

Masking both apprehension and irritation. Anne rose gracefully. "I suppose I should go congratulate my little girl on her luck."

Vance took her arm. Though he applied no pressure, the meaning was very clear. "You'll do nothing of the kind. What you're going to do is pack your bags and get out."

Enraged, Anne jerked away from him. "Who the hell do you think you are? You can't order me to leave."

"Advise," Vance corrected. "You'd be wise to take the suggestion."

"I don't like the tone of your suggestion," she retorted. "I intend to see my daughter—"

"Why?" Vance stopped her cold without raising his voice. "You won't get another dime, I promise you."

"I haven't any idea what you're talking about," Anne

claimed with frigid dignity. "I don't know what nonsense Shane's been telling you, but—"

"You'd be wise to think carefully before you say any more," Vance warned quietly. "I saw Shane shortly after you left her last night. She had to tell me very little before I got the picture." He gave her a long, hard look. "I know you, Anne, every bit as well as you know yourself. There'll be no more money," he continued when Anne fell silent. "You'd be smarter to cut your losses and go back to California. It would be a simple matter to stop payment on the check she's already given you."

That annoyed her. Anne cursed herself for not getting up early and cashing the check before Shane thought better of it. "I have every intention of seeing my daughter." She gave him a glittering smile. "And when I do, I'll have a few words to say to her about her choice of lovers."

His eyes neither heated nor chilled, but became faintly bored. Nothing could have infuriated her more. "You won't see Shane again," he corrected.

Under the silk, her lovely bust heaved. "You can't keep me from seeing my own daughter."

"I can," Vance countered, "and I will. If you contact her, if you try to wheedle another dollar out of her or hurt her in any way, I'll deal with you myself."

Anne felt the first prickle of physical fear. Warily, she stepped back from him. "You wouldn't dare touch me."

Vance gave a mirthless laugh. "Don't be too sure. I don't think it'll come to that though." Casually, he set down the glass of liquor. "I have a number of contacts in the movie industry, Anne. Old friends, business associates, clients. A few words in the right ears, and what little career you have is out the window."

"How dare you threaten me," she began, both furious and afraid.

"Not a threat," he assured her. "A promise. Hurt Shane again and you'll pay for it. You're getting the best of the deal, Anne," he added. "She doesn't have anything you want."

Smoldering, she took a step toward him. "I have a right to my share. Whatever my grandmother had should be split fifty-fifty between Shane and me."

He lifted a brow in speculation. "Fifty-fifty," he said thoughtfully. "You must be desperate if you're willing to settle for that." Without pity, he shrugged off her problems. "I won't waste my time arguing legalities with you, much less morals or ethics. Just accept that what Shane gave you yesterday is all you'll ever get." With this he turned toward the door. In a last-ditch effort, Anne sank down on the bed and began to weep.

"Oh, Vance, you can't be so cruel." She lifted an already tear-drenched face to his. "You can't mean to keep me from seeing my own daughter, my only child."

He studied the beautiful tragic face, then gave a slight nod of approval. "Very good," he commented. "You're a better actress than they give you credit for." As he pulled the door to behind him, he heard the sound of smashing glass on the wood.

Springing up, Anne grabbed the second glass, then hurled it as well. No one, *no one,* she determined, was going to threaten her. Or mock her, she fumed, remembering the cool amusement in his eyes. She'd see he paid for it. Sitting back on the bed, she clenched her fists until she could bring her temper to order. She had to think. There had to be a way to get to Vance Banning. *Riverton Construction,* she reflected, closing her eyes as she concentrated. Had there been any scandal connected with the firm? Frustrated, she hurled her pillow across the room. She could think of nothing. What did she know about a stupid firm that built shopping centers and hospitals? It was all so boring, she thought furiously.

Grabbing the second pillow, she started to toss it as well when a sudden glimmer of memory arrested her. Scandal, she repeated. But not about the firm. There had been something…something a few years back. Just a few whispers at a party or two. *Damn!* she swore silently when her recollection took her no further. Sheila Hourback, Anne thought, tightening her lips. Maybe the stuffy old bird could be useful. Scrambling over the unmade bed, Anne reached for the phone.

Shane was busy detailing a skirmish of the Battle of Antietam for three eager boys when Vance walked in. She smiled at him, and he heard enthusiasm in her voice as she spoke, but she was still pale. That alone brushed away any doubts that he had done the right thing. She'd bounce back, he told himself as he wandered into the antique shop, because it was her nature to do so. But even someone as intrinsically strong as Shane could take only so much. Spotting Pat dusting glassware, he went over to her.

"Hi, Vance." She sent him a quick, friendly grin. "How're you doing?"

"I'm fine." He cast a look over his shoulder to be certain Shane was still occupied. "Listen, Pat, I wanted to talk to you about that dining-room set."

"Oh yeah. There was some mix-up about that. I still haven't gotten it straight. Shane said—"

"I'm going to buy it."

"You?" Her initial surprise turned into embarrassment. Vance grinned at her, however, and her cheeks cooled.

"For Shane," he explained. "For Christmas."

"Oh, that's so sweet!" The romance of it appealed to her immediately. "It was her grandmother's, you know. She just loves it."

"I know, and she's determined to sell it." Idly, he picked up a china demitasse cup. "I'm just as determined to buy it for her. She won't let me." He gave Pat a conspirator's wink. "But she can hardly turn down a Christmas present, can she?"

"No." Appreciating his cleverness, Pat beamed at him. So the rumors were true, she thought, pleased and interested. There was something going on between them. "She sure couldn't. It'll mean so much to her, Vance. It just about kills her to have to sell some of these things, but that's the hardest. It's…ah, it's awfully expensive though."

"That's all right. I'm going to give you a check for it today." It occurred to him that it would soon be all over town that he had a great deal of money to spend. He would have to talk to Shane very soon. "Put a Sold sign on it." He glanced back again, seeing Shane's three visitors were preparing to leave. "Just don't say anything to her unless she asks."

"I won't," Pat promised, pleased to be in on the surprise. "And if she does, I'll just say the person who bought it wants it held until Christmas."

"Clever girl," he complimented. "Thanks."

"Vance." She lowered her voice to a whisper. "She looks kind of down today. Maybe you could take her out for a while and cheer her up. Oh, Shane," she continued quickly in a normal tone, "how did you manage to keep those little monsters quiet for twenty minutes? Those are Clint Drummond's boys," she explained to Vance with a shudder. "I nearly ran out the back door when they came in."

"They were thrilled that school was called off because of the snow." Instinctively, she reached for Vance's hand as she came in. "What they wanted was to work out the fine details of a few engagements so they could have their own Battle of Antietam with snowballs."

"Get your coat," Vance told her, planting a kiss on her brow.

"What?"

"And a hat; it's cold outside."

Laughing, Shane gave his hand a squeeze. "I know it's cold outside, fool. There's already six inches of snow."

"Then we'd better get started." He gave her a friendly swat on the seat. "You'll need boots too, I suppose. Just don't take all day."

"Vance, it's the middle of the day. I can't leave."

"It's business," he told her gravely. "You have to get your Christmas tree."

"Christmas tree?" With a chuckle, she picked up the duster Pat had set down. "It's too early in the season."

"Early?" Vance sent Pat a grin. "You've got just over two weeks until Christmas, and no tree. Most self-respecting stores are decked out by Thanksgiving."

"Well, I know, but—"

"But nothing," he interrupted, taking the duster from her and handing it back to Pat. "Where's your holiday spirit? Not to mention your sales strategy. According to the most recent poll, people spend an additional twelve-and-a-half percent in a store decorated for the holidays."

Shane gave him a narrow glance. "What poll?"

"The Retail Sale and Seasonal Atmosphere Survey," he said glibly.

The first genuine laugh in nearly twenty-four hours burst from her. "That's a terrible lie."

"Certainly not," he disagreed. "It's a very good one. Now go get your coat."

"But, Vance—"

"Oh, don't be silly, Shane," Pat interrupted, giving her a push toward the stairs. "I can handle the shop. We're not likely to have customers pouring in with all this snow. Besides," she added, shrewd enough to know her employer, "I'd really love a tree. I'll make a place for it right in front of this window." Without waiting for a reply, Pat began to rearrange furniture.

"Gloves too," Vance added as Shane hesitated.

"All right," she said, surrendering. "I'll be back in a minute."

In little more than ten, she was sitting beside Vance in the cab of his small pickup. “Oh, it’s beautiful out here!” she exclaimed, trying to look everywhere at once. “I love the first snow. Look, there’re the Drummond boys.”

Vance glanced in the direction she indicated and saw three boys pelting each other violently with snow.

“The battle’s under way,” he murmured.

“General Burnside’s having his problems,” Shane observed, then turned back to Vance. “By the way, what did you and Pat have your heads together about when I went upstairs to get my things?”

Vance lifted a brow. “Oh,” he said complacently, “I was trying to make a date with her. She’s cute.”

“Really?” Shane drew out the word as she eyed him. “It would be a shame for her to be fired this close to Christmas.”

“I was only trying to develop good employee relations,” he explained, pulling up at a stop sign. Taking her by surprise, he pulled her into his arms and kissed her thoroughly. “I love that little choking sound you make when you try not to laugh. Do it again.”

Breathless, she pulled away from him. “Firing a trusted employee is no laughing matter,” she told him primly, and adjusted her ski hat. “Turn right here.” Instead of obeying, he kissed her again. The rude blast of a horn had her struggling out of his arms a second time. “Now you’ve done it.” She ruined the severity of the lecture with a smothered chuckle. “The sheriff’s going to arrest you for obstructing traffic.”

“One disgruntled man in a Buick isn’t traffic,” Vance

disagreed as he made a right turn. "Do you know where you're going?"

"Certainly. There's a place a few miles down where you can dig your own tree."

"Dig?" Vance repeated, shooting her a look. Shane met it placidly.

"Dig," she repeated. "According to the latest conservation poll—"

"Dig," he agreed, cutting her off.

Laughing, Shane leaned over to kiss his shoulder. "I love you, Vance."

By the time they arrived at the tree farm, the snow had slowed to a gentle mist. Shane dragged him from tree to tree, examining each one minutely before rejecting it. Though he knew the color in her face was a result of the cold, the spark was back. Even if he sensed some of the energy was a product of nerves, he was satisfied that she was bouncing back. The simple pleasure of choosing a Christmas tree was enough to put the laughter back in her eyes.

"This one!" Shane exclaimed, stopping in front of a short-needle pine. "It's exactly right."

"It doesn't look much different from the other five hundred trees we've looked at," Vance grumbled, slicing the point of his shovel into the snow.

"That's because you don't have a connoisseur's eye," she said condescendingly. He scooped up a handful of snow and rubbed it into her face. "Be that as it may," Shane continued with remarkable aplomb, "this is the one. Dig," she instructed, and stepping back, folded her arms.

"Yes, ma'am," he said meekly, bending to the task.

"You know," he said a few moments later, "it suddenly occurs to me that you're going to expect me to dig a hole to put this thing in after Christmas."

Shane sent him a guileless smile. "What a good idea. I know just the place too. You'll probably need a pick though. There are an awful lot of rocks." Ignoring Vance's rude rejoinder, she waved over an attendant. With the roots carefully wrapped in burlap and the tree itself paid for—by Shane over Vance's objection—they headed home.

"Damn it, Shane," he said in exasperation. "I wanted to buy the tree for you." The truck rumbled over the narrow wooden bridge.

"The tree's for the shop," she pointed out logically as they pulled in front of the house. "So the shop bought the tree. Just as it buys the stock and pays the electric bill." Noting that he was annoyed, Shane walked around the truck to kiss him. "You're sweet, Vance, and I do appreciate it. Buy me something else."

He gave her a long, considering look. "What?"

"Oh, I don't know. I've always had a fancy for something frivolous and extravagant…like chinchilla earmuffs."

With difficulty, he maintained his gravity. "It would serve you right if I did buy you some. Then you'd have to wear them."

She rose on her toes, inviting another kiss. As he bent down, Shane slipped the handful of snow she'd been holding down his back. When he swore pungently, she made a dash for safety. Shane fully expected the snowball that bashed into the back of her head, but she didn't expect to be agilely tackled so that she landed facedown in the snow.

"Oh! You really aren't a gentleman," she muttered, hampered by a mouthful of snow. Vance sat back, roaring with laughter while she struggled to sit up, wiping at her face.

"Snow looks even better on you than mud," he told her.

Shane lunged at him, catching him off-balance so that he toppled onto his back. She landed with a soft thud on his chest. Before she could deposit the snow she held in his face, he rolled her over and pinned her. Resigned, she closed her eyes and waited. Instead of the cold shock of snow, she felt his lips crush down on hers. In immediate response, she pulled him closer, answering hungrily.

"Give?" he demanded.

"No," she said firmly, and dragged him back again.

The urgency of her response made him forget they were lying in the snow in the middle of the afternoon. He no longer felt the wet flakes that drifted down the back of his neck, though he could taste others on her skin. He fretted against the bulky clothes that kept the shape of her from him, against the gloves that prevented him from feeling the softness of her skin. But he could taste, and he did so greedily.

"God, I want you," he murmured, savaging her small, avid mouth again and again. "Right here, right now." Lifting his head, he looked down on her, but whatever he would have said was cut off by the sound of an approaching car. "If I'd had any sense I'd have taken you to my house," he mumbled, then helped her to her feet.

Hugging him, she whispered in his ear, "I close in two hours."

While Shane dealt with a straggle of customers who touched everything and bought nothing, Vance made himself useful by setting up the tree. Pat's lighthearted chatter helped cool the blood Shane had so quickly heated. Following Shane's instructions, he found the boxes of ornaments in the dusty attic.

Dusk was falling before they were alone again. Because she was still looking pale, Vance bullied her into a quick meal before they began to sort through the ornaments. They made do with cold meat from the rib roast neither of them had touched the night before.

But as well as alleviating her hunger, the meal reminded her forcibly of her mother's visit. She struggled to push away the depression, or at least to conceal it. Her chatter was bright and mindless and entirely too strained.

Vance caught her hand, stopping her in midsentence. "Not with me, Shane," he said quietly.

Not bothering to pretend she didn't understnad, Shane squeezed his hand. "I'm not dwelling on it, Vance. It just sneaks up on me sometimes."

"And when it does, I'm here. Lean on me, Shane, when you need to." He lifted her hand to his lips. "God knows, I'll lean on you."

"Now," she said shakily. "Just hold me a minute."

He drew her into his arms, pressing her head to his heart. "As long as you want."

She sighed, relaxing again. "I hate being a fool," she murmured. "I suppose I hate that worse than anything."

"You're not being a fool," he said, then drew her

away as he came to a decision. "Shane, I went to see your mother this morning."

"What?" The word came out in a whisper.

"You can be angry if you like, but I won't stand by and watch you be hurt again. I made it very clear that if she bothered you again, she'd have me to deal with."

Shaken, she turned away from him. "You shouldn't—"

"Don't tell me what I shouldn't have done," he interrupted angrily. "I love you, damn it. You can't expect me to do nothing while she puts you through the wringer."

"I can deal with it, Vance."

"No." Taking her shoulders, he turned her around. "With an amazing number of things, yes, but not with this. She turns you inside out." His grip lightened to a caress. "Shane, if it had been me hurting, what would you have done?"

She opened her mouth to speak, but only released a pent-up breath. Taking his face in her hands, she pulled it down to hers. "I hope I'd have done the same thing. Thank you," she said, kissing him gently. "I don't want to know what was said," she added with more firmness. "No more problems tonight, Vance."

He shook his head, acknowledging another delay in making everything known to her. "All right, no more problems."

"We'll trim the tree," she stated decisively. "Then you're going to make love to me under it."

He grinned. "I suppose I could do that." He allowed her to pull him down the stairs. "What if I make love to you under it, then we trim it?"

"There's nothing festive in that," she said gravely as she began unpacking ornaments.

"Wanna bet?"

She laughed, but shook her head. "Absolutely not. There's an order to these things, you know. Lights first," she announced, pulling out a neatly coiled string.

It took well over an hour as Shane shared her memories about nearly every ornament she unpacked. As she took out a red felt star, she recalled the year she had made it for her grandmother. It brought both a sting and a warmth. She'd been dreading Christmas. It hadn't seemed possible to celebrate the holiday in that house without the woman who had always shared it with her. Gran would have reminded her that there was a cycle, but Shane knew she would have found a tree and tinsel unbearable had she been alone.

She watched Vance carefully arranging a garland. How Gran would have loved him, she thought with a smile. And he her. Somehow she found it didn't matter that the two people she loved most in the world had never met. She knew both of them, and the link was formed. Shane was ready to give herself to him completely.

If he doesn't ask me to marry him soon, she mused, I'll just have to ask him. When he glanced over, she sent him a saucy smile.

"What are you thinking?" he demanded.

"Oh, nothing," she said innocently, stepping back to view the results. "It's perfect, just as I knew it would be." She gave a satisfied nod before taking out the old silver star that would adorn the top.

Vance accepted it from her, then eyed the top branch.

"I'm not going to be able to get this on there without knocking half of everything else off. We need a ladder."

"Oh no, that's okay. Let me up on your shoulders."

"There's a stepladder upstairs," he began.

"Oh, don't be so fussy." Shane jumped nimbly onto his back, hooking her legs around his waist for balance. "I'll be able to reach it without any trouble," she assured him, then began scooting up to his shoulders. Vance felt every line of her body as if he'd run his hands over it. "There," she said, settled. "Hand it to me and I'll stick it on."

He obliged, then gripped her knees as she leaned forward. "Damn it, Shane, not so far; you're going to fall into the tree."

"Don't be silly," she said lightly as she secured the star. "I have terrific balance. There!" Putting her hands on her hips, she surveyed the results. "Step back a bit so I can see the whole thing." When he had, Shane gave a long sigh, then kissed the top of his head. "It's beautiful, isn't it? Just smell the pine." Carelessly, she linked her ankles against his chest.

"It'll look better with the overhead lights off." Still carrying her, he moved to flick the wall switch. In the dark, the colored lights on the tree seemed to jump into life. They shimmered against garland and tinsel, glowed warmly against pine.

"Oh yes," Shane breathed. "Just perfect."

"Not quite yet," Vance disagreed.

With a deft move, he pulled her around into his arms as she slid down from his shoulders. "This," he told her as he laid her on the rug, "is perfect."

The lights danced on her face as she smiled up at him. "It certainly is."

His hands weren't patient tonight, but neither were hers. They undressed each other quickly, laughing and swearing a bit at buttons or snaps. But when they were naked, the urgency only intensified. Their hands sought to touch, their mouths hurried to taste—everywhere. She marveled again at his taut, corded muscles. He filled himself again on the flavor and fragrance of her skin. They paid no more notice to the warmth of the lights or the tang of pine than they had to the chill of the snow. They were alone. They were together.

Chapter 13

It wasn't easy for Shane to keep her mind on her work the next day. Though she made several sales, among them the tilt-top table she had so painstakingly refinished, she was distracted throughout the morning. Distracted enough that she never noticed the discreet Sold sign Pat had attached to the Hepplewhite set in lieu of a price tag. She could think of little else but Vance. Once or twice during the morning, she caught herself glancing at the Christmas tree and remembering. In all of her dreams, in all of her wishes, she had never imagined it could be this way. Each time they made love it was different, a new adventure. Yet somehow it was as though they had been together for years.

Every time she touched him it was like making a fresh discovery, and still Shane felt she had known him for a lifetime rather than a matter of three short months. When he kissed her, it was just as thrilling and novel as the first time. The recognition she had felt the instant she had seen him had deepened into something much more abiding. Faith.

Without doubt, she was certain that the excitement and the learning would go on time after time over the comfortable core of honest love. There was no need to romanticize what was real. She had only to look at him to know what they shared was special and enduring. With another glance at the tree, she realized she'd never been happier in her life.

"Miss!" The customer considering the newly caned ladder-back chair called impatiently for Shane's attention.

"Yes, ma'am, I'm sorry." If the smile Shane gave her was a bit dreamy, the woman didn't seem to notice. "It's a lovely piece, isn't it? The seat's just been redone." Calling herself to order, Shane turned the chair over to show off the workmanship.

"Yes, I'm interested." The woman poked at the caning a moment. "But the price…"

Recognizing the tone, Shane settled down to bargain.

It was just past noon when things began to quiet down. The morning's profits weren't extraordinary, but solid enough to help Shane stop worrying over the large chunk of her capital which she had given to her mother. The wolf wasn't at the door yet, she told herself optimistically. And with luck—and the Christmas rush—she could hold him off for quite some time. Two or three good sales would keep her books from dipping too deeply into the red. Professionally, she wanted little more at the moment than to calmly tread water. Personally, she knew precisely what she wanted, and she had every intention of seeing to it quickly.

She was going to marry Vance, and it was time she told him so. If he was too proud to ask her because he didn't yet have a steady job, she would simply have to persuade him to see things differently. Shane had made up her mind to take a firm stand that very day. There was an excitement bubbling inside her, a sense of purpose. Today, she thought, almost giddy from it, nothing could hurt her. She was going to propose to the man she loved. And she wasn't going to take no for an answer.

"Pat, can you handle things if I go out for an hour?"

"Sure, it's slow now anyway." Pat glanced up from the table she was polishing. "Are you going to another auction?"

"No," Shane told her blithely. "I'm going on a picnic."

Leaving Pat staring behind her, Shane raced upstairs.

It took her less than ten minutes to fill the wicker basket. There was a cold bottle of Chablis inside it, which she had splurged on madly. It might be a bit rich for the peanut butter sandwiches, but Shane's mind wasn't on proprieties. As she raced out the back door, she was already picturing spreading the checked tablecloth in front of Vance's living-room fire.

Wet, slushy snow sloshed over her boots as she stepped off the porch onto the lawn. The perfect day for a picnic, she decided, letting the hamper swing. The air was absolutely still. Melted snow dripped from the roof with a musical patter. The fast water in the creek broke through thin sheets of ice with an excited hissing and bubbling. Shane paused to listen a moment, enjoying the mixture of sounds. The feeling of euphoria built. She found it the most exquisite of days, with the sky coldly blue, the snow-laced mountains rising and the naked trees slick with wet.

Then the low purr of an engine intruded. She looked back, then stopped as she recognized Anne pulling up in the drive. All of her joy in the afternoon slipped quietly away. She hardly noticed the fingers of tension which crept up to the base of her neck.

With her faultless grace, Anne picked her way over the melting snow in calfskin boots. She wore a trim fox-fur hat now to match her coat, and a small, smug smile. There were ruby studs, or clever imitations, glinting at her ears. Though her daughter stood rigid as a stone, she glided up to greet her with the customary brush of cheeks. Without speaking, Shane set the hamper down on the bottom step of the porch.

"Darling, I had to drop by before I left." Anne beamed at her with a cold gleam in her eye.

"Going back to California?" Shane asked flatly.

"Yes, of course, I have the most marvelous script. Of course, I'll probably be weeks on location, but…" She gave a gay shrug. "But that's not why I dropped by."

Shane studied her, marveling. It was as though the ugly scene between them had never taken place. She has no feelings, she realized abruptly. It meant less than nothing to her. "Why did you come by, Anne?"

"Why, to congratulate you, of course!"

"Congratulate me?" Shane lifted a brow. It was easier somehow knowing that the woman in front of her was simply a stranger. A few shared genes didn't make a bond. It was love that did that, or affection. Or at the very least, respect.

"I admit I didn't think you had it in you, Shane, but I'm pleasantly surprised."

Shane then surprised both of them by giving an impatient sigh. "Will you get to the point, Anne? I was on my way out."

"Oh, now, don't be cross," she said placatingly. "I'm really thrilled for you, catching yourself a man like that."

Shane's eyes chilled. "I beg your pardon?"

"Vance Banning, darling." She gave a slow, appreciative smile. "What a catch!"

"Strange, I never thought about it quite that way." Bending, Shane prepared to pick up the hamper again.

"The president of Riverton Construction isn't just a mild triumph, sweetheart, it's a downright *coup*."

Shane's fingers froze on the handle. Straightening, she looked Anne dead in the eye. "What are you talking about?"

"Only your fantastic luck, Shane. After all, the man's *rolling* in it. I imagine you'll be able to turn this little shop of yours into an antique palace if you want a hobby." She gave a quick, brittle laugh. "Leave it to cute little Shane to land herself a millionaire the first time around. If I had a bit more time, darling, I'd insist on hearing the details of how you managed it."

"I don't know what you're talking about." Cold panic was beginning to rush through her. She wanted to turn and run away, but her legs were stiff and unyielding.

"God knows why he decided to dump himself in this

town," Anne went on mildly. "But it's your good fortune he did, and right next door too. I suppose he means to keep it for a little hideaway once the two of you move to D.C." *A fabulous house,* she thought on a flash of envy. *Servants, parties.* Carefully, she kept her tone gay. "I can't tell you how thrilled I was to learn you'd hooked up with the man who owns virtually the biggest construction firm in the country."

"Riverton," Shane repeated numbly.

"Very prestigious, darling Shane. It does give me cause to wonder how you'll fit in, but…" She shrugged this off and aimed her coup de grâce. "It's a shame about that nasty scandal though." Shane merely shook her head and stared at Anne blankly. "His first wife, you know. A terrible tangle."

"Wife?" Shane repeated faintly. She felt the nausea rising in her stomach. "Vance's wife?"

"Oh, Shane, don't tell me he didn't mention it!" It was exactly what she'd hoped for. Anne shook her head and sighed. "That's disgraceful of him, really. Isn't it just like a man to expect some wide-eyed girl to take everything on face value." She clucked her tongue in disapproval, thinking with inner appreciation that Vance Banning was going to take his knocks on this one. She didn't think of Shane at all.

"Well, the very least he might have done was tell you he was married before," she continued primly. "Even if he didn't go into the nasty business."

"I don't…" Shane mangaged to swallow the sickness and continue. "I don't understand."

"A spicy little scandal," Anne told her. "His wife was

a raving beauty, you know. Perhaps too much so." Anne paused delicately. "One of her lovers put a bullet in her heart. At least that's what the Bannings would have everyone believe." The shock in Shane's eyes gave Anne another surge of gratification. Oh yes, she thought grimly, Vance Banning was going to get back some of his now. "Hushed it up rather quickly too," she added, then brushed the matter away with the back of an elegantly gloved hand. "An odd business. Well, I must run, don't want to miss my plane. *Ciao,* darling, and don't let that handsome gold mine slip away from you. There are plenty of women just dying to catch him." Pausing, she touched Shane's cap of curls with a finger. "For God's sake, Shane, find a decent hairdresser. I suppose he thinks you're…refreshing. Get the ring on your finger before he gets bored." She brushed Shane's cold cheek with hers, then dashed off, satisfied she'd paid Vance back for his threats.

Shane stood perfectly still, staring after her. But she didn't see her. She saw nothing. Trapped in the ice of shock, the pain was dormant. That would have surprised Anne had she given it any thought. As a woman who knew nothing of emotional pain, she would assume Shane would feel only fury. But the fury was surrounded by pain, and the pain lay waiting to spring out.

The sun bounced glaringly off the melting snow. A breeze, chill and sharp, whipped through her carelessly unbuttoned coat. In a flash of scarlet, a cardinal swooped over the ground to roost comfortably on a low branch. Shane stood absolutely still, noticing nothing. Sluggishly, her mind began to work.

It wasn't true, she told herself. Anne had made it up for some unexplainable purpose of her own. *President of Riverton?* No, he said he was a carpenter. He *was,* she thought desperately. She'd seen his work herself… He'd…he'd worked for her. Taken the job she had offered. Why would he—how could he—if he was everything Anne had said? *His first wife.*

Shane felt the first stab of pain. No, it couldn't be, he would have told her. Vance loved her. He wouldn't lie or pretend. He wouldn't make a fool of her by letting her think he was out of work when he was the head of one of the biggest construction firms in the country. He wouldn't have said he loved her without telling her who he really was. *His first wife.* Shane heard a soft, despairing moan without realizing it was hers.

When she saw him coming down the path, she stared blankly. As she watched him, her whirling thoughts came to a sudden halt. She knew then she'd been a fool.

Spotting her, Vance smiled in greeting and increased his pace. He was still several yards away when he recognized the expression on her face. It was the same stricken look he'd seen in the moonlight only a few nights before.

"Shane?" He came to her quickly, reaching for her. Shane stepped back.

"Liar," she said in a broken whisper. "All lies." Her eyes both accused and pleaded. "Everything you said."

"Shane—"

"No, don't!" The panic in her voice was enough to halt the hand he held out to her. He knew that somehow she had learned everything before he could tell her himself.

"Shane, let me explain."

"Explain?" She dragged shaking fingers through her hair. "Explain? How? How can you explain why you let me think you were something you're not? How can you explain why you didn't bother to tell me you were president of Riverton, that you—that you'd been married before? I *trusted* you," she whispered. "God, how could I have been such a fool!"

Anger he could have met and handled. Vance faced despair without any notion of how to cope with it. Impotently he thrust his hands into his pockets to keep from touching her. "I would have told you, Shane. I intended—"

"Would have?" She gave a quick, shaky laugh. "When? After you'd gotten bored with the joke?"

"There was never any joke," he said furiously, then clamped down on his panic. "I wanted to tell you, but every time—"

"No joke?" Her eyes glittered now with the beginnings of anger, the beginnings of tears. "You let me give you a job. You let me pay you six dollars an hour, and you don't think that's funny?"

"I didn't want your money, Shane; I tried to tell you. You wouldn't listen." Frustrated, he turned away until he had himself under control. "I banked the checks in an account under your name."

"How dare you!" Wild with pain, she shouted at him, blind and deaf to everything but the sense of betrayal. "How dare you play games with me! *I believed you.* I believed everything. I thought—I thought I was helping you, and all the time you were laughing at me."

"Damn it, Shane, I never laughed at you." Pushed

beyond endurance, he grabbed her shoulders. "You know I never laughed at you."

"I wonder how you managed not to laugh in my face. God, you're clever, Vance." She choked on a sob, then swallowed it.

"Shane, if you'd try to understand why I came, why I didn't want to be connected with the company for a little while…" None of the words he needed would come to him. "It had nothing to do with you," he told her fiercely. "I didn't expect to get involved."

"Did it keep you from being bored?" she demanded, struggling against his hold. "Amusing yourself with a stupid little country girl who was so gullible she'd believe anything you said? You could play the poor working man and be entertained."

"It was never like that." Enraged by the words, he shook her. "You don't really believe that."

The tears gushed out passionately, strangling her voice. "And I was so willing to fall into bed with you. You knew it!" She sobbed, pushing desperately at him. "Right from the first I had no secrets from you."

"I had them," he admitted in a tight voice. "I had reasons for them."

"You knew how much I loved you, how much I wanted you. You *used* me!" On a moan, she covered her face with her hands. "Oh God, I left myself wide open."

She wept with the same honest abandon he'd seen when she laughed. Unable to do otherwise, he crushed her against him. He thought if he could only calm her down, he could make her understand. "Shane, please, you have to listen to me."

"No, no, I don't." She pulled in breath after jerky breath as she struggled for release. "I'll never forgive you. I'll never believe anything you say again. Damn you, let me go."

"Not until you stop this and hear what I have to say."

"No! I won't listen to any more lies. I won't let you make a fool of me again. All this time, all this time when I was giving you everything, you were lying and laughing at me. I was just something to keep the nights from being dull while you were on vacation."

He jerked her back, his face rigid with fury. "Damn it, Shane, you know better than that."

Her struggles ceased abruptly. As he watched, the tears seemed to turn to ice. Without expression, she stared up at him. Nothing she had said so far had struck him to the core like that one cool look.

"I don't know you," she said quietly.

"Shane—"

"Take your hands off me." The command was devoid of passion. Vance felt his stiff fingers loosen. Freed, Shane stepped back until they were no longer touching. "I want you to go away and leave me alone. Stay away from me," she added flatly, still looking directly into his eyes. "I don't want to see you again."

Turning, she walked up the steps and to the door. After its final click came absolute silence.

Far beneath the window, the streets were packed with traffic. The steady fall of snow increased the confusion. Beneath the overhang of the department store across the street, a red-cheeked Santa rang his bell, ho-hoing when someone dropped a coin into his bucket. The scene below was played in pantomime. The thick glass of the window and well-constructed walls allowed no street sounds to intrude. Vance kept his back to his plush, spacious office and continued to watch.

He'd made his obligatory appearance at the company Christmas party. It was still going on, with enthusiasm, in a large conference room on the third floor. When it broke up, everyone would go home to spend Christmas Eve with their families or friends. He'd refused more than a dozen invitations for the evening since his return to Washington. It was one thing to do his duty as the head of the company, and another to put himself through hours of small talk and celebrating. *She wouldn't be there,* he thought, staring down at the snowy sidewalk.

Two weeks. In two weeks, Vance had managed to straighten out a few annoying contractual tangles, plot out a bid for a new wing to a hospital in Virginia, and head a heated board meeting. He'd dealt with paperwork, and some minor corporate intrigue he might have found amusing if he'd been sleeping properly. But he wasn't sleeping properly any more than he was forgetting. Work wasn't an elixir this time. As she had from the very first moment, Shane haunted him.

Turning from the window, Vance took his place behind the massive oak desk. It was clear of papers. In a fury of frustrated energy, he'd taken care of every letter, memo and contract, putting his secretary and assistants through an orgy of work over the last two weeks. Now, he had nothing but an empty desk and a clear calendar. He considered the possibility of flying to Des Moines to supervise the progress of a condominium development. That would throw the Iowa branch into a panic, he thought with a quick laugh. Hardly fair to upset their applecart because he was restless. He brooded at the far wall, wondering what Shane was doing.

He hadn't left in anger. It would have been easier for Vance if that had been the case. He had left because Shane had wanted it. He didn't blame her, and that too made it impossibly frustrating. Why should she listen to him, or understand? There had been enough truth in what she had flung at him to make the rest difficult to overturn. He had lied, or at the very least, he hadn't been honest. To Shane, one was the same as the other.

He'd hurt her. He had put that look of helpless despair on her face. That was unforgivable. Vance pushed away from the desk to pace over the thick stone-colored carpet. But damn it, if she'd just listened to him! If she'd only given him a moment. Going to the window again, he scowled out. Laughed at her? Made fun of her? No, he thought with the first true fury he'd felt in two weeks. No, by God, he'd be damned if he'd stand quietly aside while she turned the most important thing in his life into a joke.

She'd had her say, Vance told himself as he headed for the door. Now he was going to have his.

"Shane, don't be stubborn." Donna followed her through the doorway from the museum into the shop.

"I'm not being stubborn, Donna, I really have a lot to do." To prove her point, Shane leafed through a catalog to price and date her latest stock. "With the

Christmas rush, I've really fallen behind on the paperwork. I've got invoices to file, and if I don't get the books caught up before the quarter, I'm going to be in a jam."

"Baloney," Donna said precisely, flipping the catalog closed.

"Donna, please."

"No, I don't please." She stuck her hands on her hips. "And it's two against one," she added, indicating Pat with a jerk of her head. "We're not having you spend Christmas Eve alone in this house, and that's all there is to it."

"Come on, Shane." Pat joined ranks with her sister-in-law. "You should see Donna and Dave chase after Benji when he heads for the tree. And as Donna's putting on a little weight," she added, grinning at the expectant mother, "she isn't as fast as she used to be."

Shane laughed, but shook her head. "I promise I'll come by tomorrow. I've got a very noisy present for Benji. You'll probably never speak to me again."

"Shane." Firmly, Donna took her by the shoulders. "Pat's told me how you've been moping around. And," she continued, ignoring the annoyed glance Shane shot over her shoulder at the informant, "anyone can take one look at you and see you're worn out and miserable."

"I'm not worn out," Shane corrected.

"Just miserable?"

"I didn't say—"

Donna gave her a quick affectionate shake. "Look, I don't know what happened between you and Vance—"

"Donna..."

"And I'm not asking," she added. "But you can't expect

me to stand by while my best friend is unhappy. How much fun can I have, thinking about you here all alone?"

"Donna." Shane gave her a fierce hug then drew away. "I appreciate it, really I do, but I'm lousy company now."

"I know," Donna agreed mercilessly.

That made Shane laugh and hug her again. "Please, take Pat and go back to your family."

"So speaks the martyr."

"I'm not—" Shane began furiously, the broke off, seeing the gleam in Donna's eyes. "That won't work," she told her. "If you think you can make me mad so I'll come just to prove you wrong—"

"All right." Donna settled herself in a rocker. "Then I'll just sit here. Of course, poor Dave will spend Christmas Eve without me, and my little boy won't understand where his mother could be, but..." She sighed and folded her hands.

"Oh, Donna, really." Shane dragged her hand through her hair, caught between laughter and tears. "Talk about martyrs."

"I'm not complaining for myself," she said in a long-suffering tone. "Pat, run along and tell Dave I won't be home. Dry little Benji's tears for me."

Pat gave a snort of laughter, but Shane rolled her eyes. "I'll be sick in a minute," she promised. "Donna, go home!" she insisted. "I'm closing the shop."

"Good, go get your coat. I'll drive."

"Donna, I'm not..." She trailed off as the shop door opened. Seeing her friend pale, Donna turned her head to watch Vance walk in.

"Well, we have to run," she stated, springing quickly to her feet. "Come on, Pat, Dave's probably at his wit's end keeping Benji from pulling over the tree. Merry Christmas, Shane." She gave Shane a quick kiss before grabbing her coat.

"Donna, wait…"

"No, we just can't stay," she claimed, making the reversal without blinking an eye. "I've got a million things to do. Hi, Vance, nice to see you. Let's go, Pat." They were out the door before Shane could fit in another word.

Vance lifted a brow at the hasty exit but made no comment. Instead, he studied Shane as the silence grew long and thick. The anger that had driven him there melted. "Shane," he murmured.

"I—I'm closing."

"Fine." Vance turned and flicked the lock on the door. "Then we won't be disturbed."

"I'm busy, Vance. I have…" She searched desperately for something important. "Things to do," she finished lamely. When he neither spoke nor moved, she sent him a look of entreaty. "Please go away."

Vance shook his head. "I tried that, Shane. I can't." He slipped off his coat and dropped it on the chair Donna had vacated. Shane stared at him, thrown off-balance by his appearance in a trimly tailored suit and silk tie. It brought it home to her again that she didn't know him. And, God help her, she loved him anyway. Turning, she began to fiddle with an arrangement of cut glass.

"I'm sorry, Vance, but I have a few things to finish up here before I leave. I'm supposed to go to Donna's tonight."

"She didn't seem to expect you," he commented as he walked to her. Gently, he laid his hands on her shoulders. "Shane—"

She stiffened immediately. "Don't!"

Very slowly, he took his hands from her, then dropped them to his side. "All right, damn it, I won't touch you." The words came out savagely as he whirled away.

"Vance, I told you I'm busy."

"You said that you loved me."

Shane spun around, white with anger. "How can you throw that in my face?"

"Was it a lie?" he demanded.

She opened her mouth, but closed it again before any impetuous words could be spoken. Lifting her chin, she looked at him steadily. "I loved the man you pretended to be."

He winced, but he didn't back away. "Direct hit, Shane," he said quietly. "You surprise me."

"Why, because I'm not as stupid as you thought I was?"

Anger flashed into his eyes, then dulled. "Don't."

Shaken by the pain in the single word, she turned away. "I'm sorry, Vance. I don't want to say spiteful things. It would be better for both of us if you just went away."

"The hell it would, if you've been half as miserable as I've been. Have you been able to sleep, Shane? I haven't."

"Please," she whispered.

He took a deep breath as his hands clenched into fists. He'd come prepared to fight with her, to bully her, to plead with her. Now, it seemed he could do nothing but try to fumble through an explanation. "All right, I'll go, but only if you listen to me first."

"Vance," she said wearily, "what difference will it make?"

The finality of her tone had fear twisting in his stomach. With a strong effort, he kept his voice calm. "If that's true, it won't hurt you to listen."

"All right." Shane turned back to face him. "All right, I'll listen."

He was quiet for a moment, then began to pace as though whatever ran through him wouldn't allow him to keep still. "I came here because I had to get away, maybe even hide. I'm not sure anymore. I was still very young when I took over the company. It wasn't what I wanted." He stopped for a moment to send her a direct look. "I'm a carpenter, Shane, that was the truth. I'm president of Riverton because I have to be. *Why* doesn't really matter at this point, but a title, a position, doesn't change who I am." When she said nothing, he began to pace again.

"I was married to a woman you'd recognize very quickly. She was beautiful, charming and pure plastic. She was totally self-consumed, emotionless, even vicious." Shane's brows drew together as she thought of Anne. "Unfortunately, I didn't recognize the last of those qualities until it was too late." He stopped because the next words were difficult. "I married the woman she pretended to be." Because his back was to her, Vance didn't see the sudden change in Shane's expression. Pain rushed into her eyes, but it wasn't for herself. It was all for him.

"For all intents and purposes, the marriage was over very soon after it had begun. I couldn't make a legal break at first because too many things were involved. So, we lived together in mutual distaste for several years. I involved myself in the company to the point of obsession, while she began to take lovers. I wanted her out of my life more than I wanted anything. Then, when she was dead, I had to live with the knowledge that I'd wished her dead countless times."

"Oh, Vance," Shane murmured.

"That was over two years ago," he continued. "I buried myself in work…and bitterness. I'd come to a point where I didn't even recognize myself anymore. That's why I bought the house and took a leave of absence. I needed to separate myself from what I'd become, try to find out if that was all there was to me." He dragged an agitated hand through his hair. "I brought the bitterness with me, so that when you popped up and started haunting my mind, I wanted nothing more than to be rid of you. I looked…I searched," he corrected, turning to her again, "for flaws in you. I was afraid to believe you could really be so…generous. The truth was, I didn't want you to be because I'd never be able to resist the woman you are." His eyes were suddenly very dark, and very direct on hers. "I didn't want you, Shane, and I wanted you so badly I ached. I loved you, I think, from the very first minute."

On a long breath, he moved away again to stare at the flickering lights of the tree. "I could have told you—should have—but at first I had a need for you to love me without knowing. Unforgivably selfish."

She remembered the secrets she had seen in his eyes. Remembered too, telling herself they were his until he shared them with her. Still, she felt the hurt of not being trusted. "Did you really think any of it would have mattered to me?"

Vance shook his head. "No."

"Then why did you hide it all from me?" Confused, she lifted her hands palms up.

"I never intended to. Circumstances—" He broke off, no longer sure he could make her understand. "The first night we were together, I was going to tell you, but I didn't want any past that night. I told myself it wasn't too much to ask, and that I'd explain things to you the next day. God, Shane, I swear to you I would have." He took a step toward her, then stopped himself. "You were so lost, so vulnerable after Anne had left, I couldn't. How could I have dumped all this on you when you already had that to deal with?"

She remained silent, but he knew she listened very carefully. He didn't know she was remembering very clearly the things he had said to her their first night together, the tension in him, the hints of things yet to be told. And she remembered too his compassion the next evening.

"You needed my support that night, not my problems," Vance went on. "From the very first, you gave everything to me. You brought me back, Shane, and I knew that I took much more than I gave. Until that night, you'd never asked me for anything."

She gave him a puzzled look. "I never gave you anything."

"Nothing?" he countered with a baffled shake of his head. "Trust, understanding. You made me laugh at myself again. Maybe you don't see just how important that is because you've never lost it. If I could give you nothing else, I thought that for a few days I could give you some peace of mind. I tried to tell you again when we argued about that damned dining-room set." Pausing, he sent her a narrowed look. "I bought it anyway."

"You—"

"There's not a thing you can do about it," he stated, cutting off her astonished exclamation. "It's done."

She met the angry challenge in his eyes. "I see."

"Do you?" He let out a quick, rough laugh. "Do you really? The only thing you see when you lift your chin up like that is your own pride." He watched her mouth open, then close again. "It's just as well," he murmured. "It would be difficult if you were perfect." He moved to her then but was careful not to touch her. "I never set out to deceive you, but I deceived you nonetheless. And now I have to ask you to forgive me, even if you can't accept who and what I am."

Shane lowered her eyes to her hands a moment. "It's not accepting so much as understanding," she said quietly. "I don't know anything about the president of Riverton. I knew the man who bought the old Farley place, you see." She lifted her eyes again. "He was rude, and nasty, with a streak of kindness he did his best to overcome. I loved him."

"God knows why," Vance replied, thinking over her description. "If that's who you want, I can promise I'm still rude and nasty."

With a small laugh, she turned away. "Vance, it's all hit me, you see. Maybe if I had time to get used to it, to think it through…I don't know. When I thought you were just…" She made an uncharacteristically helpless gesture with her hands. "It all seemed so easy."

"Did you only love me because you thought I was out of work?"

"No!" Frustrated, she tried to explain herself. "I haven't changed though," she added thoughtfully. "I'm still exactly what I seem. What would the president of Riverton do with me? I can't even drink martinis."

"Don't be absurd."

"It's not absurd," she corrected. "Be honest. I don't fit in. I'd never be elegant if I had years to practice."

"What the hell's wrong with you?" Suddenly angry, he spun her around. "*Elegant!* In the name of God, Shane, what kind of nonsense is that? I had my share of elegance the way you mean. I'll be damned if you're going to put me off because you've got some twisted view of the life I lead. If you can't accept it, fine. I'll resign."

"W-what?"

"I said I'll resign."

She studied him with wide, astonished eyes. "You mean it," she said wonderingly. "You really do."

He gave her an impatient shake. "Yes, I mean it. Can you really believe the company means more to me than you do? God, you're an idiot!" Furious, he gave her an unloverlike shove and strode away. "You don't yell at me for anything I've done. You don't demand to hear all the filthy details of my first marriage. You don't make me crawl as I was damn well ready to do. You start spouting nonsense about martinis and elegance." After swearing rudely, he stared out the window.

Shane swallowed a sudden urge to laugh. "Vance, I—"

"Shut up," he ordered. "You drive me crazy." With a quick jerk, he pulled his coat from the chair. Shane opened her mouth, afraid he was about to storm out, but he only pulled an envelope out of the pocket before he flung the coat down again. "Here." He stuck it out to her.

"Vance," she tried again, but he took her hand and slapped the envelope into her palm.

"Open it."

Deciding a temporary retreat was advisable, Shane obeyed. She stared in silent astonishment at two round-trip tickets to Fiji.

"Someone told me it was a good place for a honeymoon," Vance stated with a bit more control. "I thought she might still think so."

Shane looked up at him with her heart in her eyes. Vance needed nothing more to pull her into his arms, crushing the envelope and its contents between them as he found her mouth.

Shane's answer was wild and unrestricted. She clung to him even as she demanded, yielded even as she aroused. She couldn't get enough of him, so that the desperate kisses incited only more urgent needs. "Oh, I've missed you," she murmured. "Make love to me, Vance. Come upstairs and make love to me."

He buried his face against her neck. "Uh-uh. You haven't said you're taking me to Fiji yet." But his hands were already searching under her sweater. As his fingers skimmed over her warm, soft skin, he groaned, pulling her to the floor.

"Oh, Vance, your suit!" Laughing breathlessly, Shane struggled against him. "Wait until we go upstairs."

"Shut up," he suggested, then assured himself of her obedience by crushing his mouth on hers. It only took a moment to realize her trembling came from laughter, not from passion. Lifting his head, Vance studied her amused eyes. "Damn you, Shane," he said in exasperation. "I'm trying to make love to you."

"Well, then at least take off that tie," she suggested, then buried her face against his shoulder and laughed helplessly. "I'm sorry, Vance, but it just seems so funny. I mean, there you are asking if I'll take you to Fiji before I've even gotten around to asking you to marry me, and—"

"*You* asking *me?*" he demanded, eyeing her closely.

"Yes," she continued blithely. "I've been meaning to, though I thought I'd have to overcome some silly ego thing. You know, I thought you were out of work."

"Ego thing," he repeated.

"Yes, and of course, now that I know you're such an important person… Oh, this tie is *silk!*" she exclaimed after she had begun to struggle with the knot.

"Yes." He allowed her to finger it curiously. "And now that you know I'm such an important person?" he prompted.

"I'd better snap you up quick."

"Snap me up?" He bit her ear painfully.

Shane only giggled and linked her arms around his neck. "And even if I refuse to drink martinis or be elegant, I'll make an extremely good wife for a…" She paused a moment, lifting a brow. "What are you?"

"Insane."

"A corporate president," Shane decided with a nod. "No, I don't suppose you could do any better. You're making a pretty good deal now that I think about it." She gave him a noisy kiss. "When do we leave for Fiji?"

"Day after tomorrow," he informed her before he rose and dumped her over his shoulder.

"Vance, what are you doing?"

"I'm taking you upstairs to make love with you."

"Vance," she began with a half laugh. "I told you before I won't be carted around this way. This is no way for the fiancée of the president of Riverton to be treated."

"You haven't seen anything yet," he promised her.

Exasperated, Shane gave him a hearty thump on the back. "Vance, I mean it, put me down!"

"Am I fired?"

He heard the telltale choke of laughter. "Yes!"

"Good." He tucked his arm firmly around her knees and carried her up the stairs.

* * * * *